TELL TALE

Five years ago, someone murdered DI Charlotte Savage's daughter and got away with it. Now Charlotte knows who was responsible — but the killer's father is a seemingly untouchable high-ranking official, and therefore his son is well protected. Before Charlotte can work out how to get her revenge, disturbing events start to unfold on Dartmoor: a woman's naked body is found near an isolated reservoir on the bleak winter moors. As the body count mounts, and the crimes are linked to mutilated animals and a sinister cult, Charlotte knows she must move fast. But in a police force tainted by corruption, her hunt for the killer won't be easy . . .

SPECIAL MESSAGE TO READERS

THE ULVERSCROFT FOUNDATION
(registered UK charity number 264873)
was established in 1972 to provide funds for
research, diagnosis and treatment of eye diseases.
Examples of major projects funded by
the Ulverscroft Foundation are:-

- The Children's Eye Unit at Moorfields Eye Hospital, London
- The Ulverscroft Children's Eye Unit at Great Ormond Street Hospital for Sick Children
- Funding research into eye diseases and treatment at the Department of Ophthalmology, University of Leicester
- The Ulverscroft Vision Research Group, Institute of Child Health
- Twin operating theatres at the Western Ophthalmic Hospital, London
- The Chair of Ophthalmology at the Royal Australian College of Ophthalmologists

You can help further the work of the Foundation
by making a donation or leaving a legacy.
Every contribution is gratefully received. If you
would like to help support the Foundation or
require further information, please contact:

THE ULVERSCROFT FOUNDATION
The Green, Bradgate Road, Anstey
Leicester LE7 7FU, England
Tel: (0116) 236 4325

website: www.foundation.ulverscroft.com

TELL TALE

MARK SENNEN

LARGE
PRINT

First published in Great Britain 2015
by
Avon

First Isis Edition
published 2016
by arrangement with
Avon
A division of HarperCollins*Publishers*

This novel is entirely a work of fiction. The names, characters
and incidents portrayed in it are the work of the author's
imagination. Any resemblance to actual persons, living or
dead, events or localities is entirely coincidental.

A catalogue record for this book is available
from the British Library.

ISBN 978–1–78541–149–6 (hb)
ISBN 978–1–78541–155–7 (pb)

Published by
F. A. Thorpe (Publishing)
Anstey, Leicestershire

Set by Words & Graphics Ltd.
Anstey, Leicestershire
Printed and bound in Great Britain by
T. J. International Ltd., Padstow, Cornwall

This book is printed on acid-free paper

For Gitte . . . again!

Acknowledgements

Tell Tale is the fourth book in the DI Savage series and by now you'd think that Charlotte and I would know what we are doing . . . not so! Without continuing help and advice from many people too numerous to mention we'd be stuck on page one, book one. Thanks to one and all.

Thanks to HarperCollins/Avon for agreeing to take the series onward to books four, five and six. *Tell Tale* was a struggle to write, but was made easier by my editor Katy Loftus offering much encouragement and many suggestions. Thanks to the rest of the Avon team for all the behind the scenes work without which there'd be no book.

A special mention must go to my wife and daughters for putting up with moody author syndrome whilst I endeavoured to whip *Tell Tale* into shape. A whole summer went AWOL — I promise it won't happen again!

Finally, as always, thanks to *you* for reading.

Prologue

Stars. Pinpricks of light vaulted across the sky. Hundreds of them, thousands, more than he can count. Perhaps, he thinks, there are even as many stars in the sky as there are girls in the city. He licks his lips, the notion exciting him. That's one hell of a lot of stars. A hell of a lot of girls.

You know what you do with stars, Chubber? Make a wish.

"Oh yes, a wish!" Chubber whispers to himself as he swings his eyes earthward, down from the heavens. "I wish, I wish . . . I wish I could find her!"

In front of him, the moor is a heaving landscape of shadows rolling towards the distant orange glow of civilisation. All around, tors rise from the scrub and heather, grey granite forms that watch and wait. Chubber is waiting too, crouched behind a prickly clump of gorse, well wrapped in a homemade sheepskin cloak. The night is cold and frosty. A lacework pattern of ice glitters amongst the bog plants. Chubber's eyes follow the silver trail as frozen water winds up towards a spring. She's up there. Hiding. If Chubber hadn't slipped over he'd have caught her by now.

Silly Chubber!

Yes. Silly. She'd been safely locked away but he'd wanted to give her a chance. The game was more exciting when he gave them a chance.

Exciting, yes! The thrill of the chase. You love it.

Chubber scans the hillside hoping his wish will come true, but there's nothing moving, nothing living out here. Not at this time of year.

December, Chubber. Nearly Christmas.

He should have waited for the big day, he thinks. Now he'll have nothing to look forward to but a ready meal from the microwave and the chocolate orange he's been saving. If only she would . . . there! His heart leaps as he spots her eyes sparkling green in a shaft of moonlight. He jumps up and starts to run. She runs too, but now Chubber's grinning, he's getting closer. Gaining. Soon he'll catch up with her.

"There, there," Chubber shouts out. "No need to run from Chubber, my little beauty. Chubber'll be nice and gentle. Promise. Just a bit of gliding and sliding and then . . . and then . . ."

She lets out a little cry, the noise disappearing into the dark of the night, the moor sucking the sound down into the boggy ground, where centuries of secrets lie hidden in the peaty soil. Chubber stumbles after her, but then pauses. There she is, standing on a ridge in the distance, for a moment silhouetted against the starry sky. She's found harder ground and now she darts away, across the moor and into the night; disappearing behind a tor, the hunks of granite sheer black against the sprinkling of stars.

Bugger.

Chubber stands and pants. Hard work, chasing. Bloody hard work. Especially when you don't catch them. Air wheezes in and out of his lungs. A hand moves down to loosen the tie on his baggies. Slips inside. Touches himself and then scratches his bollocks.

Double bugger, he thinks. Waste of an evening. She's well and truly gone. Disappeared behind that . . . Chubber feels a breeze glide across his exposed tummy. He shivers. Realises he's chased his prey far over the moor.

Too far, Chubber. Much too far.

Yes, because he knows this place. The tor. What lies beyond.

Chubber moves slowly now, climbing to the ridge so he can see down into the valley beyond. A group of rocks stands in a circle, the hunks of granite clustering like sentinels, guarding a large, flat boulder at the centre. This place is bad, cursed, he thinks. An ancient place of witches and ghouls, spirits and will-o'-the-wisps. In the daytime you might sit and eat a picnic, but at night . . .

Ch . . . Ch . . . Chubber!

Chubber looks again. The rocks are moving, dancing, one with a towering headpiece of antlers.

Not rocks, Chubber — people!

Six standing stones and six people dancing in and out, weaving some sort of pattern. A soft wind carries a plaintive melody across the ground, a woman's voice, as sweet and clear as the cold night air. Then other voices join in, a low hum providing a background drone.

Chubber tries to understand the song, but the words mean nothing, the language foreign to him, alien.

He stares down and his lip quivers. He moves to the tor and slides behind a large boulder. His head peeks round as the six figures begin to move faster and faster, back and forth between the stones. The tall figure with the antlers starts to sing a different chant, the figures whirling until there almost seems to be more than six. As if the very stones have somehow come alive and are joining in.

Chubber, run!

But he can't, he's frozen to the spot, mesmerised. Seconds pass, minutes, hours maybe. He doesn't know. The figures race round and round until their chants conflate to a single drone. Chubber blinks. Something has happened. The six figures have rushed away from the circle. They are pulling something from behind a stand of gorse. It's a person. A man. He's limp, not resisting. Now they shove him down next to the flat rock and push him into a shallow trench alongside it. The six figures position themselves around the huge slab and slowly push the boulder over the hole in the ground. The scraping echoes into the night and the rock moves the final few inches and seals the chamber.

Chubber turns from the tor and runs back down the hill. Twice he tumbles over and rolls in the bog, clothes soaking, body cold. When he's put two ridges between himself and the stone circle, he finally pauses for breath. He thinks of the man, the one in the hole. Chubber looks to heaven, raises his hand and passes his palm across his eyes, recreating what happened back at the stone circle. The tapestry of moon and stars and galaxies soaring overhead are wiped away, replaced by the utter blackness of the tomb.

Chubber whimpers at the thought of it. He knows he's a bad man, but what he's just witnessed goes far, far beyond bad. Those people, they were . . .

Evil, Chubber, those people were evil.

Evil. He doesn't like the sound of that. He quickens his pace again. Not long to the track where he's parked his van. Just a few more steps and he'll be there.

Chubber!

Oh God! There's the track and there's the van and . . .

And, Chubber, and?

And standing by the car is a hooded figure with a towering headpiece of antlers.

Dead Sheep Attributed To Students

Local residents are said to be shocked by the discovery of a dead lamb on Midsummer Common. The animal appeared to have been ritually slaughtered and was found alongside a number of candles and other paraphernalia relating to devil worship. Police have dismissed the residents' concerns and say they believe the killing to be the work of students. "This was an end-of-term prank which got out of hand," Detective Sergeant John Simpkins told the Gazette. "Nevertheless, there's no excuse for this kind of barbarity and the public should rest assured we intend to do everything we can to catch the perpetrators." The Gazette understands that college authorities are also undertaking their own investigation.

CHAPTER
ONE

Sunday 24th August

"Bee, Mummy, Bee." Jamie pointed at a blur of wings hovering over the food. "Buzzy bee."

"It's a fly, sweetheart," she said, swatting the insect away with a hand and offering her son another Dairylea sandwich. "They're like bees, only they don't make honey."

"Bee," Jamie repeated before he took the sandwich and chomped it down. There was the tinkle of a bell and Jamie looked up. "Horse."

She turned to follow his gaze. Samantha and Clarissa were riding up and down the narrow lane on their bicycles, every now and then one of them uttering a "trot on" or a "woah" to control their mounts.

"Pretend horses." She turned and scanned the horizon until she picked out a group of Dartmoor ponies grazing near a clump of gorse. "There're some real ones, darling."

Jamie had by now lost interest in the local wildlife and turned his attention to his collection of chunky plastic cars. She cleared away the picnic things, then lay back on the woollen blanket, shielding her eyes from the light. The respite wouldn't last long, she knew. Jamie would need attention or the girls would all of a sudden come over and profess extreme boredom. But for the moment she would enjoy the warmth of the sun, the sound of birds in the heather, the stillness of the surrounding wilderness.

"Vroom," Jamie said. "Vroom, vroom, vroooooom."

She felt something on her thigh. The wheels of a truck climbing the impossibly steep hill of her body. She worried about Jamie sometimes. His sisters were nine — seven years older — and they played with him only when it suited them, so he was, in effect, an only child. With her husband away for much of the time, Jamie only had her to spice up his life. Of course he went to nursery five days a week; she figured the girls there spent many more hours playing with Jamie than she did. Not for the first time she felt a pang of guilt, but then dismissed the thought. She wondered if her husband ever had the same doubts as he lay on his bunk at night.

"Car, Mummy." The wheels rolled up and onto her stomach. "Vroom, vroom."

"Yes." She reached out a hand, keeping her eyes closed and groping for the toy. "Let me have a go."

"No, Mummy, car! Car!" Jamie's voice went up in pitch. "Car coming!"

She opened her eyes and sat up, hearing the revving of an engine, something like a racing car, a guttural exhaust spitting and crackling, the squeal of tyres on tarmac. Somewhere the tinkling of a bicycle bell and a shout. She turned her head towards the road and heard a scream silenced as metal screeched against metal. She pushed Jamie away and scrambled to her feet, aware of a flash of blue haring away down the lane, her daughter lying like a rag doll in the road next to the mangled frame of the bicycle, one wheel still spinning round. Even as she ran towards the accident she could hear the tick-tick-ticking as the wheel rotated, and as she reached Clarissa it was the only thing moving, the only thing still making a sound in the whole wide world.

Then she woke up.

Charlie Kinver cast out once again. He had no real expectation of another fish. Two nice ones in an hour was a good bag. Especially for Fernworthy. The reservoir's surface dimpled with little wavelets as the earlier breeze died to a zephyr. A duck set out from the far bank and a dozen swallows skimmed the surface, sweeping up the last of the morning hatch. The heat of the late August sun warmed Charlie's back. The bright light would be driving the trout deeper. Unlikely he'd get another bite now. But still . . .

He wound in, thinking he'd have one final cast. Behind him, in his fishing bag, the two brown trout almost shouted out to be taken home and placed in a pan. A knob of butter, a few minutes' heat and then served atop a slice of toast made from the bread his wife had baked that very morning. They'd had an argument before she'd gone to church and he'd headed off fishing, so the catch would serve as a peace offering.

He cast out a final time, and almost as soon as the fly touched the water, a fish struck. Kinver raised his rod.

The reaction was instinctive, but this time he was too late. The fly flew out of the water and caught in the low branch of a tree to his right. He could see the line had somehow wrapped itself around the branch. He pulled on it, hoping it would slip over the branch. It didn't. Instead, the hook caught in the bark. Charlie put the rod down on the bank. Pointless getting cross. He had waders on, so he could simply wade along the bank a few metres and free the hook. Since this was his last cast he'd cut the line, pocket the fly and then reel in.

Charlie stepped into the water and began to make his way down the bank. He reached the tree, put a hand up and held the fly. With the other hand he took his knife, sliced the line and freed the hook. He pulled the line to make sure it would come round the tree and then began to wade back to the gravel beach.

A flash of white caught his eye. On the bankside, wedged in the crook of an old stump, was a plastic carrier bag. The carrier bulged, something within. He waded closer. The bag seemed to be filled with some kind of material. One of yesterday's picnickers had forgotten their blanket or water-proofs. Charlie grabbed the bag and carried it to the beach. He'd walk round to the car park and leave the bag on the wall. First though, he'd take a look inside. There might be some personal item to identify who the bag belonged to.

He delved into the bag, finding a pullover, a flimsy top, a short skirt. Then a black bra, and some black, lacy knickers. He opened his mouth. There was something about finding a pair of knickers in the middle of nowhere. It meant somebody was going around without a pair. He thought of his wife. Perhaps after he'd wooed her with the trout he could persuade her to climb the stairs to their bedroom, to remove her own knickers.

At the bottom of the bag was a lightweight windcheater and beneath that a slim leather wallet. Charlie flipped the wallet open. Forty quid. A driving licence with a picture of a pretty girl bottom left. Was she the owner of the knickers? He stared down at her. Long hair, high cheekbones, a real babe.

On the top left of the licence there was a familiar circle of yellow stars on a blue background. An EU flag. In the centre of the stars sat the letter "H". On the top right, in capitals, the word "MAGYAR". Charlie looked at the pile of clothing again. Finding a bunch of women's clothing had for a moment provided a frisson of excitement. Certainly the girl in the picture was one he'd like to see naked. But, as his eyes returned to scan the surface of the water where dark blues and browns and blacks shimmered in the sun, he thought of what might be hidden in the depths of the reservoir. He reached for his tackle bag and pulled out his phone, knowing it was now unlikely he'd be eating the brace of trout for lunch.

For DI Charlotte Savage, Sunday morning came around all too soon. A pale glow seeped past the edges of the curtains, the daylight intruding on a dream about her daughter, Clarissa. It was getting on for five years now. Savage stared up at the ceiling, trying to discern an image of Clarissa in the soft shadows. Nothing. She had to turn to the bedside table and the little picture frame on it to see her daughter smiling out from a face fringed with red hair. Savage reached up and touched her own red hair. She twirled a long length with her fingers until one by one the strands slipped from her grasp.

Ever since Clarissa had died, Savage's sleep had been plagued with bad dreams. She was used to spending half the night tossing and turning, often waking in a sweat and a tangle of duvet. Recently though, the dreams had become more vivid, with the same scene repeated over and over. Savage knew why. It was because she'd discovered who was responsible for the death of her daughter. The official report had the death down as a road traffic collision, or RTC. In old money, an RTA: road traffic *accident*. But Savage had never seen what had happened as an *accident*. The hit-and-run driver had been travelling way too fast for the moorland lane — but it was the "run" bit of "hit-and-run" which had compounded Savage's anger. The driver hadn't hung around to see the consequences of his actions, and, having never been caught in the following investigation, he'd escaped punishment.

"He" being a young lad by the name of Owen Fox.

Savage sat up, her husband, Pete, stirring for a moment before settling back to sleep. She hadn't told Pete about Owen Fox. Pete was a Royal Navy officer, had been for all his adult life. He'd been commander of a frigate until recently, when the ship had been scrapped. Now he was shore-based, training naval cadets while waiting for another command. On-board the ship everything was governed by rules and regulations. You did the right thing. You served your country. Even when you gave the order to fire a cruise missile, you knew the destruction you were about to wreak was backed up in law. What Savage wanted to do to Owen Fox was far, far from legal.

She climbed from the bed and headed to the kitchen. The kids wouldn't rise for another couple of hours, but Pete would be up soon. With Stefan, their unofficial Swedish au pair, away racing yachts for the summer, Pete had to juggle his new duties with looking after the children. Often he'd wake early and come downstairs to read some document or other. Savage needed to be out of the house by then. She'd leave a hastily scribbled note explaining that a call had come in. Not the first time she'd have lied to her husband, but she told herself the deception was necessary. Pete simply wouldn't understand or accept the truth — and what she intended to do about it. It didn't make her feel any less guilty.

Breakfast was a bowl of cereal, a piece of fruit and a cup of black coffee. She slid the patio doors open and took her food onto the deck. An area of lawn spread from the deck to a hedge, beyond which cliffs fell sheer to the sea. It was still early but a couple of yachts had slipped their moorings and were cruising down the Sound. They'd be catching the tide, intent on getting a free lift westward to Fowey and beyond. If they'd set off a couple of hours later then they'd end their journey pushing against a foul current, getting nowhere fast.

Savage sat at the garden table, watching the yachts. Timing was the issue. Owen Fox wasn't just another boy racer. When she'd found out the name she'd been shocked for the first few seconds, but then everything had become clear. How the lad had managed to remain under the radar and escape detection. Dozens of officers had gone well beyond the call of duty trying to find Clarissa's killer, and yet they had failed. Not surprising really — for Owen Fox was the son of Simon Fox, the Chief Constable of Devon and Cornwall Police.

She finished her breakfast as the yachts passed the break-water and turned west. A puff of pink exploded from the lead yacht as the crew launched a colourful spinnaker, the huge sail filling and billowing as the breeze caught it. For a moment Savage felt an almost overwhelming sadness that she wasn't aboard the boat. What joy it would be to have Plymouth at the stern, the bow forging through clear blue water, perhaps — if she was lucky — dolphins racing alongside.

Then she gathered her breakfast things and went back inside the house.

DC Jane Calter glanced at the clock on the dashboard and then out at the open moorland stretching away in all directions. Nothing moved in the bright summer sun, other than a heat haze rising from the undulating terrain. She thought for a moment of the man she'd left lying in her bed and wondered if he'd woken and seen the note she'd left on top of his clothes. Wondered if he'd be there when she got back.

Calter slumped sideways in the passenger seat, as next to her DC Patrick Enders swung the car round yet another sharp bend. Her stomach heaved and she hoped she'd be able to hold on to her breakfast — a slice of toast, plus half a Mars Bar, courtesy of Enders. Last night had been epic in more ways than one, but if she'd known she would be subject to an hour's car journey with Enders at the wheel she'd have taken things a little easier. Enders was as chirpy as ever, prattling away as Calter tried to doze. The DC was the same age as her — mid-twenties — but already married with three kids. He was Irish and usually Calter found his accent soothing. Right now though she was so, so tired she wished he would shut the fuck up.

The call had come at eight, just a couple of hours after she'd fallen asleep.

"That misper from last week," the voice had said. "Her clothes have turned up at Fernworthy Reservoir. Looks like she either topped herself or . . ."

It was the "or", left hanging by the officer on the end of the line, that had pulled Calter from a state of half-slumber to wide awake. As the officer had given her the details she'd headed for the bathroom. In five minutes she was washed and dressed and in the kitchen, a slice of toast popping up as she gulped down a pint of water and tried to banish her hangover and focus on the task in hand.

The missing person was a twenty-two-year-old Hungarian by the name of Anasztáz Róka. She'd been in the UK for six months, working as a waitress in a coffee bar. A week ago a housemate had reported her missing. The report had been logged but other than a few preliminary enquiries, no action had yet been taken.

"We're here, Jane," Enders said as the car rumbled across a cattle grid, woodland closing in on both sides. "Fernworthy Reservoir. Been up here many a time with the kids. Lovely spot for a . . . you alright?"

Calter nodded and glanced at the Forestry Commission sign by the side of the road, interested in another nearby which said it was but three hundred yards to the car park and toilets. If she needed to be sick she'd prefer to do the business away from the gaze of other officers.

Enders turned off the road and was ushered into the car park by a couple of uniformed officers. Calter caught sight of the reservoir for the first time. The surface of the water was alive, little wavelets reflecting the sky, a tinge of brown in with the blue. Even on a hot day the water would be cool. Only the foolhardy would ignore the "no swimming" signs.

"D Section," Enders said. He stopped the car and pointed across the car park, where three men were unloading boxes of equipment from the back of a large van. "Hope they've packed their beach ball."

D Section provided water-borne tactical support and had expertise in underwater search operations. The head of the section, Inspector Nigel Frey, stood next to one of two patrol cars, talking to another uniformed officer. Frey was dressed in black, military-style boots on his feet, only a peaked cap and a Heckler & Koch submachine gun missing from his usual attire. He waved when he saw Calter and Enders get out of their car. Calter sucked in a few mouthfuls of fresh air and tried to banish her hangover.

"Morning, sir," Calter said as she crossed the car park to Frey. "What's the story?"

"You tell me," Frey said. "Thought we were coming out here on an emergency. But it looks like this could be more of a recovery operation. Am I right?"

"The girl's been missing for a week, so yes, unfortunately you might be." Calter turned to look at the lake. "What's it like in there?"

"Don't know yet, I've only had a quick shufty. Cold and deep. The water clarity's not too bad though. If she's in there we'll find her, but it will take a while. Going to work up a search grid now and then I'll get the lads in the drink." Frey nodded over to where two of his men were struggling into drysuits, the third preparing an inflatable dinghy. "Got the light with us this time of year, but there's no way we'll complete today."

Calter left Frey and moved over to the car park entrance where Enders was talking to one of the uniformed officers.

"Found by a fisherman," Enders said, pointing down to a plastic carrier bag which sat on the road verge next to a small boulder. "Unfortunately the fisherman moved the bag and touched the contents, but they haven't been touched since except to examine the driving licence to confirm ID."

"Sorry, I didn't wear gloves." The officer Enders had been talking to shrugged his shoulders. "But I thought I

17

was dealing with something either as simple as lost property or as tragic as a drowning. I never —"

"Not a problem," Calter said. "Can you show us where the bag was found?"

The man nodded and then beckoned one of the other officers over to take his place at the car park entrance. Calter and Enders followed the man as he led them through a small gate and across a patch of neat grassland designated as a picnic area. At the water's edge he headed along the foreshore, crunching over the exposed lake bed where the water level had dropped over the summer, dry for once in Devon. After a few minutes the officer pointed to a section of bank where a tree had fallen into the water.

"There. Just to the right of the stump of the tree. The fisherman says he found the bag by the stump. You'd not see it unless you were wading or you'd pushed through the vegetation to get to the water's edge."

"What the hell was she doing out here?" Enders said. "We're miles from her digs, in the middle of nowhere and she didn't have any transport. Not even a bike. I suppose she could have hitched a lift, but why?"

"Is all her clothing in the bag?" Calter said to the officer.

"Yes, everything." The officer blushed. "Even a pair of knickers and a bra."

"I don't like it, Jane," Enders said. "I don't like it one little bit."

"Neither do I," Calter said. "She either came here of her own free will, stripped off and went for a swim —

18

possibly with the intention of killing herself, possibly she succumbed to cramp or the cold — or else . . ."

"It's that bit I don't like. The 'or else'."

Five minutes later and they were back at the car park. Frey's men were already in the water, the divers in the shallows, a man in the dinghy dropping weighted buoys to demarcate search areas.

"I'd be surprised if she's down there," Frey said, looking out across the lake. "If she's been in the water any length of time she'd have been a floater. There's a lot of people around here in the summer so somebody would have seen the body before it sunk again."

"And the water level's lower than usual, isn't it?" Calter pointed to the strip of exposed lake bed around the edge. "So she couldn't have been swept through the outflow."

"No. The underwater outlets will have grilles on too."

"But if this wasn't an accident or a suicide then she could be on the bottom."

"Sorry, I don't get you?"

"If the body had been weighed down with rocks for instance, put in a sack. She could have been taken out in a boat and dumped in the deepest part of the reservoir."

"Possibly, but when? Middle of the night? We're at the height of the tourist season, so any other time of day and there'd be witnesses. I suppose bad weather would keep the tourists away, but we haven't had any recently." Frey paused. He glanced at the water and then back at the surrounding woodland. "It's a big job, all this. Is Charlotte coming out?"

Calter felt put out for a moment. Frey plainly believed the situation merited the attendance of more than a couple of junior detectives.

"No, sir," Calter said. "She isn't. I'm sure she's got better ways of spending her Sundays."

CHAPTER
TWO

Savage slipped out of the house unnoticed. She drove from Plymouth to the outskirts of Newton Abbot and a large park and ride, slotting her car into a bay, the vehicle anonymous amongst hundreds of others. Being spotted here, being seen with the man she'd arranged to meet, was a definite no-no. She got out of her car and looked around until she saw the Range Rover. She walked over and opened the door.

Kenny Fallon turned and looked at Savage as she got in. "Unfinished business, Charlotte. Is that what this is?" He reached for the ignition and started the car. "Or are we just going over to have a recce?"

Unfinished business.

Yes, you could call it that, Savage thought. Only the business was personal.

The Range Rover glided out of the car park and onto the main road heading for Paignton. Fallon's hand went up and rubbed his goatee beard.

"Well, Charlotte?" He glanced at her and the hand moved from the beard to stroke his huge mane of white hair. The hair tumbled down to well beyond his shoulders. Plymouth's premier gangster might have resembled a sort of cuddly Hell's Angel, but in Fallon's case appearances were definitely deceptive. More than one or two rivals had misjudged the man's intelligence and guile and not all had lived to regret their mistakes.

"I just want to see him, that's all," Savage said. "I'll decide what to do afterwards."

"Right." Fallon chuckled. "Ask him if he'll say sorry and then kiss and make up? After that maybe send each other Christmas cards every year."

Savage didn't respond. She stared at the traffic rushing towards them on the other side of the road. Headlong. That's what it felt like sometimes. Her family had been wronged, Clarissa killed. Nobody punished. How could that be right?

"Whatever." Fallon spoke again. Took one hand off the steering wheel and patted her on the knee. "Uncle Kenny will sort things for you. Mind you, considering who the killer is, we'll need to go careful. You don't go messing with the Chief Constable's son."

When Savage had discovered the truth, it had at first seemed unbelievable. But then, turning things over in her mind, it had made more sense. How, for instance, the driver of the car which had hit Clarissa had managed to avoid detection. The police had known the make and model — a Subaru Impreza — yet they hadn't been able to track down the owner. That Simon Fox was behind this failure to find and implicate Owen, was in no doubt in Savage's mind. The trail must've been covered up, records obfuscated, perhaps even officers told to keep quiet.

A few minutes later and they were on the outskirts of Torquay, the Range Rover purring through a recently built estate. Neat little lawns with brick-paved driveways stood in front of two- and three-bedroomed houses. This was the preserve of newly formed families, the first or second step on the housing ladder. Owen lived here with his wife and young children. Did he sleep easy at night in the serenity of his suburban idyll? Or did he toss and turn with worry, Clarissa Savage haunting his dreams?

"There," Fallon said, his head turning to the left as they drove past a house with a red door, a car sitting on the driveway. Not an Impreza; a Ford. "Happy families, hey?"

Fallon drove on and pulled up a short way along the road. Savage craned her neck to look back. As she did so the front door of the house swung open and a young woman appeared holding a baby in her arms, an older kid of four or five by her side. She stepped out of the house, closed the door, and went over to the car. Savage turned away as the woman busied herself with strapping the baby into a car seat, while the other child climbed in.

This wasn't what she had been expecting at all. She needed to hate Owen, to see him as some sort of demon. Instead Savage was wondering how on earth she was going to go through with what she'd planned.

"Can't stop long, Charlotte," Fallon said, nodding through the windscreen to where a woman had raised her head from a flower bed and was paying them rather too much attention. "My motor. A bit flash for round here. Time to move on."

Move on.

Could she? There had to be some sort of resolution, some settling of the score. Or did it go further than that — maybe stretching to something approaching vengeance? She wasn't sure what she wanted any more.

"Go," Savage said. "Just fucking go."

Fallon raised his eyebrows, then put the vehicle into gear and eased forward. The road was a close, at the end a turning circle. Fallon manoeuvred round and headed back past the house. Owen's wife had by now reversed into the road and she drove off, with the Range Rover following.

"We could tail them," Fallon said. "Her and the kiddies. Find out where they're going. Might be useful if we need to come back and give them a bit of a scare."

"No!" Savage thumped the dash. "My argument is with Owen. We leave them alone, got it?"

"OK, love. It was just a bloody suggestion."

"Look, Kenny, it's not that I'm ungrateful for what you've done. Finding out who did it, tracing Owen, all that. But I'm the one who has to make the decision as to what to do."

"Sure." Up ahead the Ford indicated left. Fallon drove straight on. "But you're going to make him pay, aren't you? After all, it would be a shame to waste all the effort me and DS Riley put into finding him."

DS Darius Riley.

Working off his own bat, he had followed a lead provided by Fallon. The lead had led to Owen via a breaker's yard and a dodgy car body repair shop. Riley was part of the problem, part of the reason Savage had spent so many nights lying awake trying to decide what

24

to do. If Riley hadn't been involved she was pretty sure she'd have done something by now. Something stupid.

Savage watched the Ford disappear down the side street.

"It won't be wasted," she said. "And I do mean to make him pay. I do."

"Well then, let's go and find the lad shall we?" Fallon slowed the Range Rover and pulled in at the entrance to a brown-field site where the gates to a half-completed development hung shut for the weekend. Savage stared at a big yellow digger and then at Fallon as he reached across and opened the glove compartment. "But first . . ."

"What are you doing?"

"This." Fallon pulled out something wrapped in an oily towel and plonked the parcel on Savage's lap. "A present from Uncle Kenny. Birthday, Christmas, whatever."

Savage felt the weight of the object on her legs. Knew what was inside the towel without looking. "Kenny?"

"Untraceable. A full clip. More if you need them but one is all it takes."

"Shit. I don't know if —"

"Think on it." Fallon engaged first gear and eased the car back onto the road. "My old man always told me regrets are for losers. He was right. Winners don't have doubts, do they?"

"No," Savage said as she folded back the rag to reveal the automatic pistol. "I guess they don't."

Then she picked up the weapon and slipped the cold steel into her jacket pocket.

DS Darius Riley stood on a desolate stretch of moorland some five miles to the west of Fernworthy Reservoir. Apart from the track he'd driven down and the dark granite of a couple of nearby tors there was nothing but grass, low scrub and heather in all directions. Not for the first time since his arrival in Devon some two years ago, he reflected on the way his life had changed since then. South London seemed a very long way away, his Caribbean heritage even further.

For a moment Riley looked east where, far away, something hung in the air above the moor, hovering like a kestrel. But he knew the object wasn't a bird. The smudge was a helicopter. Call sign NPAS-44. Air Operations. The helicopter was looking for the missing Hungarian girl, and there'd be people on the ground too. He shook his head. That's where the action was. Officers hunting for clues, piecing the evidence together, coming up with theories. He gave a silent curse and turned back to the job in hand.

"Crap." That from DI Phil Davies. Pissed-off too. He articulated Riley's thoughts. "Call this police work? I don't. We should be over at the reservoir or knocking on a few doors and unsettling some of the local nonces. Sort it, Darius, because I want to get back home in time for Sunday lunch."

Davies turned and strolled away, hands reaching into his pocket for lighter and fags. Davies was something of an enigma. With his lack of respect for regulations, a well-worn face with a more-than-once broken nose, cheap shirts and aftershave and even cheaper jokes, the

DI appeared to be a dinosaur from a previous age of policing. Davies was known to associate with various members of Plymouth's criminal classes. "In the line of duty" was his excuse. "Lining his pocket" was how Riley saw it. But there was another side to Davies. He was the main carer for his wife, disabled after a riding accident. Riley rated her as one of the most attractive and graceful women he'd met. The contrast with Davies was unsettling.

Davies trudged away with a cigarette in his mouth, leaving Riley to continue.

"Are you sure this wasn't natural causes?" Riley said to DC Carl Denton, walking in a circle around the body so he could view it from all angles. "Something getting at the corpse? A stray dog or a fox?"

"Sorry, sir. The pony was slaughtered." Denton's eyes moved to the rear of the animal. He reached up and scratched the pronounced scar on his cheek. "And worse."

"Tell me you're joking?" Riley said, wondering what his old friends on the Met would say if they could see him now. The sick jokes would be coming thick and fast.

"No, sir. He's been interfered with, something shoved up his rectum and the genitals cut off. No way a dog did that. Anyway, what about those burn marks on the ground?"

The burn marks were apparent in several places, piles of white ash surrounded by black earth and scorched grass.

Boy racers up on the moor for a party, Riley had thought at first. But the positioning of the fires was too uniform. Five of them. Straight lines had been scratched in the earth from each fire to the ones opposite and a circle had been drawn through all the points too. The result was a pentagram with the dead animal in the centre.

"Jesus," Riley said, shaking his head and then laughing at his use of the word. "Or not."

"Not, sir." Denton seemed unamused at Riley's quip. The lad knelt at the head of the pony and peered at the neck, where the jugular vein had been severed. A pool of red-brown earth showed where the animal had bled out. Flies buzzed, flitting from the blood to the neck. There was already a whiff of something bad in the air. "Not Jesus by a long way."

"We've had this before though, yes? Animals being tortured?"

"Sort of." Denton looked up at Riley and then stood. "But not like this. We had that deer with a crossbow bolt through the head in Plymbridge woods a while back. There was a horse shot with an air gun last year. Then there was a pony slashed in the genitals over on Bodmin Moor. The animal survived though. Not like this one."

Denton stared past Riley, his eyes roaming the vista of moorland, farther away, a tor rising to pierce the blue sky. The poor lad looked shell-shocked, Riley thought. He knew Denton had been off sick for a couple of months. "Gone mental" was the squad room gossip, but as one of the few people Denton confided in, Riley knew better. Denton had become infatuated with DC Calter but she'd been having none of it. A bunch of flowers bought as a Valentine's present had been returned with a polite "no thank you". An invitation to dinner had been rejected. Riley reckoned poor old Denton would have been OK, had a close relative not died soon after. Rejection followed by loss had pushed him over the edge and into full-blown clinical depression. On his return to duty he'd gone on various training courses and had come back to a new position working as a Wildlife and Countryside officer in DI Maynard's newly formed Agricultural Crime Squad. The role was a largely solitary one and Riley wondered if Denton was coping with the isolation. At least Denton was his own boss. Riley and Davies came under the direct control of Maynard, and the DI never failed to let them know he was in charge. Thankfully Maynard was off on his annual birdwatching holiday, and for a couple of weeks at least Riley had a little more freedom.

"So is this of interest to the ACS or not?" Riley said. "Only we've got some sheep rustlers to catch."

Denton turned back to Riley, not catching the irony. "Could be if we want it. Those other incidents were down to kids or bored city folk. 'Having a laugh', they'd call it. This is something different. I wouldn't have thought the pentagram was the kind of thing some kids would think up. I reckon we've got something much more disturbing."

"You're talking about the occult? Animal sacrifice? I thought that sort of stuff belonged in movies."

"That's your job to find out, sir. If the ACS's remit extends that far."

"Shit." Riley shook his head again. He and Davies had been stuck with Maynard for the best part of six months. The sheep rustling case the pair of them were working on was to be their last one, Detective Superintendent Conrad Hardin having belatedly decided Riley's talents were wasted in the ACS. "I guess it does, although I'm not sure what Maynard's going to make of all this. Especially if it means a bit of covert ops watching a bunch of gothic types frolicking naked under a full moon."

Denton didn't smile. "The animal's been brutally slaughtered, sir. You've seen what they did to the rear end. It's not a joke."

"Sorry, of course not," Riley said. "We'll get on it. You'll give me a written report and let me know if you find anything else, OK?"

Denton nodded, then Riley turned and walked away, leaving the lad staring down at the corpse. Davies stood over by their car. He dropped his fag and stubbed the butt out on the ground.

"Any good? I know I was moaning earlier but if this case can get us away from those bloody sheep for the rest of the month I'll bite."

"Carl reckons some kind of ritual took place. Not sure it's our bag or one for the RSPCA. Depends on whether it goes any further than this I guess."

"Ritual?" Davies grinned as he opened the door to the car. "You mean orgies and nude chicks on altars? Right up my street."

30

"Don't mention that to Carl, sir." Riley went round to the driver's side and got in. "He's a wee bit sensitive on the issue."

Half an hour later, Savage stood staring out across Brixham. A jumble of white houses tumbled down the hillside to the harbour while seagulls wheeled above fishing boats unloading their catch. Tourists thronged the harbour walls, many with ice creams or chips in hand, even though it was still only mid-morning; Brixham was a downmarket version of Dartmouth, not quite as picturesque and strictly for the kiss-me-quick brigade.

Savage turned from the view and eyed a row of shops on the quayside. At the far end of the row stood an estate agency, one belonging to a local firm with a sprinkling of offices in South Devon. There were branches in Exeter, Sidmouth, Teignmouth and here, in Brixham. Inside the tiny waterfront box a shape moved. Somebody fiddling with the window display.

Owen Fox.

Owen resembled his father, the Chief Constable, only in the fact that he had jet-black hair. His facial features were much softer, a cherub-like face reminding Savage that the lad was only in his early twenties. He already had a wife, two children, a mortgage to pay. He'd already killed someone.

Fallon had dropped her at the harbour a little while earlier, giving her directions and another pep talk.

"Take a look, Charlotte. See what you think. The lad took away something you loved and in my book that makes what you've planned legit. I'll park up and grab myself some breakfast. Call me when you're done."

Now, her eyes still on Owen, Savage let her hand go to her pocket. Her fingers closed around the grip. Killing Owen, or even just hurting him, wouldn't bring Clarissa back, but only a fool would say it wouldn't make things a whole lot better. Savage had never had a liberal view of punishment. Too often the bad guys served a few years while the victims and the families received a life sentence. If that was what justice was then the whole system needed ripping up.

Owen Fox, of course, had never even been caught. He'd escaped punishment entirely.

Savage blinked as the door to the estate agency opened. Owen strode out and wheeled to the left, a set of keys in his hand. Brixham was all steep hills and tiny streets and suffered from a lack of parking. Owen was walking to an appointment.

Her heart rate rose and she moved away from the quay wall and followed as Owen strolled along the edge of the marina and then turned left. He headed up a steep hill and turned left again. A couple of hundred yards later he swung right into the driveway of a large detached house. On the opposite side of the road there was only a stone wall. The house had an amazing view over the harbour, was right in the centre of the town and yet the location was secluded. Perfect, Savage thought, just perfect. Owen's clients would arrive. He'd show them around and then they'd leave. He'd go back into the house to check it over. Savage could slip inside and confront him. No one would see her. No one would know.

She put her hand in her pocket and touched the gun. Fallon said one bullet was all it took and he was right. One bullet to end all her worries. She carried on walking and went past the house without looking up. At the end of the street a bench on the pavement faced the sea. She went over and sat down and stared across the harbour. Barely a minute went by before something vibrated in her pocket. Not the gun, her phone.

Shit. Her phone. All of a sudden she realised her mistake. The phone could be tracked, her location pinpointed. If anything happened to Owen Fox in Brixham today she'd be the first person his father suspected.

Savage pulled the phone out and glanced at the display. DC Calter. She answered, then rose from the bench and began to walk back down the hill towards the town.

CHAPTER
THREE

Savage arrived at Fernworthy Reservoir shortly before midday. The drive up from Brixham had given her time to ponder. What would she have done if her phone hadn't gone off? If she'd come face-to-face with Owen Fox today? As her car climbed onto the moor her mood darkened to match the black of the granite tors. Up here was where Clarissa was killed and where a sort of living hell had started for Savage. By the time the road wound up towards Fernworthy she knew she had to do something. One day soon she'd return to Brixham with Fallon and confront Owen. Hurt him over and over. Maybe, if he begged, she'd stop. Then again, maybe she wouldn't.

The car thrummed across a cattle grid and a minute later she was turning into the car park at the reservoir. On the far side of the car park a young female DC sat behind the wheel of her car with the door wide open and the seat reclined. The woman's eyes were shut, the officer enjoying forty winks in the sunshine. A blonde bob curled round her cheeks and the short-sleeved shirt revealed healthy biceps.

DC Calter.

Savage got out and strolled over. Her shadow fell across Calter's body.

"Don't tell me, Patrick," Calter said, her eyes still closed.

"You've just wet yourself because you've found some fucking geocache."

"Is that what he's up to then?" Savage said.

"Ma'am!" Calter opened her eyes and sat up. "Sorry, just taking a break."

"And DC Enders?"

"He's off somewhere with his precious GPS. Something about search parameters."

"That's the PolSA's job, isn't it?"

"Yeah, but the search adviser hasn't turned up yet. Inspector Frey's taken control of the lake but we're at sixes and sevens about the rest." Calter climbed out of the car and Savage listened as Calter explained about the discovery of the bag of clothes. The PC who'd first attended the scene had found the driving licence and called the details in, flagging up Ana's name on the missing person list.

"Remember her passport was missing?" Calter said. "We concluded she'd probably returned to Hungary. Seems unlikely now."

"Yes," Savage said. "The driving licence changes everything."

"She's got to be here somewhere." Calter swung her arms wide to encompass the water, the forest, and the surrounding moorland. "But to be honest I don't think she'll be alive when we find her."

Savage followed Calter's gesture. The lake was cold and deep, the forest a vast area criss-crossed with tracks and paths. And then there was the moorland, an upland wilderness of tors and bogs stretching for miles in three directions. Only to the east was there the comfort of civilisation. A few farms and hamlets and then the town of Chagford. Was it possible the girl had gone that way? Or maybe that's where she'd come from. Chagford was a little bit of London on the moor. Hideaways for the rich and famous. Perhaps Ana had been at a house party which had turned sour. Drugs or sex, she'd overdosed or been raped. Either way, the hosts had ended the night with a body on their hands. In London you'd struggle to dispose of the evidence, but up here?

Savage kept silent, not wanting to confirm Calter's suspicions. Then she nodded towards the entrance to the car park as a vehicle swung in past the two uniformed officers.

"About bloody time. The PolSA. Let's see what he has to say."

The police search adviser turned out to be new in the job. He'd done half a dozen courses and knew a string of buzzwords, but by the end of the conversation with him Savage wasn't convinced by his proposed strategy. And neither was Calter.

"He couldn't locate a burger in a bun," Calter said, as the PolSA went to find Frey. "Search the lake and five hundred metres around where the bag of clothes were found? I could have told you that. But where else?"

"He doesn't want to squander resources, Jane," Savage said. She pointed up at the forest rising from the far side of the lake. "And you can see his point. It would take hundreds of officers to search the woodland, and with the density of the trees and scrub you could pass within a couple of metres of a body without seeing anything. On the other hand you're right; what he's come up with is hardly rocket science. I'd have liked something else."

Savage left Calter at the car park and strolled along the road which bordered the reservoir. To the left the woodland was a mixture of new plantings, half-grown trees, and full-grown pines. Beneath the mature trees light scrub hugged the ground, but the canopy high above prevented much of it from growing. Searching those areas would be easy. Likewise with the sections of forest which had been clear felled. It was the areas with half-grown trees that would prove a problem for the search teams. The pines were five to ten metres high and their branches reached down to near ground level. The result was a mass of almost impenetrable greenery. Anything other than a cursory search would prove near impossible. In its entirety Fernworthy comprised several square kilometres and the terrain was by no means flat. There was steep hillside, streams and gullies, and here and there rocks pushed up from the peaty ground. Although there were a few forest tracks, access along those would need to be in four-wheel-drive vehicles and the majority of the searching would have to be done on foot.

Savage paused and felt the warmth of the sun. With the water and the forest this place was as perfect a beauty spot as one could imagine. And yet there was something unsettling about the place. She looked into the tree line on the other side of the reservoir. Beyond the first few trunks there was nothing but shadow, thick, black and impenetrable. She blinked and turned away, her eyes drawn to a movement on the water. For a second her heart skipped a beat as a monster-like hump rose from the reservoir near the centre. But the black bump was no beast, rather, it was one of Frey's men. The man raised his arm and made a signal. At once a whine from an outboard filled the air as the officer in charge of the dinghy gunned the engine and surged towards the diver. It looked, to Savage's uneducated eye, as if the diver had found something.

The sunken treasure lay on the bank side, stretched out on a blue tarp. A long strip of green webbing with a loop and a ratchet mechanism at one end and a big hook at the other.

"A tie-down," Frey said. "Not been in the water long. No weed or slime and no tarnishing of the metal."

"What makes you think this has anything to do with the girl?" Savage said as she knelt at the edge of the tarp. "Looks like a piece of rubbish to me."

"Maybe. But if so then it's expensive rubbish. Do you know how much a set of good quality tie-downs cost?"

"Tell me."

"A lot. Certainly enough that you don't chuck one away without good reason."

"So what would that 'good reason' be?"

"Say if it's broken. Which this one isn't. Or if the material has some sort of incriminating evidence on it." Frey knelt alongside Savage and pointed to the end of the tie-down with the hook. "There, take a look."

"There's a stain." Savage could see a discoloration where some sort of liquid had worked its way into the webbing. "Blood?"

"Could be." Frey stood. "But I think it looks more like oil. Examine the material near to the hook. What do you see?"

"Not a lot." Savage leaned in closer and shielded her eyes from the sun. Now she could see some fraying on one side of the webbing. A wisp of material like fine fishing line. No, not fishing line. "A hair?"

"Yes." Frey stared across the water. "If we can find a matching one amongst the girl's clothing or maybe at her lodgings, then we've got our first major lead."

"So she's tied up with the webbing and brought out here." Savage followed Frey's gaze and then looked back to the bank to where the bag of clothes had been found. "He strips her, kills her and throws the webbing out into the lake."

"Which leads me to think she's not out there." Frey turned from the water and looked towards the forest. "If she was then surely she would be with the webbing. But my diver says there's nothing else down there."

"Unless the perp forgot about the webbing until the last minute and then had to dispose of it in a hurry.

39

Either way we're getting a little ahead of ourselves. I guess we'll need to wait to see if the CSIs can get some sort of match on the hair."

"And then?"

"Then I'll get onto that idiot PolSA and get him to widen the search."

Charlie Kinver was the fisherman who'd found the bag of clothes and yet, apart from his initial statement to the PC, he'd not been questioned. Savage berated Calter and went off to do the job herself.

The man's place lay about three miles from Fernworthy. A narrow lane ducked into a tunnel of trees and emerged after a quarter of a mile into a tiny valley where a stone cottage sat beside a brook. Ducks muddied the shallows as they probed beds of watercress and as Savage slowed the car, a heron rose from the water and flapped away. The house was from a postcard, honeysuckle climbing over a wooden porch, flowers in bright window boxes, a vegetable garden with rows of produce bursting from the neatly tended beds. To one side a number of chickens scratched bare earth in a pen, while a cat watched from the shade of a nearby fruit tree.

Savage got out of the car and went across to the front door. The door stood open and she knocked and called out a "hello". Someone answered from the gloom inside and a figure stooped forward down the hall and held out a hand.

"Charlie Kinver," the man said. The hand was dinner plate-sized and felt rough and calloused as Savage shook it. Kinver was in his forties but with a weathered face, short hair prematurely greying. "You must be the police, right?"

Savage nodded and introduced herself as Kinver led her through to the back of the house. The kitchen had oak units and wooden worktops with a deep sink and an old Rayburn stove. Very rustic, Savage thought, wondering if rustic wasn't exactly the right word to describe Kinver too.

"Made them myself, I did," Kinver said, noting Savage's interest. "Carpentry. About all I'm good for. At least that's what the wife says."

"They're beautiful," Savage said. Kinver's eyes had wandered to the window and she followed his gaze. In the back garden a woman lay on a sun lounger positioned beneath the shade of a tree, a book in one hand. "Is that your wife?"

"Yes. She's had a hard morning baking bread and then singing in the choir. Not like me, off for a spot of fishing, catching our food."

Savage looked back into the room. On the kitchen table a hunk of bread smeared with butter and layered with cheese lay half-uneaten, while a salad had wilted in the heat. Kinver, for some reason, hadn't been able to finish his meal.

"Can you go through it again for me? What happened this morning?" Since Kinver didn't offer, Savage pulled a chair out from the table and sat down. "It must have been a shock, finding the girl's clothes."

"Sorry." Kinver appeared to realise he'd neglected to be a good host and now he moved to pick the kettle up and fill it at the sink. "No, not a shock. At least not at first. I didn't think much of it until I saw the underwear. Then the logic sunk in. She was either in the lake or lying naked and dead somewhere in the woods."

"Why did you think that?"

"Well, there weren't any other possibilities which came to mind. I could see she wasn't close by sunbathing. Anyway it was too early for that."

"How often do you go fishing, Charlie?"

"This time of year it'd be a couple of times a week, sometimes three. I don't catch something every trip, but when I do it's nice to have a piece of fresh fish for lunch. Only today I didn't feel hungry. I cut off their heads, gutted them, gave the scraps to the cat and put them in the freezer for another day."

"When you were last at Fernworthy did you fish the same spot?"

"Yes, as a matter of fact I did. Usually I'll try to vary which swims I fish from, but this was only a short trip and I couldn't be bothered to walk round the lake."

"And that was when?"

"Day before yesterday. I had no luck but I spotted a couple of nice fish. That's partly why I returned to the same place. And no, the bag definitely wasn't there."

"And in your recent trips you haven't noticed anybody acting suspiciously?"

"I'm usually there too early to notice anyone. The tourists don't start arriving until mid-morning. There'll be some walkers, of course, but it's rare I see anybody before eight. Once the kids start splashing in the shallows you can say goodbye to any chance of a bite so I usually try to do morning or evening sessions. This morning I didn't see anyone and if I recall t'was the same the day before yesterday."

"You said you sometimes do evening sessions?" Kinver nodded. "Do you ever get people at the reservoir then? Couples maybe?"

Kinver smiled. "Sometimes. They'll turn up at dusk usually. They might take a walk but if they were thinking of a spot of alfresco the mossies usually put them off. All that bare flesh? — supper time for the little vampires, isn't it?"

"You've seen them though?"

"Sure. Stood and watched a few times." Kinver held up his hands. "Don't get me wrong, I'm no perv, but when I'm stalking fish round the edge of the lake I'm invisible, hardly make a sound. Once, late evening, I came across two guys and a woman. She were being spit-roasted, I think that's what they call it. Me and the wife had a good laugh about it when I came home. Spit-roasted the brace of brownies I caught too."

Savage shifted in her chair, aware that Kinver was leering. The man was a little free and easy with his descriptions for her liking. She was glad his wife was out in the back garden.

"And apart from that one time, have you ever seen anything dodgy?"

"The occasional couple in a car. With the lights on you can see everything. I've reported a vehicle that's been broken into a couple of times. Once I rang the rangers to alert them to a bunch of teens who were camping and had lit a big fire. The camping was fine, but I reckoned the fire was a bad idea considering the dry weather we were having. I'd have had words myself but I didn't want no trouble."

"And that's the extent of it?"

"As far as I know. I've never seen a guy in an old mac, hands down his trousers, leering after young girls." Kinver looked up from his tea-making duties and leered himself. "Young, *pretty* girls, know what I mean?"

"I'm not sure I do, Mr Kinver," Savage said, thinking Kinver was again giving her way too much information. He seemed keen to show her the extent of his lasciviousness. Was it an act? — or maybe he was trying to flirt, even though his wife was but steps away. "Anyway, what makes you think this girl was young and pretty?"

"Hey?" Kinver cocked his head, nonplussed. Then he returned his attention to the kettle and poured water into two mugs, adding teabags to each afterwards. "Her picture, of course. On the driving licence. Cute little thing, I thought."

Shit, Savage had forgotten about the licence. For a moment she'd thought Kinver had let slip something. Kinver was squeezing the teabags with a spoon while gazing out the window at his wife. He was mumbling about how he was very much in favour of the EU if the migrants were all like Ana.

"Send 'em over, I say," he said as he turned and deposited the mugs on the table. "The more the merrier."

"But you've never seen her before?"

"No." Kinver grimaced. "And I don't reckon I'm likely to get the chance now, am I?"

"You're jumping to conclusions. Most missing persons turn up at some point. Fingers crossed this girl does too."

"Oh she'll turn up all right." Kinver pulled out a chair and sat down. He raised a finger to his mouth, licked the tip and then lowered his hand and ran his finger along the smooth edge of the tabletop. "But she won't be winning any beauty contests when she does, will she?"

Irina Kryukov sat on a bench on the Hoe and cried. The sun shone down from a clear blue sky and out to sea the water sparkled. Yachts crawled back and forth, wallowing in the light airs. A rib loaded with divers carved a foamy white trail in the water as it sped towards the breakwater. Close at hand, on the huge grassy expanse of the Hoe, people lounged around with ice creams or a beer or two. A family had just unpacked a substantial picnic and a young kid of three or four was grasping for the bottle of Coke. Nobody seemed to be taking any notice of Irina, everybody seemed to be enjoying themselves. But they hadn't had to find out what she just had.

The knock on the door had come first thing in the morning. A uniformed female police officer stood on the step outside, reluctance written all over her face.

"It's about your housemate, love," the officer said. "Anasztáz Róka? We've found some of her things on

45

Dartmoor. Somebody will be round to take a statement later, OK?"

Job done, the woman had turned and walked away.

Irina sniffed and used a paper tissue to wipe away some of her tears. The little boy with the picnicking family looked up and pointed at Irina, but his mother grabbed his arm and wheeled him round. Irina felt completely alone, as if nobody cared.

It was a feeling she'd had when she'd first come to the UK from Russia a couple of years ago. She'd arrived in London pretty much penniless, planning to spend a few days there before heading off to start her course at Plymouth University. After seeing the sights of London, which — truth be told — were pretty poor fare compared to Moscow, she'd hitch-hiked west. A lorry driver had offered her a lift and then halfway down the M4 he'd pulled off at Membury services and asked for payment. "I'm going as far as Bristol. A blow job'll get you there. Or you could let me fuck you and I'll bung you twenty quid so you can get a train the rest of the way."

Irina had wrenched the door of the cab open and tumbled out into the drizzle. The man had cursed and asked her what the problem was? After all, weren't all Russian girls whores? Then he'd chucked her rucksack down, started the truck and roared off. Irina had lain on the wet tarmac, nursing a bruise and a bunch of shattered illusions. Maybe, after all, England wasn't the Promised Land. Maybe people were pretty much the same wherever you went.

She remembered her father's reaction on hearing the news she intended to leave Russia. "Different seas," he'd said. "Different salt in the water. You either like the taste or you don't." Certainly her first taste had been sour, but after a nightmare few weeks things had improved, and over time some of her faith had been restored. She had a nice room in a shared house and a part-time job in a cafe. The winters were warmer, if wetter, than Moscow, and this year the British summer had been a scorcher. She'd had a brief fling with a lifeguard who'd taught her how to surf and although the relationship had ended she'd enjoyed herself while it lasted. The UK, all in all, wasn't so bad.

Until now.

Although Ana Róka had only come to Devon half a year or so ago, the Hungarian girl had quickly become Irina's best friend. She guessed it was because they shared a common experience in making the physical and psychological journey from East to West. When Ana had gone missing, Irina had been distraught. But the police had seemed uninterested. They had carried out a few checks and then told her they could do nothing more. People went missing all the time, they had said. Especially foreign immigrants. She'll likely as not turn up. That story seemed to have changed now.

Irina screwed up the paper tissue and lobbed it into a nearby bin. She stood and weaved her way across the Hoe, dodging the picnickers. Perhaps in the UK people did go missing all the time, she thought. But in Russia, when somebody went missing you knew something very, very bad had happened to them.

CHAPTER
FOUR

Colours whirl on the huge outdoor screen, most people on the plaza paying little attention as the soundless pictures flash by. Chubber's paying attention though. Chubber's *interested*. The newsy news is always interesting, but today's is especially so.

The screen shows a presenter talking to the camera. Behind him cars and vans. People in uniform. The blue of water. Trees and granite tors. Moorland.

Moorland, Chubber? We don't like the moor, do we?

That's not right, Chubber thinks. The moor is fine — as long as it's not dark and you avoid stone circles and the man with the antlers on his head. That's when things get scary. When the man starts talking and Chubber starts listening and the man tells Chubber things he doesn't want to hear about demons and ghosts and the devil and people who get hurt if they open their mouths to tell stories to anyone who might listen only they won't listen because the stories are just stories so it's better to keep quiet and do what they say than be caught and suffer for ever in the fires of h . . . h . . . h . . .

Don't think about it, Chubber, don't!

Chubber opens and closes his mouth like a fish out of water. A rush of panic fills his chest. He checks the sky for the sun. The big ball of fire is up there, hot and yellow and high and a long, long way from the horizon. Chubber breathes deep. No need to worry. He's done exactly as Antler Man asked. Everything is OK. He focuses once again on the huge screen and the subtitles that scroll along the bottom.

Breaking news: police searching Dartmoor reservoir after clothing of missing waitress found . . .

Chubber stares. Reads the words. Feels excitement tingle across the back of his hands. Feels a swelling *down there.*

Chubber! That's naughty! Down there *is very bad.*

"Hot chocolate?"

Black and white blocks Chubber's view for a moment. The black of a dress, the white of an apron, more black flows like liquid down legs cosseted in sheer hosiery. He looks up, smiles, and meets the eyes of the girl as she places the drink in front of him.

"Thank you," he says. Nice girl. Lovely girl. Beautiful girl. "Thank you very much."

The girl half smiles back but there's a sadness behind her expression. Chubber wonders if the girl has been crying. Wonders if she needs comforting. Maybe the smile is an invitation. Does she want him to reach out and touch her thigh? Her leg is so close, clad in shimmering nylon, the inner part not thin, but fleshy, soft, succulent.

Succulent, Chubber?

Yes. The word reminds him of ripe fruit, a plum or a nectarine perhaps. Sink your teeth into a plum and the goodness flows out. Forget touching, maybe he should bend his head and bite her down there. Where she's juicy.

No Chubber! This place is much too public for that! Too many people.

Chubber stares around. Tables lie scattered outside the cafe. People are walking back and forth across the plaza. Yes, much too public; far too many people. Instead of bending and biting he lets his eyes follow the waitress as she moves away, glides and slides between the tables and heads back inside the cafe. The uniform suits her, he thinks. The way the material flares out from the waist, accentuating her shapeliness. Making the most of her curves, her hourglass figure.

Hourglass. Like an egg-timer, Chubber. Sand. Trickling downward. Marking time while the eggs boil dry.

Chubber shakes his head. He doesn't like time. The way the seconds slip past. Clocks tick. Hours go by and Chubber finds things haven't changed much. He needs to do something about that. He needs to act.

"Oh well," Chubber says aloud. "Faint heart never won fair maiden."

"Pardon?" An elderly woman sitting at the next table looks across. "Did you say something?"

"Huh?" Chubber says and then crunches his nose in a sneer. "My business. Not your business. You mind yours and I'll mind mine, OK?"

He scrapes his chair around so he won't have to look at the crone. Concentrates instead on the waitress. He can see her in the cafe, talking to a customer. Then she slips behind the counter. Uses a pair of tongs to retrieve a cream éclair from the cake cabinet. The tongs squeeze the cake, the cake lets out a long sigh and the cream oozes out.

"Ah!" Chubber says. "Lovely. What a lovely, lovely girly girl."

A snuffle comes from behind him. Chubber hopes the old dear is choking on her dentures. He pauses. He really shouldn't be doing this, shouldn't even be here. If Antler Man knew, he'd be angry. Very angry. Still, he can't know, can he? Chubber reaches into his pocket and pulls out his pencil. Licks the tip. Takes a napkin and flattens it. Bends to the table and writes a note to the waitress. She'll read the note and maybe next time he comes into the coffee shop she'll ask him out.

He slips a ten-pound note on top of the napkin and moves back his chair. The girl looks over from another table, mouths a "thank you" and starts to move towards him.

"Oh Chubber-Chub-Chubs," Chubber says as he hurries away. "Chubber's been a bad boy. Naughty Chubber. Bad Chubber."

He doesn't look back as he pushes across the plaza. He kicks the side of a pushchair as a young mum comes by. Barges past an elderly man who is as slow as a snail on coarse-grit sandpaper.

Sand again, Chubber? It's slip, slip, slipping away. Marking time. Hours rushing past.

"Busy, busy, busy," Chubber says as he skitters away and turns off the plaza, heading down Royal Parade.

"Got things to do today. At home. Best get back. Kettle on the boil. Things on the go. Deary, deary, deary, me my Chubber-Chub-Chubs."

Major Crimes operated out of Crownhill Police Station, located on the north side of the city, away from the centre. The building was a modernist brute of a structure in brown concrete, the colour choice not lost on the officers within or on a number of the more quick-witted of their clients. Savage arrived back from the moor mid-afternoon and went straight to the crime suite, where a DC informed her that DSupt Hardin wanted to see her.

"Pronto, ma'am," the DC added. "As in, now."

Savage about-turned, headed to Hardin's office and rapped on the door. Hardin's "enter" came with a splutter and when Savage pushed the door open she found him attempting to pat himself on the back with one hand while wiping up a pool of coffee on the desk with a bunch of tissues held in the other. The DSupt's bulk filled his chair and most of the space behind the desk. He was a big man, often mistaken for an ex-rugby player. However, Savage reckoned Hardin would never have had the dexterity for ball games; tug-of-war would have been much more his thing.

"Just had a phone call, Charlotte," Hardin said, screwing up the tissue paper and chucking the soggy mess in the bin. "Dan-bloody-Phillips, the crime reporter on the *Herald*. He tells me they're going to town with this one. 'Moorland Killer on the Rampage' is to be the headline. Nightmare."

"'Killer'? Where did he get that from? I'm still hoping the girl is alive and there's some rational explanation for her disappearance."

"Hey?" Hardin raised one eyebrow. "Come on. You and I both know it's only a matter of time."

Savage sighed. "Yes, sir. You're right. But how does Phillips know that?"

"That photographer of his. He's been up at the reservoir. Got some shots of Frey retrieving the webbing strap. Phillips reckons lorry driver. Only he's made the leap from there to killer. He tells me the Yorkshire Ripper was a truck driver. That right, Charlotte?"

"Yes, but it's a stretch isn't it?"

"Not really." Hardin leant over the desk, careful to avoid the damp patch. "You see, Phillips reckons the presence of a certain female officer lends credence to his argument. DI Charlotte Savage is, apparently, Devon's hotshot detective. When she turns up, you know the bodies can't be far behind."

"Fiction, sir. Headlines to sell newspapers."

"Of course," Hardin clucked. "Anyway, he wants an interview with you. A feature with pictures and everything. He told me he's already come up with some taglines. 'Killer Thriller'. 'Red Handed'. 'Juliet Bravo'. I'm thinking of passing this one to the PR guys. They love this sort of stuff. If you're up for it?"

Savage cocked her head on one side and tried to read the grin that had appeared on Hardin's face. "Respectfully, sir, I'd rather resign from the Force than do that sort of publicity shit."

"Ha!" Hardin laughed. "That's what I told him you'd say. Now, about this lorry driver business. Phillips may have something there. I've got the preliminary report on the webbing from John Layton. It's a heavy-duty tie-down most often used by hauliers to secure loads. The hair is still being analysed, but the stain is most likely a commercial oil of some type. That does say lorry driver to me."

"Possibly. But he didn't drive up to Fernworthy Reservoir in his vehicle, did he? The roads on that part of the moor are way too narrow. If you did somehow get up there you'd struggle to turn around. And whoever dumped Ana's clothing up at Fernworthy Reservoir knows the area well. I think they're local."

"What about these boys on North Hill? Reckon it could be something to do with them?"

Hardin was referring to an as-yet unidentified group of men who were targeting female students walking home from the centre of town. The police suspected that the men were using mobile phones to communicate information about women who looked so drunk they could barely walk. They'd identify those women as easy targets and one of the gang would home in and persuade — or force — the victim to have sex with them.

"There have been a number of rapes, but nothing like this."

"Maybe something went wrong. The girl banged her head or choked on her own vomit. Somebody decided to hide the body."

"Possible, but there's no evidence to suggest she was out on that night. True, if she was she would have walked home along North Hill, but Fernworthy is a heck of a long way to go to dispose of a body. If, of course, a body is what we are looking for. But then the clothes by the lake are pretty conclusive. She had no transport of her own so I can't see how she could have got there without someone else's involvement. This doesn't look like suicide to me, nor do I think she's gone back home to Hungary."

"So where the hell do you think she is?"

"Well, Inspector Frey is almost positive she's not in the reservoir. Which just leaves the woods, the rest of the moor and anywhere else that might have taken the killer's fancy. I understand the search and rescue teams are out today and the helicopter is going to be taking a second look too, but to be honest, sir, Frey is right when he says searching for her without a better idea of where to focus is a complete waste of time."

"Bloody gun-touting idiot. I'll decide whether it's a waste of time or not. The man's not happy unless he's steaming in somewhere with a machine gun nestled under one arm and an Andy McNab paperback under the other."

Savage tried not to smile. Hardin's view of the tactical support group was that they were a bunch of trigger-happy nutters.

"The police search adviser pretty much concurs, sir," she said. "Until we get some more information, we are better off not spreading our resources."

"The PolSA? Right." Hardin drummed his fingers on the desk. "Well if we're not going to look for the girl just what the heck *should* we be doing? Appealing to the killer's better nature and asking him to turn himself in?"

"An appeal is a good idea. Finding the clothes means we might be able to put together some form of reconstruction. Fernworthy is a busy place this time of year, so if anybody saw Ana there an appeal will jog their memories."

"Relying on the public. You know I don't like that, Charlotte." Hardin nodded over at his phone. "All we ever get are hoax calls, dreamers and people with nothing better to do than waste our time. Sure, we'll go with an appeal, but have you got any better ideas?"

Savage almost snapped back, "have you?" But instead she said: "We need the usual pulling-in of known sex offenders and then I think we should conduct a full-scale search of Ana's house, forensics and everything. When the initial misper report came in there was a cursory examination of her room but that was the extent of it. Now we can ratchet up the investigation a level or two."

"Three or four I think," Hardin said. "We just so happen to have the honour of the Crime Commissioner visiting us for a tour tomorrow. And he's bringing some other dignitaries with him. Charles Milner for one."

"The MP?"

"Yes. Milner's local, of course, but he's also on the bloody Home Office Select Committee. He can pull strings and raise budgets. Conversely, he can cut them.

So for the moment, this case is a priority, right? I want officers redeployed from the stabbing on Union Street and see if you can draft people from some other lesser investigations too. We need to sort this fast — and establish Anasztáz Róka's disappearance has nothing to do with any kind of serial killing. That should wipe the smile from Dan Phillips' face and hopefully put this station in the Crime Commissioner's good books."

Simon Fox, the Chief Constable of Devon and Cornwall Police, sat inside his car in his garage. He wore his full uniform, the silver buttons reflecting the sterile light from a fluorescent tube mounted on the wall above a workbench. On the bench an array of tools lay in neat rows, the light glittering off them too. He'd spent many happy hours in here, the bonnet up on whichever car he happened to own at the time, tools clinking on metal, an oily rag to wipe his hands on. In the end though, he couldn't kid himself he was doing much more than tinkering. These days modern cars were so complicated that tinkering was all you could really do.

Fox reached over to the passenger seat for the bottle of whiskey. He'd drunk half the contents but he needed more. Dutch courage. Hell, any sort of courage. He unscrewed the cap and took a deep draught. He'd long ago passed the drunk stage and now every extra gulp added clarity to the situation. And the clearer things became, the clearer the solution to his problems.

He peered over his shoulder into the rear of the Jaguar. The car was an estate, an XF Sportbrake.

Perhaps it was a bit of a cliché for a senior officer to have such a vehicle, but Fox didn't care. His grandfather had owned an XK150 from new. Fox wondered what might have happened to the car, where it was now, how much it would be worth. There was of course nothing to say the car was still around. It could have rusted away, crashed, or been crushed.

In the rear of the car a vacuum cleaner hose tumbled over the back seat. Fox had attached the hose to the exhaust pipe using gaffer tape and then led the tube up through the hatchback. He'd pulled the hatch shut as best he could and secured it with a bungee cord. Then he'd stuffed a couple of blankets in the gap. Not airtight, perhaps a bit of a bodge job, but good enough.

Tinkering.

The word summed up his career, his life. Fox wondered whether fiddling around was all anyone could hope to do. You tried to make a difference, to change people's lives for the better. In the end though, whatever you did, you ended as dust. Atoms spinning in the infinite void, never again to experience anything. Fox wallowed in a growing feeling of despair. Many years ago he'd been faced with depression, but he hadn't let it get the better of him; he'd beaten it and come out stronger. This time, he knew it was different. This sort of depression couldn't be beaten. This time he couldn't win.

Fox took a final swig from the bottle and then screwed the cap back on. He placed the bottle carefully on the passenger seat and then his hand strayed to the keys in the ignition. He turned them a notch. The lights on the dash lit up, the aircon began to hum and the navigation system came on. A blinking icon indicated that the sat-nav couldn't lock onto any satellites to fix its position. Lost, Fox thought. Completely and utterly lost.

The wrong turn had come miles back, an error of judgement undoubtedly, but one made with what at the time had seemed the best of intentions. Covering up his son Owen's involvement in a hit-and-run accident in which a young girl had died had been a remarkably easy decision to make. Owen had been high on drink and drugs, and the effect on Fox's career had the truth come out would have been cataclysmic. At the time Fox had told himself he'd done it for Owen and his young fiancée — Lauren, pregnant with the couple's first child — and not for his own selfish reasons, but deep down he now wondered at the veracity of that. Sure, Owen had reformed. Fox had forced him into a boring job, forced him to begin to accept the responsibilities that came with fatherhood. The lad had abandoned his old friends and was now a model citizen. Still, there'd been a heavy price to pay. Fox had had to call in favours and make promises to keep the truth from coming out. The problem was corruption had a stink about it and however hard you tried to keep things airtight, sooner or later there was always a leak.

There was the human cost as well, not just to his own sense of psychological wellbeing but to the parents of the victim. And that the mother should be one of his own workforce compounded the situation. Every time he met her he worried that she could read the guilt on his face. He, in turn, could see the pain on hers. She'd never got justice, never found peace. The latter, Fox reckoned, would never come, but justice? Well, some sort of resolution to the whole stinking mess lay just around the corner, the next turn on his journey.

Fox lay back in the seat and closed his eyes. Imagined the classic XK150 with his grandfather at the wheel. Soon, perhaps, he'd be sitting beside him, rolling through countryside bathed in the sunlight of an endless childhood summer. They'd park up somewhere on a village green where they could watch a game of cricket. His grandfather would reach into the glove compartment and pull out two tins and his pipe. The first tin contained boiled sweets, and Fox was allowed one every time a four or a six was scored or a wicket went down. His grandfather would take the other tin and tap his pipe on the lid three times, open it and fill the pipe with tobacco. Then he'd light up and they'd talk about the game in front of them or football or rugger. Whether Simon would like to come fishing with him. The same life but another time, a simpler time. A better time.

Fox felt tears welling in his eyes. Disgusted with himself for his lack of courage he blinked the moisture away. Then he turned the keys another notch. The engine started and exhaust fumes began to pump into the car.

CHAPTER
FIVE

When Savage pulled the car into her driveway, the sun hovered low above the Cornish coast; Plymouth Sound bathed in light. Sunday was all but gone. Back at Fernworthy the search teams had given up for the day, the latest report from Frey stating there was a high probability Anasztáz Róka wasn't in the reservoir. The bankside and woodland area designated by the PolSA had been scoured inch by inch and nothing had been found. Results from the search and rescue groups engaged in a wider sweep of the moor were equally disappointing.

Savage paused at the front door, taking a moment to switch off and leave the day's events behind. Her kids didn't need to know that a girl was probably lying naked and dead in a shallow grave somewhere on Dartmoor. Her husband wouldn't want to be filled in on the minutiae of misper procedures. Her role as a police officer ended at the threshold to the house. And yet she couldn't leave behind everything that had happened today. Seeing Owen Fox, holding the pistol in her hand as she'd watched him go about his business, unfettered by guilt, had made her realise she couldn't let things go on as they had. She owed it to herself, to her family and most of all to Clarissa, to find a way to make Owen pay for what he'd done. She just needed to think of a way to do it without endangering everything she loved. Savage took a deep breath and then went inside.

In the house she found Pete in the kitchen tossing a salad, an apron tied round his waist. Pete was the epitome of a good-looking, clean-cut naval officer, but he still looked ridiculous wearing the apron.

"From absent husband to househusband in just a few months," Savage teased. "I might just be the only person in Plymouth grateful for the defence cuts."

"Careful," Pete said, waving a wooden salad spoon at her. "I still hold a high rank in the Navy and as such am in charge of an array of formidable weapons."

"Really?"

"Yes." Savage ducked as Pete used the spoon to launch a cherry tomato across the room. "Mind you, I might be in need of some gunnery practice."

Savage laughed and then picked the tomato up and lobbed it back at Pete, running from the kitchen before he had a chance to retaliate. In the living room, Jamie and Samantha were arguing over which movie the family were going to watch for their regular Sunday film night. Jamie wanted something with cartoon animals while Samantha was keen on anything with vampires and pale, unhealthy-looking males. By dinner time they'd plumped for some Disney movie and they sat with bowls of pasta on their laps, pigging out.

An hour and a half later, with the end titles streaming up the screen, Savage's mobile rang. She pushed herself up from the sofa, reached for the phone and stumbled out of the darkened room and into the hallway.

"Ma'am, it's me." It was DC Enders, his Irish accent providing all the introduction needed.

"Yes, Patrick?" Savage said, closing the door to the living room to shut out the kids' conversation as they played out the funnier bits of the movie.

"The Hungarian girl." Enders paused, but Savage knew what was coming next. "We've found her."

Savage sighed, the laughter coming from the children suddenly grating. She walked into the kitchen, opened the back door and went out into the garden. Pete had set a sprinkler to water the lawn and as she walked across the grass a fine mist caressed her face.

"Tell me."

"At the reservoir. Not far from where the fisherman found her clothes. In fact, he was the one who found the body. Dodgy, if you ask me, ma'am."

"Right. Are you up there now?"

"No, I'm at the station. John Layton and Inspector Frey are there though. The pathologist has been called."

"Thanks, Patrick. I'm leaving now, tell them I'll be there in an hour."

Savage hung up and stared across Plymouth Sound towards the lights of the city where, despite it being a Sunday, the night would be getting into full swing. A wash of tiredness swept over her. A fitful night had been followed by a long day. The stress of seeing Owen Fox had worn her out and the news about the Hungarian girl was the last straw. She felt as if she barely had the energy to climb the stairs to bed. For a moment she considered phoning Enders back and telling him she couldn't make it, that a family crisis had intervened. Then she remembered the passport photograph of Anasztáz Róka. A blonde girl far from home. Lost and now dead. She was somebody's daughter too.

"You selfish cow," Savage said to herself.

Then she wiped the moisture from her face and went back inside.

Darkness had enveloped the moor when Savage arrived at Fernworthy. A patrol car guarded the lane to the reservoir, its blue strobing light casting pale fingers into the trees. An officer waved Savage through and she drove to the car park. Then she was directed to where the body lay, some two hundred metres west of the reservoir in dense woodland, in an area that had supposedly been searched at least once.

"It's not good enough, Nigel," Savage said, trying to contain her anger as she walked up to Frey in the near blackness beneath the canopy of trees. "The girl should have been found at the first attempt. Your search pattern was mucked up or somebody boobed."

"No," Frey said. "I won't have that. You can see the paper-work if you like. The quadrants the PolSA laid out were dealt with methodically. I'll stake my job on it."

"Well, you may have to."

John Layton had insisted on a fifty-metre perimeter around the scene, and from where she stood Savage could see a patch of bright light in which several suited figures worked. The CSIs were moving away from the body, trying to establish a safe route back and forth. It was another thirty minutes before Layton came across to Savage and Frey. The senior CSI had abandoned the Tilley hat he was usually seen in because it wouldn't fit beneath the hood of his white suit. As he approached, he pulled the hood down. Layton was mid-thirties, maybe a little older. He had dark hair and a slim face, beady eyes that missed nothing. The eyes flicked back and forth between Savage and Frey. Then he scratched his pointed nose and nodded at Frey.

"You're off the hook," he said. "She's not been there long. An hour or two at the most. She's lying on several fronds of bracken that have only been crushed recently. There's no way she was here this morning."

"That doesn't make sense," Savage said. "Are you saying she was dumped *after* the initial search?"

"Yes. Right under our noses. Sense and science can sometimes contradict each other, however difficult that makes things for us."

"Nigel," Savage said, turning to Frey. "I guess I owe you an apology."

"Accepted, Charlotte," Frey said.

"How long has she been dead?" Savage turned back to Layton.

"You'll have to wait for Nesbit for an estimate, but nothing like a week for sure. The body's in a bit of a state though. Little cuts and scratches all over her. Something like she was running through the woods naked and the branches and brambles scoured her skin."

"Cause of death?"

"Haven't got a whiskers. There don't seem to be any major external injuries. I guess she could have been strangled. Do you want to take a look?"

Savage nodded and went to find a suit and all the other paraphernalia. Suitably attired, she followed Layton down the little trail he had prepared. Festoon lights had been hung between the trees, creating a corridor of luminance which wound through the woodland, almost as if the path was leading to a fairy grotto. At the end of the path the burning glare of several halogen bulbs turned night into day. Beyond the circle of light the surrounding forest disappeared into utter blackness. As they approached the CSIs, Layton put out a hand.

"Close enough, Charlotte," Layton said. "We haven't completed our detailed search of the immediate area yet."

Savage nodded and stared through the undergrowth to where white skin contrasted with black peat. The body lay half in a drainage ditch, the face partially submerged in the dirty water. The right eye was open and gazed out across a film of scum and forest detritus, while the left was below the surface. The girl's peroxide-blonde hair floated in a fanlike pattern, individual strands moving as a slight current washed past. A blob of dark mud had splattered one cheek and several pine needles had drifted into a nostril. Savage looked closer. The girl's body was tumbled in an odd way. The right leg came out at a weird angle to the body while the right arm was twisted underneath her head. A contortionist would have struggled to adopt such a pose.

"It's a strange position," Savage said. "Whatever the killer meant by posing her like that is beyond me. If she was posed."

"I can't see how she fell with the arm behind her head," Layton said. He gestured at the trees and the undergrowth. "It would take some effort to force it into that position. I don't think it could have happened by accident."

Savage noticed the scratches Layton had mentioned. They were shallow enough to have been caused by brambles or cat's claws or fingernails. They certainly weren't terminal. Her eyes followed the outstretched leg from the toe up to the thigh to the dark triangle of pubic hair.

"Any sign of sexual assault?"

"No." Layton shook his head. "Nothing I can see from an external examination. Small blessing that it is."

Savage moved her attention to where the woodland encroached on the circle of light. There were no paths and the scrub was dense. Layton was right, Ana couldn't have run fast enough to cause her limbs to twist round in the way they lay. Yet the scratches suggested she had been running. Savage tried to imagine her last moments. How long had Ana been stumbling around the woodland naked? Had she managed to avoid the killer for hours and then somehow come across him again? She'd fallen and the killer had pounced on her. As his hands had closed around her delicate neck she'd screamed and thrashed. The killer had hit her and then pinned her leg with his body. In the struggle her arm had been twisted behind her neck. Maybe the killer had used his forearm to crush the girl's windpipe while the other hand held her arm. And yet, Savage reminded herself, none of that had happened here. If Layton was correct the body had been dumped recently. It was even possible Ana had been alive as the teams had searched for her that very morning.

"Any sign of which way the killer came?"

"No," Layton said. The CSI sighed. "In fact I can't find any meaningful footprints. That could be because he — or she — came up the drainage ditch. I'm thinking of damming the ditch and draining the water to see if I can find any footprints. The only other conclusion would be that she'd flown here by magic, right?"

Savage nodded. "Where's Nesbit got to? The sooner we can get the time of death the better."

"On his way," Layton said. He turned and padded back towards the body to join the other CSIs. Savage stood for a moment and then made her way down the avenue of lights back to the perimeter and from there to the car park. She stood next to her car and gazed across the ink-black water, where pinpricks of starlight speckled the surface. After dark, there was no reason for anybody to come here, but in the day Fernworthy Reservoir was a popular place. There would be families picnicking, fishermen fishing, walkers and mountain bikers exploring the woodland. It was inconceivable Ana had been attacked anywhere near here in the daytime — or even been moved here — without somebody noticing. Unless, as Layton had suggested, magic was involved.

Savage stood next to the mobile incident room van and watched Dr Andrew Nesbit, the pathologist, climb out of his car in the gloom. He put his black bag on top of the car and began to put on a protective suit, pulling the outfit up over a tweed jacket and tie. She guessed he'd be unimpressed with John Layton's hypothesis concerning magic. The methodical way he put on the suit, gloves, hat and mask said it all. When it came to performing his job, scientific method was everything. There was no room for spirituality. His gangly form had been compared by many to a spider, but Savage wondered if a robot might be a more apposite choice. His matchstick-like limbs moved efficiently to ensure the gear went on with the minimum of fuss, although Savage was surprised when he performed a small flourish as he snapped the latex gloves in place. Perhaps the pathologist didn't realise anybody was watching.

"Charlotte," Nesbit said, as he walked over to the van. He looked up at the clear sky above, and as he did so, starlight glinted on his half-moon glasses. "Beautiful evening. I must admit I don't get up on the moor as much as I'd like. Then again, I don't get anywhere as much as I'd like these days. And to be honest, you guys don't help. Catching them, Charlotte, that's the thing, hey?"

"We do try, you know?" Savage gestured towards the woodland. "Sometimes we need help though."

"She's in there, then?" Nesbit followed Savage's gaze. "Not in the lake?"

"No, but it was an easy mistake to make. Her clothes were found by the water's edge."

"And nobody thought to search the woodland just to make sure?"

Savage sighed. "Moot point. The entire area was searched but somehow they either missed the body or it wasn't there."

"So the clothes were dumped first and then the killer returned with the body?"

"I'm hoping you might be able to explain that." Savage pointed at the wood once more. "Shall we?"

As they reached the scene, Savage paused, and let Nesbit continue on his own to where Layton was bent over a nearby bush, torch in hand.

"Fingertipped ten metres all around and found nothing," the CSI said, straightening. "Not even a footprint. Got a pump coming to drain the ditch."

Nesbit nodded and peered at the corpse of Anasztáz Róka, the girl's flesh white as porcelain in the light from the floods. "I can see why you wanted me out here. She's in a strange position, isn't she? Let's see . . ."

Nesbit dropped his bag down onto a nearby tree stump and then stepped over to the body. He moved his head in small movements, taking in every aspect. Then he reached down and took the girl's lower leg in both hands. He flexed the leg back and forth and then mumbled to himself. Next, he reached for the arm and did the same.

"Andrew?" Savage said. "Anything interesting?"

70

"Dislocated." Nesbit looked over at Savage and then at the ground surrounding the body. "The knee and the shoulder. Difficult to see how this happened here. A considerable amount of force must have been used and there's no sign of a struggle. Am I right, John?"

"Yes. As I said there's nothing on the ground. No indentations, no scuffing, no footprints. There are some small marks to one side of the body, possibly made when she fell or was placed."

"There's some bruising on the arms and legs and also the torso." Nesbit bent and examined the legs again. "Some marks on her ankles too. Indentations, as if something has been wrapped around them. Rope or chain maybe. The dislocations happened while she was alive. Painful as they would have been, they aren't what killed her."

"Any idea what did?" Savage said. "Strangulation, possibly?"

Nesbit bent to the body again. His fingers moved to the girl's forehead and he lifted each eyelid in turn. Then he examined the neck, spidery fingers creeping across the pale skin.

"No signs of petechiae in the eyes, no marks on the neck, no sign a ligature was used." Nesbit looked across at Savage and shook his head. "I'll know more when I get her on the table back home."

Savage forced herself to suppress a smile. She assumed Nesbit was talking about the mortuary rather than where he lived.

"What about the time of death, anything you can tell me?"

71

"If you give me a moment I'll take a temperature reading, but the rigor stage has passed. Looking at the appearance of the body I would think something between twenty-four and forty-eight hours, no longer."

"The bag containing Ana's clothing was found this morning. The fisherman who found the bag had been in the same spot two days before and swore it wasn't there then. So we're looking at some time in the night before last."

"That would work, yes. But there's still some explaining to do about the body. How it got here and why it was moved."

Savage said nothing as Nesbit continued to work on the corpse. He removed a thermometer from his bag and inserted its remote probe into the girl's rectum. He spoke into a small dictation device as he went over the body again, concentrating on the process of pulling apart the evidence, everyone else all but forgotten.

She left him to his work and headed back to the incident room vehicle in search of Inspector Frey. She found him inside the van, staring at a laptop screen.

"Can't fathom it, Charlotte." Frey's finger hovered over a map of the reservoir and surrounding woodland. "The area where the body was found was searched not once, but twice. She definitely wasn't there. But how did the bugger manage to enter the area with the body when the place was swarming with us lot?"

"Maybe he didn't arrive with the body." Savage pointed at the screen. "The boundary to your search grid is only a hundred metres from the dump site. My hunch is the body was somewhere beyond the boundary. The killer returned sans body, picked up the corpse from the initial hiding place, and carried the body back to where we found it."

"To what purpose?"

"To prevent the body being found."

"Because we'd already searched the area." Frey nodded as if in agreement, but then shook his head. "But who would be stupid enough or bold enough to do that?"

"Kinver?"

"The fisherman?"

"Yes. Seems a bit too much of a coincidence that he found the clothes *and* the body, don't you think?"

"He said he was walking back from his fishing position along a woodland path. He claims he heard something, went to investigate, and found the body." Frey smiled and then jabbed a finger at Savage. "He's seen too many detective shows on TV too. Knew he shouldn't approach the body, so he never went within ten metres. Layton pointed out the man's footprints to me. There's a distinct trail coming and going."

"Could he have thrown the girl that distance?"

"Be sensible, Charlotte. Kinver's telling the truth."

"You believed him?" Savage wondered what Frey was on. Kinver, in her book, should at least have been arrested and brought in for questioning. "Nigel, I don't want to —"

"No, of course not. But I believed his wife. She and a friend were with him. Unless they're in it together, Kinver's in the clear."

"Shit."

"Yeah. We're back to Layton's version. Hocus pocus and witchcraft."

CHAPTER
SIX

Monday 25th August

Some time later Fox heard the tap, tap, tapping of the pipe on the tobacco tin. Then a faint acrid aroma caressed his nostrils. His grandfather. Fox kept his eyes closed, not wanting to believe. He waited for the old man to say something.

Again: tap, tap, tap.

"Simon?" His grandfather's voice sounded muffled, as if the sound was coming from far off in the distance. "Simon, wake up."

He'd been dozing, the warmth of the sun soporific, the slowness of the game of cricket lulling him to sleep. He'd open his eyes now and his grandfather would suggest they drove off to a pub where the old man would buy a pint of Guinness for himself and water with a splash of lime for Fox. Maybe, if he was lucky, a lemonade. Now he did believe. This wasn't the ending, it was the beginning. Whatever had gone before was done. He could start all over again, full circle.

Tap, tap, tap.

Fox opened his eyes. He was still sitting in his car, the tools still gleaming on the rack in front of him. His eyes flashed to the rear-view mirror. The garage door stood open now and the early morning light streamed in, pale, cold and unwelcome.

Tap, tap, tap.

"Simon, what on earth are you doing? I woke up and didn't know where you'd gone. Thought you'd been called out."

Fox turned his head to see Jennifer, his wife, bent to the window. She clicked the door open and looked to the rear of the car where the hose curled across the back seat. Wafted her hand in front of her face to disperse the exhaust fumes.

"Oh God, Simon. Why?" Jennifer reached in and turned the key to the off position. She collapsed to her knees, her hands grasping at the door sill, her head bowed. When she looked up, tears were streaming down her face. "Whatever's happened?"

"The air-conditioning," Fox said. "Positive pressure."

"What are you talking about?"

"Kept me alive. Despite everything. I fucked up. Again. I should have known better than to even try and make things right."

"Simon. Please."

"I tried, didn't I? Made sure the reports got mixed around. The teams checked the wrong cars. They never found out. Until now."

"I don't understand. What are you on about, darling? Tell me."

"Tinkering, bloody tinkering." Fox moved a hand to the top of his wife's head and stroked her hair. Then he

76

reached for the ignition and pulled out the keys. "Let's go inside."

In the living room, Fox bade his wife to sit. He stumbled across to the drinks cabinet and took out an unopened bottle of premium malt and two tumblers. The glasses clunked down on the occasional table and he unscrewed the whiskey and poured a generous measure into each.

"No," Jennifer said. "You had enough last night and it's not even breakfast time."

"Drink up, you're going to need it." Fox considered his own glass for a moment and then returned to the drinks cabinet. He selected a fistful of mixers: bitter lemon, ginger ale, tonic water. With an opener in one hand and the bottles in the other he went and sat on the sofa. The bitter lemon fizzed open and he took a gulp straight from the bottle. Three more gulps and he'd drained the contents.

"Simon, I —"

"You remember a few years ago that lass was killed up on the moor? A hit-and-run accident?"

"No, I can't —"

"DI Charlotte Savage's kid. Nine years old. We never caught the driver, never traced the vehicle."

"Oh yes, of course, I remember now. The poor woman. Losing a daughter must be awful. I can't imagine what I'd have done had anything like that happened to our children."

"No, I dare say you can't." Fox pointed to Jennifer's glass. She'd drunk a mouthful. "More."

Jennifer took another sip. "What's this got to do with you, Simon? Have you caught the driver?"

"In a manner of speaking, yes." Fox fizzed open another mixer. Tonic. He downed the bottle, the bubbles catching at his throat. He swallowed a burp. "Owen was up on the moor on the day of the accident. He'd camped out the night before, somewhere north of Princetown, with a few friends. They'd had a party way off in the wilds. Plenty of beer, a couple of bottles of spirits, other stuff as well. Lauren was with him too."

"Other stuff?"

"I'll come to that. Back then Owen drove that Impreza, didn't he? All souped-up like a rally car. The important thing is, Owen's route back the next day took him past the spot where DI Savage and her family were picnicking."

"He was a witness to the accident? He saw the hit-and-run car?"

"Oh yes, he saw the car alright. Owen and Lauren were *in* the car. Owen was the driver."

"*What?*" Jennifer's hand went to her mouth. "Our son? He killed the young girl?"

"Yes." Fox paused. His wife's eyes glistened as they filled with tears. Fox wanted to move across and hug her, but he couldn't. He had more to say. Much more. "Owen drove off. He panicked. He called me and I went round to his place. He showed me the damage to his car, confessed everything. He wanted me to bring him in. He was a complete mess, blubbering and ranting. Crying like he was a baby again."

"So what happened?"

"The other stuff I mentioned along with the drink? Drugs. Amphetamines, cocaine, cannabis."

"Owen was taking all those?"

"He was on speed, yes. The other drugs, he was selling. That night on Dartmoor he'd shifted a load to his friends. Wouldn't have looked good on the news, would it? Chief Constable's son arrested on drug and murder charges."

"*Murder?*"

"I don't know what the CPS would have come up with but you can be sure it wouldn't have been a speeding ticket."

"But you said Owen wanted to turn himself in?"

"Yes, but I told him I'd handle it. And I did."

Jennifer put her hands to her face. Fox rose and walked across to her. He knelt in front of the chair and reached out for her.

"We'd have lost all this. Our son, my job, this beautiful house. For God's sake, Lauren was pregnant with our grandson, I had to do something to protect my family. The child was dead. It was a terrible accident, but why compound the situation by bringing Owen, Lauren and the other kids into it?"

"So you covered it up?" Jennifer stared at Fox, her mouth half-open, as if she didn't believe he was capable of such a thing.

"Owen sorted out the car with a new front wing. He got a rush job done. The place I sent him to was suspect and dealt in stolen motors, dodgy insurance, that sort of thing. Besides, they didn't know who he was and he paid cash. The police team investigating the accident began to trace Imprezas and I made sure Owen knew when to expect a visit. The car remained in his garage and when an officer came round and inspected the Impreza nothing was spotted. The officer knew I was Owen's dad. No way was he going to press things any further."

"And after that?"

"The team worked on, but got nowhere. Using contacts I've got with Special Branch I had a flag put on the registration number of the car. If anybody did a search for the details on the DVLA system I'd know about it. I told Owen to wait a few months and then sell the car, which he did. A year went past, then another. Apart from a parking infraction for the new owner, the car fell off the radar. It changed hands again and ended up somewhere in the Midlands. I thought that was the end of the matter. It was hell for a while, but I believed it was for the best, that the past could stay that way. Then a couple of months ago we had another hit-and-run on Dartmoor. You'll remember a prison officer was killed? That got me worried, as I knew old accidents would be investigated. Yesterday I get an email from my Special Branch contact. He'd been away on holiday and had returned to find that the flag on the vehicle registration database had been triggered. An officer from Devon and Cornwall Police had requested the full details of the Impreza. He'd viewed all the records, going back years. The officer was a detective in the same squad as DI Savage. I knew then the game was up." Fox sighed and then went on. "Last night was stupid though. I drank way too much. All I could see was how my life was going to be destroyed, piece by piece. The newspaper stories, the media circus. Imagine me — a senior police officer — serving a long prison sentence. To be honest, I was a coward. Ending it seemed like the only way out."

"Oh, love." Fox bowed his head and let Jennifer stroke his hair. "Why didn't you tell me? We could have worked through this together."

"The fewer people who knew, the better. Now of course there are others. What I can't understand is why I've heard nothing from this officer or Savage."

"Perhaps he hasn't told her."

"Possibly. More likely he's got plans to blackmail us or, worse, DI Savage *does* know, but she's got plans too."

"So if neither of them has made this official, what does that mean?"

"I'm not sure." Fox shook his head. "But I know what I have to do now. It's time to stop digging myself deeper into a hole. It's time to face the music. I'm going to turn myself in, admit to what happened, plead for leniency."

"No, Simon. The man I married all those years ago would never give in so easily and he certainly wouldn't plead."

"What?" Fox felt his wife's hand under his chin. She lifted his head and met his eyes. "What else can we do?"

"We're going to fight this. What about Owen, his wife and children? We can't let this destroy everything. There must be friends who can help us."

Fox stared at Jennifer. All these years she'd stood at his side; doing the little wifely things he'd always dismissed as largely irrelevant. She cleaned the house, raised the kids — a life on the sidelines done well, but a life anonymous and largely meaningless. Now he realised just what she was made of. How hard she was willing to fight for them and their family. She was stronger than him, no doubt about that.

"Yes," Fox said, thinking his wife was correct. On Sunday night he'd given in too easily to the feelings of self-pity and guilt. Now the effects of the alcohol had worn off, he could see that. He smiled at Jennifer. "You're right as ever, darling. There *are* friends who can help us."

Savage was woken by Jamie at a little after nine on Monday morning.

"Mummy?" he said, bouncing on the bed. "Daddy says it's time to get up."

Savage glanced at the clock and groaned. She hadn't arrived back until four a.m. and it seemed mere seconds ago she'd collapsed on the bed. She reached out and pulled Jamie to her and gave him a hug.

"No huggles, Mummy!" Jamie wriggled free, slid off the bed and ran to the door. "Breakfast time!"

A couple of minutes later Jamie returned with Pete, her son holding a glass of orange juice, Pete a tray with toast and tea.

"What's this?" Savage said as Jamie plonked the glass down on the bedside table while Pete placed the tray on the bed. "Room service?"

"You were working all day yesterday and had a late one last night," Pete said. "Thought you might need a lie-in and then a pick-me-up."

"Thanks. Both of you."

Jamie grinned and then scampered off.

"It's all over the news," Pete said. "Sounds horrible."

"They always are. Especially close up."

"Look . . ." Pete sat on the edge of the bed. He said nothing for a few seconds and then touched Savage on the shoulder. "I've been thinking. This break I've been having since I've been ashore . . . well, it's done me the world of good. Training the cadets, spending more time with you and the kids, getting out on our boat. Perhaps you —"

"No." Savage shook her head and then, aware she had snapped, smiled. "I'm fine. Really."

"But seeing this sort of thing week in, week out. Can't be good for you. And this latest one. Another girl. I mean . . ."

Savage knew what Pete meant and there was an element of truth in what he'd said. "The girl isn't the problem, is she?"

"No, of course not."

"I'll get over it. I *am* getting over it. It takes time."

"It's been years, Charlotte. None of us find it easy, but lately I've been wondering if time's moved on for you at all. You haven't slept well for months. You're tired, grumpy. The last few weeks —"

"I'm sorry," Savage said. "I've had things on my mind."

"You need to talk to me, love. Tell me what's going on. I know I haven't always been here, but now I am . . . I want to help."

"You *are* helping," Savage said. She indicated the toast and then reached for the cup of tea, wanting to bring the conversation to a close. "And everything will be OK, I promise."

Pete leant over and kissed her on the cheek. "Sure?"

"Yes." Savage blinked. Saw Clarissa tumbling over the bonnet and hitting the road. Imagined putting the gun Fallon had given her to Owen's head. "I'm sure."

Despite the grand name, the Agricultural Crime Squad had been allotted but a small corner of the crime suite. The "pigsty", as Davies called it. Three tables in a "U" shape were home to several terminals and monitors and beneath the tables there was room for a few file boxes. DI Maynard had gone all proprietorial over the area and pulled a couple of freestanding whiteboards to act as a wall between the space and the rest of the room.

"So we can't see them sniggering," Davies had said, adding, "and they can't see us crying."

There was, Riley thought, as he walked into the crime suite armed with breakfast for himself and Davies, an element of truth in the DI's statement. Tracking down a missing tractor or arresting a bunch of sheep rustlers was never going to be as glamorous as working on the Major Crimes Investigation Team. Still, just a few more weeks and hopefully he'd be right back where he belonged on the MCIT, penance for his past sins well and truly served. Riley believed the punishment had been unfair; it was Davies and Savage who'd delved into the murky elements of Plymouth's underworld and got a little too close to Kenny Fallon. He'd been guilty only by association.

He paused halfway across the room. There'd been a vicious racially motivated killing in the city centre and several detectives were poring over a set of CCTV stills showing the last moments of the victim. This was real crime. Put the guys who did this away and you were removing scum from the streets, helping the family, proving a moral point. Lord knows what good tracking down a bunch of pony perverts would do.

Davies seemed to be thinking along similar lines, because when Riley plonked the sandwich down in front of the DI he contemplated the food for a moment, then smiled.

"They eat horses in France, don't they?" He shook his head and began to unwrap the sandwich. "So quite what we're getting so excited about, I don't know. Still, at least the case is a little more interesting than trying to catch these sheep rustlers."

Riley nodded and glanced up at one of the whiteboards where a map of South Devon was dotted with yellow stars. Each star represented a farm where sheep had been stolen from. Mostly it was single animals, leaving the farmer concerned unsure as to whether the sheep had simply escaped. By tracking all the reports of missing animals, Riley and Davies had ascertained there were too many for that to be the case. So far they'd identified over one hundred. At the top of the board a wag from MCIT had stuck a printed message: *Devon's most prolific cereal killer. Have ewe seen him?*

Riley had wanted to take the message down, but Davies had stopped him. "We take it down and they put up something else. We leave it and they'll get bored." Davies was right. The banter they'd endured at the beginning had now all but ceased and they'd been left to get on with their work. Clear up the rustling case and figure out what was going on with the pony on the moor and they'd be done with Maynard for good.

"Where to start?" Davies said. "The internet?"

"Not sure, sir," Riley said. "Type 'devil worshippers' into Google and I reckon you'll get all sorts of rubbish. I think we need some sort of expert, although where we'll find one I have no idea. First I'm going to look on the PNC and see if there are any similar incidents in the area."

"Good idea." Davies unfolded his newspaper and began to eat his sandwich. He mumbled through his BLT. "Let me know if you find anything, OK?"

An hour later, showered, dressed and at least partially refreshed, Savage drove to Crownhill. On the way in she took a call from John Layton. The CSI was round at Anasztáz Róka's digs in Mannamead, turning the room upside down. The team had nearly finished, so if she wanted to come across for a gander she was more than welcome.

The Mannamead area of the city was home to wealthy middle-class professionals. Solicitors, lecturers, junior consultants, maybe even middle-ranking police officers, jostled for the best double-fronted Victorian and Edwardian houses, pushing prices up and up. Ana's place was on Fernleigh Road, and usual student fare it wasn't. Savage parked behind John Layton's crusty old Volvo and got out, wondering why the landlord would decide to rent to students and low-paid youngsters rather than tenants who might be able to afford more money.

A fence of iron railings sat atop a stone wall with a gate leading to a flagstone path. The path ran through a low-maintenance gravel garden to the front of the period property, which had bay windows and an imposing porch. Savage walked up the path to the front door, where a CSI stood trying a Yale key in the front lock.

"Found this on her bedside table," the CSI said. "It doesn't seem to fit this door though."

"It could be for her home in Hungary," Savage said.

"Don't think so, ma'am. Says Timpson on the key. Unless they've got branches in Europe, this is for a property in the UK."

Savage nodded and went through the door. From behind her the CSI called out that Ana's room was upstairs. Savage walked down the hallway and climbed the wide staircase, which had a decent carpet secured with polished brass stair rods. She once again wondered why the high-end property had been rented to Ana and her housemates. At the top of the stairs a door to the right stood open, a mess visible within. Layton stood next to the bed, arranging several evidence bags on the mattress.

"Blitzed it, Charlotte," Layton said, indicating the upturned room where the doors to a wardrobe hung open, drawers had been removed from a chest, and the furniture moved away from the walls. "Take a look."

On the bed several polythene packets held the girl's clothing. A cardboard box contained some of her student work. Layton indicated the pillows at the head of the bed.

"I'm pretty sure I'm going to get a match from the hair we found on the webbing at the reservoir. There are a number of blonde hairs on the pillow and a quick look with my big magnifier leads me to think they're the same."

"Great," Savage said. She waved a hand around at the room and its furnishings. "This place is all a bit plush for a student."

"Prostitution, you mean?" Layton smiled. "Well, since you've brought up the subject of sleaze, I've found something else of interest which might explain things."

He moved across to the chest of drawers where a picture of Ana cuddling a small white dog sat to one side of an open jewellery box. The box contained trinkets, nothing of more than a few pounds value. Above the chest of drawers was a large mirror. Layton reached out and tapped the glass.

"Sorry?" Savage stared at the mirror and at her reflection. She needed a haircut.

"Look." Layton moved alongside Savage and reached out. He lifted the mirror from the wall and put it to one side of the chest of drawers. "Smile, you're on camera."

On the wall, a little way below the hook the mirror had hung on was a hole the size of a penny. A flash of light came from a piece of glass set back in the hole.

"The landlord?"

"Got to be, hasn't it?" Layton smirked. "Dirty bastard's been getting a peep show for free."

"How's the camera connected up?"

"Wireless I expect. He'll have installed the camera when he redecorated the room. Hard-wired the power supply into the mains. Wouldn't mind betting he's got the other rooms covered too."

"That could explain a lot about the house. High-quality rooms, attracting high-quality girls. How many other tenants are there?"

"Four. Girls only, and all of them are foreign."

"Do you think Ana knew?"

"If she did then why hide the camera? I'll need a warrant to search the other rooms properly, but I could take a quick peek now . . ."

"How would you get in?"

"These." Layton held up a bunch of keys and jangled them. "The landlord gave me his master set. What do you say?"

"Absolutely not." Savage bit her lip, then nodded at the camera and winked at Layton. Then she went towards the door and stepped out onto the landing. Layton followed and Savage lowered her voice to a whisper. "Thirty seconds in each room, wear gloves, and don't touch any of the girls' stuff. Oh, and it never happened, OK?"

"Sure." Layton chuckled. "But the subterfuge isn't necessary because I've unplugged the internet router and bagged it for evidence. The camera is dead."

Layton was still laughing to himself five minutes later as he came down from the second floor.

"Well?" Savage said. "Any more?"

"All four rooms. There's a big full-length mirror in the shared bathroom too, but I can't remove that without a major DIY job. We've got the router though, so we can call Hi-Tech Crimes out here. They can plug the router back in and see all the devices that are connected wirelessly. If we find more than Ana's camera, which of course we will, then we can ask the other girls for permission to look inside their rooms and make the discovery official."

"How's the landlord viewing the material?"

"Remotely. He could log on from anywhere as long as he had a connection."

"Nice work if you can get it."

"I couldn't possibly comment, Charlotte. Not without finding myself in front of the Professional Standards Department, keen to know about my attitude to women. But four nubile Eastern European girls? Well, that's a lot of flesh to get excited about."

"And it went further than that, didn't it? Voyeurism to violence. It's not the first time and I doubt it will be the last."

Savage thanked Layton and went downstairs and out onto the street, where she phoned through to the station to set up interviews with the other tenants and the landlord. There'd need to be considerable tact involved in speaking to Ana's housemates, but from what she had seen inside tact was the last thing she'd be using when she interviewed the landlord.

CHAPTER
SEVEN

Police. On the moor. In the wood. In the big dark wood.

Police, Chubber?

Yes, police. Poo lice. Chubber doesn't much like poo, nor lice for that matter. He once had lice, down there. Caught them from some dirty whore. Itchy they were, the little buggers. He should've gone to the doctor, but the doctor would have asked too many questions. Difficult questions. So instead he squirted on neat bleach. The liquid burned and turned his pubic hair white. Killed the lice though.

Get to the point, Chubber.

The point is the police have found the missing girl. They've been down near the reservoir looking for secrets. Chubber's got secrets, but luckily they're not down near the reservoir. No, they're in the wood, the big dark wood, and at home too.

Right now Chubber is sitting on his sofa in his living room watching TV. The police haven't come visiting. Not yet. Chubber doesn't think they know where he lives. They couldn't. But he's already decided he should be a bit more careful.

The blue of the lake flashes on the screen. A presenter explains about the girl. Asks how did she get there? Was this some crime of passion, something to do with the Eastern European mafia, or was she abducted, raped, killed and butchered by some mad chocolate-drinking psychopath?

Chubber! The presenter didn't say that.

No.

Chubber shifts on the sofa and the springs protest beneath him. He can't get comfortable because something isn't right.

Not right, Chubber?

No.

The TV picture has moved on to another story. Still Dartmoor, still about butchery. There's a pony at a stone circle and someone's been at it with a knife. Slicing and dicing. Chopping off the poor animal's knackers. Nasty. Painful. Chubber feels a loosening in his bowels, a queasy sensation of gas rising in his stomach. *Uncomfortable.*

Uncomfortable what, Chubber?

Uncomfortable truths. Things that happen in stone circles at night when Chubber's been watching.

Chubber pushes himself up from the sofa, stumbles across the room, fast-food packaging rustling like autumn leaves as he wades through the detritus. All of a sudden he needs the toilet, needs to take a crap, thinks he's going to be sick. The two actions are essentially incompatible. He rushes down the hallway, clumps up the narrow stairs, bile rising in his throat. He lurches into the bathroom, his face over the sink, vomit exploding from his mouth. He grasps and reaches for the tap, water splashes out as he retches again.

Chubber rubs water on his face, spits into the sink, and then releases the buttons on his trousers. They drop to the floor and he lowers his boxers and turns to sit on the toilet. His bowels open and a long heavy mass of shit drops out. He breathes out a huge sigh of relief, but while the sick and the shit and the stale air have been expelled from his body there's still something remaining inside. As he reaches for the toilet paper he sees his hand shaking.

Yes, Chubber. Consequences. Haven't you heard the word?

Of course he's heard the word, it's just up until now he's never thought it would apply to him. Consequences happen to other people. People who piss him off. Kids who tease him on the street. Girls who wear push-up bras in cafes.

Chubber rips off a length of tissue paper, wipes himself, repeats the action, then gets up from the toilet. He washes his hands in cold water and thinks about the cold night up on the moor just before Christmas. The man with the antlers standing by the car. About the next day, when he went back in daylight.

"Help me!"

The voice had come from the rock. The one in the centre of the circle.

Chubber moved forward, padding across the ground. He scanned the horizon. Nothing. The weather had turned from cold to wet and on this part of the moor there wasn't a soul to be seen.

"Is somebody there? Please! Help me!"

The voice was muffled. Like a rock would sound if it *could* talk.

Didn't like that, did you Chubber?

No. Voices in head, OK. Voices from a rock, not good. But Chubber had to see, to check. He'd moved even closer. The rock was still talking, crying, sobbing. Screaming.

"HELP ME!"

Chubber had stopped right next to the big flat stone and put his ear down on the cool granite.

"HELP ME! FOR GOD'S SAKE HELP ME!"

Silly Chubber. Not the rock. Somebody *beneath* the rock. Chubber shook his head. Trouble. Not his business. Won't get involved. Antler Man said he'd be watching Chubber and he'd know if Chubber told tales.

Best keep quiet then, Chubber.

Exactly.

Riley had hunkered down at the computer but he'd hardly got into his work before there was a scraping of chairs and a few coughs. All around the crime suite officers were sitting up straight and clearing their desks of detritus.

"Hey?" Riley tapped Davies on the shoulder. "What's going on?"

"Bloody hell," Davies said, sweeping his sandwich wrapping into a nearby bin. "It's our tour party. Didn't you read the memo this morning? Half a dozen councillors, the Crime Commissioner and a bloody MP who sits on the Home Office committee. Lively, Darius, or you'll be on dog poo collection duty for the rest of your days."

Riley straightened and smoothed his shirt as DSupt Hardin showed several men into the room. He recognised two of them as the Commissioner and the local MP. Davies pulled a tie from a drawer and hurriedly put it on.

A little while later Riley wondered why they had bothered to make any effort at all. The visiting party had kept to the other side of the room where the real action was taking place. Sheep rustling didn't interest them.

The excitement over, Riley resumed his search. After another hour he wasn't any wiser. He went over to Davies and fanned a sheet of printouts in front of the DI.

"Stuff from the PNC and some bits and pieces from the internet," Riley said. "Neither of much use."

"No?" Davies eyed the sheets with suspicion.

"No." Riley waited for a moment. Davies didn't look interested. "The PNC flagged up various incidents countrywide, which at first sight appeared to be connected to devil worship. In reality, nearly all turn out to be animals killed by natural causes or kids pranking around."

"Nearly all?"

"There was a case over in Norfolk connected with child abuse. A load of chickens seem to have been slaughtered ritually in a house where three children had to be taken into care. A man and a woman were convicted. Not ponies, and the rituals seemed to be a sham designed to indoctrinate other adults. Nothing like our situation."

"So we're done?" Davies appeared disappointed.

"Well, I've found someone at the university — a Professor Falk — he's an expert in cults and that sort of thing. I'm going to set up a meeting with him to see if he can suggest any new avenues of investigation."

"We're back to orgies then?" Davies perked up again.

"Yes."

"Well? What are you waiting for, Sergeant?" Davies pointed across to a phone. "Get onto this Falk pronto. As in now, OK?"

Riley nodded and moved back to his desk. Ten minutes later, with the appointment made, he turned back to Davies. Before he had a chance to call across his phone trilled out. DC Denton.

"There's a second pony," Denton said. "A DPA ranger just called it in."

"DPA?" Riley said.

"Dartmoor Park Authority. He said it's pretty bad." There was a pause. "Look, I can't make it up there until later. I'm working on something to do with the first killing. I said you'd go, OK?"

Riley glanced over to the next desk where Davies had started on his post-breakfast snack; a cup of coffee and a custard doughnut. "Sure, mate. Be my pleasure."

The landlord lived three streets away in a similar period property to his tenants'. It took Savage five minutes to walk there, and when she arrived DC Jane Calter was waiting for her.

"Ma'am?" Calter said. "The desk sergeant said you wanted me over here, right?"

"Yes." Savage nodded up towards the house. "I think this guy might be just your type."

The big brass knocker reverberated through the street and a minute or so later the door swung open to reveal a man in his thirties with close-cropped hair. Kevin Foster wore a diamond stud in his left ear and a Bluetooth microphone hung from his right. He was speaking to a caller as he opened the door.

"Sorted, mate." Foster made a quizzical expression with his eyebrows and looked at Savage and Calter in turn. "No. Three-fifty at least. I won't go lower and if they piss me around any more you can tell them it's off the fucking market, understand?"

Savage produced her warrant card and held the identification out for Foster to read.

"Right then. Be seeing you." Foster reached up and unhooked the headset from his ear. "'bout the girl, isn't it? Worried myself, to be honest. Good-looking lass like that goes missing you can only think one thing, can't you? So when one of your lads came round earlier and told me the bad news I was only too pleased to help. Do anything to find her killer, I would."

"May we, Mr Foster?" Savage gestured inside and Foster nodded and indicated they should come in. He showed them through to the front room, which was some kind of office. To one side of the room several computers, each with multiple screens, sat atop an array of glass tables. On the other side a large leather sofa was angled towards a wall-mounted screen on which a twenty-four-hour news channel played in silence. Foster pulled out a swivel chair and sat down while Savage and Calter plonked themselves down on the sofa.

"Anasztáz Róka was a tenant of yours, correct?"

"Yes," Foster said. "Although she was behind with the rent. She hadn't paid for three months."

"I see. But you let her stay anyway for free."

"Well, I'm not an ogre. Bloody nightmare now though, isn't it?"

Ana, he explained, had come to him pleading poverty. Money she'd been expecting from Hungary hadn't come through and she'd begged for a grace period. One month became two and then three. Foster tutted to himself.

"I was too soft, but the lass was foreign and I felt sorry for her."

"And was that all you felt?"

"Hey? I don't get your drift?"

"What about her, Mr Foster?" Calter said. "Did *she* get your drift?"

"I —"

"'Good-looking lass like her goes missing you can only think one thing.' Wasn't that what you just said to us, Mr Foster? Sounded a little bit like a confession to me."

"Don't be bloody ridiculous. As soon as Ana went missing I was concerned about her."

Savage pointed at the office set-up. "What is it you do, Mr Foster?"

"This and that. A bit of trading, a few properties, some other stuff."

"This other stuff, wouldn't happen to involve the internet, would it?"

"Sure. What doesn't these days? I used to work up in London, but now I do everything from here. Some people moan about progress, but I say bring it on."

"So you know a bit about technology then?" Savage looked across at the computers again. "You know how to set up networks and that sort of thing?"

"Of course." Foster swivelled his chair from side to side, something like a nervous twitch. "What's this got to do with Ana's disappearance?"

"We've found a hidden webcam in her room," Savage said. "Was that part of the deal? Is that the reason you were quite happy for her to stay, despite her being in arrears? Or maybe there were other reasons. Maybe you had something else in mind too."

"Web —" Foster coughed and then swivelled back to face his desk. He reached for a bottle of spring water and unscrewed the top. Three gulps, and he'd composed himself. "Don't know nothing about no webcam. Those girls, well they get up to all sorts, you know. Little minxes, the lot of them."

"Minxes, really? So if we were to examine the camera for fingerprints we wouldn't find any of yours on there? If we took a look at your computers or phone there'd be nothing to indicate you've ever accessed this webcam?"

100

"There . . . I . . ." Foster raised the bottle to his lips again.

"Yes?"

"Accidental. Might have just taken a look when my laptop connected without me knowing."

"You take your laptop to the property, do you?"

"Yes, I mean no. Not usually. Now and again maybe if I need to sort out the internet connection in the house."

"And you used the laptop to view this webcam which you knew nothing about?"

"Yes, that's about the gist of it."

"You watched Ana stripping off and you got excited, didn't you? I don't blame you. From the pictures I've seen of her she was a very attractive young woman. You must have found it hard to resist going inside and telling her how much you enjoyed watching her. Maybe you didn't resist. Maybe *she* was the one who resisted. Maybe you didn't like the way she repaid your kindness."

"You're crazy. I never touched the girl."

"The camera, Mr Foster." Calter had stood. Full height, she cut an imposing figure. "The explanation of how it got there would go some way to getting you out of the sticky situation you're in."

"The camera . . .?"

"Don't mess around with us," Savage said. She crossed to one of the desks and jabbed at a screen. "Because I'm jumping to conclusions and there's only two of them. One, you're a dirty little pervert who got off on watching Ana. Two, ditto the first conclusion, only — to coin a phrase — watching wasn't enough. It's your call, Mr Foster, which is it to be?"

"This is a fucking stitch-up." Foster was on his feet now as well, his chair rotating round and round as he pushed it away. "Hobson's bloody choice. Either way I'm in a whole heap of trouble."

"You said it. Best you tell us the truth then, hey? We're going to be examining these computers, looking at your business receipts, checking to see if anybody else could have placed that camera in Ana's room."

"Shit." Foster put his arm out to stop the chair revolving. Shook his head and then reached out for a nearby phone.

"Put that down please," Savage said. "You're coming with us."

"Sure. But I get to make a phone call first, right? My lawyer. I pay her enough — 'bout time she got off her fat arse and did some work."

It was the best part of two hours later before they arrived at the scene. Davies had insisted on lunch. "Something warm inside us," he'd said. "Be cold up there."

Riley had shaken his head, not much impressed. Now though, he was glad they'd eaten. He stood with his back to a strong breeze, his waterproof flapping wildly until he managed to zip up the front. The wind came from the east, scudding over a ridge and down a hill scattered with low bracken and gorse. Above them the sky was blue, nothing to obscure the sun's rays, but Davies' meteorological prediction was spot on. Unlike yesterday, the air temperature was struggling to get into the teens. In August.

Waterproof secured, Riley looked down at the pony again. The animal lay at the centre of a small stone circle, the circle on a plateau set into the hillside. A dozen jagged rocks poked above the heather and grass, the largest barely above knee height, the whole circle with a diameter of perhaps fifteen metres. Stonehenge, it wasn't. This time though, Riley thought, there really wasn't much doubt about the cause of death.

The animal lay on its back, a huge gash down the centre running from the base of the tail to the neck. The ribcage had been opened, all four legs forced back and down so the beast was spread-eagled. A mass of entrails lay on the ground to one side; heart, lungs, kidneys and other blobs of flesh Riley couldn't identify. A little farther away some of the intestines had been laid in a rough circle, the remaining lengths criss-crossed in triangle shapes over the top. Another pentagram.

"Fuck." That from Davies. The DI had lumbered over and now stood alongside Riley. "Enough to make you go veggie, isn't it?"

Riley nodded. A horde of flies blackened the guts of the animal and despite the cool wind, a distinct smell hung in the air. He kept his breathing shallow and tried not to swallow. He usually had a pretty strong stomach for this kind of thing, but the sight of the animal had unsettled him. Violence done to humans was one thing, cruelty to animals quite another. Irrational, he knew, but true.

"These places," Riley said, indicating the rocks. "They must have some significance."

"It'll be fairies and pagans and all that stuff. Sacrifice to the Gods. Deflowering virgins. Sticking candles up your bottom for all I know."

"Candles?"

"Old case." Davies winked. "You had to be there, but I'll tell you over a pint someday."

"We need to see that professor, sir. We're out of our depth."

"What the hell is he doing here?" Davies turned towards the track where a blue Volvo bounced along, pulling up next to Riley's car. "Mr Dippy Hippy from Totnes."

"He owed me so I called in a favour. I thought he might be able to help."

The car stopped and the door opened. A figure got out, reached back in and pulled out a Tilley hat. Plonked the hat on his head. Scratched his Roman nose.

"Layton?" Davies said. "What does he know about this?"

"He's New Agey, isn't he? Green, spiritual, Earth Mother wife. All that dancing he does. I figured he might know a thing or two."

Riley ignored Davies' chuckling and walked back to the car park. "John. Good of you to come out."

"For a horse?" Layton nodded. "Yeah, wasn't it? Don't know what the DSupt's going to say when he finds out I've joined the ranks of the RSPCA."

"I'll take the rap. This is the second one and they seem to be getting nastier. Your expertise would be welcome and we could hardly get Nesbit to come."

"He'd probably welcome the change, but I get your point." Layton moved to the rear of the car and hefted the tailgate up. He pulled out a large toolbox. "Let's go see then."

As they strolled back to the circle Riley told Layton about the two ponies and then asked if he had any knowledge of the occult. Had he ever seen or heard of this sort of thing?

"Hey?" Layton paused as they reached the central stone. "You think living in Totnes qualifies me to speak on animal sacrifice? A bit of hummus in a canvas shopping bag from the wholefood shop and next you're slicing ponies in half?"

"No, John." Riley couldn't help but glance down at Layton's feet, bare in sandals. "But you know more about this than I do, right?"

Layton sighed. "Yes, I guess I do. But let me get a good look at what you've got first, OK?"

"Sure. No problem." Riley held his hands up in apology, stepped back and then strolled over to where Davies was sitting on an isolated boulder some distance away.

A few minutes later and Layton finished up and came across.

"Not much to say. Butchered by amateurs playing at rituals. Probably used a machete, along with some kitchen knives. The ground's too hard for any footprints, but I got a butt from a roll-up spliff." Layton stared at Davies. "Assuming it's not yours of course."

"No." Davies shook his head. "B&H, me."

"There's also a can of Carlsberg with some dregs in the bottom over by one of the stones. Fresh, by the smell of it."

"Dope and lager?" Riley said. "Doesn't sound much like the sort of thing you'd be taking in the middle of some ritual."

"No." Layton turned back towards the circle. "I'm not sure this is the real deal."

"What do you mean?"

"I think these people are playing. They've got an idea of what this sort of thing is *supposed* to be like, probably from the internet. And they got some things right. You saw the intestines arranged in a pentagram shape? But they don't know what they're doing, what they're messing with."

"*Messing with?*" Riley said. "You sound like a character from some horror film."

"Science doesn't tell us everything. Whichever way you want to look at it there's things we don't know, that we can't explain."

"Tell us then," Davies said, plainly impatient.

"This circle is well off the beaten track, right? You might wonder why anybody would bother coming all the way across the moor to be here. Well, a little way to the north lies an important ley line — the St Michael's line — which runs across the country all the way from Bury St Edmunds down to St Michael's Mount in Cornwall. Leys are supposedly corridors for spiritual energy. Worshippers think that they can draw on that energy from this point. A bit like plugging into a power socket on the wall."

"You don't believe this crap?" Davies said. "You'll be telling me little green men use this place to recharge their flying saucers next."

"Hang on." Layton held up his hand and turned and pointed at the pony. "It doesn't matter if I believe it or not. Somebody believes it enough to murder that animal. Look." Layton reached into his bag and pulled out a map of Dartmoor. "So the ley line is somewhere here. It runs through St Michael's at Brentor to the west and crosses the moor heading towards Crediton." Layton traced a finger across the map. "Now, the first pony was killed up near Postbridge. Here we're some way north of Princetown. Join the two sites and you have a line *exactly* parallel to the ley line."

"Bloody coincidence," Davies said. "You may as well string together public houses. Make for an entertaining journey at least."

"No coincidence. The sacrifice of the ponies points to somebody being familiar with the alignment of ancient sites. So someone in this group is not such an amateur."

"Shit," Riley said. "You're sure it's not just kids messing around?"

"I shouldn't think so."

"What the hell do we tell Hardin?"

"I suggest you tell him to start worrying." Layton pointed across to the remains of the pony. Pieces of flesh hung on the white bones and the viscera had

107

darkened in the sun. "Do this to an animal, and it's only one step further to doing the same to a human being."

CHAPTER
EIGHT

Kevin Foster was the type of person who lent credibility to the theory that physical attributes were a marker to deviancy. He was, as Calter had said, "a right specimen". Now, sitting in a room at Charles Cross dressed in a paper jumpsuit, some of the effect was lost. Gone was the gold bracelet round his wrist, the bunch of keys on a long chain and the jeans without a belt. Still, his stocky frame with numerous tattoos, cropped hair and the way he kept nodding his little round head as it swivelled back and forth was good enough for Calter to utter another one of her classic lines.

"Imagine *that* watching you as you got undressed in the evening, ma'am. Think I'd prefer to dance naked through the squad room."

Foster muttered under his breath as they entered the interview room, expletives just audible until his lawyer provided a gentle rebuff by way of a hand on his arm. The lawyer turned to Savage, a row of brilliant white teeth glistening as she parted her lips in an approximation of a smile.

Amanda bloody Bradley. Savage cursed and stepped into the room as Bradley stood and held out her hand, red fingernails sharp and curved like an eagle's talons.

"Charlotte." The hand was proffered as if Bradley was a member of the royal family. "So *nice* to see you again. And you're looking a little better than last time we met. I do hope it won't be too long before you're back to full health."

Every time they met Bradley made some comment on Savage's looks or dress sense. It was her way of trying to gain some kind of advantage before the sparring had even begun. Savage resisted the temptation to spit on Bradley's hand. Instead, she ignored her and sat down opposite Foster. Getting Bradley to represent him was probably one of the more intelligent things Foster had done. The solicitor had a reputation for getting her clients off the hook using fair means or foul. An array of contacts usually meant she had somebody she could call on for help, and if that didn't work she wasn't afraid to use all her feminine wiles to get what she wanted.

Savage nodded at Calter and the DC guided Foster through the interview procedure and explained about his rights and the recording equipment. Foster glanced up at the camera in the corner and smiled, the irony obviously not lost on him.

"Inspector," Bradley said when Calter had finished the preliminaries. "My client has decided to admit the cameras were his and that he filmed the girls in the house over several months. The material was for his own personal use and not for wider dissemination. However, any implication he was involved in the murder of the girl is way over the top."

"Is that right, Mr Foster?" Calter said, ignoring Bradley's attempt to bring Savage into the interview and control the situation. "You're happy to make a statement to that effect?"

"Yes. Seems best." Foster glanced at Bradley and then back at Calter. Smiled. "Get it all out in the open and bare my chest. So to speak."

"Very droll." Calter tapped the printout in front of her as Bradley grimaced across at her client. "I hope you manage to keep your sense of humour when you're banged up."

"I . . ." Foster held up both hands by way of apology. "Sorry. My bad."

"Where did you get the idea to install the cameras from?"

"Saw some guy on the news. Up in Birmingham. Had a load of student accommodation and wired up some of it. Police found a room in his house where the live feeds were displayed on half a dozen screens. The fucker just sat there and brought up whatever property he fancied watching. Teens on tap. I thought 'I'll have some of that.' I know a bit about computers, so setting the thing up was easy." He saw the expression on Calter's face and hurriedly went on. "I lost my wife a few years ago. The cameras were just a bit of harmless fun to keep me entertained."

"I'm sorry to hear about your wife's death, Kevin, but it doesn't excuse your actions."

"Well, when I say 'lost', I don't mean she died. She walked out on me. She's alive and kicking, more's the pity." Foster glanced at Bradley as she coughed. "Not that I'd wish her any harm or anything, just she got a rather large divorce settlement. I had to sell three of my properties to pay her off."

"Right." Calter looked at Savage. A cue for her to take over.

"Mr Foster," Savage said. "Anasztáz Róka vanished a little over a week ago. Yesterday we find her body. Today we discover you have a bit of a thing about voyeurism. Coincidence?"

"Yes, of course. Look, she owed me money. When she disappeared I figured she'd probably gone back home or done a bunk to some other part of the UK."

"When you watched her on the webcam you were aroused, weren't you?"

"No."

"No? A nubile teen naked on screen just for you and you weren't aroused? No wonder your wife left you if —"

"Hey! OK, I was aroused."

"You masturbated over the images, didn't you?"

"Jesus! I've admitted filming, what more do you want?"

"The police want the truth, Kevin," Bradley said. "Just tell them what you got up to and everything will be fine."

"OK, OK." Foster looked sideways down at the floor like a naughty schoolboy in a headmistress's office. "I wanked off. That's all. They were beautiful, right? I was only doing what was natural."

"And what would be more natural than wanting something more than your own hand? Maybe one of

112

those lithe bodies under yours? Did you ever think of that?"

"Of course I *thought* of it, but thinking was as far as it went."

"Really? I think you went further. Much, much further."

"No."

"After seeing Ana on the screen, you had to have her. You propositioned her but she rejected you. So you decided to force her. She struggled, maybe things got out of control, you didn't realise your own strength. At the end of it she was dead."

"No!" Kevin jumped up. "You've got it all wrong, it wasn't like that! You fuckers are trying to twist the story around. I watched the girls, I wanked over them, I wanted them, but that was all."

"Are you sure? I reckon you came on to Ana. Made it clear you'd let her off the rent if she let you have sex with her."

"OK, so what if I did? I *said* the wrong thing, but I never fucking *did* anything."

Savage let his admission hang in the air. Foster held her eyes for a moment and then slumped back in his chair.

"Tell us what happened, Kevin." Calter. Leaning forward, soft words; Foster's new best friend.

Foster shook his head and then looked across at his solicitor. Bradley nodded.

"Ana came to me a week or so ago. She told me she was still unable to pay the rent and could see no way she could in the foreseeable future. I told her I had an

113

idea. I said I'd buy her lunch and explain what I wanted. When I told her we'd go over to a pub in the countryside she got nervous, but still agreed to come. I'm pretty sure she expected me to want to stop off on the way and have sex. But she still said yes, OK?"

"And is that what happened?"

"No — I mean, at first I wanted it to." Foster held his hands up. "Like you said, she was young and attractive. What hope does a man like me have of getting to make out with a girl like her?"

"Not much to be honest, Mr Foster," Calter said. "Go on."

"While we drove, another idea came to me. I enjoyed watching Ana and her housemates on screen, but really I never got to see very much. The cameras weren't positioned in the right places and the girls got dressed and undressed far too quickly. The camera in the bathroom worked a treat until they took a shower. Then the bloody mirror steamed up. Plus none of the girls had boyfriends so I never got to see any sexual activity, apart from a couple of the lasses playing with themselves under the covers. So I thought I'd let Ana and her housemates off their rent for good and pay them some money if they would make sure to display a bit more flesh. If they could put on a couple of lezzie shows, get a lad or two in, so much the better. I'd seen sites on the web where you could watch the action in houses pretty much twenty-four-seven. Sounded like a money-making opportunity to me. Better than just a one-off fumble."

"So you put this to Ana?"

"Yeah. We were driving along up near Widecombe-in-the-Moor, heading for a pub, and I told her about the camera in her room. She went mental. Started calling me all kinds of names and then demanded to be let out. I told her to shut up but she started screaming so I stopped the car and she jumped out. She told me to drive off or she'd start shouting 'rape', so I did. Honestly, that was the last time I saw her. I never killed her. I never even touched her."

"Were there any witnesses to see this, being as you were close to Widecombe?"

"No, I'd stopped just outside. There was nobody else around. But she walked into the village, I'm sure of it."

"I'm sure you are, Kevin, but the ending to your story sounds a little too convenient." Calter turned to Savage. "Ma'am, what's your opinion?"

"I think it's total bullshit," Savage said.

Riley was back at Crownhill mid-afternoon. He dropped Davies off and continued into town for his meeting with Professor Graham Falk, slightly surprised that the academic had suggested Starbucks as a rendezvous point. He sat outside the coffee shop, watching out for Falk. His first latte had been and gone when he glanced up to see a man standing beside his table.

"DS Darius Riley?"

Riley was taken aback to see the voice belonged to a man some way the right side of fifty, the epitome of tall, dark and handsome. Well, perhaps he wasn't tall, but the other two attributes certainly applied.

"Yes." Riley made to get up, but Falk waved him down.

"Please." He glanced down at Riley's empty cup. "Can I get you another?"

Riley nodded and Falk walked off. Five minutes later he was back with a cappuccino for himself and a fresh latte for Riley.

"Is this your usual place for a meeting?" Riley asked. "I was expecting to find you in an office surrounded by musty old books."

"I'm a social anthropologist." Falk waved a finger around. "You could say this is as good as an office for me."

"I thought you were in the sociology department?"

"*Was* being the operative word. In order to save money the department has been swallowed up by the new School of Government. Sociology has always been a dirty word. Politicians don't like the subject because it raises too many questions, but doesn't provide an equal number of answers. Anyway, I don't have to worry. At the moment I'm attached to the Centre for Culture, Community and Society. I have a bursary and apart from a few light teaching duties I'm on sabbatical writing a book which I hope might become a TV series."

"On Satanism?"

"Hell no!" Falk smiled. "Excuse the pun. No, it's on the changing nature of belief. How we got to the twenty-first century and left God behind."

"Controversial?" Riley said, thinking the man was certainly the type of male eye candy TV executives

116

would rush to sign up. Middle-aged women from middle England would swoon at his every word.

"I hope so." Falk smiled again and leaned forward. He reached down into his bag and brought out a copy of the *Herald*. "Now, to your problems. I see the local paper isn't helping much."

"No." Riley read the headline: *Satanic Ritual Pony Horror*. "I guess they're in the business of selling papers, not helping the police."

"What annoys me is they make most of the stuff up. Their ideas come from watching Hammer horror movies. Would you believe they contacted me for an interview, but they wanted to conduct it in a churchyard at night? Of course I said 'no'. They want buckets of blood, naked virgins and plenty of sex."

"What we discovered on the moor was certainly bloody. Are you going to tell me that's not what it's all about?"

"Not really." Falk shook his head. He gazed across the plaza to where two Goths were pushing a baby in a buggy. "See those parents? Plonk them in a graveyard sans child and they'll be viewed entirely differently. Everything comes down to context and one's point of view."

"I don't get it."

"Relativism, Mr Riley. One man's meat is another man's murder. There are no absolutes."

"Those ponies suffered. That's an absolute. I can't see why anybody would do such a thing."

"*You* can't see." Falk smiled. "You have to understand that people believe in things for different

117

reasons. Science has eliminated deities but people still feel the need for something spiritual. They want something to use as a tool to structure their lives. No different from Christianity. Over the twentieth century, God as a supernatural being has been swept aside by materialism. Your identity is no longer formed from what you believe, but rather from what you possess." Falk put his hand in his pocket and pulled out his mobile phone. "This is what people worship nowadays."

"Right." Riley stared at Falk. He considered himself something of an intellectual, but he had no idea what Falk was talking about. He lived in a different world. A world of ivory towers and grants which enabled you to write pure garbage for a living. He tried again.

"Could I ask you to take a look at these?" Riley pulled out a sheaf of photographs and passed them across to Falk. "Fact, not the fiction of the newspapers."

Falk took the pictures and looked at them one by one. Then he put them down and pushed them across the table back to Riley.

"Well?" Riley said. He looked across to a nearby table where the Goth couple had sat down. The father held the baby, spooning some yogurt from a pot into the child's mouth. "What do you think?"

"I can tell you this stuff isn't genuine. In my experience true believers don't go cutting up ponies. In fact atheistic Satanists don't believe in any form of human or animal sacrifice. The members of the groups I've studied are just like you and me. Ordinary people, not monsters."

118

"Professor Falk, what I need from you is help tracking down these nutters."

"Killing a couple of ponies does not make you a nutter, not clinically."

"Maybe not, but what if the next step is to go further?"

"I doubt it will come to that. These people are just having a laugh, no more."

Riley sighed. This wasn't what he was expecting. "We still need to find them. They've committed a serious crime. I was hoping you might be able to give me one or two names. Somebody connected with this sort of thing. In the scene. We're at a loss as to where to start."

"I'm sorry to disappoint you. There is no 'scene' to speak of. By their very nature these groups are secretive. You don't join in the same way you join a golf club. There's no easy way in."

"You must have interviewed people."

"Yes, but my research is confidential. I can't go passing on names to you. I have to protect my sources. And, as I just told you, the killers of these ponies have got nothing to do with Satanism. Speaking to the people I know wouldn't get you anywhere."

"And if you're mistaken about these pony killers not progressing from animals, if they are already carrying out some form of human sacrifice?"

"Human sacrifice?" Falk shook his head, laughing. "Fantasy, Mr Riley. Pure fantasy."

The academic bent to his cappuccino and took a sip and for a moment Riley saw a chink of something beyond the suave good looks. Doubt, or guilt?

Whatever, when Falk lifted his head again the expression had gone.

Savage was back at Crownhill by late afternoon. She went to the crime suite in search of Gareth Collier, the office manager, intent on getting a summary of where they were at the end of day one. She found him working up different scenarios on a whiteboard, every now and then raising a hand to scratch his crewcut hair as he puzzled over some minuscule detail. The case had moved up several notches now it had become a full-blown murder investigation and Collier was assigning actions as if he had unlimited resources. Ana's fellow tenants had been interviewed when she went missing but now they'd be seen again. Other friends and acquaintances were being lined up for questioning too. Layton was having a full search of the house carried out, the college where Ana had studied was being contacted and an officer had been assigned to liaise with the Hungarian police.

"Ana had a part-time job at that coffee bar on Armada Way, Bean There," Collier said. "One of the other housemates worked there as well. The Russian student. Name of Irina Kryukov. Ana will have come into contact with loads of people at the cafe. It's possible she made friends there too."

As Collier began to expand the circle of people Ana had come into contact with, Savage held up her hand. She explained about Kevin Foster, the cameras and how he'd admitted taking Ana up onto the moor.

"We focus on Foster for now," Savage said. "His car's getting a going over from Layton so if Ana has been in there then we'll soon know. The clothes we found up at the lake are also being tested. Any trace of Foster on the clothes and then I reckon we can start to build a case."

"*Start* to build." Collier scratched his close-shaven head. "I can foresee all sorts of problems. He's already said that Ana had been in his car. There could be loads of legitimate reasons why her clothes could have traces of Foster on. We need motive and as far as I can see the last thing Foster would want to do is jeopardise his potential new income stream."

"Foster got off on filming the girls," Savage said. "He said it himself. He liked what he'd seen on cam and wanted more. She rebuffed him, so he tried to take what he wanted by force. Or an alternative could be that Ana found out what he was doing and he had to shut her up somehow."

"OK, but his story about her being in the car cuts out half the forensic. Unless we get blood or something. He's ensured he's got a reason for being on the moor and his statement places Ana being dropped close to somewhere nice and safe. Clever."

"Maybe too clever. Widecombe in mid-August at lunch-time would have been heaving. If Ana was there somebody must have spotted her. She was striking. If nobody else the male pensioners on one of the coach trips would remember."

"Jesus." Collier rubbed his head again. "Tracing those people is going to be a nightmare. They'll have come from all over the country. How the hell are we going to know which companies to contact?"

"There's a couple of inns in Widecombe, a cafe too. Likely they'd have had bookings. A coach party can't just turn up unannounced and expect to be fed. Get onto them and find out if they had any large parties in on the date concerned. As you say, finding the passengers is going to be tricky, but at least we've got something to work with."

"I think what you mean," Collier said as he picked up a fat marker pen and began to scribble on the whiteboard, "is *I*'ve got something to work with, right?"

Cornish Guardian, *December 20th, 1995*

Butchered Cow Down To Satanists Says Farmer

A cow stolen from a farm near St Breock, Wadebridge, and later found with its throat cut, was killed by devil worshippers, says local farmer Reggie Collins. Mr Collins claims the heifer was taken from a shed on his farm last Friday. The animal was found by a dog walker on Bodmin Moor on Sunday morning. The cow's throat had been slit and some of the entrails removed. Several fires had been lit nearby.
Police enquiries are continuing.

CHAPTER
NINE

Tuesday 26th August

First thing Tuesday and Savage headed for Mannamead to interview Irina Kryukov, Ana's Russian housemate. When she arrived at the rental property she found Layton's blue Volvo parked on the kerb. The front door stood open and the sound of hammering echoed down from upstairs. Savage knocked anyway and halfway down the hall a door opened. A dark-haired girl of about twenty-five poked her head out. She had high cheekbones, red lips and pale skin. Russian women, Savage decided, must have different sensibilities than the average Brit. Or maybe they were just made of tougher material. It was the only explanation for Irina Kryukov choosing to remain in the house even though her fellow tenants had packed up and left.

"More police?" the girl said. Savage nodded and Irina shrugged and led the way through to a front room with two big Ikea sofas and a huge flatscreen television. "Please, sit."

Savage sank down into one of the sofas as Irina went and stood by the television. The screen was showing a news programme but the sound was off. Still, Savage could tell from the scrolling news ticker at the bottom of the screen that the channel wasn't British.

"He paid for the foreign programmes," Irina said, taking a remote control and blipping the TV off. "Kevin Foster. I thought that was nice of him. But yesterday your Mr Layton showed me the cameras so now I know different. I learn many things since coming to England. Mostly about men."

"I'm sorry for what happened, Irina," Savage said. "I can tell you Mr Foster is facing serious charges concerning the cameras he used to spy on you and he is the number one suspect in the murder investigation."

"Yes."

"It means the investigation is now extremely high priority. We've got dozens of officers on the case."

"Yes."

"We're doing everything we can to get the evidence we need for a conviction, but we need your help."

"Yes."

Savage stared at the girl for a moment. She spoke good English but her answers were monosyllabic, as if she didn't understand. But she did, Savage was sure of that. There was something else.

"Irina," Savage said. "Is something bothering you?"

"Yes."

"Well?"

"My job." Irina moved from the TV and strode across to the second sofa. She sat, avoiding Savage's gaze and instead looked down at her lap and examined her fingernails. "I'm worried that I might lose it."

"I'm guessing you shouldn't be working. Am I right?"

"Yes. My visa doesn't allow me to."

"I can't make promises for other agencies but I can assure you that the police are not interested in your immigration status or whether your employer is breaking the rules. It's catching Ana's killer we're interested in."

"OK." Irina lifted her head and nodded towards the television. "Mr Foster is — how do you say? — a dirty old man?"

"In police work we call them sex offenders, but yes, he is."

"It's nothing. There are many Russian men the same. They have money, they think they can have girls too."

"And Foster wanted Ana, right?"

"He wanted all of us. He would come round every week. Always an excuse about fixing this and that so he could have a flirt. We always had a laugh about him when he'd gone."

"This is good, Irina. Little details like this help us build a case. With enough pressure we can get him to admit he took Ana."

"No."

"Sorry?"

"Mr Foster, he is not the one. He's a sad man. He's the type who pays for prostitutes and kids himself they enjoy it. He watches porn, he believes women are there for him." Irina turned and looked Savage squarely in the eye. "But he didn't have anything to do with Ana's murder. It was another man."

"Why didn't you say so before?" Savage shook her head. "Your job, right?"

"Not just that. The police in Russia. In a barrel of apples you expect to find one or two bad, but not the whole lot. When they're all rotten you stop eating apples."

"Thankfully, we do things differently here."

"You do?" Irina shook her head. "I'm not sure. I've seen your bad cops on the news. And not just one or two."

"Look, Irina, I'm not a 'bad cop', OK? I'm going to do my utmost to find out who killed Ana and I promise you they'll pay for what they've done." Savage waited for Irina to respond but the woman stayed silent and then just shrugged. "Now, can you tell me about this other man?"

Irina said nothing for a few seconds. Then she nodded. "I work in the same coffee shop as Ana. The money, it's not good, but the tips make up for the low pay. We split the tips between whoever's on. Me and Ana, well, we always get plenty. To be honest it's about how we look. We bought some really nice nylons and a push-up bra each. When we work we make sure we smile and show plenty of cleavage. The men, they're so easy, so stupid. You should see them drooling. On a good shift we can easily double or treble our basic pay."

"OK." Savage wasn't sure where this was going, wasn't sure if she approved. "So what's this got to do with Ana going missing?"

"There're quite a few regulars, guys who come every lunch-time, or after work. They like to flirt and to be honest so do we. They're funny, make us laugh."

"There's more though, isn't there?"

"Yes." Irina bit her lip, and then sucked in a gulp of air. Savage could see moisture in the girl's eyes. "There's this one man, I first saw him a couple of months ago. He's weird, creepy. Fat, disgusting. He has a hot chocolate, sometimes something to eat. And the way he watches us, it's unsettling. He looks at our legs, our breasts."

He would, Savage thought. They all would.

"The thing is, his tips are very generous. A couple of quid when he's just had a drink. If he's had a snack sometimes he'll leave a five-pound note. I guess that's why we put up with him leering."

"And how long has this been going on for? The tips?"

"A month or so, maybe a bit longer. He started coming in, how do you say in English? Regular, like clockwork? Eleven o'clock on the dot. At first it wasn't so bad, just the leering, but when the messages started I didn't like it."

"Messages?"

"They were creepy." Irina stood and went across to the mantelpiece. She lifted a small ornament and removed something from beneath it. A paper napkin. "This is one he left a few weeks ago. I kept it because I was going to show the owner of the cafe. In the end I didn't. The job. I need it, you understand? I don't want to make trouble."

Irina passed the napkin to Savage. Scrawled across the surface was some writing beneath a crude heart shape. Savage flattened it out to read the writing.

I'm watching you and I love you.

128

Savage stifled a smile. Was this so bad? She looked across at Irina. The girl was beautiful, a heartbreaker. Add in a sexy outfit to the girl's Slavic looks and it was understandable how a man could fall in love with her.

"And you're saying Ana got these letters too?"

"Yes. In fact to start with the messages were always left for Ana. Later he began to send notes to both of us. It made me sick."

"Irina," Savage said, passing the napkin back across the table. "I don't want to sound unsympathetic, but this isn't enough to make me suspect this man of anything. If you know where we can find him then perhaps I can send someone to question him. Have a word about the notes. Perhaps he knows something about your friend, but I doubt he's her killer."

"He is!" Irina snatched the napkin back and returned it to the mantelpiece. "You aren't listening to me, there's more. A few weeks ago I saw him outside here hanging around, in the dirty old coat he wears, carrying a plastic bag. He was walking up and down the street, eyeing the house."

"Why didn't you report this when Ana went missing?" Savage shook her head. "Let me guess, you didn't trust the police, right?"

Irina nodded. She pulled something out from her pocket. Another napkin. "He left this for me on Sunday. With a ten-pound tip. It's disgusting."

She passed the napkin across and Savage took it. There was the same heart and the same scrawl of pencil, but this time the message was different.

I love you and I want to fuck you and then I want to eat you.

Savage read the message again. She looked up at Irina. The girl's hands had gone to her face and she was crying. Between the sobs she mumbled Ana's name again. Then she looked up at Savage, the eyes cold, the stare like a blast of winter wind from the Russian steppes.

"Is that enough?" Irina said. "Is that *fucking* enough?"

Morning. Another day for Chubber and another cafe. Another *three* cafes. Two hot chocolates and some breakfast. Cheese on a weird type of bread. Cia . . . cia . . . cia . . . Foreign, but tasted nice. He thinks of the waitresses. They're foreign too, and finger-licking-good. Chubber rises from his seat. He likes cafes, but that's quite enough for today. He walks across town towards the multi-storey where he's left his car.

"Chubber's got to checker, check, check," he says as he looks around. "Best not be followed by the munchkins."

He pauses at a shop window. Notes the reflections passing by. Mere ghosts shimmering over a display of pine furniture. Ghosts worry him, scare him. They really exist, he's sure of it. Ghouls too. Zombies, wraiths, spectres, apparitions. Chubber touches the glass. Cold, these ghosts. But not following.

Checker check check again, Chubber?

Yes. Always need to be sure. Don't like surprises. Especially not when the surprise is the man with antlers on his head.

130

Told you, Chubber, didn't he? Told you what to do.

Yes. Said he needed Chubber's help. To keep an eye on someone. At first. And when he'd finished helping with the first girl there was another one.

But Antler Man said be discreet, didn't he? Watch from a distance. Don't talk to them. If he ever found out what you'd been up to with the notes . . .

He won't. And there's no harm in being friendly.

But say he did find out, Chubber . . .

He can't.

But just supposing . . . then there'd be harm, wouldn't there?

Oh yes, Chubber thinks. Antler Man would be cross and he'd start talking about the devil and damnation and the fires of h . . . h . . . h . . .

Don't think about it, Chubber, don't!

Chubber opens and shuts his mouth. Sucks in air. Tries to focus on something else. He lurches along the street and then ducks into the car park. His car's on the third floor, a little white Micra car derived van. Rust patches at the bottom of the doors, filler on the nearside rear quarter, the wing mirror gone that side too. But Chubber doesn't care about the state of his car any more than he cares about the state of himself.

Chubber gets in and drives off.

Not far home. A few minutes and Chubber is there. It's a little terrace house, door opening from the road straight into the living room.

Chubber steps round the shopping trolley with the bent wheel. He negotiates his way past a stack of carrier

131

bags bound with string. He clambers over the pile of food packaging at the foot of the stairs.

"Bit smelly," he says, as he spies some green residue creeping over an empty pizza box. "Must remember to put the rubbish out."

But there's no time to clear up. Never any time. Chubber is busy busy busy.

Time again, Chubber. The clock ticking. Tocking. Mocking.

The stairs run up the side of the living room to two small bedrooms and a bathroom.

Up we go Chubber. Up, up, up!

Into the bathroom to wash his hands. Wash wash wash. Then into the back bedroom to unpack his things. Lay them on the bed. Lovely. Been to that kitchen shop in town. The fancy one with the fancy stuff and the fancy staff at the checkout. Uniforms. Black and white with frills. Like waitresses. Pretty maids all in a row. But no time for lusting or thrusting because he's got shopping to do. Yes, they've got them. Hanging on the wall in plastic sheaths. Shiny. Expensive. But Chubber doesn't care about the money. Oh no, no, no. Chubber's got to have the best for this job.

Chubber looks out the back window. There's a yard, tiny, nothing but paving slabs. A bicycle leans against an old concrete shed. A clanky manky bicycle but the wheels go round. Gets him where he wants to go if he doesn't need to carry anything heavy.

Heavy heavy heavy. Difficult to move. Sort of thing you need to heft over your shoulder.

Oh my, my Chubber! Naughty Chubber!

In the shed are other things too. Chains and ropes for hanging up stuff, sacks for storing things in, crates for moving things which are a bit slippy sluppy yucky mucky.

But not mucky here. There are neighbours. Fences. Neighbours and fences and a lot of peering over. Chubber needs a place quiet. Quiet and peaceful and a long long way from anywhere. Because when you do the things Chubber does, oh yes indeed you do not want neighbours.

You don't, Chubber?

No, Chubber doesn't.

Collier had chosen the one person who wouldn't moan about doing the research on the coach parties up at Widecombe-in-the-Moor: Jane Calter. She was certainly a grafter, Savage thought, as she went over to see what progress Calter was making. The DC was a keen runner and Savage reckoned the training gave her discipline. For a marathon or half marathon you had to prepare, put in the miles, do the legwork and stick to your schedule. Only the legwork in this case took place using the tip of your finger.

Calter explained that she'd managed to track down a coach company who'd had a coach in Widecombe-in-the-Moor on the day Foster claimed to have dropped Ana at the village. The coach had stopped for two hours so the passengers could explore and have lunch. The good news was the company had a passenger list.

"Nathans, ma'am," Calter said. "Hebden Bridge. Really helpful. There were fifty-one people all told, and they sent me an email with the names and addresses. I reckon if Ana was in Widecombe at lunchtime then it's likely one of the party would have seen her."

"We'll need help from West Yorkshire Police then."

"Already in hand. Most of the people come from the town so it shouldn't be too hard to speak to at least a few of them today. I've sent a picture of Ana up to Hebden Bridge."

"Great stuff," Savage said, and then went across to speak to Collier about the possible new suspect Irina had told her about.

"Really, Charlotte?" Collier said in disbelief. "Because 'weirdo in dirty mac writing love notes' doesn't rate high on my radar."

"Not if he's stalking the girl?"

"And is he? From what you've told me he's not gone beyond a few clumsy attempts to make a pass at the waitresses, and visited them at home once. He sounds like a sad, lonely bloke lusting after pretty girls. If we arrested everyone like him we'd have to convert Cornwall into an open prison to hold them all."

"He's worth a look, surely?"

Collier sighed. "Go on then, give me his name." He pulled the cap of a marker pen and sniffed the tip as if sampling the bouquet of a fine wine.

"I don't have a name." Savage held up her hands as Collier shook his head and tutted. "I know he comes to the cafe where Irina works."

"So what do you expect me to do? Write 'man, weirdo, no name'? Sorry, Charlotte, I can't spare officers for surveillance on an unlikely suspect who might not even turn up at the cafe for several days. If he turns up at all, that is. A surveillance op would require at least four officers to watch the cafe during opening times, and there'd need to be back-up cover too. Those officers would have to be pulled from somewhere. You know how stretched we are, it's just not possible."

"But . . ." Savage looked at the whiteboard where lines of Collier's neat writing indicated actions he had been only too happy to agree to. She tried again. "Irina told me the man's a regular."

Collier bit his lip before continuing. "OK, if, for some reason, perv number one — Mr Foster — fails to come good today, then you personally can take a look. Can't say fairer than that, can I?"

Savage nodded, not for the first time wondering if she was in control of the investigation, or if it was the office manager.

CHAPTER
TEN

Irina placed another book in the cardboard box on her bed. She'd filled three boxes already and had just her clothes and a few personal possessions left to pack. This morning she had asked the student housing office to find her some new accommodation; they'd been reluctant at first until she told them about Foster. Irina argued that the university had supposedly inspected the place. Weren't they partly responsible? After that, the housing officer couldn't move fast enough. From tomorrow she'd be in a nice little bedsit in a purpose-built block, with the university paying the first three months' rent.

"Not that we're liable, love," the man behind the desk said, giving her a glance up and down. "Anyway, you look like you can take care of yourself, right?"

Arsehole.

A man in a white paper coverall walked past the open door to her room, carrying a plastic crate down the corridor. Irina put a foot out and kicked the door shut. She was fed up with the police. She hadn't thought much of them the first time they'd been around. They'd shown little interest in Ana's disappearance, dismissing Irina's concerns almost as if she was telling them about a lost pet rather than a human being who'd gone missing. Now, with Ana dead and officers swarming all over the house, she hadn't seen anything to change her opinion of their competency.

Earlier, she'd been interviewed by a woman detective. Attractive, with red hair, she'd nevertheless had an edge to her which Irina found unsettling. She hadn't believed Irina about the fat man in the coffee shop and seemed to be more concerned with Kevin Foster. Irina went over to the window. The terrain fell away from the house and she had a good view across the city. Somewhere out there the fat man was walking the streets with his dirty old coat and his plastic bag. He was the one the police should be questioning. He was the one the police should be following. They didn't even know who he was or where he lived, so how could they be so sure he had nothing to do with Ana's disappearance?

Back home in Russia the corruption amongst the police was endemic. Here in the UK they just seemed lazy. The public seemed to accept everything at face value. They were unquestioning, a blind faith in the authorities. At least in Russia if you wanted something doing you could grease someone's palm and they'd do it. Irina remembered asking her father what you did if you didn't have any money to pay.

"You get off your backside and you do it yourself," he'd said. "That's the only way to get on in life."

Irina had taken his advice at face value. She'd got off her backside and tried her best to better herself. At school she'd worked hard and along with her studies she'd been a gymnast. Early morning training sessions, weekends away competing, the camaraderie of the club. She'd loved it and she'd been good at it too; good enough to win several national competitions at junior level. In the end though she'd had to choose between studying and sport, and she chose studying. Her father had told her he was proud of her choice. Not whether one option had been better than the other, but that she'd come to the decision herself. "Always remember to follow your own path, Irina," he'd said.

Do it yourself . . . follow a path.

Irina returned to the bed, placed a final book in the box and flipped shut the flaps. She'd made her mind up. If the police wouldn't do anything about the fat man then it was down to her. She picked up her phone. Five minutes later and everything was arranged. She was working the first shift at the coffee shop tomorrow morning.

An hour later, they had confirmation from Hebden Bridge. At least three members of the coach party had made a positive ID of Ana.

Savage went across to tell Collier.

"Corroborates Foster's story," she said. "Looks like he did leave Ana at Widecombe. However, he could have met up with her again afterwards, so he's not out of the frame yet."

"'fraid he is, ma'am," Collier said as he put a line through Foster's name on the whiteboard. "The bugger's no saint but I don't think he killed Ana."

"Go on."

"Don't know how we missed it," Collier said. He proffered a printout with a calendar for August on. "Kevin Foster reckons he took Ana up to Widecombe-in-the-Moor on Thursday. That was the fourteenth. The cafe where she works say she came in on the thirteenth and picked up her pay."

"So?" Savage said as Collier showed her another bit of paper. "Maybe she had an inkling of what was going on with Foster and had already made plans."

"Possibly." Collier pointed at the statement where Savage could see the date marked with yellow highlighter. "But there's been a mistake with the day. The owner's statement says, I quote: 'It was the thirteenth I last saw her. Yeah, late Thursday afternoon. I remember she'd come in to collect her pay packet.'" Collier shook his head. "Thursday was the *fourteenth*, not the thirteenth. The date was extracted from the statement but nobody noticed the mix-up with the day of the week."

"Have you checked this?"

"Yes. I've spoken with the cafe owner again. His payroll day *is* Thursday. He checked his books, Ana's pay was made up to that day. Ana definitely returned to the cafe *after* her car ride with Foster."

Savage slapped her hands to her head. "Jesus. And that makes sense, doesn't it? She's just discovered Foster has been spying on her. She's had enough, so she decides to get out of the house, out of Plymouth. Late afternoon fits with her having to get back from the moor."

"But her things? She didn't return to her place to collect anything."

"Understandable. Think about it, Gareth. She's just had a rather nasty shock. Foster has told her he's been watching her naked. He's come on to her. Would you want to go back to the house? She probably thought he'd be waiting there for her."

"So where the hell did she go? None of her friends had any further contact with her. The cafe owner appears to be the last person we have on record who saw her." Collier shook his head and then ran his hand over the short stubble on top. The mannerism was the closest thing Collier got to a meltdown. "Unless . . ."

"The man who's been bugging the girls at the cafe."

"Shit," Collier said.

DC Carl Denton lay in deep shade, his body wedged beneath an overhanging slab of granite. He tried not to think of the hundreds of tonnes of solid rock above him. The tor had been standing here for thousands of years and it wasn't about to come tumbling down any time soon. Dampness seeped in through his waterproof trousers and a mosquito zipped around his head. He swatted at it and adjusted his position. He'd been lying beneath the rock for a good two hours. The Cornish pasty he'd brought along for supper had long gone and the bottle of cola nestled by his side had only a dribble left inside. Maybe, Denton thought, he'd made a mistake. Maybe he'd got the location completely wrong.

140

He looked out of his tiny cave through several fronds of bracken. The landscape fell away, boulders scattered in a haphazard fashion down the steep side of the tor. A drystone wall stood where the ground levelled and beyond lay a clearer patch of ground. He could make out the stone circle, the rocks casting lengthening shadows as the sun moved closer to the horizon.

Denton glanced down at his map. He'd used a pencil to reproduce the lines John Layton had shown them. To the north of his position was St Michael's Ley, the line running across the undulating contours, crossing Dartmoor from east to west. Parallel to that was a second line, which joined the two stone circles at Postbridge and Princetown. Denton rated Layton; the chief CSI was one of the good guys. However, Layton had missed the next step in the theory: extend the line from the Postbridge and Princetown sites and you got a line which ran straight to the Merrivale ceremonial complex with its stone rows, kistvaens and stone circle. To Denton it was obvious something was going to happen here next.

He shivered, partly from the cold now that the sun had dipped below the horizon, partly from the excitement. The first killing had taken place on Sunday, then there was one yesterday. Logic told him there'd be another one today. If he was lucky he'd catch the perpetrators red-handed.

Denton pulled the zip on his coat up. He yawned. This morning he'd been in early to complete bits and pieces of paperwork. Tonight he had no idea when he'd get to bed. He stared down the hillside. The landscape had greyed now the sun had gone. The night would be clear and cold. The forecast for the rest of the week was good. More sun than rain, temperatures pushing up into the mid-twenties. With the fine weather she'd be out on a run tomorrow, he thought, then later in the week out clubbing.

She being DC Jane Calter.

Denton closed his eyes for a moment. There was rarely a moment when Calter was out of his thoughts these days. Everything she did mattered to him, every word she said had some kind of hidden meaning which he tried to decode. At the start of the year he had realised he was in so deep he was drowning, the water closing above his head as he sank down. The crunch had come a couple of months before when he'd overheard Calter talking to a female colleague. "He's a sweet boy," she'd said, "but a total drip. I like someone with a bit more guts."

Guts? He'd once tackled someone armed with a cutthroat razor and received a slash across his face for thanks. That fact seemed to have passed Calter by. After that comment and the depression that had followed the death of his grandma, Denton had tried to rescue himself by leaving CID and taking up a role as a Wildlife and Countryside officer. He still had contact with Crownhill but not on a day-to-day basis. He'd thought it would help but it hadn't. Who was he kidding? He was still in love with Calter and she, as far as he could tell, didn't even notice him.

Now, though, Denton had come up with a better plan to impress. Women, he knew, always had a soft

142

spot for animals and he'd heard Calter talking about her gran's dog and how she hated any type of cruelty. What better way to show not only his softer side but also his bravery than by tackling a load of devil worshippers intent on sacrificing Dartmoor ponies?

Denton blinked his eyes open. A pale glow faded in the west while to the east, stars began to emerge as darkness fell. In the distance a succession of headlights swept the moor, cars heading to and from Princetown. As each one passed he tried not to get excited. These would be people returning home from a night out. Whatever was going to happen here would happen much later.

The stone circle had by now all but vanished into the night. He yawned again. If nothing happened by three or four he'd pack it in, head back to his car, and then drive home and snatch a few hours of sleep. Still, it would be worth it in the end when Calter threw her arms around him and said he was so brave for saving the pony, told him she loved him.

Denton yawned again, then moved his day-sack into a position where he could use it as a pillow. He stared up at the stars for a moment and then closed his eyes. A nap was what he needed, just a short nap.

Simon Fox had taken Monday morning off to recover. He spent some quality time with his wife and then went over to see Owen. He said nothing of his fears to his son. By the afternoon he was at force HQ and during a visit to the PR department, he'd caught sight of a monitor showing the local news. A reporter stood outside Crownhill Police Station. Then the story cut away to Fernworthy Reservoir, long panning shots of the water and officers on the shoreline, DI Savage's face springing out at one point. Fox's mouth had dropped open and a question from a colleague went unheard and unanswered until the officer had repeated it. Fox had blinked and dismissed the incident as a rush of déjà vu. Later, in his office, he'd wondered if the appearance of Savage on the screen had been an omen, not something to brush off at all.

Monday evening had seen him at a social — a retirement party for a distinguished officer. Fox hadn't managed to get away until after midnight so it wasn't until the following evening — Tuesday — that he'd had a chance to act on his discussion with his wife.

He'd eaten dinner in near-silence as Jennifer looked on, concerned. The bottle of fine red had emptied by the time she asked him if he wanted some cheese and biscuits.

"I'll have it in my study please," he said. "I need to make a phone call."

Five minutes later and Fox sat at his desk. Three digestives and a chunk of Stilton lay on a plate alongside a tumbler of whiskey. He heard the television go on in the living room and reached out to push the door shut. He cut a slice of cheese and laid the piece on one of the digestives, noticing as he did so that his hand was shaking. He considered the food for a moment and then slid the plate away, a bitter taste in his mouth. Then he picked up the phone.

144

The man on the end answered on the second ring. Like Fox, he often worked late. Even so, he sounded gruff.

"It's Simon," Fox said. "Simon Fox."

"Simon, of course." The man sounded cheered. "Sorry, other things on my mind. Want my advice? — don't ever think about going for a job like mine. It's a thankless task. You try to help people but they just don't see it."

The man, Fox thought, had never served anybody but himself, but he let that pass and leant back in his chair as the voice on the end of the line talked about the problems he was having balancing his various interests. Fox reflected that he had similar issues. The job of Chief Constable involved managing budgets and expectations. Bridging the gap between the two was a task for a juggler with Machiavellian instincts. You had to keep a number of balls in the air, while kicking at the faces of those who continually sniped from the sidelines. Provide the public with what they wanted and your colleagues might just hold off stabbing you in the back.

Bread and circuses.

Perhaps a clown would have been better suited to the task.

Fox took a sip of whiskey as the man continued. Unlike him, with his old boys club, Fox had been educated at a comprehensive, risen from the ranks of a bobby on the beat to his present position through hard work alone. No dodgy handshakes, no nods or winks. Few could claim to have done likewise; certainly not

145

the man on the other end of the line. Fox imagined him surrounded by paperwork, his loyal wife keeping him supplied with coffee and biscuits. Coffee and biscuits and sex — although that didn't come solely from his wife. He was a large man, with large appetites. Appetites which had led to him living dangerously on a number of occasions. The incidents involved scandal rather than illegality and Fox had turned a blind eye for the sake of their friendship. Truth be told, he'd done more than turn a blind eye in one instance.

"Sorry to butt in," Fox cut across a stream of words which had turned into a rant about the EU. "I've got a bit of a problem. Or should I say *we've* got a bit of a problem."

Dead air came from the phone and for a moment Fox thought the connection had broken. Then the voice came through, low but clear.

"What is it, Simon? You sound stressed."

"Yes. Somebody's tracked down the Impreza. They know Owen was driving that day. It won't be long before they work out that strings have been pulled and there's been a cover-up."

"*What?*" More dead air. "This is bad, Simon. Very bad."

"Yes," Fox said. "Everything will come out. The fact that your daughter — Lauren — was there with Owen. That they were both dealing drugs. Once the press get hold of the story they won't let go. You and I, we're the bubbles, the fizz. The story is flat without us. Just an everyday tale of drugs and a hit-and-run. With us it's a very different cocktail. The journalists will lap it up right down to the very last dregs."

"Shit, Simon. I've got my own set of problems at the moment. You can't even imagine the hell I'm going through. I don't need this."

"Of course not, but back then I covered things up as much for Lauren's benefit as Owen's. As much for yours as mine. I did my bit. Now I need you to return the favour." Fox paused. The meat of it was coming next. "Your friends. The ones in high places. You're going to have to pull some strings. We need to do something about Savage."

"Hell, has it come to that?"

"Yes, I'm afraid it has. It's a shame, because I've always rated the woman. I guess I felt sorry for her, guilty, but that was before she became a threat."

"And you want her stopped, whatever it takes, whatever the price. Right?"

"Yes." Fox waited, half-expecting a response, but he was unsurprised when the line went dead.

A few seconds later the door to the study swung open, to reveal his wife standing there. It was clear to Fox she'd been listening from the hallway.

"Did you call him?" she said.

"Yes." He tried to make his voice sound firm, resolved.

"And?"

"And he's going to do what's necessary."

Jennifer nodded and turned and walked away. Fox heard her fiddling in the kitchen, the sound of the kettle being filled and set to boil. He picked up the glass from the desk and considered the contents. The gold liquid rippled as his hand shook. Then he lifted the glass to his mouth and necked the remainder of the whiskey.

Denton lay on his back and gazed up at Calter. She sat astride him, moving her hips back and forward, one hand pressing down on his chest, the other touching herself. Her breasts were small but perfect and Denton reached up to cup them. Calter gasped once and then let out a whine of ecstasy as she came.

Then Denton woke up.

Above him, stars shone unblinking in a crystal clear sky. The whine came again. Not Calter. Denton blinked. The cry was more like a whinny. He pushed himself up into a sitting position. The stone circle was just about visible. In the centre some figures stood around something lying on the ground. Something about the size of a pony.

He scrabbled in his day-sack and pulled out a pair of binoculars. They had huge optics, designed to suck in all the available light. He raised them to his eyes. Men, three of them. Hoods cowled their faces in black as they moved around the pony. The animal wasn't moving; likely, Denton thought, it was already dead. One of the figures bent to the rear of the animal and made a slashing motion.

Shit. So much for saving the pony.

Denton lowered the binoculars and scanned the moorland around the stone circle. There. About a hundred metres to the right of the circle, some sort of vehicle stood with its sidelights on. A small horse trailer was attached to the rear of the vehicle. Denton shoved the binoculars into the rucksack and swung it onto his back. He scrambled away from his hiding position and down the side of the tor, traversing the slope and heading for the vehicle. The figures at the circle were still doing something to the pony. They'd also lit several small fires. The gathering seemed a little chaotic, not like a ceremony at all. Maybe that was the point.

He worked his way down a small gully and approached the vehicle from a point directly opposite the circle. Denton went to the rear of what turned out to be a Nissan 4X4 and unhitched the trailer, resting the tow hitch on the rear bumper. Then he moved to one of the wheels on the 4X4, unscrewed the cap on the air valve, and pressed in the valve so the air began to hiss out. The men were larking around now and didn't seem to be in a hurry to leave. When the tyre had deflated, Denton moved on to the next one. When that too was flat he moved away, first crouching, then scuttling across the ground like a crab, then running flat out until he'd reached the dark shadow of the tor again. Then he reached for his phone.

CHAPTER
ELEVEN

Wednesday 27th August

"Irina, I don't know what to say," Dave, the proprietor of Bean There said as Irina came into the cafe. He put his arms around her. "The news about Ana is shocking. Truly shocking. Do the police have any leads? And are you sure you're ready to come back to work?"

Dave was a nice guy, Irina thought, not like most of the British men she'd met. She told him about the police investigation and how they believed her landlord was involved in Ana's disappearance and murder. She left out her hunch about the man who'd been coming to the cafe. Instead she assured Dave she wanted to get back to work, if only to take her mind off it all.

Time to act. It was nearing the end of the school holidays, and with the sun beaming down, the cafe was packed inside and out. There was only one other waitress and the two of them struggled to keep up with the orders.

"Hustle, hustle, hustle," Dave shouted from the kitchen, where he was making up baguettes as fast as he could. "What we take today makes up for a soggy, sloppy Wednesday in mid-October."

Irina smiled and half-laughed as she completed yet another cappuccino, finishing it off with a little flourish, a star drawn in the creamy foam. Rushed off her feet, she had forgotten all about Ana and the fat man. She loved this job when the weather was fine. The blue skies and hot sun brought out the best in the customers and they reciprocated her happy mood and big smile with generous tips. Irina danced between the outside tables, almost as if she was a gymnast again. She twirled away from a trio of businessmen she'd been flirting with and into the arms of the fat man.

"Oh my," he said. "Careful careful, Chubber's all fingers and thumbs. Catching little beauties is thirsty work, tiring work. Hot chocolate, please. And plenty of creamy cream on the top as well."

The man's hands grasped Irina's bare arms for a moment and he stared down at her breasts, his mouth opening and closing as if he was chewing something.

"Cle . . . cle . . . cle . . ."

What was the man trying to say? Cleavage? Irina stepped back, revolted. He let go.

"Cle . . . clever, that," the man said and plonked himself on a chair, reaching for a paper napkin, a pencil appearing in his right hand. "Nice big t . . . t . . . tips."

Irina headed for the counter. He was here! The person who'd killed Ana. Irina tried not to shake as she prepared the man's drink. She frothed up the milk and mixed the chocolate. She squirted some instant cream onto the top and dusted the cream with sprinkles. Then she carried the cup of steaming liquid back to the man's table.

When she reached the table she saw he was still writing on the napkin. He snatched the napkin away and looked up at her.

"Chubber's got secrets," he said. "Don't want just *anybody* to see, do we? Only the special ones get to know my secrets."

"One chocolate with extra sprinkles," Irina said. "Just how you like it."

"Lovely jubbly."

The man reached up to take the hot chocolate from Irina but as he did so she emptied the cup into his lap.

"Owwweee!" The man scraped the chair back and stood. "Hot! Hot! Hot!"

"I'm so sorry!" Irina raised a hand to her mouth, aware other customers were staring, Dave looking concerned from behind the counter. "How stupid of me."

"Aaahhheee!" The man peered down at the mess of chocolate and cream at his crotch and attempted to pull the material of his trousers away from his body. "Oh my, oh my, oh my. What a mess! What a yucky mucky mess!"

"Here, let me help you." Irina pulled out the little hand towel she had hanging at her waist and handed it to the man. She gestured towards the cafe and at the same time reached for the canvas bag down by the man's feet. "The bathroom, quick. Don't worry about your bag, I've got that."

"Chubber's wet wet wet. Burning bits. I've got to get to the bathroom quick quick quick."

The man shuffled away from the table and headed for the cafe entrance with Irina following, his bag clutched tightly in her left hand.

Chubber stood in the disabled toilet with his trousers and boxer shorts round his ankles. One hand held the little towel the girl had given him while the other rubbed his crotch.

Naughty Chubber.

No, Chubber thought, it was the girl who was naughty. Very naughty. Like the other one. The first waitress Chubber had watched. According to Antler Man she'd been very, very naughty. What was it with waitresses?

He rubbed the towel up and down his thighs and around his groin area. Scritchy scratchy. Nice. He closed his eyes and imagined the girl doing the rubbing. Perhaps doing more than just rubbing. Was that why she'd spilled the drink? Did she want to see him like this, half-naked?

Chubber opened his eyes and stared at the hairy pink form reflected in the mirror.

No, that wasn't it. Couldn't be. She'd poured the chocolate over him for some other reason. Maybe she hadn't liked the little notes he'd been leaving. But she'd taken the tips, hadn't she? Time after time he'd left a couple of pound coins, a fiver, more. She'd snatched the money up without question, given him a little smile, led him on.

Naughty girly girl. Chubber could see why Antler Man got so cross about waitresses. If they went around

153

spilling hot drinks in people's laps then they deserved punishing.

Now then, Chubber. Careful what you say. Careful what you wish for.

Oh yes, Chubber would be careful. He was always careful.

He dried himself off and pulled up his underwear and his trousers. A huge dark stain had spread from the crotch area and down one leg. There was a white patch on one side and a brown encrustment of chocolate on the other. It didn't look good. People would be mumbling as he passed by. They'd be sniff sniff sniffing as if he was some kind of dirty old incontinent codger. But Chubber would show them, show the girl too. She needed to be taught a lesson. Knickers down around *her* ankles. A little spank on the bottom.

Chubber! Antler Man didn't say anything about that.

But Antler Man couldn't know everything. Chubber washed and dried his hands. Maybe the day wasn't turning out to be so bad after all.

Riley had to attend a meeting with several Neighbourhood Watch representatives, three councillors and a local policing team first thing on Wednesday. There'd been a number of tractors stolen from farms over Yelverton way and the councillors wanted to know what the police were doing to prevent further thefts and catch the perpetrators. "Sod all," Riley could have said, but he stuck to the standard spiel. Several investigative avenues were being pursued but in the meantime the police and the local community had to work together. Neighbourhood Watch, he informed them, had a very important role to play.

Half-a-dozen self-important egos salved, Riley headed to Crownhill where he found Davies in a less-than-cheerful mood.

"Those Satan-worshipping pony killers," Davies said. "They're at Charles fucking Cross. DC Denton nabbed them in the early hours. He's a bloody hero. Apparently."

"Right." Riley nodded. "Why aren't you over there questioning them?"

"Drunk. All of them. Mid-afternoon before they're sober, the custody sergeant reckons."

"So what happened?"

"Super Denton happened," Davies said. "He was watching a stone circle on the off-chance and these three guys turn up with a pony and horsebox. They kill the pony and Denton sabotages their van so they can't get away. He calls it in and three cars on blues and twos arrive from Plymouth and arrest them. Full plaudits to Denton, except Hardin's blown his top. This was our case, not his. He shouldn't have been there, definitely shouldn't have been single-crewed."

"Still, we've got them, right?"

"Got some people who killed a pony, sure, but I'm not altogether convinced these guys are a bunch of Satanists. Here, look." Davies handed Riley a couple of sheets of paper. "These three hardly know how to read. The closest they've come to esoteric is a bit of thrash metal."

"Thanks." Riley peered down at the sheets. "Nigel Branson, Greg Randall, and Andy Howson. Do we know them?"

"Know them? This lot have spent more time in the custody centre than they have in their own beds. Three of North Prospect's finest. Howson's twenty-five and he's already got two girls up the duff and found time to spend eighteen months inside. Carjacking, burglary, assault. Randall's done time for dealing and the baby of the three, Branson, is nothing like his more famous namesake other than he's partial to virgins. Bugger all on the rap sheet about mutilating horses though. To be honest, I'd have thought Howson was more used to backing the three-thirty at Kempton than killing a nag on Dartmoor. According to Denton they were tanked-up, but there was no ceremony of any kind. Looks like they unloaded the pony from the horsebox, took the animal into the circle, and then butchered it. They also lit a number of fires."

"In a pentagram shape?"

"Yes. But there was nothing in the van or the box associated with Satanism. No regalia, nothing."

"And the pony was assaulted as before?"

"Yes, but it happened after the animal was killed. Not that it makes it any more palatable. I'm struggling to understand what the hell these lads were up to."

"What have they said so far?"

"Sod all. They've been busted so many times they know the ropes. Keep schtum and wait it out." Davies grinned.

156

"They reckoned without yours truly though, didn't they? Come this afternoon I'll be down there pressing them hard. They'll be crying for their mummies by the time I've finished with them."

Savage had tried to ring Irina's mobile several times but on each occasion the call went through to voicemail. She spent Wednesday morning in the crime suite, but by lunchtime, still with no word from Irina, she resorted to going round to her place. She found Kevin Foster on the pavement outside talking to two men beside a large box van. Foster sneered as she got out of her car and moved away from the van towards her.

"Bloody cheek," Foster said. "Showing your face round here. I've had reporters outside my place this morning, snapping away with their cameras and asking silly questions. My picture's going to be all over the front page come tomorrow."

"Just deserts, Mr Foster," Savage said. "You might be off the hook as regards Ana's murder but you're guilty of plenty else."

"Yeah?" Foster gave a sneer. "Well the whole thing wouldn't be so bad except a number of my other tenants have banded together to take legal action against me. Psychological trauma or some other bollocks."

"Well, Amanda Bradley should relish the fight." Savage pointed up towards the front door of the property. "Is Irina inside?"

"No, as it happens she's not."

"Do you know her whereabouts?"

Foster explained he'd seen Irina that morning. She'd informed him she was moving out and wanted a refund on the last six months' rent. If he gave her the money she wouldn't press charges. Meantime she was headed for work.

"Canny lass," Foster said as Savage turned to go back to her car. "Bloody canny."

The Bean There cafe was one of a number on Armada Way. Groups of tables and chairs clustered together under an array of large parasols as seagulls and pigeons wheeled in the air above. The patrons consisted largely of tourists with the odd group of businessmen and women taking an early lunch or holding an impromptu meeting.

When Savage introduced herself to the proprietor — a guy called Dave — he was apologetic.

"Gone," he said. "She's a good girl, Irina, but she was a little absentminded this morning, asked to leave halfway through the day. Can't say I blame her after what happened to Ana. Shocking."

"She's not at home, so have you any idea where she went?"

"No, sweetheart." Dave spread his arms wide. "And I could have done with her today. When the sun's out all people want to do is drink coffee. Maybe I shouldn't have let her leave but she was getting clumsy. Knocked a hot chocolate over one of my regulars. He wasn't happy, I can tell you. Wrote down my name and number on a napkin and said he'd send me the laundry bill."

"Hot chocolate . . . napkin . . ." Savage whispered to herself. Irina had mentioned something about a weirdo drinking hot chocolate and that he'd written messages to Ana and Irina on paper napkins. "Do you know this man's name or where he lives?"

"Sorry, love, no. He's a regular but I'm not friendly with him. He is a bit of an odd one to be honest. Mind you, I couldn't help but laugh at the sight of him all covered in hot chocolate. It was all Irina could do to keep up with him as he rushed for the toilets. He shut himself in and she had to wait outside holding his bag. Then he came out, had words with me, and scuttled off. Irina said she wasn't feeling well afterwards so I sent her home, only from what you told me she's not there. I expect she's gone round a friend's place or something."

"Yes," Savage said, already moving from the counter towards the street, fumbling for her phone at the same time. "I expect she has."

CHAPTER
TWELVE

By end of play Wednesday, Davies was far from happy. The lads from North Prospect had gone "no comment", each telling Davies and Riley they could "get stuffed" if they thought they were going to split on their mates. A second night in the cells had seemed a step too far for what was a relatively minor offence and they could only get an extension to hold them if they thought fresh evidence would be forthcoming.

Back at Crownhill after a frustrating afternoon Davies slumped down in a chair while Riley stood at the whiteboard. The board had pictures of the slaughtered animals, the pentagram shapes, and several shots of the stone circle and the surroundings.

"Crying for their mummies, you said." Riley tapped the board with a finger, trying to suppress a laugh. "Eating out of your hand. Spitting on it more like."

"Fucking scrotes." Davies leant back, feet up on the desk. "Old days and I'd have had something. That Branson's a little whiner. He was about to crap himself before his lawyer stepped in."

"Trouble is, sir, these days the boys are wising up. What was it Howson said? 'Human rights'?"

"Fuck human rights, those scum are animals."

"And there's the rub. They've sliced up several animals and, as John Layton says, it's only one step to doing the same to a human. Thing is, we can't charge them with much more than animal cruelty. They won't be looking at a custodial. A slap on the wrist, a fine — which they won't pay — and some community service for a community that would prefer to see the back of them."

Davies mumbled something about grabbing a coffee and swung his legs down, pushed himself out of his chair and headed out of the room, leaving Riley staring at the board.

He tapped the board again for his own benefit. The mystery here was why on earth three lads from North Prospect had ventured onto the moor in the first place. Were they really Satanists or were they just larking about? Cans of lager, a spliff and the general lack of seriousness at the scene described by DC Denton suggested the latter. On the other hand the sheer effort involved in stealing a horsebox and then finding and catching a pony and bringing the hapless creature up to the stone circle pointed to something different.

"Sir?" One of Layton's junior CSIs hovered at Riley's shoulder. He held out a ziploc bag. "We've finished up at the circle. Not much more to report, but we did find this."

Riley took the bag. Inside, silver glistened alongside a twist of leather twine.

"What is it?" Riley said, touching the piece of jewellery through the plastic. An infinity symbol was joined to a sort of double cross. "A New Age sign?"

161

"Something like that." The CSI held up several photographs and pointed to one. "It was found here, right next to the kistvaen."

"I've seen this on the web," Riley said, turning the bag round and examining the object within more closely. "It's a Satanic cross. A sigil."

"Sorry?"

"Never mind." Riley shook his head and thanked the CSI.

With the man gone he looked again at the piece of jewellery. He'd learnt about the Satanic cross while researching devil worship and knew it was based on the alchemical symbol for sulphur and supposedly had magical powers. This one was made from silver and appeared to be high quality. On the back there was a tiny inscription. Riley squinted, but couldn't make out the wording. He carefully removed the item from the bag, placed it on a desk and reached for his phone. A few seconds later and he was zooming in on a picture he'd taken. The inscription came up clear as day: RazCaz Design. A web search brought up the company's address: New Street down in the Barbican.

"Figures," Riley said to himself. "Tourists and all that."

The Barbican was an old part of Plymouth that had escaped the wartime bombing that had levelled much of the city centre. A maze of tiny streets and alleyways hugged the quayside, and the area had numerous galleries, bookshops, bars and cafes. A little boutique selling handcrafted jewellery wouldn't be out of place at all.

He placed the piece of jewellery back in the plastic bag. RazCaz had made this — but for whom and why? A sigil was connected to the occult. Could it belong to one of the North Prospect boys? Unlikely.

Riley returned to the whiteboard and looked again at the pictures of the crime scenes. There were three stone circles, the final one with a kistvaen at the centre. A kist was an ancient burial site chamber dating from thousands of years ago. The board was peppered with images of similar historical sites that Riley had printed from the web in order to get a handle on the number of such places on Dartmoor. Denton had guessed correctly which one would be next and, turning to the map at the centre of the board, Riley could see how. The three sites lay in a line. A game of join the dots. His eyes flicked from picture to picture once more. There was something wrong, a difference between one of the images from the web and the crime scene photos. Now he saw it.

"Oh fuck!"

"Hey?" Davies materialised beside him, the steam from two cups of coffee wisping under Riley's nose. "Found something?"

"Take a gander at that." Riley pointed to the web picture of the kist and then at the crime scene photo that showed the spot where the sigil had been found. "Tell me what you see."

"Whoever took the crime scene pic is no David Bailey," Davies said. "Other than that, I don't know what you're on about."

"Notice anything unusual?"

"What's this, Darius? Spot the difference?"

"Yes, exactly. The picture on the left is from the National Park Authority website. It was taken a couple of years ago. The image on the right is one John Layton took when we were out there after the pony had been removed. Can you see it yet?"

Davies stared again. "No, son, I can't. They're taken from different angles but apart from that —"

"The centre stone. The one covering the kistvaen."

"Hang on, it's bloody moved!"

"Yes. In the first image the stone isn't over the old grave. Many of the kistvaens are like that. The graves were plundered over the centuries."

"But . . ."

"In the second picture the stone has been returned to what must have been its original place."

"What are you saying?"

"I don't know what I'm saying, but what I'm *seeing* is a stone that has walked a couple of metres sometime in the last couple of years."

"So this is something to do with the killing of the pony?"

"Got to be, hasn't it? I'm going to contact the DPA and English Heritage and see if they know anything about the site. If the rock has been moved without their permission then we'll need to get up there with the appropriate authorities and get to work."

"Get to work?"

"Yes." Riley nodded and stared at Davies, feeling a rush of excitement and realising he bloody loved this

164

job. "We're going to move the stone and see what's underneath."

Fox had spent the day at a community partnership forum in Newton Abbot. He had smiled, made the right sort of comments, pushed the third sector buttons when needed. Privately he thought the forum a complete waste of time. There were too many do-gooders there, too much talk about deprivation being a route into crime, as if these poor animals had no choice. The little darlings thought they had it tough as they sat drinking lager while watching satellite TV, their fingers gliding over the latest mobile phones. Fox could tell them a thing or two about tough. He'd grown up when poverty meant going hungry, not going without expensive gadgets.

After the handshakes all round, the photographs with the local dignitaries, and the promises to act on the page after page of waffle the forum had produced, Fox headed for his car. Within minutes he'd escaped the late afternoon traffic surrounding Newton Abbot and was gliding east along the dual carriageway towards Exeter.

The medley of light classical music was interrupted by a call. Fox flicked the hands-free button and answered the phone.

"Simon," the disembodied voice said. "Thought I'd better catch up. Let you know how I'm dealing with this problem of yours."

"Not mine," Fox said, flooring the accelerator for the climb up Haldon Hill. "Ours."

"Yes." Silence. Just the sound of the engine as Fox guided the car around the sweeping bends.

"And?"

"And I've had a word with somebody. Up in London. Understand?"

"You mean —"

"Yes. You don't need to know the details. Suffice to say it's all in hand."

"Good," Fox said. "I'll just pray you're successful."

The call ended and the radio leapt back into life, a wash of violins filling the interior of the car. For a moment Fox felt elated, a huge weight lifted from his mind.

Whatever the price . . .

Then he recalled the man's words from the night before and wondered if he'd made a mistake involving him. He had an edge, a sinister side. And if this played out he'd be back to extract payment.

The man had taken an age to come out of the toilet and Irina had wondered what on earth he was doing in there. When he finally emerged he'd grabbed his bag from Irina and stomped off, mumbling something about "having words with the manager". He'd threaded his way through the tables and disappeared. Irina had breathed a sigh of relief and then she'd taken her phone from her pocket and stared at the picture she'd just taken. An electricity bill, the man's name and address top right. Mr Adam Creasey, thirty-three Glenmore Avenue.

166

Now Irina sat on a bench in a small park at the end of the road. She could see the front door of number thirty-three through the hedge bordering the park, and as far as she knew, Mr Creasey was inside. She'd been sensible enough to grab a can of Coke and one of Dave's egg mayonnaise baguettes, along with a cinnamon swirl. For the first thirty minutes she'd sat and fiddled, but now the warm sun relaxed her and she reached for her lunch. The Coke can fizzed open and the baguette tasted wonderful. She simply had to sit, wait, and watch. At some point Creasey would emerge and Irina could take a closer look at his house.

It was several hours later when Creasey pulled open the front door and stepped out. Irina had been dozing, and it was the sound of Creasey dropping some plastic crates onto the pavement beside his van that woke her. She blinked and peered through the hedge. Creasey disappeared back inside the house and came out a minute or so later with a couple of black bin liners. He opened the boot of the van and put the crates and bin liners inside. For a moment he stood behind the van, staring across the road towards the park. Irina turned her head away until she heard a door slam and an engine start. When she turned back, Creasey was driving off.

She left the remains of her lunch on the bench, crossed the park and exited through a little iron gate. Creasey's house was in a long terrace, the doors opening directly onto the pavement. At the rear of the terrace a cut ran behind the houses. The houses had little backyards and stone walls separated the cut from the yards, wooden gates allowing access. Irina crossed the road and headed up the alley. The cut was cobbled and uneven. A motorbike with its rear wheel missing sat chocked on a couple of blocks nearby, while farther down a silver 4X4 with tinted windows was parked close to an abandoned shopping trolley. Tall green bins stood out the back of each property.

Irina glanced up and down the cut. Nobody. She started walking, counting the houses as she did so. She needn't have bothered, because Creasey's house was recognisable by the stack of plastic boxes that tottered above the fence. She stood for a moment at the gate. A crack in the wood revealed a bare yard with a concrete shed in one corner. An old bicycle leant against one wall and a green hose ran across the slabs in spirals, a trickle of water seeping from the end. Irina could see now that the concrete was wet. Creasey had been washing down the yard. She took another glance up and down the cut, then reached for the handle on the gate. The catch lifted and the gate swung open. She stepped into the yard, closed the gate behind her. Beneath the latch she found a bolt which she slid across.

Although the yard was overlooked on both sides, Creasey had erected a sort of pergola structure topped with translucent plastic roofing sheets. The shoddy arrangement hid the back of the yard from the neighbours. Irina scanned around the yard. A plant pot with a sad-looking fern stood to one side of the back door. She went over and tilted the pot. Underneath several woodlice scuttled away from the light, but there was no sign of a key. Too obvious, she thought. She searched round some more. A broken slab revealed more woodlice and the gap near the fence at the rear of the yard was filled with weeds, dirt and not much more. Damn. She examined the pergola and wondered about climbing it to access a first floor window. She had the strength in her arms to lift herself, but the wood felt soft and rotten. It was when she reached up to touch one of the supporting beams that she saw the glint of metal. Pushed under one end of the plastic roofing was a set of keys on a loop of string. She hooked her finger in the loop and pulled them down. There was a Yale lock, two keys for deadlocks, and a number of smaller keys.

Irina turned to the concrete shed. A rusty iron hasp had a large padlock threaded through its eye. The second of the smaller keys Irina tried clicked open the lock. She removed the padlock and placed it on the floor, then pulled back the hasp and opened the door. Inside there was a smell of something metallic and another odour, stronger. Something like drains gone bad. The floor of the shed glistened with moisture.

Irina bent and touched the floor. Wet. Creasey had used the hose in here too. She stood and looked around. Tools hung on the wall. A range of saws, some large knives and a meat cleaver. Over to one side, several lengths of rope dangled from a beam along with a section of chain. There were more white crates as well and Irina moved closer to investigate. The crates too had been washed and when she put her face down she could sniff a faint aroma of bleach.

There was nothing else of interest in the shed so she moved back out into the yard. For a second she hesitated. Maybe it was time to go to the police. The trouble was that there was nothing further to go on. No trace of Ana. Just a sense that something wasn't right. Irina pulled out the bunch of keys again. She walked across to the back door and tried one of the big flat deadlock keys. The key slotted in and she turned it, hearing the lock click. She pressed down the handle and pushed open the door.

A short corridor led past a small pantry to a kitchen-cum-dining room. It was a mess. A pile of bin liners stood on one side and several had split, spilling their contents of scraps and food packaging onto the floor. There were more of the white plastic crates, a bicycle wheel, a large cantilevered toolbox open displaying a rusty set of tools, a heap of clothing including several off-white boiler suits, a shoebox, a stack of newspapers, and an array of Tupperware boxes spread across a grubby Formica table.

Irina didn't know what she was looking for. Some evidence of Ana, she supposed. But there was nothing to suggest she'd been here. Anyway, would Creasey really be so stupid as to bring Ana to his house?

At one end of the kitchen diner an arch led through to the living room. Irina hesitated again. She'd bolted the rear gate so Creasey would have to come through the front door. If he did so while she was in the kitchen she could make her escape. If she was anywhere else she'd be trapped.

170

Sod it, she was out of here. She turned and went back into the corridor and then into the yard, closing and locking the rear door. She popped the keys back up beneath the roof and slipped across the concrete and unbolted the rear gate. What a waste of time. It might have been a better idea to follow Creasey but she had no transport and could hardly jump in a taxi and shout "follow that van".

Irina opened the gate and stepped out into the alley. A figure emerged from the side of the green bin.

"I was thinking 'bout coming looking for you, girly," he said. "Saved me a journey, haven't you?"

CHAPTER
THIRTEEN

Thursday 28th August

Irina awoke to the sound of birdsong and a warm shaft of sunlight stroking her face. She reached up and touched the area under her chin where there was a throbbing. Sore.

She pushed herself up into a sitting position, the ground beneath her hand smooth and cold. The sunlight came from high above, a crack in the ceiling letting in a beam that struck a wall and reflected off its mirror-like surface. Metal. The walls and floor. Irina looked around. The room was a few paces square and lined to well above head height with aluminium sheeting. The air smelt dry and dusty and husks of corn lay scattered across the floor. In one corner a pile of large paper sacks had been bound together with orange string. Irina crawled over and looked at the sacks. Bird food, a picture of a pheasant on the front of the sack.

In the centre of one wall a recess held a door. The door too had been covered with aluminium, but a handle protruded through where the metal had been cut away. Behind the metal was dark oak. Irina stood and went across to the door. She pressed the handle down and pushed. The door rattled but didn't open.

The locked door broke the drowsy state she had been in. Until that moment she'd been in a dream, half-conscious, but not really aware of the situation. Now the truth came washing over her. Creasey had abducted her. Soon he would be back.

I love you and I want to fuck you and I want to eat you.

Irina felt a wave of panic rise in her chest. She thought of the butchery equipment she'd seen hanging on the walls of Creasey's outhouse. Saws, knives, that huge meat cleaver. She tried the door again, now in a panic. It was no good. The door was secured on the outside. There was no escape. Irina's breathing quickened and she tried to prevent herself from screaming. Screaming would only bring Creasey running to silence her. He was somewhere out there, prowling around, sharpening those knives, preparing. Soon, he'd be coming. Irina tried not to think about what he might do, but it was all too easy to imagine the door swinging open, Creasey's grubby hands outstretched as he came towards her, his fingers clawing at her clothing, his dirty coat flapping open . . . No!

Irina shook her head. She was making the situation worse. Better to occupy her mind with something practical, to try and figure a way out of her predicament. She moved from the door over to the only other thing in the room worth investigating. The pile of paper sacks. There were dozens of them, the stack about a metre high. If nothing else, she could use the pile as a bed. She pulled the bundle out from the corner and as she did so something slipped from between the layers of sacks and fell to the floor. She knew what it was even before she picked it up. A little notebook with a piece of elastic on one side for holding a pencil. She'd used an identical one the day before when she'd been working at the cafe. She bent and picked up the order pad and flipped to the first page where pencil scrawl filled each line.

My name is Anasztáz Róka . . .

The first thing Savage did on Thursday morning when she arrived at the station was scan the overnight reports for any sign of Irina Kryukov. Nothing. All officers had been told to keep a lookout but the girl had vanished. Neither was there any sign of the man who'd tried to get friendly using a five-pound note and a paper napkin. It was Collier who drew Savage's attention to Irina's statement.

"Comes in at eleven," Collier said. "Regular. Least that's what the girl told you. Whether he turns up or not is another matter, but it's worth a try."

Now Savage and Calter sat at an outside table in front of Bean There, two cappuccinos ordered and on the way, Dave the cafe owner in on the act with a conspiratorial wink. Savage hoped he wouldn't give them away.

"Long shot, ma'am," Calter said. "Do you think he'd really return if he had anything to do with Irina's disappearance?"

174

"I don't know," Savage said. "According to Irina he's a creature of habit. He might not be able to stay away. Anyway, long shot or not, this is our only option."

The drinks arrived and Savage leant back in her seat and scanned the cafe patrons. Several groups of tourists, some students, an elderly man with a large dog. No sign of anybody matching the descriptions given by Irina or Dave. The first set of cappuccinos went and were replaced by another. Savage took a glance at her watch: just before eleven.

An hour and a half later the second set of cappuccinos had long gone and a couple of tuna salad baguettes sat on two plates. A third plate held a salad. Savage played with a piece of shredded lettuce and then popped a cherry tomato in her mouth. Calter drummed her fingers on the table.

"Eleven was a while back, ma'am," she said. "How long are we going to give this?"

"We'll eat these and then call it a day, yeah?"

Calter nodded. The DC bent to her baguette. Feeling full of coffee, Savage got up to use the toilet. A couple of minutes later she returned to find Calter making a face at her.

"There, ma'am," Calter said as Savage sat back down. She removed the wooden stirrer from her drink, placed it on the table, and swivelled it to point diagonally away from Savage. "He matches the description Irina gave us to a T."

Savage lifted her cup to her lips and at the same time turned a fraction to see. Close by, a man in a suit tapped his fingers on a tablet. Over his shoulder at the next table a figure sat hunched over, right leg jiggling up and down. He was mid-thirties, overweight, with a smooth hairless head. Round glasses sat on a sharp nose, the shape of the nose at odds with the pudgy face. In his right hand he held a stubby pencil which he was using to write in a wire-bound notebook. Despite the summer weather he wore a long overcoat, white, but grubby.

"You're right." Savage turned back to Calter, who was trying hard not to stare. "Exactly as Irina said. Now we wait."

The man appeared agitated, not happy with the male member of staff who took his order. The waiter returned with a hot chocolate and the pair engaged in conversation, the waiter shaking his head several times, before moving away to take somebody else's order. After just a couple of minutes the man scraped back his chair and barged his way through the maze of tables. A howl of protest went up as a coffee tumbled over, but the man ignored the shouting and went off along Armada Way, head down and oblivious.

"Something's not right," Savage said.

"No time to ask the waiter," Calter said as she rose to her feet. "I'm away."

The DC dashed after the man on foot while Savage went for their car. Five minutes later she was swinging onto Notte Street and stopping halfway up for Calter, who was waving her arms frantically.

"Just got in a white van parked up the road," she said, breathless from having run back to Savage. "Hurry up and we'll catch him."

Calter leapt in and Savage moved off. The van pulled out in front of her as they rounded a corner. It headed off in the direction of the city centre and Savage followed, Calter carrying out an index check on the vehicle. The van circled Derrys Cross roundabout three times before taking the exit onto Union Street.

"Owned by a Mr Adam Creasey," Calter said, listening as the dispatcher gave her the registration details. "He lives in the Stoke area. Glenmore Avenue. A couple of driving offences but no criminal record."

Savage nodded and concentrated on driving. Creasey headed north, passing Central Park on the right and eventually pulling up outside a row of terraced houses. The man got out and left the engine running. He shuffled over to a front door which opened onto the street, unlocked it, and went inside. Three minutes later he was back with a couple of plastic crates and something resembling a tool wrap.

"No idea, ma'am," Calter said when Savage looked across at her. "But he looks like he's off somewhere."

Calter was right. This time the route was direct. They followed the van out of the city and took the A38 heading east. Creasey zipped along the dual carriageway past Ashburton and Buckfastleigh and then turned off the main road and took a lane heading north.

"The moor," Savage said. "Fernworthy."

Riley's enthusiasm for the job waned during Thursday morning. He'd expected to phone a couple of people and be up on Dartmoor by midday, ready to shift the stone from the kistvaen. No such luck. After speaking to John Layton it turned out this sort of thing needed paperwork. Reams of the stuff. An archaeologist from English Heritage would need to be present, representatives from the Dartmoor Park Authority too. There'd need to be a risk assessment conducted before any work could begin, because moving a rock that size could be dangerous. On top of that the archaeologist needed to come from Bristol and it just wasn't possible at short notice. Riley wanted to scream, but he knew vocalising his anger wouldn't do any good. Breathe deep, he thought, realise procedure means process leading to progress and take it one step at a time.

With any chance of getting up onto the moor before Friday vanishing fast, Riley decided to focus on the piece of jewellery they'd found. The lads from North Prospect had been released and informed that charges would follow. The more information Riley could get, the better, so he headed into town intent on visiting RazCaz Designs. He parked on Madeira Road and walked down to the Barbican. To his right the sea sparkled with light. A fishing boat was hovering near the entrance to the marina and Riley heard the klaxon sound as the gates to the swing bridge began to close.

Down in the Barbican, New Street was a narrow cobbled lane that wound between old buildings. It wasn't hard to imagine the place centuries ago. Probably, Riley thought, the whole area was once the haunt of pirates and brigands. What they would have made of either the daytime tourist crowd or the night-time rabble of hens and stags, Riley had no idea.

178

RazCaz Designs was squeezed between something labelled as a sixteenth-century eating place — now home to a Nepalese restaurant — and a small museum known as the Elizabethan House. A narrow window displayed a couple of select pieces and to the right a step led down through a fly curtain comprising several silk scarves.

Riley pushed through the scarves, a line of tiny bells jangling as he disturbed them. Inside, wisps of smoke hung in the air, a scent of incense permeating the whole interior. A stand to one side showed a number of items of jewellery, but Riley was drawn to the rear of the shop, where a figure worked on something beneath a large magnifier. For a moment Riley couldn't tell whether the person was male or female — long blond hair hung down over the head which was bent low. Then Riley saw the hands. A man's hands, fingernails bitten to the quick, long fine hairs on the backs. A pentagram tattoo on the right wrist.

The man looked up. The blond hair framed a rough face with several days' beard growth. He laid down the silver chain he was working on and scratched his chin. "Can I help you?"

"DS Darius Riley." Riley showed his identification and then swept an arm around. "Are you the proprietor?"

"Proprietor, janitor, cleaner, general dogsbody." The man held out a hand. "Rasmus Yarnic."

"Is that the 'Ras' in RazCaz Designs?" Riley asked, shaking the man's hand.

"Yes." The voice became hesitant as Yarnic withdrew his hand. "What's this about?"

"Did you make this?" Riley pulled out the silver necklace still in its plastic evidence bag.

The man took the bag and turned it over in his hands. "I guess I did. Must have been a while ago because I don't recall anything like this in the last couple of years. I think it was a commission. I'll have a record somewhere out the back."

"Know what the symbol is?"

"Yes." Yarnic rolled his sleeves down and covered the pentagram on his wrist. "A Satanic cross."

"Know anything more?" Riley nodded down at the man's arms.

"This pentagram is Wiccan, mate. Nothing to do with Satan. It's when the star is inverted it represents evil."

"And which way up is the one on your wrist?"

"Depends on which way you look." Yarnic smiled. "From your side you'd probably say I'm a fully paid-up member of the devil-worshipping brigade; from over here I'm all good."

"But you made the cross?"

"Of course. People have the right to believe what they like, don't they?"

"Would you have made somebody a swastika?"

"Might have. To be honest though I can't see a skinhead fascist coming in here, can you? Anyway the swastika predates anything to do with Nazism. It's a Hindu symbol, amongst others."

"Fascinating." Riley reached out and took the bag back. Yarnic was beginning to annoy him. He had a self-assuredness about him that bordered on arrogance. "What I need to know is who commissioned the piece and when?"

"Evidence is it? Only maybe I need to call my lawyer."

"Only if you're guilty of something, Mr Yarnic."

Yarnic met Riley's eyes and held his gaze. Moved his head almost imperceptibly from side to side.

"No," he said, before turning and walking to a small door which led to some sort of storage room. "Records, sketchbooks, accounts. They're all out the back. Five minutes, OK?"

Riley nodded and then went to browse the displays. He could hear Yarnic moving boxes around, pulling things from shelves, cursing to himself as he searched the store room. Then the commotion stopped. After a while longer, Riley moved closer to the room. Now he could hear the man talking in a low whisper. Riley was unable to make out what was being said, but he was pretty sure Yarnic was on the phone.

It's a long way there, Chubber, isn't it?

Yes it is. Sixty minutes minimum. Fast to start with but then there's a whole load of lanes. Chubber's shack is in the back of beyond. In the big dark wood. Out of the way. Space to play. Chubber hums to himself as the car weaves and wends. Chubber likes humming. The road follows the contours, heads up a valley, deep into the moor. The blacktop becomes a track, a gate to unlock and then it's carving between two tors, grey granite looming either side, like sentinels on guard duty. Chubber carries on humming. A wood slips and slides down the rolling hill, closes in and throttles the track. The van bounces up the track. Bounces and crashes.

Slow down, Chubber.

Yes, there's no need to rush. She'll still be there. Five minutes more will make no difference. Ah, here we are.

He parks the car, gets out and listens. Checker check check. Nobody coming up the lane behind him. No fucker nosing into his business. Oh no, no, no. Better not nose into Chubber's business. Chubber's business is Chubber's business and a mucky yucky business it is too.

What about Antler Man's business? Have you forgotten that?

No, Chubber hasn't. But today is all about Chubber. Antler Man does things one way and Chubber does things another way. Chubber's done everything Antler Man said. Listened carefully. Got the waitress sorted. Now it's Chubber time.

Chubber time?

"Yes," Chubber says to himself. "Fun time."

He goes around to the back of the van and opens the boot. Now he's got to unload and walk. Carry things up to the shack.

Up?

Yes, up. Up through the big dark wood. Chubber picks up his stuff and follows a path all wibbly and windy amongst the trees. Rows of pine, the ground tan with needles, ditches black with peat, silver water trickling along.

Chubber walks on, a backpack and two bags. Four empty crates stacked and tied to the top of the pack. Need the crates later. For the slippy sluppy yucky mucky bits.

Hot, hot, hot. Hard work this walking. Up, up, up. Weaving and wending amongst the trees. Should be humming. Can't be humming. Need to breathe. Hot work, hard work. The way back will be heavier, but downhill. Easy.

Here.

Here, Chubber? Are you sure?

Yes, Chubber's sure. The tree with the little rock beside. The rock with a little piece of quartz. Crystal. The track carries on up, but step to the right, duck under the branch and walk down the row of trees. A hundred paces and here we are. The trees thin, the sun shines down, and ahead posts and wire stand in the shafts of light. The remains of a pheasant pen. The mesh is rusty, the posts are rotten. No gamekeeper has been here for years. A couple of fifty-gallon drums stand on little platforms. Bird feeders. A stream bubbles across the clearing into a small pool. Clear water. Pond skaters skitter skatter as Chubber approaches.

Dump the stuff down, Chubber!

Yes, good idea. Bend and take some water. Cool, but tasting of peat. Phew.

A noise, Chubber.

Yes. Chubber looks over to the shed. Not concrete like the one in the backyard. Corrugated. She's in

183

there. But Chubber knew she would be. Chubber put her there. Now Chubber needs to prepare. Set out the crates. Ready the ropes. Get out his tools. His shiny *new* tools.

Oh Chubber Chub Chubs. This is going to be good, isn't it?

Yes it is, Chubber thinks. Better than good. *Awesome.*

Half an hour later and Riley was back in his car. A bag of chips sat on the passenger seat and he ate them with one hand while he looked through several jotter pads given to him by Rasmus Yarnic.

"It'll be in one of these," Yarnic had said. "All the designs are in there. Names, contact details and invoice amounts too. No way to run a business, I know."

Too bloody right, Riley thought after he'd got halfway through the first pad. Scratchy line drawings filled each page. Figures, phone numbers, reminders to buy milk or bread. Every so often there was a completed design, circled and with a name or number next to it. Yarnic had a strange way of working.

Riley popped another chip into his mouth. He was nearing the end of the third pad when he found the cross. Several attempts at sketching the symbol had been abandoned, but down the bottom right of the page was a neat drawing, the lines fluid, the design complete. Yarnic had obviously been meticulous in his work because the silver cross matched the drawing exactly. Alongside the sketch he'd written "350" followed by a question mark. The sum seemed like a lot

184

of money to Riley for what you might pick up in the market for a few quid. Then again this was a one-off item, handmade and in silver. Only it wasn't a one-off. In neat pencil towards the bottom of the page Yarnic had printed out the words: "The client requires seven exact copies."

Yarnic was playing games. Surely he'd have remembered making seven crosses? Riley glanced at the pad again. The final invoice figure amounted to near two and a half grand. In anyone's book the sum was a nice little earner, not an amount you'd forget in a hurry, even if it was several years ago. Below the invoice amount was a phone number. Riley pulled out his phone and dialled the number.

You have reached the voicemail of Helen Peacock . . .

Riley hung up. There was something familiar about that voice. Helen Peacock? *The* Helen Peacock? Surely not? He heard her almost nightly on the local BBC TV news show, *Spotlight*. What would a BBC presenter be doing buying seven Satanic crosses? More importantly, if she was the owner, how did the cross get up on Dartmoor at the site of the gruesome killing of a pony?

Riley glanced at the clock on the dash. Just twelve-thirty. The presenters rotated, but if Helen Peacock was on the evening show she'd likely be at the studio now. He could pop over and catch her before she headed off.

He flipped the pad shut and reached over for the last of his chips.

Chubber doesn't really think he's a bad man. But sometimes Chubber is a little bit naughty.

Yes, Chubber, you are!

Right now is one of those times.

Chubber's standing by the corrugated shed in the big dark wood. He's about to do the business. *His* business. He's taken off all his clothes and put on a boiler suit. Nothing underneath. Naked, the rough cotton scratchy scritchy. The boiler suit is white. Well, off-white really. Grubby. Red stains. Going to be a messy mess mess. Doing the business.

But wait! Chubber thinks he'd like to have a little fun first. Fun can't hurt, can it? All those girls in all those coffee shops. None of them took kindly to his invitations. Hot chocolate after hot chocolate, hundreds of pounds in tips and he barely got a smile in return. But this one in the shed, she's different. He doesn't have to ask her permission. He can do what he likes.

Oh Chubber Chub Chubs. You're not going to do what I think you're going to do, are you?

Chubber knows this kind of thing is against the law. That people don't talk about this kind of thing in polite society. But Chubber doesn't care about polite society, does he? Chubber isn't polite and he doesn't do society. Chubber wants some fun, wants that feeling. Gliding, sliding. Oh! Ah! Urgh! Nice. Lovely. Beautiful.

Go on then, Chubber. If you must.

Chubber must.

He unties the twine holding the door closed and opens up. Dark inside. Smelly. Urine. Soaked into the earthy floor, but still stinky. Inside, the shed is divided into two inner sections. Two, because one is never

186

enough. He moves to the left and pulls back the bolt on one of the doors. He stares round. Empty? Empty! No!

No. There she is. Lying up against the back wall. Cowering. Chubber makes noises. Clucking noises. He hopes they might reassure her.

"There, there," Chubber says. "Nothing to worry about. Don't fret, Chubber's here."

She looks across at Chubber. Big eyes. Green. She blinks. Chubber creeps forward and reaches out with his huge hands. All fingers and thumbs. More all thumbs actually. Then she moves. Fast.

She's up on her feet making a dash, a dart. But Chubber grabs her as she comes past. He tries to hold on, but she's loose, out through the door and away.

Chubber! Don't just stand there. After her!

He runs, falls on his face in the mud.

Chubber. Quickly!

And then he's up and running after her through the big dark wood.

CHAPTER
FOURTEEN

Savage put her hands on her hips and looked back down the track. Their car was just visible where they'd left it next to a locked gate. They'd followed the van into the depths of the moor; up past Widecombe and then twisting through narrow lanes, further into the wilderness. Savage had stayed well back, inching round corners to make sure they weren't spotted. Then the van had turned off the lane and the driver had got out and unlocked the gate, driven through and then relocked it. As soon as he'd disappeared up the track in a cloud of dust, Savage and Calter had rolled up and Calter had leapt out and examined the chain securing the gate. It was no good, the only way through was on foot.

The track climbed to the right and then followed the course of a small stream between two towering tors.

"Where do you think he's heading for?" Calter said.

Savage looked upwards to where the track became lost amongst the thick greenery of a dense pine wood.

"No idea. Somewhere in the wood I guess."

"Fernworthy's a good few miles from here," Calter said. "A different wood."

"You're right. Why dump the clothes in such a public place when you've got this all around?"

They plodded on up the track, continuing when it entered the woodland. After another quarter of a mile the track reached a dead end where a small quarry enveloped a turning circle. The van sat to one side next to a huge pile of scalpings.

"Gone, ma'am," Calter said as they approached the van. The DC pointed to a small trail which led up a grassy bank and disappeared into the dark at the tree line. "Up there I reckon."

"Let's go then," Savage said.

"Is that wise? My mother always told me never to follow strange men into dark woods."

"Sensible advice, but unfortunately not applicable when you're one of Devon and Cornwall's finest."

They started up the path, Calter leading, the dense woodland rising all around, rows of conifers clustered together, shadows beneath. The corridors of trees stretched away into the gloom and Savage thought she saw something move far in the distance. When she stopped to look, there was nothing. Apart from the sound of their feet trudging in the dirt there was silence. No birds flitting in the branches, no animals scuffling in the undergrowth, not a living creature to be seen.

"We should have brought dogs," Calter said. "This place is vast, he could be anywhere."

"You know how I feel about dogs."

"Whatever, ma'am, but I'd feel a lot safer with a couple of big German Shepherds to keep us company.

This place is like something out of Middle Earth. There could be anything up there. Trolls, orcs, goblins."

"I think you'll find worse in a Union Street club on a Saturday night."

"You're right there."

The path wound in amongst the trees, turning left and right, curling back on itself before forging upwards again. Every now and then they had to duck under a fallen branch or struggle through a clearing where brambles and bracken fought for supremacy. The little glades were bright, green oases in an otherwise sterile environment of black peat and a carpet of fallen pine needles. They paused next to a shallow leat, clear water within moving slowly along the contour line. Savage took her jacket off and tied it around her waist. She needed a rest. Calter leant against a tree to wait for her, hardly drawing breath.

"You need to come out with me, ma'am," Calter said. "Start easy, just five K a couple of times a week. How about it?"

Savage nodded. She'd been meaning to start running again for years, ever since she'd had Jamie. Somehow she'd never got round to it. Maybe she'd take Calter up on the offer. But five K sounded anything but easy.

The route levelled out for a while and then began to rise again. Savage paused again at a tree, wishing they'd brought some water with them, and then carried on. In another twenty minutes the trees thinned and then all of a sudden they were walking on rock, the granite of a tor rising before them.

190

Savage cursed. There was no sign of the man, no sign of anything much aside from the trees circling the little peak.

"We're lost," Savage said. "Let's get to the top of the tor to try and get our bearings."

"Actually, we know where we are." Calter held her phone up, the screen glinting in the sunlight. "The trouble is my map shows sod all but a huge patch of green."

They scrambled up the last few metres and then stood atop the crag. The forest dropped away in all directions. To the south they could see the valley with the track that led back to where they'd left the car. Savage looked at her watch; it was an hour and a half since they'd parked up at the gate.

"Loath as I am to admit it," Savage said as she plonked herself down on a boulder, "but I think we've bitten off more than we can chew. Call it in. Get a response unit up here ASAP. We'll take a short rest and then head on down."

"Ma'am?" Calter had raised her phone, but then stopped. "Can you hear that?"

Savage stood and listened. A faint chopping sound echoed amongst the boughs. Thud. Thud. Thud. Both Savage and Calter whirled round, trying to make out where the sound was coming from.

"There," said Savage, pointing down into thick woodland. "Let's go."

Chubber's caught her now. He managed to corner her up against a fallen tree. Grabbed her and carried her back to the shed. This time, Chubber uses the ropes.

Not so stupid Chubber Chub Chubs, are you?

No, not so stupid.

Chubber's had his fun and now he's strung her up by the legs. There's a block and tackle slung over a branch. A few pulls on the rope and she's swinging there. Swing, swing, swinging. Cruel. Nasty.

You don't like cruel do you, Chubber Chub Chubs?

No. Not cruel. Time to act then. Using the knife, slipping the point in at the neck to cut the jugular. Bleeding her out. Soon dead. No more pain. Hot work. Take a little break. Another gulp of water from the pond and then back to the job.

Skin her first rather than gut her. If the gutting comes first then there's a danger of staining the skin. And Chubber doesn't want that. The skin is useful. Precious. Skilful job, taking the skin clean off in one piece. But Chubber's worked in a slaughterhouse. Knows what he's doing does Chubber Chub Chubs. Oh yes, Chubber does. Absolutely compos mentis Marks and Spencer's is our Chubber.

Yes, we is!

Stop doodling and dawdling then, Chubber. Onward!

Chubber slips the knife in. Pulls. Teases the skin away from the muscle. Slip, pull, tease. Slip, pull, tease. Comes off like a glove or a stocking. Rolls down easy until Chubber throws the lot to one side, the skin all loose and flippy floppy. Fillet her next. The viscera sliding out. Chubber'll deal with that later. Take the mess half a mile away and dump it. Now for the jointing. Lower her down onto the big piece of ply. Cut,

192

chop, hack. Cut, chop, hack. Easy peasy. Stack the pieces in the plastic crates. So many pieces. Amazing!

And that's it. Job done. Slaughtered. Skinned. Gutted. Butchered. Twenty minutes, half an hour max.

Chubber looks at himself. Clear-up time. Muddy, bloody, pissy. Yuk!

Come on Chubber, get yourself together!

Chubber goes to the pool and splashes cool water on his face and hands. Oh! Freezing. Brrrr! Rub a dub dub. Splish splash splosh. Chubber's cleaner now. Sloshes water over the ply and sweeps the surface down with a broom. Spots the skin and the box of guts all slurp sloppy slop. He kicks the box and they wibble wobble like a giant jellyfish. Bother. He'll leave them and the skin until his next trip. There'll be flies but it's better than getting all dirty again. Now he takes everything down to the car. Hard work. Rewarding work. Satisfying.

Are you sure you're satisfied, Chubber?

"Yes I am," Chubber says aloud to no one but the big dark wood. "Very satisfied."

Chubber sits in the car. Starts the engine. Gets his breath back. Thinks, does Chubber. Dangerous, thinking, he thinks.

Leads to problems. Oh yes and there's one big problem now isn't there? A biggy big big problem. Inside the corrugated shed, one of the rooms is empty.

Oh my my Chubber. Naughty Chubber. You know what this means don't you?

Chubber does know. Always knows. It means that by next week he'll need another one.

★   ★   ★

Savage and Calter plunged off the tor and down into the thick woodland. A path of sorts cut through the trees but it was more suited to deer than humans. Low branches tangled Savage's hair while briers snagged at her legs. The path soon gave out and they were forced to continue down between avenues of trees. After another five minutes Savage stopped.

"We're lost," she said. "Where are those leats we crossed on the way up? They run along the contours so we should have come across them."

"This is bad news, ma'am," Calter said. "Not only are we lost, we're lost in a wood with a psycho."

"If we continue to head downhill at some point we'll come out at the bottom."

"Unless we come across him first."

They headed on down and after ten minutes of pushing through branches and brambles they emerged onto another path.

"This is the way we came up," Savage said, starting to move along the trail. Then she paused. To her right, something glinted. She stopped again. There. A rock with piece of quartz on one side. Just by the rock, a footprint had been left in a patch of mud. Savage stared off the path down the line of trees. A pine sapling a few metres away lay on its side, the thin stem broken. A little further on, the lower branch of a tree had snagged a plastic bag.

"Here," Savage said, spotting another footprint as she ducked under a low branch. "Somebody has walked down the tree line. We must have missed this on the way up."

She moved on, following the line of trees. After a few minutes they came to a dilapidated chicken wire fence. Most of the fence posts lay flat on the floor, rotting. Where they stood upright the wire hung down in great sheets. The trees thinned and a clear pool sparkled in beams of sun, the light filtering down through the canopy of fir. On the far side of the pen a corrugated iron shed appeared to be more cared for than the fence, since it had benefited from a recent coat of black bitumen. Close to the shed an A-frame scaffold-like structure stood over a flat base. Beneath the frame stood a plastic crate.

Savage stepped forward over the broken fence and moved into the enclosure. The base beneath the A-frame glistened red with blood.

"Oh my God!" Calter said, pointing at the crate. "What the fuck is in there?"

The crate brimmed with grey sludge of viscera and flesh and blood.

"This is . . ." Savage didn't know how to finish the sentence. The scene was appalling.

"Irina. Got to be." Calter reached the base, a sheet of plywood.

Savage shook her head. She was struggling to keep her lunch down. In all her time in the force she'd never witnessed anything as shocking.

"Over here," Savage heard herself say as she lumbered across to the shed. There were several pieces of baler twine tying the door shut. Savage tried to unpick the knots and then gave up. She rattled the door and peered in through a crack. Black. A strong smell of urine. Something moving in the dark. "Jesus, there's somebody in there. Help me."

The DC came across and the two of them jerked the door. The baler twine held. Calter moved away and picked up a broken fence post.

"Let's try this, ma'am. We can slip it inside the twine and apply some leverage."

"OK." Savage bent to the door. "It's alright. Police. We'll have you out in a moment."

Calter took the fence post and inserted it in the loop of twine. She rotated the post and applied downward pressure. The twine snapped. As Calter threw the post away Savage swung open the door.

"Bloody hell!" Calter said. "The stench."

Urine, shit, something rotting. The smell was overpowering.

Savage moved into the shed. As her eyes grew accustomed to the lack of light she saw there were two inner rooms, the door to one standing open. She moved to the other door and slid back the bolt.

"It's OK," Savage said as she opened the door. "You're safe now."

At the back of the shed the girl coughed and then made a horrible bleating sound. A shape moved and Savage saw green eyes flash, the poor thing retreating deeper into the darkness.

"Take your time. My name is Detective Inspector Charlotte Savage and next to me is Detective Constable Jane Calter. You're not in any trouble and you're going to get all the help and care you need."

Savage stepped to one side and motioned for Calter to do the same.

Then the girl ran for the door.

But the thing on four legs with a woolly coat and a startled look flashing across green eyes wasn't a girl.

"It's a sheep, ma'am!" Calter said, starting to laugh.

The animal skipped away across the clearing and disappeared into the wood.

Savage let out a long breath. "Dear God, I nearly had a heart attack." She turned and walked back to the A-frame. A bundle of wool lay next to the box of offal. She kicked the bundle with her foot. "Sheepskin. Thank goodness. Creasey's got nothing to do with the murder of Ana — he's the phantom sheep rustler the Agricultural Crime Squad have been after."

"Where is he? Looks like he's been hard at work and then just buggered off."

"No idea. Let's get back down to the vehicles. Maybe response have blocked him in. Then we'll call Riley and tell him the score. He can take it from here."

"OK." Calter nodded. She had her phone out and was snapping a couple of pictures. "I'll just get some evidence first, ma'am. And something for the canteen noticeboard too. The day we thought we had our very own Dartmoor cannibal."

Although Riley knew the word cougar was highly disparaging, it could have been invented to describe Helen Peacock. The way the woman strode across the foyer towards him had the effect of turning his legs to jelly. Another part of his anatomy was rapidly going the other way.

"Detective Riley?" Red lips articulated the words while the woman's tongue paused for a moment, the tip caressing her top lip. A figure-hugging dress displayed a substantial cleavage to good effect. The hem was cut short. Media folk, Riley reflected, were a breed apart.

Helen Peacock was in her fifties. Riley knew she'd been a bigshot presenter up in London. Then she'd had children and moved back to her home county of Devon. Many had been surprised when she'd opted to return to work for a regional branch of the BBC rather than back at the top. Her explanation was she'd "been there, done that". Quality of life, time with her husband and children, was now what mattered, she'd said in numerous interviews.

"Yes," Riley said, getting up from the sofa. "Detective Sergeant Darius Riley."

"Darius?" The tongue on the lips again, her eyes looking him up and down. A slight nod of the head indicating all was good. "Unusual. For round here."

Riley wasn't sure whether Peacock meant his name, his skin colour, the fact he was a police officer or all three. He coughed. Peacock slid onto the sofa next to him, her legs crossing and even more thigh showing.

"It's about this," Riley said, sitting back down and showing the cross in the plastic bag. "Is it yours?"

"Where . . .?" Peacock shook her head, for a moment her BBC coolness evaporating. "Yes. Yes it is."

"So you know what the symbol represents?"

"Yes, of course. It was handmade for me. Of course I know."

"And?"

"It's a Satanic cross." Peacock touched the edge of her skirt, her hand splayed on her thigh. "Don't look so shocked, Darius. The piece was a joke. My husband always said I had a little of the devil inside me so I decided to commission the cross as a private reminder. The thing is, it was lost or stolen a while back. Where on earth did you find it?"

"When did it go missing?" Riley ignored the question and tried to ignore the woman's legs too. "And where?"

"When? Oh it must have been a year or two ago. As for where, well, I've no idea. I didn't wear it to work, obviously, so it must have been lost on a night out."

"And you don't recall the circumstances? It was valuable, Mrs Peacock. Surely you remember the occasion?"

"No, Officer, I don't. Not wanting to sound snobbish, it only cost a few hundred pounds. It was a sentimental loss only." Peacock uncrossed her legs and sat forward. "Can you tell me what this is about? The way you're questioning me suggests you aren't simply here to return the item."

"Do you go walking on Dartmoor, Mrs Peacock?"

"Is that an invitation, Darius?" Peacock smiled, the tongue in action again. "Because I'd very much like to take you up on it if it is."

"No." Riley held up the plastic bag. "This was found on the moor at a crime scene. Do you have any idea how it might have got there?"

"No." Peacock moved, her body rigid like a cat arching its back. The allure she'd been turning on had been switched off in an instant, instead replaced by a cold edge to her voice. "I don't. Will it be returned to me?"

"When we've finished with it."

"That would be good. As I said, it's not valuable, but the piece has sentimental value."

"What about the other six?"

Peacock moved again, a hand going to her thigh and a fingernail scratching her leg. As if the action might make her remember.

"For friends. Part of the same joke."

"And the names of these friends?"

"Oh, I couldn't possibly tell you that, Darius. Not unless you decide to make me." Peacock put her head on one side, smiled and held Riley's gaze for a few seconds. Then she stood up. "Until then, Detective."

Peacock strode off, even though Riley hadn't said anything about the interview being over. Halfway across the foyer she turned for a moment, Riley sure the look she gave him being an open invitation. *Forget all about the cross and you can bed me.* Or was it the other way around: *Bed me and you'll forget all about the cross.*

Women, Riley thought. Satanic or not, there was a kind of evil magic at work inside each and every one.

Chubber drives down the track until he gets to the gate. There's a car parked the other side. Somebody's been nosing, he thinks. He climbs out and checks through the windscreen. There's a sticker there, a parking permit. Like the local residents thing he's got in the front of his van. Only this one's not for residents. This is for the poo lice station in town.

Trouble!

Trouble, yes. Chubber goes back to his car. Turns it around and heads back up the track. When he reaches the quarry and the turning circle he slips the car off the side in amongst the trees. Then he's out of the car and back up the little trail as fast as he can run.

Up, Chubber, up you go!

When he reaches the rock with the little piece of quartz he turns and walks along the tree line. Then he kneels in the mud. Slippy sloppy, like the guts from the animal he's just killed. Through the low branches he can see two people nosing around. One of them is taking pictures with her phone. She's pretty and Chubber wonders what she'd do if he gave her a message with a couple of pound coins.

If she's a police officer then she'd arrest you, Chubber, that's what she'd do.

Yes. Better not risk that. Pretty girl can wait. The redhead though. She's older. Maybe she'd be more receptive?

I doubt it, Chubber.

Chubber nods to himself. No, best leave them alone. He steals backward and inches away. Pushes through the trees, heading not down to the car but climbing through the thick woodland.

You need to check on something, Chubber?

Yes. Two hundred metres up the hillside is Chubber's *other* shed. The shed once held feed for the pheasants but when Chubber discovered the building the place was falling down. Chubber restored the shed. Specially. Antler Man's orders.

DIY, Chubber?

Yes. Do it yourself. Chubber carried all the materials up from the car. Mended the walls. Re-lined the inside with metal sheeting. Repaired the beams. Sealed the roof. Good as new.

He stomps the last few paces to the shed. Three bolts adorn the heavy door. Padlocks are attached to each bolt. Everything looks secure.

That's a lot of security for a shed in the middle of nowhere.

Yes. Because this shed has to hold more than just sheep. You see, sheep aren't clever. A latch or a couple of pieces of baler twine will keep them in. Other things have bigger brains. Chubber lifts the little shutter on the peephole which lies dead centre in the door, scrunches up his left eye and uses his right to peer in.

Other things, Chubber?

Yes, Chubber thinks, pleased to see she's still in there. Other things, like girls, are a different matter entirely.

CHAPTER
FIFTEEN

Friday 29th August

Savage rose early, once more out of the house before Pete and the children had woken. She was worn out and weak after her moorland exertions the previous day and Fallon's offer of breakfast at a little greasy spoon on Union Street was too tempting to pass up. By seven-thirty she was sitting in the cafe, an anaemic slice of bacon sandwiched between two doorstep pieces of bread sitting on a plate in front of her.

"Should have had the eggs, Charlotte," Fallon said, cutting into his omelette. He raised his voice. "Barry does good eggs, don't you Barry?"

Fallon waved an arm at the proprietor who acknowledged him with a nod and a grin before returning to cleaning the grill.

"Now you tell me." Savage pushed the plate away and reached for her coffee. "I wouldn't have ordered the bacon butty if I'd known the meat was being rationed."

"You can understand Barry's reasoning, Charlotte. He's a veggie. The less bacon he uses, the fewer piggies have to die."

"Well, why doesn't he start a vegetarian restaurant then?"

"No money in it. Believe me, I've looked into running one myself." Fallon looked pained. "I thought I'd be able to get away with a few carrots and a lettuce or two. But no, the customers want couscous, mung beans, pine nuts and that sort of crap."

Savage smiled and took a sip of her coffee. She'd not spoken to Fallon since the day in Brixham. He'd been pissed-off that she hadn't confronted Owen, even though she'd explained about her mobile. Now though, he seemed to have cooled down.

"Not to worry, I totally understand." Fallon held up his hands. "A mobile is both a crook's best friend and worst enemy. Without a mobile I couldn't do half my business, but you've got to be so careful. Pay as you go, multiple SIM cards, importing foreign phones to use . . . hey, I shouldn't be telling you all this, should I?"

Savage smiled. "I don't think you need to worry about me."

"No, love." Fallon returned the smile. "I guess I don't."

"Now, why am I here?"

"Owen, isn't it?" Fallon said. "We're not done until I've helped you and so far I've done nothing."

"You helped me track him down. That's enough."

"That's not enough. He's got to pay for what he did to your little one, hasn't he?" Fallon paused and then lowered his voice to a whisper. "The thing is, I don't think you've got the guts to do it alone, am I right?"

"This week, Kenny," Savage said. "There's a girl dead, another one missing. I've had other things on my mind."

"Bollocks, love. A girl dead and you've not thought of your own daughter?" Fallon shook his head. "Well *I've* thought of her and I've thought of Owen. And I still owe you, don't I? That business with Ricky Budgeon. I could well have been toast without you."

Savage sighed. The debt, she thought, had been wiped out, the information that led her to Owen being the payment. So Fallon's motive for helping further wasn't entirely altruistic. He'd be all too pleased to have something else to hold over her. Still, he was right. In the last few days she'd tried to distract herself with police work, but Owen Fox had always been there.

"OK," Savage said. "So what have you got in mind?"

"I made a mistake the other day. I should have been there with you. To provide you with a bit of moral support. A bit of physical support too."

"Thanks, Kenny, but it's down to me."

"Yeah, in the end. But having somebody alongside you might have made things easier, right?"

"I guess."

"So, I've got a plan. You and me," Fallon chuckled, unable to contain his mirth. "We're going to be married at the weekend. Man and wife."

"Sorry?" Savage leant back and cocked her head. "Say that again?"

"Don't worry, not what you think. Just an act. You see I've made an appointment for me and the Mrs to view a pretty little countryside property near

Kingswear. Quiet, secluded and very, very isolated. Sunday at eleven. A Mr Owen Fox is going to be showing us around."

A shiver ran through Savage and she stared across at Fallon. "You're joking?"

"No, love. It's all set up, everything arranged." Fallon smiled. "Oh, and don't forget to bring that present I gave you, OK?"

The news of Irina Kryukov's disappearance had hit the broadcast networks first thing in the morning. Ordinarily a missing girl in her mid-twenties wouldn't have merited a mention, but Irina had lived in the same house as Anasztáz Róka. The coincidence wasn't lost on Dan Phillips from the *Herald* and he'd come up with a suitably lurid headline for the first edition: *Home Sweet Home*.

Savage strolled into the crime suite to see the front page of the newspaper stuck up on the central whiteboard, the headline above a picture of the house.

"The only good thing about it," Enders said as Savage came over, "is the news might help bring property prices down. As you know, I'm looking to move to somewhere in Mannamead sometime around the end of the century."

"Irina's disappearance is no joke," Savage said. "What the hell does Dan think he's playing at?"

"Being a London hack, I shouldn't wonder. But he's got a point, hasn't he? His piece says we don't have a clue, that we've already eliminated two suspects and don't have any further leads. And according to the

206

article, the remaining two tenants aren't even under our protection. I checked and he's right."

"Shit." Savage read the text of the article over Enders' shoulder. "Get some sort of safe house organised for them, Patrick."

"And the sheep shagger from yesterday?"

"Adam Creasey?" Savage sighed. "He wasn't in when a unit went to his place last night. I'm sending DC Denton from the Agricultural Crime Squad and DC Calter round there this morning. Denton will be covering the illegal slaughtering angle while Jane will ensure Creasey knows that passing erotic notes to young waitresses is a no-no."

"The way Carl is over Jane," Enders sniggered, "I wouldn't be surprised if he asks Creasey for some advice as regards women. Creasey's technique can't be any worse than his, can it?"

Savage tried to stifle a laugh as a nearby DC passed her a phone.

"Dr Andrew Nesbit, ma'am," the officer said. "Conclusions from Ana's post-mortem."

Savage took the phone and grabbed a pad and pen as Nesbit began to detail his findings. First came the usual dry, technical details about the girl's age, height and weight. Next Nesbit went on to explain that the girl hadn't been strangled or asphyxiated, nor were there any stab wounds.

"Sexual assault?"

"No."

"So how did she die?" Savage said.

"Severe concussion resulting in a cerebral haemorrhage."

207

"From a head wound?"

"She banged her head, certainly, but this is the type of injury you would expect from a severe fall or a car accident."

"Are you saying she wasn't murdered?"

"I'm not saying anything other than her head hit an object, not the other way around."

"This might sound stupid," Savage said. "But could she have run into a tree?"

"Unlikely. I found high levels of a barbiturate in the blood. Nembutal. That's a strong sedative. I don't think she would have been doing any running, she'd have been barely conscious."

"What about if she'd been in a car accident, perhaps not wearing a seatbelt?"

"Yes. However, the scratches on the skin suggest she wasn't in a car, rather she was in the wood."

"Unless she received the scratches in the wood, then had a car accident, and then was returned to the wood."

"A jumble of possibilities, Charlotte. There has to be a better explanation and I might have found it."

"Go on."

"I don't want to disparage your reputation as a polymath, but I'm sure you don't know much about dendrology."

"Polymath . . .?" Savage laughed. "I think you've got the wrong person. And I haven't a clue what dendrology means."

"It's the study of trees. In this particular instance the tree we're interested in is *Pinus Sylvestris*, better known as the Scots pine. Now, the Scots pine is a monoecious plant, meaning male and female flowers are found on the same tree. In the spring the male flowers release pollen and this is captured by the female flowers which go on to form the cones. I found a small, green cone entangled in Ana's hair. I'm sure you are aware of what a Scots pine looks like."

"Tall."

"Yes and usually no branches near the ground. The cones form high up. Do you get my drift?"

"She was up in a tree?"

"Yes. It's possible she fell and banged her head. The fall killed her. Judging from the head wound she must have been some way up, but whether this happened where the body was discovered or not I've no idea."

"But from what I know of Scots pines they're the last kind of tree you'd be able to climb. How did she get up there?"

"I'm not sure. As I mentioned before, she was drugged. Climbing a tree in the state she was in sounds unlikely, but you need to take another look at the scene."

"You don't think this cone could have been on the ground and that's how it ended up in her hair?"

"Yes, possibly. However, there was a residue of sap across part of her arm, which suggests she was climbing. Of course a recently felled tree could be another explanation."

Savage tried to visualise the area around where the body had been found. Scrub and pine trees. But climbing one of the firs would have been difficult. The branches were packed together and spindly. She thanked Nesbit and hung up.

"Problems, ma'am?" Enders stood beside her. "You look perplexed."

"Dr Nesbit," Savage said. "Usually I trust him to come up with the goods but this time his explanation just doesn't fit."

"No?"

"No." Savage paused. "You get that safe house organised, I'm going back to Fernworthy. Nesbit said I needed to look at the crime scene again and he's right."

Denton had been feeling pretty pleased with himself after the result up on the moor on Tuesday night. True, Hardin had bollocked him for not telling anybody what he'd been up to, but even Hardin was bathing in some of the reflected glory. "People will be starting to take the ACS seriously now," the DSupt had said as he'd handed Denton a celebratory custard cream. However, back in the crime suite a new printout had been stuck to one of the team's whiteboards.

"My Little Pony," Denton had said, reaching for the piece of paper and scrunching it up before DI Davies could see the way the picture had been digitally altered around the genital area. "Just a bit of fun."

The picture had been a bad omen, Denton realised. Wednesday saw Davies and Riley fail to get much out of the North Prospect boys and on Thursday DI Savage and Jane Calter had inadvertently solved the sheep rustling case. Now a disgruntled Calter was accompanying him on a trip to interview the man responsible — a

Mr Adam Creasey — with a view to pressing charges. She'd made it clear that she didn't consider the visit proper police work. So much for trying to impress her.

Creasey lived on Glenmore Avenue, over Stoke way. The terrace had no front gardens, not even a couple of feet of concrete. The doors opened onto the street, nothing more than a front step, with the pavement slicing diagonally down across each, showing the steepness of the hill as the ground fell away. Number thirty-three had a wooden door stained dark brown. A little glass window with a distorted pane sat top centre.

Calter stood to one side as Denton pressed the bell.

"Thanks for coming," Denton said.

"No problem." Calter shook her head and stared at the front door. "Come on, what's taking him so long?"

Something behind the door rattled. Keys in locks. Top and bottom. A bolt being drawn across. The door opened and a bald man stared at them through wire-framed glasses. A large wart on one side of a pudgy neck seemed to move in time with the man's laboured breathing.

"Yes?" The man reached down with one hand and rubbed his belly which extended over the top of a pair of grey jogging bottoms. "Don't need no broadband. Don't want to change leccy supplier. Don't care about no fucking Jehovah."

"Police, Mr Creasey," Denton said. "You are Mr Adam Creasey?" Denton glanced at Calter and she nodded.

"He is, Carl."

"I *might* be," the man said. "But Chubber needs to checker check check. See if *you're* who you say *you* are."

"Chubber?"

"Me. Chubber's me. Mr Adam Creasey's me. One and the same person. Mostly."

Calter held out her ID. "DC Jane Calter and this is DC Carl Denton."

"Nice," Creasey said. "Picture, I mean. Pretty."

"May we?" Denton stared past Creasey down a corridor littered with pizza boxes. A couple of black bin liners stood to one side, rubbish spilling from the top of one. "There's a few questions we'd like to ask you."

Creasey nodded and turned. The ribbed sweater he wore was several sizes too small and his arms bulged inside. Calter and Denton followed Creasey down the hallway, Calter shutting the door with a bang.

"In here," Creasey said, opening a door to a living room. "Bit of a messy mess mess. Sorry."

Several green plastic crates sat on an orange sofa and more fast-food packaging was strewn across the floor. There was no carpet, just layers of newspaper.

"The crates, Mr Creasey," Denton said. "Where did you get them?"

"Oh goodness. Sorry. Tesco. Only borrowed them. Meant to give them back. Take them, please, take them. I won't do it again. Cross my heart and hope to . . . hope to . . ."

"Let's cut to the chase," Calter said. "You've been taking sheep from farms on Dartmoor and illegally butchering them. We've found your little hideaway up on the moor, found some evidence. It would be best if you came down the station and made a full statement."

"She-she-sheep!" Creasey's jaw worked up and down. "Oh my, of course sheep! I thought you meant . . ."

"The waitresses?"

"Oh God!"

"We know all about them too, Mr Creasey."

"You do?" Creasey's hand went to his jaw. He bit his knuckle. "I . . ."

"This is a warning. Don't ever write notes like that again. If you do you could find yourself being prosecuted for harassment. I'd stay away from cafes from now on if I was you."

"Oh yes, I will! Thank you very muchly. Thank you, thank you, tha —"

"Enough. This visit is about the sheep, remember?"

"Yes, the sheep."

"You admit to it then?"

"Yes, yes. But not illegal. I used to work in a slaughter-house. I know what I'm doing. They never feel anything, the little beauties."

"You killed them."

"The knife slips in just beside the jugular and you pull the blade sideways. They're unconscious in seconds. The loss of blood pressure, see? Dead in a minute. A bit of twitching, but that's just nerves. Chubber's not cruel. Never."

"Mr Creasey, never mind the cruelty, you *stole* the sheep."

"Inflation. The cost of living crisis. Hard times. People say to me 'Chubber, where can I get my hands on some cheap meat?' I say 'leave it to Chubber' and off I go. There's thousands of sheep on the moor or in the fields. One or two don't matter. Mrs Grately, three doors up. Her pension's not enough. Chubber likes to help out. Then there's the Lawrence family. The daddy's just been made redundant and with three little ones life is —"

"Stop!" Calter said. "You're coming down to the custody centre. We're going to charge you with . . . with . . ." Calter turned to Denton for help.

"Sheep stealing," Denton said. "Running an illegal slaughterhouse, dispatching animals for food in unhygienic and dirty premises and various charges under the Welfare of Animals at the Time of Killing legislation."

"T-t-time of killing?" Creasey said. He raised a hand to his forehead and wiped a sheen of sweat away. "Chubber don't like time. Sand, slipping down. Grandfather clocks ticking in the hallway. Mother in the bed wasting away. Never liked the days going by. Saying bye-bye, nighty-night, sleep tight, snuggle down and the bugs won't bite."

"Jesus," Calter turned to Denton and muttered under her breath. "Forget the sheep, this guy's a section one-three-six job. Cuckoo. Let's take him to Charles Cross, bring in an appropriate adult and get a shrink to have a look. The sooner we can get shot of him and I can get back to some real police work, the better, OK?"

Denton looked across at Calter, feeling his heart sink even further.

"Yes, Jane," he said. "Whatever you say."

Savage headed back to Dartmoor once more, Nesbit's botany lesson fresh in her mind. The answer to exactly what had happened must lie somewhere in the wood at Fernworthy. When she arrived at the reservoir she sat in the car as a light drizzle misted the windscreen. There were a couple of other vehicles in the car park, but no sign of the owners. Savage pulled over near the entrance and got out. She put on a lightweight waterproof and hoped that the rain wouldn't get any heavier. The sky to the west was a grey fuzz of tumbling cloud and a strong breeze swept the whole mass in her direction.

She followed the path around the edge of the reservoir. Wavelets collided with the bank side with a rhythmic slap, slap, slap and at one point a coot shot out from behind a bush and skittered across the surface of the water, calling out in alarm. The route to the spot where Ana's body had been found was obvious, the trail trampled by dozens of boots as detectives, CSIs and mortuary technicians had gone about their business. She turned away from the reservoir and walked into the woodland. Pine scent hung heavy in the air and little birds flitted back and forth from tree to tree. Within five minutes she had reached the perimeter of the scene, although the blue and white tape which had marked the area was gone. She could see the mossy rock near where the body had lain and the black peat of the drainage ditch slashed through the brown canvas of needles. The trees here, like most of those which surrounded the reservoir, were mature pine. Savage moved across to one. The lower branches were crowded together, while the upper ones were thin and spindly. They weren't the kind of trees you could climb and anyway, according to Nesbit, Ana had been drugged. She may well have been conscious, but undertaking any complex physical activity would have probably been beyond her.

Savage walked forward and hopped over the drainage channel. The mossy rock lay several metres from where Ana's body had been found. Was it possible she had banged her head on the rock and then staggered across to the channel? But John Layton hadn't found any signs to indicate that and the ground was soft enough so that as Savage walked across to the rock she made visible footprints. Anyway, the body hadn't been there on the first search. The killer had dumped the body later. Unless there was another explanation. She looked back at the depression in the ground where the body had lain. Three steps away was a large Scots pine, the trunk telegraph pole straight. Savage followed the trunk upward. For several metres there were no branches, then one or two, and near the very top the greenery plumed like a Christmas tree with multiple branches. Something caught her eye. Something sparkling up there in the light.

Savage squinted against the sky. The branches were like black fingers spreading out against the clouds. Halfway up a larger branch had been broken in two so that one half hung down, the light-coloured wood splintering out from the bark. On a thinner branch a little way below hung a circle of silver.

She moved her position a few metres, trying to get a better look. Whatever the thing hanging there was, she was sure it must be connected to Ana.

Savage moved to the base of the tree, for a moment considering whether she could climb it. No, as Nesbit had said, climbing a Scots pine was near impossible. Without a ladder or rope there was no way up there. But the girl *had* been up there. Nesbit had been right.

She headed back down the trail to the lake, where she pulled out a mobile phone. There was no signal. Back at the car park there should be one. She began to walk along the path when she spotted Charlie Kinver on the shoreline, a swoosh of his rod as he cast out.

"Inspector Savage," Kinver said, winding in as she approached. "A surprise."

"I could say the same," Savage said. "Don't you feel uncomfortable being so close to where the body was found?"

"No, do you?" Kinver had been standing a few metres from the shore and now he turned and waded back to the bank side. "The girl's dead, but it was nothing to do with me."

Savage nodded. She was about to carry on along the path to the car park when a thought struck her. She looked at Kinver's fishing rod. "You fancy giving me a hand?"

Five minutes later and she stood beneath the tree with Kinver. Savage pointed up at the glinting silver.

"Do you think you can reach it?"

Kinver stared up at the branch. The object was perhaps five or six metres from the ground. Kinver pushed the fishing rod upwards, holding it by the end of the handle. The tip flexed as he waved it around and then nudged against the object. Kinver made a twisting motion with his hand and the top eye of the rod caught. He pulled and then the thing came loose, tumbling down and landing at Savage's feet.

She pulled a pair of gloves from her pocket and bent to pick it up. It was a plain silver bangle.

Savage stood. "Thank you, Mr Kinver, you've been a big, big help."

CHAPTER
SIXTEEN

Irina hadn't managed to sleep much. The pile of paper sacks was no substitute for a mattress and her reading material — Ana's notebook — wasn't the sort of bedtime tale to bring sweet dreams.

"Not just Creasey," she'd muttered to herself before she'd finally dozed off.

When she woke, Creasey's face hung for a moment in the motes of dust swirling in light shining above. Now, thanks to Ana's scrawl in the notebook, Irina knew there were others involved too. Their names meant nothing to Irina and the story barely seemed credible. And yet in Russia such tales of corruption and illegality were commonplace. Why would things be any different here?

She sat up and tasted the stale, dry air. For a moment she thought she caught a hint of Ana's favourite perfume layered over the musty smell. She shook her head. She was imagining things. Trying to bring Ana back to life. A sadness welled up inside. Ana wasn't going to come back to life because she was dead, killed by Creasey and the others. Why, Irina didn't know, but then "why" rarely counted for much. All that mattered was the fact that men used women as playthings and when they got bored, or the playthings displeased them, then they discarded the women.

Irina pushed herself to her feet. Was she destined to be a plaything? Or was her abduction for some other reason? Most likely simply turning up at Creasey's house was enough to make her a threat that needed to be eliminated. Again she thought of her home country. Rich men got what they wanted through the use of money and influence. They paid somebody to do something or pressurised them to bend to their will. But there was enough incriminating evidence in Ana's notebook to end all that, at least in this case. If Irina could escape she could see these people got what they deserved.

She looked around the room at the walls lined with sheet metal. The metal extended to some two metres from the floor and above that, wood panelling rose to where the roof pitched inward. Wooden beams latticed their way across the centre of the room, huge oak trusses supporting the roof. Up there more tin had been tacked in place, but sections of it had peeled away, old and rusty. The shafts of light which illuminated the dust particles came from several holes, but the roof was way up high, maybe seven or eight metres above. Even the beams that crossed back and forth were a good two metres beyond her outstretched arms.

Earlier she'd found a plank over by one wall. The piece of wood was a metre and a half long by half a metre wide. At the time she'd thought the discovery meaningless. The plank was too short to be of any use. Now, however, Irina nodded to herself and then smiled.

Whoever had imprisoned her in the room must have decided the place was all but escape-proof. Nobody could hope to jump high enough to reach the beams and, even if by some miracle they did, climbing any further would require the skills of a contortionist and the strength of an athlete.

Or, Irina thought, the agility and physique of a championship gymnast.

Dozens of images of Helen Peacock filled the terminal screen in front of Riley, many of the pictures looking as if they had been taken directly from the television.

"Snapped by the more obsessed members of her fan base," Riley said. "Screen caps, they call them."

"Hey?" Davies peered at the images.

"Screen captures. Peacock is all over the web forums as one of the best-looking older women on TV. Type 'cougar' into a search and she comes somewhere near the top."

"Don't these saddos have anything better to do?" Davies tapped the screen as Riley enlarged one of the images. Peacock on a studio couch, the screen capture showing the exact moment her dress had ridden all the way up her thigh. "Sitting around at home all day, waiting for that one moment. Mind you, she's certainly a looker."

"I guess they all are," Riley said. "TV people. Goes with the territory."

"Fair enough. I expect something for my licence fee. What did she have to say for herself?"

Riley recounted yesterday's meeting, leaving aside the come-on Peacock had made.

"Guilty as," Davies said. "Her explanation won't wash. She's been up on that moor, dancing naked under the stars and slicing up ponies."

"But why? She's got fame and money, a nice place in Cornwall. Why on earth would she get involved with something like this?"

"Excitement." Davies made a succession of chopping movements with his right hand and then pinched some invisible dust between finger and thumb and raised it to his nose. "Like the old laughing powder. People want more. Drugs, swinging parties, devil worship. Most of us would be happy with what she's got, but famous people don't think like normal folk. I guess that's how they got to where they are."

"You reckon?" Riley put his head on one side. Davies didn't usually get so philosophical. "Well, at the moment all we have is the sigil and she's given us an explanation as to how that got on the moor."

"Bollocks. Just because she's BBC doesn't mean you have to believe everything she says."

"Well then we need to discover the connection between Peacock and the lads from North Prospect."

"Those scrotes and a woman of her class?" Davies chuckled and then pushed back his chair, indicating to Riley he was going for coffee. "Beauty and the beasts. Doesn't bear thinking about."

By the time John Layton arrived some ninety minutes later the drizzle had turned into a cold rain, the grey sky darkening. Layton's battered old Volvo bore several sets of ladders on the roof, the ends festooned with red rags, the whole affair giving the impression of odd job builder. Savage got out of her own car and went across. Layton wound down his window.

"Not magic, then?" Layton said.

"No." Savage moved back as Layton opened the door and got out. "And if my hunch is correct it could explain why Frey and his men were unable to find the body on the first attempt."

Savage helped Layton in untying and then unloading a large extending ladder. Layton pulled on a large rucksack containing his gear and they hefted the ladder onto their shoulders, Layton at the front, Savage at the rear.

"Thank God there's no one here to see us," Layton said. "We look like a right pair."

Layton was right; they resembled some comedy duo, a circus act, maybe a scene from a Laurel and Hardy movie. Walking round the edge of the lake was easy but negotiating the woodland was harder. Unable to weave between the trees, the length of the ladder made progress frustrating. Several times they had to back up and try a different route. Under the thick canopy of leaves the rain turned into large droplets of water that splattered down. By the time they reached the scene, Savage was soaked through.

Layton sniffed, bashed some water from his Tilley hat, and then turned to Savage. Together they manoeuvred the ladder into a vertical position, pushing the upper section up through the branches until they could lean it against the tree. The feet of the ladder sank into the soft ground. Layton hopped onto the bottom rung.

"Hold tight, would you?" The CSI peered up to where the ladder disappeared into foliage and gloom. "It'll be a bit wobbly when I get near the top."

Layton tested the next step and then began to climb. Savage held on to the bottom of the ladder as Layton pushed up through the branches, cursing as he went. Savage glanced up but Layton was out of sight and all she received for her efforts was a face full of water as his movement dislodged droplets from the branches above. After a minute or so, Layton shouted down.

"She was up here, you were right." Layton's voice sounded excited, though muffled by the foliage and the rain. "Looks like she was lying on a web of branches and then she fell off when it got windy or when she was trying to move. If Nesbit's time of death is correct and Frey's search didn't miss her the first time then it all makes sense. Hang on a moment."

Savage waited, staring through the rungs at the tree trunk. Sure it made sense, Savage thought, but only in a very limited fashion. Without a ladder, the tree was unclimbable. They were back to magic again. Layton hollered down again, his voice fainter.

"I've gone up a couple of metres and I can see some strands of hair caught on a thin branch. For the life of me I can't understand how she got up this far. The branch I'm talking about would barely hold a squirrel."

A couple of minutes later Savage felt the ladder shake as Layton descended. Clump clump clump he came, moving down two rungs at a time with little care. As he came into view Savage glanced up and a drop of water hit her in the eye. She flinched, for a moment relaxing her grip on the ladder. The whole thing wobbled and Layton's feet slipped off the rungs. He tumbled down, landing prone on the soft pine needles.

"Shit." Layton lay still for a second, then pushed himself up into a sitting position and rubbed his back.

"Sorry," Savage said, stepping forward and offering him a hand up. "Are you OK?"

"Yeah. But that could have been nasty. Twist an ankle up here and you need mountain rescue to get you out." Layton took Savage's hand and pulled himself to his feet. He reached into a pocket and took out a plastic ziploc bag. He held the bag up. "Several blonde hairs, almost certainly from Ana. She was up in that tree, but how she got there I've no idea."

Layton brushed the pine needles from his back and then the two of them went about lowering the ladder. Layton explained he would come back the next day with a full team and some sort of scaffolding tower.

They walked in silence back through the wood, carrying the ladder along the lake shore to the cars. Layton tied the ladder onto the roof.

"I'll get these hairs off to the lab. I'm convinced they're Ana's though."

"John," Savage said. "I've got an idea about how Ana ended up in the tree. It's a bit off the wall, but hear me out, OK?"

"Sure. Go ahead."

"It was when you mentioned mountain rescue. I thought of the Dartmoor Rescue Group, of how they get to people deep in the moor. When you can't walk there or the casualties are too injured to be hiked out."

"And?" Layton had his hand on the door of his car. He removed his hat revealing hair plastered to the top of his head. Rain streaked down his face. He'd had enough.

"They use a helicopter." Savage paused, but Layton didn't cotton on. "What about if Ana fell or was pushed from a low-flying helicopter or light aircraft and she ended up in the tree? Maybe she was already dead, or maybe she hit her head on the way down. Whatever. Her body entered rigor mortis and was stuck up there, rigid. Then the rigor mortis wore off and the wind dislodged her. She fell to the ground after Frey had conducted his search."

"Jesus, Charlotte," Layton said, grinning, his mood brighter. "That's brilliant. Crazy, but bloody brilliant. The girl's injuries — her scratches — could have been caused by the initial fall through the canopy. She was still alive then because she wouldn't have bled if the fall had happened post-mortem. However, the shock of landing on that large branch may have caused the concussion which Nesbit talked about."

"And the bag of clothes," Savage continued. "It could have been thrown out at the same time. Maybe they wanted the girl to land in the lake but they got their timing wrong."

"I'm thinking low-flying," Layton said. He put his hand out, flat, and moved it over the roof of his car.

"From high up there would have been many more injuries and much more damage. And I think it was a fixed-wing aircraft, not a helicopter, otherwise they wouldn't have mistimed the drop. Also, it must have been in the night-time. In the daytime the flight would have been far too risky because somebody would have seen the aircraft."

"Unless it was a genuine accident."

"But you don't believe that, do you?"

"No. For a start she was naked. Unless something very kinky was going on I can't see why anyone would be without their clothes in a small aircraft. This was murder."

By Friday afternoon Riley had managed to finalise arrangements for moving the stone covering the kistvaen. English Heritage and rangers from the Dartmoor Park Authority were going to be attending as well as members from the Dartmoor Rescue Group. The search and rescue team were not only going to provide safety cover in case of accidents, they'd undertake to move the stone as well.

Davies hadn't been too interested in yet another trip into the wilderness so Riley headed off alone, leaving the DI staring at pictures of Helen Peacock in various states of undress.

As Riley drove the twisting route from Yelverton to the stone circle, rain teemed down, the drizzle of earlier now more persistent. At the circle Riley found the leader of the rescue group, Callum Campbell, leaning nonchalantly against the DRG Land Rover and talking to a park ranger, seemingly impervious to the weather. Campbell's giant frame towered over the ranger, his Scottish accent booming across the landscape. Three DRG members and a couple of DPA workers stood over by the stone circle and nearby the archaeologist from English Heritage was setting up a video camera on a tripod, struggling to keep the camera's waterproof cover secure in the wind. She looked up as Riley climbed out of his car and strolled across to Campbell.

"Buried treasure?" Campbell said. "Or did you just fancy a spot of weightlifting?"

"Neither." Riley looked at Campbell. The man had a physique that suggested he might be able to shift the stone all on his own. "But the rock has moved and I want to know why."

"Aye. I've not been over this way for a while but I remember the kistvaen being open. It's a strange little box-shaped compartment. The kids jumped in and out of the hole when I was here for a picnic a couple of years ago."

"Definitely open," the DPA ranger said, wiping a drop of water from his nose. "And messing with something like this is against the law. Damaging an ancient monument. Although to be honest, judging by the state of those ponies, there're other things the blighters could be arrested for too."

"Well," Riley said, "you'll be glad to hear we've caught them. I'm just looking for some additional evidence."

"No time like the present," Campbell said. "Let's get started."

228

The archaeologist nodded at Riley as he came over to inspect the rock.

"The stone was there," the woman said. She pointed to a depression a metre or so away. A thin covering of weeds grew from the black peat but no heather. "Those plants are recent, seeded this year. The stone was moved sometime over the winter."

While the archaeologist began to explain to Riley about the history and use of the kistvaen, Campbell and his team brought over an assortment of ropes, various oak joists, crowbars and spades. Then Campbell and the ranger argued about how they should proceed. For a few minutes a heated discussion took place, during which there was much arm waving, but they eventually settled on lifting each end of the rock in turn onto strips of wood and then sliding the rock to the side with one of the vehicles providing the motive power. Riley shook his head. It was like a bloody grannies' meeting.

Another half an hour saw everything set up, the wood joists in position beneath the rock and a wire cable stretching from a winch on the front of the DRG Land Rover to a complicated weave of ropes wrapped around the rock. Campbell operated the winch and the wire strained and began to hum in the wind. There was a creak and the rock began to scrape along the oak beams. Riley moved forward to peer into the hole but Campbell waved him away.

"Stay back," Campbell shouted. "If the wire breaks it could slice you in half."

Riley stepped back quickly. The stone inched along the twin rails of wood. Riley circled round and joined Campbell at the front of the Land Rover. The rock had moved a couple of metres when Campbell cut the power to the winch.

"That'll do it," he said.

Riley moved back towards the hole but Campbell's long stride took him there first.

"Well," he said, staring down. "Looks like dead ponies are the least of your worries."

Riley reached the kistvaen. Four vertical slabs of rock had been sunk into the ground to form a small box. A contorted shape lay jumbled inside. A colourful waterproof jacket contrasted with a pale shrunken face and eye sockets gazed empty and unseeing from beneath a fleece hat. Skin peeled from the scalp where great chunks of hair had fallen out and some animal had gnawed away at one side of the cheek. Half the jawbone jutted out through the cheek, a line of teeth exposed in a grimace. The worst thing was the hands. Nothing but dried skin stretched tight over a skeletal frame, clasped together as if in prayer.

"Fuck," Riley said.

Savage was following John Layton's car along the narrow lane away from the reservoir when the CSI put his hazard lights on and pulled over onto the verge. Savage stopped her car behind Layton's as he got out. He had his mobile in one hand and he waved the phone at Savage as if he was sprinkling holy water.

"DS Riley." Layton turned and jerked the phone to the west where the rain clouds had given way to a sun glowing red and fierce as it settled on the horizon. "He's found a body over at the stone circle. I'm heading there now. Being as you're senior to Riley I think you'd better come too."

Savage trailed the CSI across the moor until eventually Layton's car crested a small rise. Several vehicles were clustered in a pull-off. DS Riley stood next to his own car and he waved as Savage and Layton parked up and came over.

"Not a girl," Riley said. "A man. And he's been there for some time."

"Thank goodness for that," Savage said. "Any ideas as to who he is?"

"Identity unknown at the moment. But then we haven't got him out of the kistvaen yet."

"The *what?*"

"Ancient burial chamber. Hence the presence of an archaeologist from English Heritage." Riley pointed over to where a fair-haired young woman with a pale face sat in the back of a squad car. "You'd have thought she'd have been used to seeing dead bodies, but she couldn't hang on to her lunch. To be fair to her, neither could the ranger and one of his workers."

"Not near the scene?" Layton growled. "You know how fussy I —"

"No, John, well away." Riley nodded to another car where Dr Andrew Nesbit stood making the final adjustments to his PPE suit. "Talking of fusspots, here comes Dr Death himself."

"Darius!" Savage flicked Riley on the arm.

"Fine evening for it, folks." Nesbit's voice carried across the moor as he strode over, his tall, thin frame reminding Savage of a circus stilt walker. As he approached he winked, a bushy eyebrow wriggling like some huge caterpillar. "Sunshine. Most unusual."

"Like this poor fellow." Riley gestured towards the stone circle where a CSI was erecting a camera tripod.

"Yes. Can't recall coming across anything like it before. Any issues I should know about?"

Riley explained that the kistvaen had originally been in an opened state, had probably been that way for centuries, but that the stone had some time in the last year or so been moved back into place, entombing the man.

"Alive?" Nesbit's right eyebrow wriggled again.

"Why else do you think you're here?" Savage said. "A picnic?"

"Never been my thing, Charlotte. Ants crawling all over the sandwiches, wasps drowning in the wine? No, alfresco to me means a table at my favourite restaurant in Sorrento overlooking the Gulf of Naples. Vesuvius to my right, the Med to my left, good food on the table and a beautiful woman sitting opposite." Nesbit winked again and Savage wondered if he was joking. "Shall we?"

As they approached the hole the CSI was focusing his attention on the junction between two of the inset stones.

"Marks in the rock," the CSI said as he fired off a couple of pictures. "Pieces have been chipped away."

"Interesting you mentioned Vesuvius, Andrew," Savage said. "Buried alive."

"Yes." Nesbit leaned over the hole and peered at the contorted body. "But in the case of being covered in hot volcanic ash death would occur from asphyxiation within minutes. I would imagine that if this poor chap was indeed buried alive then he took considerably longer to die. Do we know the date when the stone was last seen in its old position?"

"Not exactly," Riley said. "The general consensus seems to be some time last winter."

"From the state of the corpse I'd say it's as good a guess as any. There's substantial decay, but we're talking six months, possibly a little longer."

Nesbit took a walk around the kistvaen, pausing several times. Back where he started he put his bag down, opened it and pulled out a small padded object. Savage cocked her head on one side and gave Nesbit a quizzical stare, unable to work out what the piece of scientific equipment was.

"At my age, Charlotte," Nesbit said as he placed the cushion on the ground and knelt on it, "one needs all manner of little aids to get through the day."

The pathologist turned back to the corpse and his jokey manner vanished. He supported himself with one hand and reached down with the other, using a pair of forceps to remove the hat. The CSI stepped forward with a large plastic evidence bag, put the item inside and handed the bag back to Nesbit.

"As I thought. A head wound." Nesbit fiddled with the hat through the polythene and turned it partially inside out. He held the bag up for Savage. "Look, the material is discoloured."

Savage took the bag. The hat was a dark blue fleece material, but in one area the blue had turned black. "Blood," Savage said. "How did you know?"

"He's not tied up, is he? He was surprised and knocked unconscious and then put in the ground. He didn't come round until the rock had been placed in position. Here." Nesbit leant forward and teased at the man's pale hair with the forceps until a dark splodge could be seen. "More blood."

"But he did come round, right?"

"Yes. The chipping away at the stone shows that." Nesbit adjusted the position of his cushion and moved backwards. He pointed at one of the vertical slabs. "There. More blood and pieces of skin. When he'd finished with whatever he used to do the chipping he tried his hands. I wouldn't mind betting that on the underside of the main rock you'll find more evidence of his futile attempts to escape."

"Bloody hell, Andrew," Savage said, feeling a rush of panic at the thought of being trapped in the small space. "Don't you ever hanker after simple cases? You know, the 'died peacefully in their sleep' kind of thing."

"Boring," Nesbit said. "But of course it's the way I hope to go. Here, look at the ends of his fingers."

Nesbit had reached down and lifted the skeletal hand. He indicated for the photographer to take some pictures.

"And?" Savage said.

234

"Damage to the bone at the finger tips. He got so desperate he didn't realise what he was doing to his hands. He clawed and clawed away until the tips were gone and he chipped the bone."

Savage shook her head. Didn't say anything as Nesbit swung his legs over the edge of the kistvaen in order to get closer. Who was this poor man? The way he was dressed — the waterproofs, hat, scarf and hiking boots — suggested somebody who had planned to be out on the moor. This wasn't a gangland killing by inner-city criminals, nor a clever hiding place for a murder victim killed in premeditation or heat of the moment. On the other hand, who but a gang would be present in such numbers as to move the rock? This wasn't a one-on-one killing then. Several people had been involved in concealing the body at least. That should, Savage thought, make things easier. *Should*.

"Can't see any other obvious signs of injury," Nesbit said. "But the post-mortem will tell us more. Getting him out in one piece is going to be tricky though. He'll likely as not fall apart."

"So did the head wound eventually prove fatal or . . .?"

"From the evidence so far I'd say not. He probably died of thirst, exposure or perhaps he had a heart attack. I'll probably not be able to give you a definitive cause of death, but let's hope the PM reveals some more information regarding the time of death. If we're lucky there'll be plant or animal material trapped in his clothing somewhere. That could narrow down the time period to a month or so."

Savage nodded as Nesbit got up and began to explain about taking the utmost care with the retrieval of the corpse. Nothing must be left behind and contamination was to be avoided if at all possible.

With that the pathologist was away and the CSI was left muttering to Savage about Nesbit being an "absolute stickler".

Two hours later and the body had gone, its removal supervised by John Layton. A plastic tarp had been manoeuvred beneath the man and then lifted, the whole caboodle being rolled up to ensure nothing dropped out. Then Layton did a methodical sweep of the kistvaen. He called Savage over when he'd finished.

"Blood." Layton pointed down to one corner. "Not much, but just about visible."

"So? He cut himself while trying to escape. Nesbit already pointed that out."

"Yes, but this is different." Layton pointed to one of the vertical slabs. "He used his own blood to write something on the side wall. There's no doubt about it really. Quite, quite unnerving."

"John?"

"Take a look."

Savage leaned over and stared. Several smears of red-black were visible, squiggles which might have been letters. The letters weren't evenly spaced, nor were they on a line. She put her head first one way and then another to try and decipher them.

"A. n. a. s. z. Oh fuck," she said, looking up at Layton. "Tell me this isn't true?"

"Unless we're both hallucinating, it's true."

Savage turned back to the writing. The letters weren't altogether clear, but the name they spelled out was so unusual there really could be no doubt about it.

"Anasztáz," she said. "How —?"

Layton shook his head. Shrugged. For once as lost for words as she was.

Western Morning News, *January 15th, 2008*

Missing Exeter Girl In France

Police searching for Fiona Macy say the twenty-five-year-old may have gone abroad. Macy disappeared some time in early December after a night out in Exeter city centre with friends. After exhaustive enquiries, officers say the most likely explanation is she has left the country and that foul play is no longer suspected.

CHAPTER
SEVENTEEN

Saturday 30th August

Seven o'clock in the morning. Savage stood in her living room and peered through the binoculars across Plymouth Sound to the Cornish coast. She could just make out a line of boats anchored to the south-east of Cawsand. Nestled in under the lee of the headland, shelter from the strong southwesterly was pretty good. The crews on board the boats would have had a good night's sleep, rocked by a rhythmic swell. Before long they'd wake and the smell of frying bacon would permeate the air. If only she could spare the time to get over there, she thought.

Time, unfortunately, was in short supply, thanks to the discovery of the body at the stone circle and the fact that the mystery hiker in the kist had something to do with Anasztáz Róka. Hardin wanted everybody in so they could blitz the two cases.

"Serious this, Charlotte," he'd said on the phone Friday evening. "Two — possibly three — victims. We need to nip this one in the bud, understand? Don't want to make that serial killer story come true." Hence

Saturday's meeting. Savage cursed and moved from the window to get her breakfast.

By eight she was at the station.

"Operation *Piquet*," Collier said when Savage came into the crime suite. "Nice bit of serendipity, don't you think?"

"*Piquet?*" Savage said. "Isn't that some kind of card game?"

"Exactly." Collier smiled. "Only our game is played up on the moor, a kind of puzzle."

"A puzzle?"

"Look, the man in the kistvaen wrote down Ana's name. To me it's like one of those card tricks where a magician produces a sealed envelope — in plain view all along — which contains a prediction relating to a card you have just picked randomly from a pack. Ana's name must have been written down before she even came to the UK."

"Gareth, you're making my head spin."

"Spinning is good. The Super is keen to solve this as quickly as possible."

Collier gestured across to where Hardin sat at a desk with an array of newspapers spread out before him, along with a packet of digestives and a cup of coffee.

"Have you noticed," Savage said, "how the DSupt seems to have an endless supply of luxury biscuits in his office, but that whenever he comes down here he brings plain ones?"

"Managing resources." Collier tapped his forehead. "I would imagine the skill is ingrained from birth. You

240

either have the gift or not. And if not, then don't bother trying for high rank."

Savage nodded. "OK. The first task has got to be identification. There was nothing on our hiker. No wallet, no driver's licence, no car keys, nothing."

"So I've been told." Collier began to move across the room towards where Enders sat at a terminal. "Usually that might cause us all kinds of difficulties but Patrick's had a brain wave."

As Savage approached it appeared as if Enders was taking a break. His screen showed an outdoor clothing manufacturer's website. The DC was nuts about mountaineering.

"Patrick," Savage said. "You're not being paid to shop on police time."

"The coat, ma'am," Enders said, smiling and pointing at the screen. "Top of the range Berghaus. Last year's model. Well over three hundred quid. I reckon if he bought the coat round here then we've a good chance of finding out who he is. Unless he paid cash, then we're in."

"He may have purchased it online."

"Even so, there aren't that many stockists. If we get no joy from a trawl of the local shops then it wouldn't take too much legwork to trace."

"You sure about this?"

"Yes." Enders nodded. "This piece of clothing is a seriously nice bit of kit. I had my eye on one for myself but the wife wouldn't open her wallet. Said we already had enough gear to equip an expedition to Everest."

"So which shops would have this in?"

"Blacks, Cotswold Outdoor and Go Outdoors in Plymouth, Trail in Ivybridge, Kountry Kit in Tavistock. Some other stores in Exeter."

"Apparently Patrick frequents them all," Collier said. "He's offered to do the legwork."

"I have." Enders grinned. "Getting paid to visit a load of mountaineering shops is my kind of fun."

Collier looked at Savage for confirmation. She nodded.

"Away with you then," she said. Enders raised his thumbs and scampered off. Savage turned to the whiteboard and pointed at a map of Dartmoor. "Riley said something about ley lines. Can we get them drawn on here, see if they point to anything?"

"Hey?" Collier held a marker pen in his hand, but he didn't look keen to deface his map. "You really think that's a line of enquiry? Nonsense, if you ask me."

The office manager, Savage knew, would want something concrete to work with. Not a load of mumbo-jumbo, airy-fairy, New Age mysticism.

"As I understand it these ley lines go through various ancient sites. I think we should be looking to see if any local ones deserve further investigation. Make a checklist. If you're struggling, see John Layton. Riley tells me he's an expert."

Savage turned away, Collier huffing as she did so. She walked across to where Hardin sat flicking through the pile of newspapers. With each headline she could see his mood darken.

"The missing girl," Hardin said, looking up as she approached. "There's no news, I take it?"

242

"No," Savage said, wondering if the DSupt assumed she'd been up all night searching for Irina. "Still no confirmed sighting since she left the cafe on Thursday."

"And the sheep killer, he didn't do it?" Hardin raised his eyebrows, expectant, hoping for a miracle.

"We don't think so. There's no evidence the girl was ever at his little hideout or in his van."

"She's to go on the back burner then."

"You mean forget her?"

"No, not at all. We work the murder cases and hope something turns up that leads us to her."

"But . . ." Savage didn't think hope was going to be much use to Irina if her disappearance was connected to Ana's killing.

Hardin held up a hand. "This goes way beyond a missing person and a few ponies getting their bits chopped off. We're talking two horrific murders. To which end I'm shifting Riley and Davies from the Agri Squad. Maynard won't like it but this is serious."

Savage knew what "serious" meant in Hardin's eyes and she wasn't surprised when he began muttering about media coverage, pointing to the newspaper headlines in-between taking bites of his biscuit and slurps from his tea. The devil worship element was bringing out the worst excesses of the press, he said. There'd already been one false alarm when a group of tabloid journos had attempted to reconstruct a Black Mass, complete with flaming cross and sacrificial lamb. A farmer had spotted the flames and opened up on the group with a shotgun. Three of the journalists had had to go to casualty to have pellets removed while the police had no choice but to arrest the farmer, since the shooting took place on public land and the farmer's shotgun licence had expired.

"Bloody mess," Hardin continued. "It started out as a bit of a joke, didn't it? A couple of dead horses with their bits mangled. This body's taken all the fun out the case. I don't suppose it could be entirely unconnected to the ponies and Ana Róka?"

"No chance, sir. Ana Róka and our hiker are definitely connected. Although I guess the pony killings could have been carried out by a separate group. Layton mentioned something about it being the work of amateurs. Playing at being Satanists."

"Playing?" Hardin shook his head. "I'd hardly call cutting off a horse's knackers playing."

"No, sir, but it's a step up from killing a horse to burying somebody alive."

"So you're saying there *are* two distinct groups?"

Savage shook her head. "To be honest I don't know. DI Davies and DS Riley have been working on this for a couple of days, they're more up to speed than I am."

"Talking of which, those two are well ahead of the game. Up with the larks this morning, roaming the badlands of North Prospect looking for the Holy Trinity. As for you, you'd better bloody well get up to speed, hadn't you?"

The Holy Trinity, as Davies had tagged them, were the three lads from North Prospect: Nigel Branson, Greg Randall and Andy Howson. Davies had collected Riley from his flat first thing and headed north up Alma

244

Road, Central Park on their right. The park separated the student and middle-class areas of Peverell, Mutley and Mannamead, from the rougher parts of the city: Devonport and North Prospect. The latter had spawned some infamous criminals, but, according to Davies, Howson and his mates were pale imitations.

"No hierarchy any more, see?" Davies said as he swung the car onto North Prospect Road and headed into the maze of streets that comprised the sprawling estate. "I've heard it from the mouths of the old-timers. Nothing is earned nowadays, they say. The kids have no respect for their elders. One jumped-up tosser is no better than any other."

"A breakdown of rules amongst the criminal classes," Riley said. "There's a delicious irony in that."

"There's nothing delicious about Howson."

Riley could only agree as they sat in the car up from Howson's place and watched him come out. He wore a pair of grey baggies and a running vest that showed his heavily tattooed arms. The man was sub-human, Riley thought, some kind of throwback. Or, worse, maybe this was the future. The lowest common denominator. A cockroach that could survive even a nuclear winter.

Howson headed off along the street away from them without a glance in their direction. Davies wasn't fooled.

"Even at twenty-five, Howson's a wise old fox," he said. "He'll know the score. I bet he's spotted us."

Davies started the engine and they cruised after Howson, tailing him to the local Betfred.

When Howson came out of the bookmakers his expression was indeed one of mock surprise.

"Well I never. Phil and his organ grinder," Howson said, grinning. "If you're looking for a tip you won't go far wrong with 'Shove it up your arse' running in the two-thirty at Haydock. He's a tight little number but you'll slide right in armed with a good supply of —"

"Shut it, Howson," Davies said. "We'd like you to come back down the station and answer some more questions."

"Can I say no?"

"What do you think?"

Howson shook his head and put his hands out in front of him, pretending they were cuffed together.

"Take me, but for God's sake be gentle, it's my first time."

Davies raised his right hand and for a moment Riley thought he was going to clout Howson. Instead he gestured in the direction of their car and the three of them walked to the vehicle in silence.

It took an hour and a half to get Howson booked in and to await the appearance of his lawyer. Eventually Riley and Davies entered the interview room and found Howson sitting alongside a lad not much older than Howson himself.

"Andy," Davies said. "I first busted you when you were fifteen. Intent to supply, if I recall."

"Course I remember," Howson said, shifting in his seat. "It were you and that Savage bird. Had a hard-on for weeks after meeting her."

246

"Well at least something good came of it then. If I remember the CPS dropped the charges in the end."

"I was a bit young. I had an innocent face and a mum who swore blind I was a little angel. Butter wouldn't melt and all that crap."

"I guess your poor mother's changed her opinion now. And if she hasn't, she will when she hears about this one. You're not going to be very popular around North Prospect when this gets out."

"What's that supposed to mean?"

"A little bird at the CPS tells me there'll soon be three extra names on the sex offenders register. You'll be on the list alongside the rapists and paedophiles." Davies turned to Riley. "Wasn't there a bit of fuss recently, Darius? Somebody's house getting burned down?"

"Yes, sir. Some old guy had been making a few too many bus journeys. He'd been ogling the teenage girls and taking pictures too. Made the mistake of letting his hands wander. Gives a whole new meaning to the words 'bus pass'. Anyway, because of the man's age he got off with a suspended sentence. Wasn't enough for the people around where he lived. One night last month someone lobs a Molotov in through his back door. He runs out through the front only to find a bunch of local residents waiting for him. Luckily a patrol car was cruising by at the time and they were able to take him into protective custody."

"There you go, Andy." Davies balled a fist and slammed it into his other hand. "Restorative justice in action. Saves the taxpayer a fortune. Now, where were we?"

"Inspector?" The fresh-faced cherub with the spots spoke for the first time. "It sounds like you are threatening my client. I might remind you he's had absolutely nothing to do with young girls."

"Maybe not, but he did cut off a horse's testicles with a knife and shoved a broom handle up the poor creature's arse."

"I didn't," Howson said.

"That's not what you said last time. 'No comment' was all you could manage. Anyway, a copper saw you do it. Who do you think a jury is going to believe, you, or him?"

"A jury?" The solicitor again. Eager to press home a point of law. "I don't think it will come to that though, do you, Inspector?"

"You're thinking this will go to a magistrate's court, are you? Usually you'd be right and usually I wouldn't be getting involved in a case like this. But what Andy may not have told you is we're not just talking about animal cruelty here. We're talking about murder."

"Murder!" Howson leaned forward and crashed his fist down into the table. "Where the bloody hell did you get that from?"

"There's another case involving Satanic rituals and sacrifices and as far as I can see this is directly linked."

"Woah, hold up there," the solicitor said. "You need to brief me on this before we go any further, otherwise I'm going to instruct my client to say nothing more."

248

Davies turned to Riley. Riley nodded and reached over to turn off the recording equipment.

It was late afternoon and Savage was about to call it a day when John Layton came into the crime suite, laptop in hand.

"Charlotte," Layton said, plonking the laptop down on a desk and flipping up the lid. "Take a look at this."

Savage moved across. The screen of the laptop showed a satellite image of part of Devon. Slap bang in the centre was a patch of dark blue.

"Fernworthy Reservoir," Savage said.

"Yes. For a moment let's say your crazy theory about Ana falling from an aircraft is true. Here's the forest to the north, west and south. The whole lot — forest and reservoir — is surrounded by moor."

Dark-green encompassed the western side of the reservoir and spread out in a shape like a lump hammer. To the east, moorland gave way to hundreds of irregular little squares, a patchwork of fields spreading across and beyond. Layton double-clicked on the map and the image zoomed in. On the western shore of the reservoir there was a yellow icon, and away from the shore in the woodland, another one.

"The clothes were found here," Layton said, jabbing at the first icon. "And the body was here. If the intention was to drop the girl in the lake, they miscalculated. That could have been because of wind or because it was dark or because they didn't account for the girl's forward motion."

249

"Yes. But we don't know how high the aircraft was or what route it took or anything."

"Wrong." Layton smiled and then clicked on the map again. A line sprang up joining the two dots together and exiting the map both to the east and the west. "Either they dropped the bag first or the girl first. Whatever, this line represents their flight path. To the west there are just a few degrees variation to take you directly to Newquay Airport. To the east, well, look."

Savage peered at the screen as Layton zoomed out. The line ran directly towards Exeter, and Layton had placed another star just to the north of the A30, at a village called Clyst Honiton.

"Exeter Airport," Savage said. "Your line is spot-on, not even a few metres deviation."

"They took off from either Exeter or Newquay. Either way the reservoir lies directly below the flight path. They descended low enough so they could see their target and then they pushed the girl out."

"They?"

"Well it could hardly be one person, could it? Not unless the girl was unconscious and the aircraft on autopilot."

"Is that possible?"

"I'm not an expert, but I know somebody who is. And, given the circumstances, I'm sure he's going to be keen to help."

Five minutes later and Inspector Nigel Frey was standing alongside Savage and Layton. Frey, it turned out, had a pilot's licence. His job commanding D Section involved water-borne operations, but his true love was flying. Layton explained Savage's theory to Frey. Frey nodded and then reached out and tapped the laptop screen.

"Bloody hell, you're right, Charlotte," Frey said. "The evidence has been in front of us all along."

"It has?" Savage said.

"The webbing we found in the lake isn't from a lorry. It's a tie-down used to secure a light aircraft when parked. I've got a similar set myself. I thought they looked a bit fancy." Frey chuckled and then became serious. "You think they were trying to drop her in there, Dambuster-style?"

"Can you think of any reason why not?" Savage said.

"Technically, no. Then again it's not a flight I'd like to make, not in the dark. There could have been low cloud and you'd be in IMC." Frey paused as Savage looked blankly at him. "Sorry, that means Instrument Meteorological Conditions. Basically flying blind and using the displays in the cockpit to navigate."

"From the extent of injuries on the girl's body they weren't that high when they dropped her. We're talking hundreds rather than thousands of feet."

"As I said, not something I'd have been doing, not over Dartmoor at low altitude."

"What about flight plans? Would they have to have filed one?"

"Of course. Doesn't mean they did though. But in that case they can't have been flying from Exeter to Newquay, not officially anyway."

"But if they did there'd be records, right? Some logs somewhere."

"Yes. They'd have paid for their slot and everything would be noted down by ATC."

"ATC?"

"Air Traffic Control. Aeroplanes aren't like boats, Charlotte. You can't just go off on a jaunt. There are procedures to be followed, rules to be obeyed."

"So we call up Exeter or Newquay and get details of night flights in the last couple of weeks?"

"Yes, but I've got a better idea." Frey winked at Savage. "That is if you are, um, 'up' for it."

CHAPTER
EIGHTEEN

Two hours later, lunch intervening, and they were back in the interview room, Howson now keen to give them more information.

"Five hundred quid. Each time. Easy money." Howson leant back, and locked his hands behind his head. "No-fucking-brainer to take the job, wasn't it?"

"You were paid to kill the ponies?" Riley was asking the questions now, Davies bent over in his chair, a pen doubling as a cigarette.

Howson nodded. "Yeah. We had to kill them and then slash them up a bit. Light those fires in a specific pattern. We didn't know what the fuck we were doing to be honest. Never knew it was anything to do with devil worship until we read it in the papers. Then we thought the whole thing was a bit of a laugh. We had a powwow and decided we'd carry on doing it as long as it wasn't too risky. After all, she paid us upfront. She was only going to give us a hundred a time to start with, but I figured we'd start at five hundred and meet somewhere in the middle. She just stumped up the money right away."

"She?"

Howson nodded. "Yeah, and she were a right babe too."

Riley glanced at Davies, wondering if he was thinking the same: this had to be the Peacock woman.

"And what exactly were the instructions?"

"We had to catch a pony and take it to one of three specific locations. Then we had to kill the animal, cut off its bollocks, and light those fires. We had to finish with the location where you lot nabbed us."

"And you didn't ask why?"

"No. Like I say, this woman was a complete babe. And there was the money, too, wasn't there?"

"And killing the ponies, you didn't flinch at that?"

"To be honest, I did. It was also a right faff catching the buggers. And when we killed the first one the blood went everywhere. We got a bit wise for number two and three and wore old clothing."

Riley continued. "OK, so the big question is, who is 'she'?"

"I don't know her name."

"Come on, you don't expect me to believe that, do you?"

"It's the truth. All I can tell you is that she were classy."

Riley looked across at Davies and raised his eyebrows. Davies nodded and pushed back his chair and left the room. Five minutes later, he was back with a couple of printouts. He shoved the first one across the table and Howson peered down.

"What?" Howson shook his head. "I told you she were a babe, not that piece of old scrag."

"Are you sure?" Riley exchanged a look with Davies.

"Course I am, she's not classy anyway, you daft c —"

"What about this one?" Davies slid the next photograph over to Howson.

"Yes, that's her. Told you she were a looker, didn't I?"

Davies pulled the piece of paper back and rotated it so the picture of the girl sat on the table in front of Riley.

Riley stared down at the picture of Anasztáz Róka. Then he turned to Davies and lowered his voice. "Bloody hell. What on earth do we do now?"

Irina worked out the angles carefully before she even attempted the move. This wasn't like a gymnastics competition. The floor was wooden with no padding, no deep mats to cushion a fall. When she'd been a child her gym teacher had forced her to repeat tumbles or vaults over and over again, even if she showed little sign of succeeding. "Eventually it will click," she'd say. "Until then, you do the move again." Here, the only thing clicking would be her back giving out as she smashed into the floor.

First she removed her shoes. Then she took off her tights and bundled them into a corner of the room. The nylon would be slippery and bare feet would give her soles more purchase. Next she went over to the side of the room and picked up the piece of wood she'd found earlier. She dragged the plank across the room and propped it up against one wall. The wood was riddled with worm holes, the surface pitted with dry rot, but it was all she had. With the plank in place, she paced out the strides. Four and a half. The half gave her time to accelerate, three more to build up power and full speed, the final stride being her foot on the plank at the wall. She walked back and forth across the room, visualising the way she'd hit the plank and continue vertically. Something like a wall of death motorbike rider.

A metre or so above where the plank leaned against the wall, a beam jutted out. If she could get her foot on that then she could propel herself even higher and make a leap for one of the cross-members of the roof truss. Up there she'd be able to climb and reach the roof, perhaps force her way out.

Irina stood by the far wall and took a breath. Then another. Then she ran.

One, two, three, foot on the plank, pushing hard, next foot on the beam and a final push upward.

She floated in space, her body twisting in mid-air as she pirouetted round, both hands outstretched as if she was mid-way between a set of asymmetric bars. For a moment she thought she heard her gym instructor shouting her name. And then her wrists smashed into the truss. She'd flown too high. She flailed and with one hand managed to grasp the beam, her body swinging violently across the space. She gripped hard, feeling splinters of wood rip into her skin, then she reached up with the other arm and grasped with both hands. She swung forward and then back, pushing on the upswing until she could fold herself over the beam and bring her legs up. Finally, she was sitting astride the truss.

First time, she thought. No repetitions required! She paused for a moment to get her breath back. Her heart was beating fast and she needed to regain her composure. One silly mistake now, one little slip, and it would all be over.

Irina peered up at the tangle of beams above. Now she could do it. She took another deep breath and then began to climb up through the latticework. When she reached the top, she pushed against the corrugated iron roof. It rattled loosely. She turned herself so she could kick out with one leg. Bang. Bang. Bang. A nail gave way and then another. The sheet of metal flapped open, daylight beyond. She wriggled up and eased between the sheets, bending one back so the sharp edge didn't cut her. In a few moments she sat outside on the roof, the heavy green foliage of pine trees all around.

She paused and listened. The treetops swished in the breeze but there was nothing else. She checked her pocket, feeling the bulge of Ana's notebook. Evidence, she thought. Evidence which she hoped would put Ana's killer behind bars. And yet, even as she recalled the shocking truth Ana had written in the notebook's pages, could she be sure of that? And if she could be sure, would it be enough? Irina shook her head. No, either way she couldn't take the risk.

She turned round, raised her feet, and slid down the roof. At the edge she bounced off and into space, flying free for a moment before she somersaulted and hit the ground running.

Frey, it turned out, owned a light aircraft based in North Devon and "up for it" meant exactly what he'd said. They left Plymouth, driving north and skirting the western side of Dartmoor. Then they headed for Okehampton and Winkleigh. Up here the countryside was flat and quiet. Empty lanes with nothing more than the occasional tractor bumping along. This was an area far from the tourist trails, far from beaches and attractions. No worse for that, Savage thought.

"Here we are," Frey said as they turned off a lane and into a small car park, a clubhouse at one end. "Basic facilities, but a friendlier bunch you'll not find."

Frey stopped the car. There was no sign of any airfield that Savage could make out. Just a strip of grass with some planes parked at one end. A red helicopter standing on a patch of concrete.

"The air ambulance," Savage said. "I thought it was based at Exeter."

"One aircraft there and one here. This spot is an excellent location for covering the North Devon coast, as well as Dartmoor."

They got out of the car and Frey went into the clubhouse. Savage stood and watched a little plane trundle down a taxiway, pause for a moment, and then race down the grass runway and surge into the air. She swallowed and felt butterflies in her stomach as the plane's wings tilted this way and that, before the aircraft banked to the right and quickly became a mere dot against the bright sky.

"Shit," Savage muttered to herself, wondering if she'd made a mistake coming along with Frey. She didn't mind flying — as long as there was something solid under your feet, an in-flight movie, and a glass of something stronger than water in her hand.

"Alright?" Frey hailed her from the entrance to the clubhouse and gestured to the line of planes parked at one end of the field. "She's all prepped and ready to go. I'll take you over and give you a quick briefing and then we'll get airborne. How does that sound?"

"It sounds bloody scary, Nigel," Savage said. "If I've got to be buffeted by the wind I prefer to do so down at sea level, wearing a life-jacket and attached to a safety line."

Frey led them around the edge of the field and stopped next to a small aircraft.

"Here she is. A Socata TB." There didn't seem to be much more room inside than in Savage's little MG. "Beautiful, isn't she?"

Frey spent a few minutes checking over the aircraft, explaining that even though the plane had been made ready by a couple of club members it was his responsibility to ensure she was air-worthy. The safety briefing Frey gave her was over all too quickly. Frey cocked his head as Savage bit her lip.

"Don't worry, Charlotte," he said. "You can't fall overboard, there are no ropes to get tangled in, no boom to smack you on the head and as long as you have a good forecast you can't get caught out by the weather because you're not crawling along at five knots."

Frey buckled Savage in, helped her with a set of headphones and talked through the instruments in front of them. Then he was on the radio, getting clearance for take-off.

The engine started and the plane shuddered as the prop whirred into life. Frey made some adjustments and a minute later they were taxiing down the undulating grass to the end of the runway. Then he swung the plane round and stopped. He made a final call on the radio, a visual check of the sky and the ground, and then they were rolling forwards. The engine noise increased and halfway down the runway, at a speed which seemed to Savage not much faster than a car, Frey was pulling back on the wheel.

Savage couldn't help but let out a gasp as she first felt her weight increase and then for a moment experienced a sensation of weightlessness. The ground fell away and as Frey banked the plane she thought they would slide sideways. Instead they rose farther and levelled out.

"Wow!" Savage stared out and down at the fields and hedges rushing by below. She looked across at Frey. "I can see why you like this."

Frey nodded as they rose higher and higher. Ahead, the mass of Dartmoor bubbled up from the flat landscape, a huge behemoth of brown spreading across the green fields.

"Big, isn't it?" Frey said. "From up here you get a real sense of what an amazing wilderness we have right on our doorstep."

"Fernworthy?" Savage said, gesturing through the front windscreen. They were high enough now that she could spot the area of green on the east side of the moor where a glint of blue shone in the sunlight.

"Easy to see in the daytime. At night you might well be on instruments. Still, with GPS, finding the reservoir wouldn't be difficult. We'll go north, circle round, and come in as if we were on a flight path from Exeter to Newquay."

Frey made a slight turn to the left and the plane banked and headed east. The moor came up below them and Savage was surprised how quickly they'd reached it.

"What's our speed?" she said.

"Hundred and twenty knots. Say they took off from Exeter, we're looking at five minutes to reach the reservoir. Another twenty to get to Newquay. Unless they pissed around over the reservoir, but that would defeat the purpose of the subterfuge."

They were high over Dartmoor now. Frey fiddled with the GPS unit and then they were banking again, this time to the right, making a full one-hundred-and-eighty-degree turn.

"Lining up on the waypoint," Frey said.

Below, the moor had given way to fields and a little village Savage thought might be Chagford. Through the front windscreen, the green and blue of Fernworthy loomed again. Frey took the plane lower and now Savage could see the moorland rushing by below. A group of ponies looked up, startled, and then broke into a gallop, the herd scattering in several directions.

"Jesus, Nigel!" The ground flashed past and she felt a surge of vertigo. "Do we need to be this low?"

Frey nodded, but didn't say anything. The reservoir was up ahead, a cluster of cars in the car park, Savage noting an ice cream van with a queue of families. Then they were over the water for a few seconds before they swept across the far shoreline.

"Now," Frey said. "Two, three, four, five, now."

As soon as he had uttered the second "now" he pulled back on the wheel and the plane rose, Savage feeling the seat press into her thighs.

"Six seconds," Savage said. "Bag, two, three, four, five, girl. Seems about right. The door is opened, they kick the bag out, and then tip the girl. Only, they did it all too late."

"They probably didn't count on the girl falling so far. However she was moving at a hundred and twenty knots, so her trajectory would have taken her from above the lake and into the trees. Possibly the plane had also begun to rise, giving the body a little upward push as well. At some point the tie-down fell out too. That was a mistake and could well be a vital piece of evidence. First thing would be to find an aeroplane with a set of tie-downs that are the same as the one we found. Layton might even be able to match the oil on the tie-down strapping to the type used in the plane." Frey turned the wheel and the plane banked hard to the right. He looked across at Savage and smiled. "And we might as well start looking for that plane close to home, OK?"

Savage nodded as sky and earth rotated, the horizon anything but level.

"Nigel," she said. "Could you just concentrate on *getting* home please?"

CHAPTER
NINETEEN

Sunday 31st August

Fallon picked Savage up from the park and ride on the outskirts of Dartmouth at ten o'clock.

"Alright, love?" he said as she climbed into the Range Rover.

"Yes," Savage nodded, feeling far from alright. Before leaving home she'd shouted at Jamie and Samantha and had an argument with Pete about working at the weekend. She hated lying to him again, but telling him the truth was impossible. "Let's get this over with."

"Fighting talk. Just what I like to hear."

Fallon steered the car out onto the main road and into Dartmouth. As they descended the steep hill into the town the Naval College rose on the left. The impressive building resembled some great stately home or royal palace. Pete, like all Royal Navy officers, had trained there, and Savage found herself averting her gaze as they passed by.

Down in Dartmouth proper Fallon drove along the quayside. In the air-conditioned interior of the big 4X4 Savage felt cut off from the tourist bustle outside. The pavements teemed with people, while on the river, boats of all sizes moved this way and that. A couple of months ago Savage had been here with Pete and the kids on their own little boat. They'd moored up in rain and high winds and wandered the near-deserted streets. The evening meal had consisted of fish and chips eaten whilst sheltering from the weather under the town's bandstand. Bliss, Savage thought, as she looked out at the crowds in the sunlight.

As they queued for the lower ferry to make the crossing to Kingswear, Fallon looked across at her. "You bring it?"

"Yes," Savage said. "It's in my bag."

"Good. When we get there I'll go and meet Owen on my own, I'll say you've taken a walk up the lane. You wait until we're inside and then you come, OK?"

"Fine."

"After that, it's your call. We hurt him, we slot him, whatever. Just remember not to touch anything in the house."

The ferry journey across the Dart took just a few minutes and soon Fallon was accelerating the Range Rover up through the streets of Kingswear, the village on the opposite of the river from Dartmouth. They took a couple of right turns and then followed the coast road round and into some woodland. Fallon shoved the car into low gear and they climbed out of the woodland and ran between tall hedges for a mile or two. The lane felt like a tunnel to Savage, the world rushing headlong towards her, everything blurred and indistinct. A sharp left down a track, and then they were pulling up outside a pretty country cottage. Savage swallowed, but her mouth was dry.

"Nice," Fallon said. "Chocolate box. And by the look of things the soft centre is inside."

A little Fiat stood at the front of the property, the side of the car badged with an estate agent's logo. Slabs of stone led up to the front door, which stood open. Fallon got out of the car, pushed through the wicket gate, and walked up the path. He rapped at the door and went in.

Savage pulled her bag onto her lap. She delved into its depths, feeling the hardness of the gun. She brought it out and stared down at the weapon. For a moment, she did nothing. After all this time, did she really still want this? Was vengeance going to bring her peace? She closed her eyes and saw Clarissa's face, heard her voice, heard the little "ding-ding" of a bicycle bell. She opened her eyes again, checked the gun, placed it in the waistband of her trousers, and got out of the car.

She stood at the front door, hearing voices within. She clenched her fists and then slipped in. The inside of the house was bare and smelt of paint. Savage's footsteps echoed on the stained wooden floor as she walked along the hallway and turned left into the front room. Owen Fox stood admiring the view through the window, Fallon by his side.

"Like I said, Mr Fox," Fallon said. "The wife."

"The sea view is quite —" Owen turned, his mouth dropping open at the sight of Savage. "What the fuck?"

"Hello, Owen," Savage said. "I've been waiting for this moment for a long, long time."

265

"No." Owen moved away from the window and sidled across to the fireplace. He eyed the doorway.

"No chance, son," Fallon said. "I might be twice your age but I've twice as much muscle too. Now, let's all go upstairs where there's a bit more privacy, OK?"

Owen's face lost its youthful glow and he turned pale. He stumbled towards the door and Fallon let him past, giving him a shove down the hallway. Owen turned and trudged up the stairs, Fallon and Savage following. Fallon indicated the back room and gave Owen another shove. There was no furniture in the room, but Fallon pointed to the floor.

"Sit down. Charlotte wants a word or two with you and I want you to listen. I'll be downstairs — but one hint of any trouble and I'll be back up to give you a fucking good spanking. Understand?"

Owen nodded and then went over to one corner and lowered himself to the floor. Fallon turned, left the room and clumped down the stairs.

Savage stood for a moment, unable to quite believe this moment had come. The person who'd killed Clarissa, her beautiful daughter, was sitting two steps away. She could do anything she wanted to him. Fallon had made that clear. He would, he'd said, take care of everything. "*Everything*, understand, Charlotte?"

Owen bowed his head and raised his hands to his face. Savage heard a snuffle and saw a bead of water slip from his palm. The lad was crying.

"Why?" Savage realised she had said the word so quietly Owen hadn't heard. She repeated the question, louder. "Why?"

Owen was sobbing uncontrollably now, but he raised his head and tried to look at Savage. "It was an accident. I took my eyes off the road for a second and there she was."

"You were going too fast, you were driving like a lunatic. My daughter had no chance."

"You have to believe me, I didn't mean for it to happen."

"Choices, Owen. Fucking choices. We all make them and each one has a set of consequences. The aftermath of what you did scarred me and my family and will continue to do so for ever. Every night I think of my daughter. *Every* night. Can you imagine what that's like?"

"Don't you think it affects me too? I've got to live with what happened."

"What?" Savage felt the anger rise within her. "You arrogant little shit. You think what you have to go through is in any way comparable?"

"I'm not having this." Owen pushed himself up from the floor and stood facing Savage. "I've had enough."

Savage stepped forward and shoved Owen with her left hand. He fell back against the wall and then raised his fists. Savage was aware her right hand was going to her trousers. The gun came out and she raised the weapon and pointed it at Owen.

"Well, so have I," Savage said. She reached forward and grabbed the collar of Owen's shirt with her left hand. Then she shoved the gun up against the side of his head. "Kneel."

Owen's legs seemed to turn to jelly, because he collapsed to the ground in an instant. He began to shake.

"Please, I beg you. I've got a wife and children. Think of them."

"Like you thought of me? Of my other two children and my husband? I don't think so, Owen."

"I was going to come forward. To admit to the accident."

"Yeah right, like I'd believe that. So what happened?"

"I was going to make a statement, honestly. But Dad said I couldn't, that I needed to realise what would happen if I did. He persuaded me not to. In fact, he said if I did I was on my own. You see, it wasn't just the accident. Lauren was in the car with me and we'd been to a party. We'd been dealing drugs and Dad was scared it would all come out. He told me his career would be over. That he'd lose everything, that Mum wouldn't be able to cope, that the stress would kill her."

"And you expect me to believe that?"

"I didn't want it covered up but Dad took over. I didn't know what to do. He said —" Owen started sobbing again, streams of tears running down his face. "P — please, I've changed. I . . . I don't do drugs any more. I've got a job and I'm trying to do the best for Lauren, Sam and Milly."

"Milly?"

"My daughter. Sh — she's eighteen months old. She's the most important —" Owen lost it completely.

He began to gulp and suck air in and out. "Please don't kill me."

"Shit." Savage pushed Owen away and he fell over and curled into a foetal shape on the floor. She kept the gun pointed at his head, but was aware her hand was trembling. This wasn't turning out the way she'd hoped. She looked down at Owen as he stared up at her through his fingers, cowering. She could see something in his eyes, the way his lip curled, a slight twitch of his fingers. Savage moved forward, grabbed the lad's hair and held his head up. She thrust the gun in his face. "There's something you're not telling me."

"I —" Owen blubbed, snot dribbling from his nose. "I —"

"FUCKING TELL ME!" Savage rammed the gun barrel in Owen's mouth. "TELL ME THE TRUTH!"

"Lauren!" Owen's eyes widened in terror. "Lauren was driving, not me! She was pregnant with Sam so I took the rap."

"You pathetic liar." Savage pushed the barrel farther into Owen's mouth until he began to gag. Her finger touched the trigger. "You expect me to believe that?"

"Charlotte. Stop." Fallon stood at the doorway. She hadn't heard him come up the stairs. He nodded to the window and then at the gun in Savage's hand. "We've got to move. There's a second viewing. The couple are in the back garden."

"Fuck!" Savage removed the gun from Owen's mouth. Then she whipped the barrel across his face. Owen rolled sideways, clutching at his cheek, blood oozing between his fingers. She stared down at him as he began to cry again. "Doesn't matter, I'm done. Let's get out of here. I've had enough."

Chubber's on his way back to the wood. Spent a night in the cells at the custody centre. Banged up. Frightened. People in there shouting, crying, screaming. A bunch of nutters.

Nutters, Chubber?

Friday night. Place was full of drunks and foul-mouthed youngsters with no respect. Chubber could teach them some respect.

You didn't, did you?

No. Kept calm. Waited until he was released. Charges pending. Further enquiries. Went back home Saturday to sleep. Back here this morning. Back to the wood.

You need to check, Chubber, don't you?

Yes. Checker check check. Chubber needs to see if things are OK. As he left them. He forges on up the hill, past the crystal rock and to the feed shed with the girl inside. He looks around. Nobody's been here. Not the police, not anybody. Chubber pauses to get his breath back. He looks at the padlocks securing the door. Then he bends to the peephole. In the shadows he can see the girl. She's sleeping under a pile of feed sacks. Chubber blows a silent whistle. Thanks goodness. He straightens and turns away.

Hadn't you better check her, Chubber? Properly?

Yes. Good idea. Chubber digs into his pocket for the set of keys. One, two, three. He fits each in turn and clicks the trio of locks open. He slides back the bolts and pushes open the door.

270

"Wake up, girly," he says. "Chubber's here, my dear."

Chubber clumps in, aware of a swathe of light from above. One of the tin sheets has come loose. Chubber shakes his head. That'll never do. Rain might get in. He'll need to see to that.

See to the girl first, Chubber.

Chubber moves over to the pile of sacks the girl has pulled onto herself. She must be freezing, he thinks. Perhaps he could cuddle up to her. Snuggle close, skin to skin.

"Girly, are you cold? Because Chubber could warm you up." Chubber begins to loosen the tie on his tracksuit bottoms. He smacks his lips together. This could be good, better than any sheep. "Come on, girly. Wakey wakey."

The girl doesn't stir. Chubber bites his lip. He's never been very good at this. The lovey stuff. Seduction. He crouches next to the sacks and reaches out. It would be nice to slip his hand beneath the sacks, slip his hand between the girl's —

Chubber moves his hand down and runs his fingers beneath the sacks, groping for the girl.

"Where are you, my little beauty?"

Chubber?

Reaching, groping, feeling. Deeper under the sacks. Still reaching, still groping, still —

Chubber!

Chubber flings back the top sack and then the next. Dives forward and flattens the pile with his body. There's nothing there. Nothing but a dozen sacks.

She's gone!

271

"No!" Chubber screams out, writhing around on the floor in anger. "No!"

He stands and whirls. The shed is empty. The light is shining down from above. The girl has climbed out through a hole in the roof. He notices the plank. Somehow she's used it to get out. Chubber runs to the door. Is something moving in the woodland? A girl running away?

No, Chubber. It's only the wind whispering your name. Telling Antler Man what you've done.

"No!" Chubber yells again as he falls to his knees. "I didn't, I didn't, I didn't!"

You didn't look after her properly. That's what you did.

Chubber buries his head in his hands. He can feel the ground opening up beneath him, the darkness growing, the wind beginning to howl in the trees.

Antler Man won't be amused, Chubber.

No, he'll be angry, Chubber thinks. He'll be very, very angry.

Savage was back home by one o'clock, slipping the car into the garage and walking in the front door to find a pile of life-jackets and waterproofs on the floor in the hallway.

"Going on the boat," Pete said. "We head across the Sound and drop anchor in Cawsand Bay. The kids can have a swim and then we can grab an early dinner at the pub. Assuming you'd like to join us of course?"

Savage stared at the life-jackets. She wanted to head upstairs and lie down, not have to deal with ropes and

272

sails and moaning children. The explosive few minutes with Owen Fox at the cottage had shaken her to the core. She'd allowed raw emotion to take over and had nearly — so very nearly — come close to disaster. Now she felt flat, lost, tired. She looked at Pete, empty, not knowing what to say to the man she loved, how to even start to explain the situation.

"Well?" Pete smiled. "If not, then there's this fit bird lives near the marina. I'm sure she fancies tugging my mainsheet for an hour or two. Only if I could leave the kids with you . . ."

Savage shook her head and, despite herself, she half-smiled. Pete could read her like a book. He knew when to turn on his boyish charm so as to persuade her to do something, as well as when to leave her well alone. The boat wasn't some spur-of-the-moment decision, she was sure. He'd thought about this all weekend.

"She wouldn't know how to tie the knots," Savage said. "So you'd better take me, hadn't you?"

An hour later, they were on board *Puffin*, their little Westerly. She was hard on the wind heading across the Sound. Cawsand Bay lay directly ahead and, if the wind didn't shift, they'd reach the anchorage in one tack. Water frothed over the leeward-side deck as the yacht yielded to a gust. Jamie whooped with delight, but Samantha screamed that her phone was getting wet. Pete stood wedged in the companion way, a watchful eye on the sails and nearby boats, while Savage was helming.

"Better than moping around at home," Pete shouted without looking back at Savage. "The wind and the water, the kids, the boat. Us. Puts things in some kind of perspective."

"Yes," Savage whispered to herself. She glanced across at Samantha and Jamie and back to Pete. For a moment she had an overwhelming sense that all that was worthwhile was here on the boat. The world was just the four of them, cradled safely in *Puffin*'s arms, and being carried by the wind and rocked by the waves. Nothing else mattered. "It does."

"Hey? What was that?"

"Yes!" Savage shouted.

"That's more like it." Pete turned and looked back at her. Then he pointed to a yacht crossing ahead. He reached over and grabbed the rope on a nearby winch, ready to release it. "They've got right of way. Will we clear them or do we need to change course? Your call, Skipper."

Savage weighed up the options. The other yacht was forging onward, but if she did nothing then they'd collide.

"We'll tack," she said, thinking once again how so very perceptive Pete was. "Ready about!"

CHAPTER
TWENTY

Monday 1st September

Jon Anderson's voice soared impossibly high as he implored the starship trooper not to tell a soul. In contrast to the music, Savage's MG let out a guttural cough and backfired, stalling as she pulled into a space in the car park at Crownhill Police Station on Monday morning. Anderson and the rest of the band were silenced as she turned off the ignition.

The ancient sports car had an old cassette deck and Savage pressed the eject button to pop out the tape. The compilation had been a present from her dad a few weeks ago when the family had visited her parents in their North Devon home for lunch. "You know it makes sense," he'd said, pressing the box into her hand.

Having listened to the tape filled with Seventies rock tracks twice through, Savage wasn't sure it did, but she knew her dad's heart was in the right place. Like Pete he had, she was sure, sensed something was up. Most likely he thought the issue was some minor marital difficulty. He can't have had an inkling her downbeat mood that weekend was to do with discovering who Clarissa's killer was. And had he known Savage had held a gun to Owen Fox's head, he would have been deeply, deeply shocked.

She got out of the car and stood staring up at the concrete cube of the station. Yesterday, sitting on the boat at anchor over in Cawsand Bay with Pete and the children, everything had appeared so simple. Owen Fox was inconsequential in the grand scheme of things. He wasn't worth bothering about any more. Now, arriving at the station, she found she felt differently once again. Inside the station her daily routine involved bringing criminals to justice and ensuring that they faced the music. A large part of her sense of wellbeing came from carrying out her job to the best of her abilities. There'd been rare occasions when she'd failed and on those occasions she'd had to meet with the victims or their families and tell them it was unlikely anyone would be prosecuted, that the offender would get off scot-free. That had sickened her. Now she was telling herself the same thing. She'd failed to bring Clarissa's killer to justice. Even though she had the evidence. Even though she knew who the guilty person was.

Savage shook her head, slammed the car door, and headed inside. She had to focus on the case at hand.

As she climbed the stairs to the crime suite, she figured the day would be a chaotic affair. Since the discovery of the body in the kistvaen and the link to Anasztáz Róka and the pony killings, the various threads of the case had been tangled into one almighty knot. Ana had paid the lads from North Prospect to kill the ponies in three predetermined locations. And

276

whoever the man in the kist was, he had spent his last moments writing Ana's name.

Inside the crime suite, Riley appeared sceptical.

"It doesn't make sense, ma'am." The DS shook his head and stared at the picture of Ana that lay on his desk. "Why would she pay the North Prospect lads to carry out Satanic rituals?"

Riley was right; it didn't make sense. Yet that it was true, Savage had little doubt. The story was so far-fetched it was beyond Howson's ability to make up. In his written statement the lad had gone on to elaborate. He'd been introduced to Ana in a pub. "By some bint I used to shag," were his words. The "bint" it seemed had moved on to better things and was now a student at Plymouth University. At some point she'd been a waitress at the Bean There cafe. Which explained the link to Ana. Ana had needed a job doing and didn't know who to turn to. The student had suggested Howson and Howson, once he'd seen the money, had been only too pleased to oblige. The whys and wherefores he'd not been too bothered about, not when there was cash upfront. And they'd done good, hadn't they? Howson said. Fooled the police completely.

"What if she didn't pay them to carry out any Satanic rituals?" Savage said. Riley cocked his head on one side. "What if they merely prepared the scene for us to find? DC Denton comes across the first pony and calls you and Davies in. Devil-worshipping, you think. Ditto the second pony. Denton makes the connection to the third location. You note the stone on the kistvaen has been moved, which leads to us finding the poor guy beneath the stone."

"Seems a lot of effort to go to, to point out some random man's body. She could've just called us and told us."

"Maybe she was distrustful of making such a direct approach."

"What do you mean?"

Savage lowered her voice. "I don't want to get personal, Darius, but we all know what can happen when people in power try to protect themselves. Remember Ana was from a former Eastern Bloc country; that may have made her naturally wary of approaching the authorities."

"But killing ponies?" Riley shook his head. "A girl like that?"

"You mean because she looked cute she wouldn't do such a thing? You're being irrational. What did you have to eat last night? A burger? You didn't worry too much about the cow, did you?"

"Foreigners are less concerned about animal rights than we are, is that what you're getting at?"

"No. You've got the wrong end of the stick. We, by which I mean British people, are over-emotional about animals. Ana may have been more concerned about what happened to the man in the kistvaen."

"Well it didn't work, did it? We found him, but we've no idea who killed him."

"Likely as not the people who killed him are the same ones who killed Ana. The question is, who is he

— and what did he do to deserve such an untimely and unpleasant death?"

Halfway through the morning, Enders blustered into Savage's office holding a stack of printouts, red-faced and excited.

"Found him, ma'am," the DC said. "The dead hiker. Easy. None of the stores stocked the jacket, but Cotswold Outdoor ordered one in for a customer a year ago. Had a contact name and number. A Martin Hedford. Did a reverse lookup on the number, which gave me an address here in Plymouth. Bretonside."

"Well done," Savage said. "And who is he, this Martin Hedford?"

"At first I thought he was pretty unremarkable, to be honest. A Cambridge graduate. Lived abroad for a while in the Nineties. Married here in the UK in 2001. Had a kid a couple of years after. Nothing much unusual."

"But?"

"I found some newspaper reports relating to him. 2008 and on." Enders waved the printouts at Savage. "The kid — a son — became ill. Some sort of brain tumour. There was an appeal in the local press to raise money for treatment in the States. The boy was flown over and underwent some kind of revolutionary operation. Initially the op was a success, but sadly the tumour returned, more aggressively this time. The boy died in 2012."

"Shit." Savage did the maths. Clarissa had died at roughly the same age. "So what happens next?"

"I'm afraid the story gets worse, ma'am." Enders shook his head. "Much worse. Last year Hedford's wife was killed in a car crash. I've checked the reports. Fog on the M5. Three others dead. No doubt the crash was an accident, but it's rough on Hedford."

"That's an understatement, Patrick. I can't imagine what sort of despair he was in after a tragedy like that."

"Yeah. And now Hedford's joined his wife and kiddie. No chance he could've pulled the rock over himself is there? Because any other way and I'd have reckoned on suicide as the number one explanation for his death."

Martin Hedford's flat on Bretonside overlooked Sutton Harbour marina. Pinnacle Quay wasn't far from a main road where town centre traffic rolled by, yet the outlook was incomparable. Savage strolled along the quayside while Calter went to find somebody to open up for them. A young lad in charge of sales wasn't happy.

"He's dead, love," Calter said. "The only way he's going to give you any backchat is in your nightmares. So if you'll be so good as to let us into the flat."

"Apartment," the man said he took them up one set of stairs and unlocked the door. "At least for marketing purposes."

"Thanks," Savage said, standing in the doorway to make it clear the agent wasn't welcome inside. "We'll drop the keys back when we've finished and if you could look for his mail. He must have a ton of the stuff."

"Today?" the man asked. "Only I'll need to get inside and check everything over."

"Unlikely. I'll let you know, but we'll be sealing the upper door so nobody is to enter the flat without our permission."

The lad flinched, Savage unsure if it was her mention of the word "flat" again or the idea of police officers sniffing around and annoying residents.

"Idiot," Calter said as the man walked away. "They're all the same. Them and car salesmen."

"And Wildlife and Countryside Officers? I've noticed DC Denton hanging around again."

"He's not my type, ma'am. Too keen. Too nice. I want somebody I can *make* submit, not someone who lies down so I can walk over them."

Savage pushed the door open. A waft of stale air came out.

"Nobody's been in here for months," she remarked as they walked in.

The flat was fitted out as a luxury apartment, wooden flooring stretching from the hallway and into a large open-plan area to their left. They went through to the living area. A kitchen of burnished stainless steel looked unused. Beyond, a low suite clustered round a glass table, a smart laptop open. On the far side of the room doors led to a balcony and a view across the marina.

"Talking of DC Denton, ma'am," Calter said as she ran her hand along the top of the kitchen worktops. "If he can promise me somewhere like this, I'm his. Or anyone's, to be frank."

Savage strolled to the balcony, turned the handle and slid open the door. The sound of seagulls filled the air as a group of birds flocked over by the fishing quay. Closer, the tick, tick, tick of ropes frapping against yacht masts provided a soothing rhythm. Although she loved living in the countryside, Savage reckoned she could get used to a place like this.

"Unfortunately this is a little above Denton's pay scale," Savage said. "What do you reckon, three-fifty, four?"

"Something like that." Calter had sat down at the glass table. "Laptop's dead. It's not plugged in so the battery must have gone flat."

"I'll check out the bedroom. He must have some personal papers somewhere."

Considering the luxurious nature of the flat, the bedroom was small and somewhat disappointing. A double bed occupied most of the space. Built-in wardrobes contained several expensive suits and shirts. Beside the bed was a little cabinet. Savage opened the top drawer. Envelopes. Hedford's name and an address in Budapest. Savage thumbed through them. They all bore the same postmark: Totnes, Devon. She extracted the contents of the first envelope. It was a press cutting. *Woman Goes Missing* was the headline and the story detailed the disappearance of a thirty-one-year-old nurse from Tiverton. Savage reached for the next envelope. Another cutting and a similar story, only this time the missing person was from Taunton. A third cutting and a man had vanished from Barnstaple. Savage leafed through the rest of the envelopes, eleven in all. Each had a single cutting, each detailed a missing person. Savage glanced at the postmarks. All the letters had been posted between six months and a year ago.

In with the envelopes was a manila folder, several more cuttings inside. One story told of a cow butchered on Bodmin Moor, a second concerned yet another missing person. There was also an Ordnance Survey map. Savage unfolded the map, her eyes immediately drawn to the series of pencil lines criss-crossing the surface. Thick black crosses had been drawn in three places too.

"Ma'am?" Calter stood at the door holding a book. "A history of the occult. He's got loads of other books on Satanism, paganism, witches, etcetera. Doesn't look like he was up at the stone circle by accident. He was well into all this stuff."

"Not by accident, no." Savage pointed to the pencil lines. "These show ley lines and the crosses mark where the ponies were slaughtered. One of them marks the kist where Hedford was found."

"I thought we'd established the pony killings were the work of those North Prospect lads?"

"Yes, I thought so too." Savage pointed at the spread of letters atop the bed. "There's these to consider as well. Mispers. These people went missing from the area in the last couple of years. Somebody took it upon themselves to send these cuttings to Hedford."

Calter glanced down at the book in her hand. "You don't think they're all victims?"

"I doubt it. We'll need to check but I wouldn't mind betting a lot of these people have turned up. Doesn't mean they all have though and it doesn't mean

Hedford wasn't on to something — or at least thought he was on to something."

"Trafficking? That sort of thing?"

"Could be. Whatever, it was serious enough to get him killed." Savage began to gather the pieces of paper from the bed. She looked again at the address on the envelopes. Savage placed her finger on one envelope, covered over the last couple of lines of writing and showed Calter. "He was living in Budapest. Know where that is, Jane?"

"Wouldn't normally have a clue, ma'am, but the question came up in a pub quiz a few weeks back. Hungary, isn't it?"

Savage nodded, remembering back to when she'd arrived at Fernworthy Reservoir. The PSCO had flicked open Ana's passport and pointed to the circle of stars around the country name: MAGYAR.

"Yes," she said. "Hungary."

Savage reached into her pocket and found a little ziploc bag. Inside a brass key flashed in the light. She left the bedroom and went to the front door, opened it and placed the key in the Yale lock. The key fitted perfectly and when she turned it, the lock's mechanism operated.

"Bloody hell, ma'am," Calter said. "Where did you get that?"

"John Layton found it in Anasztáz Róka's room."

"*What?*"

"After seeing Ana's name on the side of the kistvaen, I had a hunch. Now we find she knew him well enough to have a key to his flat."

"His lover, ma'am, got to be."

"She was early twenties and he was near fifty."

"Mail-order bride?" Calter gesticulated at the room and the furnishings. "He was well off. After losing his wife he went to Hungary for a few months to meet someone, brought her back?"

"No," Savage said. "That doesn't make sense. If Ana was Hedford's wife then why didn't she report him missing? And why was she living over in Mannamead when she could have been here?"

Savage left Calter perusing the press cuttings and went back to the balcony. The sun beamed down, the day bright and warm, but as she stood looking over the marina, she shivered. Hedford had died cold and frightened, scrabbling to be freed from his kistvaen tomb. Ana had experienced moments of sheer terror as she fell naked from an aeroplane.

As a yacht nosed from a nearby berth, Savage thought of Pete and the children. Maybe Pete was right; maybe — when this case was over — it was time to take a break.

On Monday afternoon Savage and Calter headed to Exeter International Airport. The journey took an hour, but from the queue of traffic crawling in the opposite direction she figured the return trip would be considerably longer.

"Bloody tourists, ma'am," Calter said. "They don't feel the holiday has started properly unless they've sat in a jam for a couple of hours. Two screaming kids — one desperately needing a wee — the car overheating, the sat-nav on the blink and the wife moaning that they should have gone to the Costa del Sol. Can't think of anything better, can you?"

The airport lay on the east side of Exeter and resembled a swish bus depot, albeit with far more car parks surrounding it. The "international" element of the title referred to a smattering of nearby holiday destinations; you weren't going to be catching a plane to Sydney or LA from Exeter any time soon. Still, the airport was the region's hub, Plymouth losing out thanks to the incompetency of local politicians who'd allowed the city's own airport to close.

Calter parked up in a car park close to the main building. They got out and walked the short distance to the terminal. Inside the place thronged with travellers, those who had just landed easily identifiable by their tans. The PA announced the final call for passengers bound for Alicante, adding that an inbound flight from Madrid had been delayed by thirty minutes.

"Peak season," Calter said. "Dead of winter and there's not a tenth of this number of people."

They approached the information desk and made themselves known. They had an appointment with a Ms Karen Sharpe, an administrator in air traffic control. The clerk at the desk gave them directions, and five minutes later they were sitting in her office as Sharpe paced before a huge window, beyond which lay the runway. Her appearance was one of formality and neatness, her dark hair groomed and stiff, her clothing precise. Those sort of attributes were, Savage thought, most likely welcome in her line of business.

286

"Night flights from Exeter, first couple of weeks in August, right?" Sharpe asked, eyeing a plane that had just landed and then completing another set of paces. "And in a light aircraft or helicopter. Don't get many of them, to be honest. Can I ask why you need this information?"

"We need to find a plane that flew over Fernworthy Reservoir," Savage said. "Since it's on a direct route from Exeter to Newquay we figured this was the best place to start. I was hoping you'd have records."

"Yes. Not only for safety but for billing purposes. Every landing and take-off incurs a charge." Sharpe turned and went to her desk. She retrieved a sheet of paper and handed it to Savage. "I've prepared the details for you. There were only seven flights."

"Is that all?"

"Some pilots aren't licensed for night flying and many small airstrips don't operate then either. Plus it's the summer and the days are long, so there's no real reason to be flying after dark."

Savage looked down at the list. Three of the aircraft movements involved the same plane, an air taxi. Only one detailed a flight to Newquay.

"What size plane is that?" Savage pointed at the Newquay flight.

"Tiny. A two-seater."

"Not good, ma'am," Calter said. "We're looking for something larger."

"Any chance you could miss one?" Savage said.

Sharpe faced Savage and then wheeled about and tapped the glass. "Out there, nothing can happen without us knowing about it. Airside these days is strictly controlled, but that's not true everywhere. Have you considered a private airfield? Quite a few individuals have a grass strip. You don't need much space."

"Private?"

"I assume you've checked out all the club fields, so that seems to be your best bet. You're sure it's not a helicopter you're looking for? They can take off from someone's back lawn."

Savage shook her head. Layton had all but ruled out a helicopter for the reason that the drop wouldn't have been botched if the pilot had been able to hover.

"Definitely a light aircraft. Would there be a list of these private strips somewhere?"

"Yes, but you'll need to contact the Civil Aviation Authority. They have a register. Of course, an unauthorised strip could be just about anywhere."

"Shit," Savage said. Sharpe turned from the window and for a moment Savage thought the woman was going to admonish her for swearing. Instead, she simply smiled.

Half an hour after leaving the airport they hit the back of the queue. Calter drummed her fingers on the steering wheel and cursed. Savage wound her window down, leaned back and closed her eyes. Yesterday had been a long day. The trip out on the boat had taken away some of the anguish over Owen Fox, but the effect was temporary. Now she had a headache and felt drained. She dozed until her mobile rang.

DS Riley.

"Data from Hedford's laptop, ma'am," Riley said. "Clean as a whistle. Not much of interest to us."

Riley explained that, according to the Hi-Tech Crimes department, the laptop was near enough brand new. Hedford hadn't used it more than a dozen times and he'd only connected the machine to the internet to register some software and to browse a few websites.

"Late December. The last time the machine was accessed was on the twentieth. Seems like he didn't get much use out of it before he got popped."

"OK. What about these websites?"

"BBC News, a couple of shopping sites and a place called Avalon Books. I've looked the business up and it's a specialist bookshop dealing with New Age, witchcraft, the occult, NLP, that sort of thing. The location is interesting though."

"Go on."

"Totnes."

"Which is where the letters we found in Hedford's flat were posted from."

"Yes." There was a pause before Riley continued. "By the way, I've arranged another interview with Professor Falk — that expert I told you about. I'll ask him about Hedford and see what he knows about this bookshop."

Savage thanked Riley and hung up. She tapped Calter on the arm. "Turn off at the next junction, we're going to take a detour."

CHAPTER
TWENTY-ONE

Totnes' main shopping street was Fore Street. Traffic eased up the narrow road. On either side, miniature versions of national chains were sandwiched between independent retailers; butchers, designer clothes shops, places selling tat to tourists. Savage and Calter followed a white delivery van up the street to where it passed under a narrow arch. Through the arch and up on the right Calter pulled over and parked next to The Green cafe and they got out and walked a few metres back the way they had come. A tiny alley with a sign in the shape of a book led between the cafe and a jewellers.

"Avalon Books," Calter said. "Camelot for the ageing middle-class hippies of Totnes."

"You mean John Layton?" Savage said, laughing. "I'm not sure if he'd call himself either ageing, middle-class or a hippy."

They walked down the alley, pausing to step aside and let an elderly man pass through. Savage noticed the book he was carrying, all glossy, the curves of a naked woman on the cover, "sex" part of the title.

"Must be in the water, ma'am," Calter said. "Maybe I'll move here when I retire."

Avalon Books stood on the left as they exited the alley. Several small round tables had been placed in front of the shop window. At one a young man sat reading a heavy tome, while at a second table two women with babies chattered over coffee.

A little bell tinkled as Savage pushed the door open and her nostrils were assailed with a scent of dust, leather and paper. The shop appeared to be comprised of a maze of shelves, each of which reached the ceiling and was stuffed with books and periodicals. Meticulously handwritten labels were fixed everywhere and over by one wall a life-sized cardboard cut-out of Harry Potter pointed his wand deep into the recesses of the shop. A little sign dangled from the wand: Avalon.

Savage gestured at Calter and they ducked beneath a low lintel, leaving natural light behind and moving through a series of small ramshackle rooms. Again, white labels had been stuck to the shelves, although now they were in the realms of science fiction: space opera, hard SF, cyberpunk. Weighty hardback books had been replaced by paperbacks, pages yellowing. In the era of the eBook and the tablet Savage wondered if any of these books would ever be read again. Perhaps they'd be pulped or used as fuel.

After a room full of classic Penguins the space opened out and natural light flooded down from a huge roof lantern. They were in a kind of atrium, tables in the centre, shelves round the edges, a high-level balcony running the circumference of the room. From the ceiling multi-coloured silk scarves tumbled from pots hanging on chains and various ornaments such as dream catchers spun in the air.

"We're here," Calter whispered.

Avalon or not, they'd certainly reached a sort of New Age literary heaven. There were books on aromatherapy, acupuncture, self-sufficiency, conspiracy theories, tantra. The range seemed to cover anything alternative, anything a few steps from the mainstream.

At the far end of the room stood a desk with a till. Savage stared across. She could've sworn that a moment ago there was nobody there and yet now a rather distinguished-looking man with dark hair stood behind the desk. He met Savage's eyes.

"Can I help you, ladies?" he said.

Savage negotiated the tables piled high with books and approached the till. "Have you got any books on Satanism?"

If the question surprised the man, he didn't show it. "Over here." He gestured with an arm to one corner. "Just to the right of paganism. What are you interested in, LaVeyan Satanism or the theistic type? We have quite a range of books on both."

"Actually," Savage said, "I don't have a clue what I'm talking about. I'm more interested in whether you do."

"Sorry?" The man paused and then looked from Savage to Calter. "You're not journalists, are you? If so, I've nothing to say. You don't understand any of this. Why don't you take yourselves back up to London?"

"Detective Inspector Charlotte Savage," Savage said. "And DC Jane Calter."

Savage pulled out her warrant card and showed it to the man. He nodded.

"Not this horse killing stuff. Why do you think the perpetrators come from Totnes? It's victimisation if you ask me."

"Nothing to do with horses, Mr . . .?"

"Thor Wodan." A snigger floated across the room from Calter but the man ignored it. "Police. I see."

"Do you know this man?" Savage said, pulling out a photograph of Hedford.

Wodan shuffled across and peered down at the picture as Savage held it out.

"Why, of course, that's Martin." Wodan looked up at Savage. "Martin Hedford."

"And he's a customer here?"

"More than a customer, he's a friend. Although I haven't heard from him in a while. I thought he was out of the country. What's . . .?" The expression on Wodan's face changed from one of puzzlement to horror. "No, please don't tell me anything has happened to him."

"Why would you think that, Mr Wodan?"

"No reason." Wodan dodged past three stacks of books and sidled back behind the till. He fiddled with some sort of invoice book on the countertop, turning the pages back and forth as if trying to find the answer to something. "What do you want?"

"How well did you know him, Thor? Was he just a friend, or was he something more?"

"What are you inferring, Inspector?"

"Martin Hedford is dead."

Savage's words had an immediate effect. Wodan's mouth dropped open and his hands rose to his face. He slumped backwards into the bookcase behind him and Calter ran across and caught Wodan as he began to slip to the floor. She held him up as Savage found a nearby chair and brought it across.

"No." Wodan slumped down in the chair. "No."

Denial of the truth always came first and Savage reckoned she could often tell whether the denial was, in itself, truthful. In this case she was pretty sure Wodan had had no idea Hedford was dead, because he began to sob. Savage touched Calter on the shoulder and made a drinking motion with her hand. The DC nodded and went off to find a glass of water. A minute or two later she was back, Wodan accepting the glass and taking a couple of gulps. He looked up and smiled weakly.

"Thank you," he said. "It was the shock. I haven't seen Martin for months, before then, only occasionally."

"But you've been sending him letters, haven't you?" Savage reached into her pocket and pulled out a wad of photocopies. "Newspaper cuttings to do with missing people. Strange occurrences on the moor. Can you explain?"

"Martin, how did he die? I mean . . . was it . . .?"

"Martin was murdered. We believe in some sort of ritual, something to do with the occult or devil worship. He was found up on the moor at a stone circle. We're not sure when he was killed but it was several months ago."

"Murdered." Wodan shook his head and bit his lip. He stifled a sob. Then he took a deep breath and visibly tried to calm himself. "When I didn't hear from him I worried, but I never believed his fears would come to pass. It seems as if he was right all along."

"Right about what, Mr Wodan?"

Wodan stared down at the floor, his head now nodding back and forth. He appeared oblivious to Savage's question.

"I told him to leave it be, that he couldn't do anything. The problem with Martin is he had a guilt complex, he felt he needed to do penance, to take these people down."

"What people?"

"Hey?" Wodan raised his head and looked at Savage, as if noticing her for the first time. Then he pushed himself up from the chair and walked shakily across the room to a corner. "Here. Paganism, the occult, Satanism. All these books, they're theoretical, essentially harmless. Look, *The Satanic Bible* by Anton LaVey." Wodan pulled out a slim volume from the shelves. "This is atheistic Satanism. Its precepts are little different from a form of individualism. There is no animal sacrifice here, no evil. It's about using one's power, sure, crushing enemies, but it's not about being bad. But these people . . . I told Martin not to get involved, but he was vulnerable, at the end of his tether."

"You mean his son?"

"You know about Hughie then, what happened to him?"

"Yes."

"After Hughie returned from the States and the treatment failed Martin became desperate. He was in here often, searching the shelves for answers. At first it was herbal remedies, acupuncture, homoeopathy. Before long, those avenues exhausted, he'd moved on to religion. I told him to make his peace, that none of this was good for Hughie, but he wouldn't listen. He just said he had to keep trying."

"Understandable," Savage said.

"Yes." Wodan shook his head and then reached for another tome. "In desperation, Martin became involved in theistic Satanism. Or, to use a more tabloid term, worshipping the devil."

"By picking a book up?" Savage took the volume from Wodan. It was an anthropological study of various forms of devil worship. The author was one Professor Graham Falk, the academic Riley had mentioned.

"No." Wodan gave a half-smile. "An old acquaintance from Cambridge contacted him. At university there'd been a group of them — SPS students mostly — who'd dabbled in Satanism. Back then the whole thing had been a joke, a student prank. Basically an excuse for dressing up, getting drunk and having lots of sex. Martin had left all that silliness behind when he graduated in 1989, but some of the group had carried on, believing their activities to be having a beneficial effect over their lives. Over the years they became more serious and committed, convinced they'd discovered some source of ancient power. At some point Martin was invited to re-join. Foolishly, he accepted."

"Foolishly?"

"He became as delusional as the others. He thought by following their ceremonies and rituals he'd be able to save his son. Unfortunately the opposite happened and Hughie died. By that time Martin was in so deep he refused to listen to me. Hughie's death had the opposite effect to what one might expect. For a time I lost him as a friend."

"For a time?"

"The death of his wife pulled him from his madness. He came to me and apologised. He said he wanted to expose the group for what they were."

"Charlatans, you mean?"

"No, Inspector." Wodan took the book back from Savage and slid it back onto the shelf. "Murderers."

"Murderers?"

"Yes. According to Martin at least."

"And you believed him?"

"Not really. The story was so outlandish. After his wife's death, Martin told me he was moving abroad for a while to try and escape from the group's influence. He asked me to start sending him any reports of people going missing in the area. He told me he'd already gathered evidence going back years. With that and his testimony he said he'd be able to bring the group down."

"We found the press cuttings you sent him. Others too."

"I mailed him everything I could, even though I knew it was probably feeding his obsession. I didn't know what else to do. He was so insistent. And then late last year he told me he was returning to the UK soon. He said he was coming back to see that justice was done. But until you told me I didn't even know he was here in Devon."

"Why didn't you or Hedford report this, come to the police?"

"I thought Martin's ideas were . . . slightly off the wall. Maybe the death of his son and wife had pushed him to flights of extreme fancy." Wodan shook his head. "He'd been sucked into a belief system but his faith had been rewarded with only tragedy. It was understandable he should try to blame the others. Now, of course . . ."

"The names, Mr Wodan. We need the names of these people. Your friend was murdered and you can't let them get away with that, can you?"

"No, I can't, but —"

"Their names. Please, Thor."

"Look, my relationship with Martin was, how to say this? Dangerous?" Wodan shook his head and turned to a photo frame propped against the side of the till. Wodan, two young children, and a woman. "If I tell you I'll lose everything."

"You were lovers. You and Hedford." Calter. She pointed to the picture. "But you're married."

"Very perceptive. We *were* lovers, yes, a long, long time ago." Wodan gestured around at the shelves. "Avalon. A mystical place. For me, a place where one can indulge one's fantasies, try out new things, explore different ways of thinking. If there is only one life, then why not try all the fruits?"

298

Why not indeed, Savage thought. "You still need to tell us who these people are."

"Yes, I do. I owe that to Martin at least. It's been a shock though. I need some —" Wodan stopped mid-sentence. He looked across at the entrance to the room where a man and a woman had come in. The man strolled across to one side of the room to browse the Zen Buddhism section while the woman headed for a shelf labelled "NLP". Wodan opened his mouth as if to continue but then closed it again.

"Mr Wodan?"

"I . . ." Wodan clenched his fists together, his hands shaking. "I need some time. If we could leave it until tomorrow, Inspector, please." Wodan's eyes flicked in the direction of the man. "We close early. I'll come into Plymouth and make a full statement."

"Mr Wodan, I rather think —"

"No!" Wodan's lips trembled and tears welled in his eyes. "I'm too distressed, OK? I promise I'll tell you everything tomorrow."

Savage nodded. Given his state, there didn't seem much point in pressing the man further. She took out her business card and handed it to Wodan. "Anything you need to tell me before then, you just call."

Wodan managed a tight smile. "I'll do that, Inspector, I promise."

Irina sat on the lumpy bed and stared at the poster fixed on the wall opposite. Smooth sea, a sandy beach, a yacht gliding through the blue water. "Visit Devon", the caption read. "Escape the stresses and strains of daily life."

Yeah, right, Irina thought.

At least now she was safe. For the moment.

After escaping from Creasey's shed she'd walked for hours across the moor, eventually coming to a road, where she'd managed to hitch a lift from a German couple in a large motorhome. They'd seemed more enamoured of Devon than she was, but they had also realised she was in some kind of trouble. As they dropped her at a service station in Bovey Tracey the woman had pressed a hundred-euro note into Irina's hand and told her to be careful.

Irina had bought a sandwich and a cup of coffee and then used a payphone to call directory enquiries. A little while later, armed with a number, she'd got through to one of Ana's friends, Ben. The boy had been soft on her, a bit of a nerd, not good socially. Irina tried to sound sweet and a little bit vulnerable. She needed a favour, could he help?

Which was how she'd ended up in a little log cabin in the garden of a guest house in a village in the middle of nowhere. She'd been here for two days and still hadn't decided what to do.

Irina sighed and then reached for the object on the bedside table.

Ana's notebook.

Her friend had crammed a lot of detail into the tiny order pad, but the story was like a heavily abridged novel and Irina was having trouble following the plot. She'd flipped through the pages several times, trying to make sense of Ana's pencil scrawl, but the names didn't mean anything to her and the story was so outlandish she had trouble believing it could possibly be true. At least Ana had had the foresight to write in English, but Irina had wondered if some of the meaning had been lost in translation or in the way the text had been condensed to fit onto the small pages.

After several read-throughs Irina had more of a handle on what had happened, although she still wasn't sure she had it right. As she understood it, Ana had come from Hungary looking for a man she referred to as "Tata". Tata had disappeared and Ana had been convinced he'd been killed by the members of some kind of cult. The cult used a number of stone circles on Dartmoor as places of worship and the sites were on some kind of invisible line called a ley. Bizarrely, Ana had arranged for three ponies to be killed at the circles so the police and media would become involved and the group's activities would be disrupted. It appeared as if Ana hoped the killing of the ponies would spark some sort of wider investigation which would lead to the cult members being exposed.

Stone circles and ley lines? Cults? Three ponies killed? At first Irina found it hard to believe. Was Ana living in some kind of a fantasy world? Had she gone crazy, her writing the result of fear, an injury or from drugs? Irina's doubts were swept away when, on the second evening, she'd turned on the little TV sitting in the corner of the room to watch the local news. There'd been nothing about her, but there had been a piece about the discovery of the body of a hiker near to where a pony had been ritually slaughtered. Whether Ana's account was entirely accurate or not, here was evidence that she'd been on to something.

Ana's plan had failed though, Irina thought. She'd been captured by the cult members. If she'd been going to come forward and present the police with her evidence it was too late for that. The only evidence now was in the notebook and most damning of all was the final paragraph:

They take me in the aircraft tomorrow. I know because I overheard him talking on the phone. This is the end. They are going to kill me and make it look like some kind of accident. As if I drowned in a lake. But I have an idea. I will try to crash the plane. My plan is desperate but it's the only way I can escape. At least nobody else will have to suffer in the same way as Tata and the others.

Irina had read the final section over and over again, her heart pounding each time. Poor Ana must have been so scared in those final hours, so frightened. Irina felt tears flow down her cheeks at the thought of the suffering her friend had gone through. They couldn't be allowed to get away with it. Somebody had to pay.

"Hello?"

Irina looked up. Mrs Hannaford, Ben's mother and the owner of the guest house, stood at the cabin door with a tray. Tea, some biscuits and a newspaper.

"You OK, love?" the woman said, stepping up into the cabin and placing the tray down on a table. "Only if there's anything you want to talk about . . .?"

"No, thank you," Irina shook her head and tried to smile. "I'm just a little homesick."

Mrs Hannaford nodded. "Well, if you need me, you know where I am." She gave Irina a squeeze on the shoulder and then left.

Irina reached for the cup of tea and took a sip, her eyes wandering to the newspaper — the *Kingsbridge & Salcombe Gazette*. She stared down at the main picture, the face meaning nothing. But then she looked at the caption and a name jumped out from the page. A name she'd spotted only minutes before in Ana's notebook. The cup went down heavily, tea slopping out onto the tray. She picked up the paper, her hands shaking. This was the man who'd abducted Ana and killed her. This was the man who needed to be made to pay. Irina nodded to herself. She'd take the notebook to the police. They'd have to act then, wouldn't they?

Irina read on, realising as she did so that the police were unlikely to help. The man was one of the elite, one of the rich and powerful. In Russia, such men were virtually immune. It would, she thought, be little different here. For a second she was despondent, but then she remembered her father's words again.

Do it yourself, Irina.

It was up to her to make the man pay — and as she read the rest of the story, she decided here was a perfect opportunity to make him do just that.

CHAPTER
TWENTY-TWO

This time, Riley did meet Falk in his office at the university. The academic rose from his swivel chair and shook Riley's hand.

"So, are you ready to become a fully paid-up Satanist?" Falk's serious expression threw Riley for a moment, but then he smiled. "Gotcha! You should've seen your face."

Riley didn't laugh. He pulled back his hand and sat in a nearby chair. Falk's humour had thrown him. It seemed misjudged.

"Sorry, I've had some good news this morning," Falk said, as if in explanation. He sat and tapped some notes on his desk. "The budget for my television series has been approved."

"Congratulations," Riley said, grudgingly. He pulled out his notepad and pencil. "But I'm in a more sombre mood. They've gone further. It's not just a case of animal cruelty now; it's murder."

"The man you found on the moor." Falk nodded. "The TV news said he was a walker who'd got lost."

"That's just a story we're putting out there at the moment. In reality the man was murdered. Likely as not in some Satanic ritual."

"I think that's far-fetched, Detective. The scenario you're suggesting is the stuff of fiction. It's a lot of fun and makes good headlines, but the reality is far more mundane."

"How can you be so sure?"

"Look." Falk turned his hands palm up. "I'm sorry if I seemed obstructive the other day. I want to help. But I also want to make sure you don't go banging up the wrong people."

"What do you mean? Who are you protecting?"

"There's a group round here I'm involved with. I'm sure they are entirely innocent."

"*Involved with?* What does that mean?"

"I'm studying them, but really it's a more in-depth process than simply asking them a few questions. I watch, sometimes I take part."

"You mean participant observation?"

"Yes." Falk put his head on one side. "To be honest, I'm surprised you've heard of it. You must be better educated than the average copper."

Riley ignored the dig. "And when you take part, what do you get up to?"

"No killing ponies, if that's what you're thinking." Falk stopped and thought for a moment. "I'm going to be publishing all this shortly, so I guess it's no secret. I attend meetings, I go along with their rituals. Some of their activities might be unpalatable to God-fearing Christians, but I can assure you there's nothing illegal, nothing like murder."

"You've been trying to steer me away from this group then?"

"To be honest, yes. My study could be compromised. It's taken me years to gain the trust of these people."

"I'm sorry about that, Professor Falk, but it can't be helped. We're talking about a murder investigation."

"The man was probably killed by a lone nutter."

"We think not." Riley glanced down at his notepad. "Do you know a man called Martin Hedford?"

"Hedford?" Falk began to laugh. "Now you are talking about a nutter. He *does* believe all this crap. More than that, he thinks there's some kind of conspiracy. A cabal of influential people worshipping the devil in order to gain special powers. The problem here is that if the people who make up this cabal *are* influential then they are *already* powerful. He assumes they must have used some sort of magic, but it's a self-fulfilling prophecy."

"So you do know him?"

"Yes. He came to me a few months ago and pestered me to investigate his crazy theories. To be honest the man was a nuisance, but I humoured him, tried to deal with each of his points in a rational way. He refused to listen, said I had my head in the sand."

"So did he tell you the names of these people?"

"No, but he assured me they were the great and the good. I didn't take much notice once I had him pegged as a lunatic."

"And you're sure he wasn't on to something?"

"*On* something, more like. He's got mental problems and wants to blame others for his own inadequacies." Falk cocked his head to one side and tapped the table

306

with a finger, sudden realisation on his face. "Hang on, you're not saying Hedford is the guy on the moor?"

"Yes," Riley said.

"Shit." Falk shrugged. "I'm sorry. You shouldn't speak ill of the dead, isn't what they say?"

"Professor Falk, do you have any idea who could have killed Hedford?"

"No. I can only assume he hooked in with the wrong kind of people. Druggies, bikers, undesirables. Perhaps somebody got fed up with him. He was an annoying little man, so persistent. I can well imagine he irritated somebody to the point where they would want to kill him."

"Did he irritate you?"

"Yes." Falk held up both hands. "But if you're suggesting I'm the one who killed him then you're way off the mark."

Riley reached into his pocket and pulled out a polythene bag containing the jewellery found at the stone circle. He showed the bag to Falk.

"Do you recognise this?"

"Of course." Falk moved his hand to his chest. "It's a necklace with a Satanic cross pendant. Common enough, I would have thought."

"This one is a bespoke piece of jewellery. There were seven made and I believe the people who own them are members of this cabal of Hedford's."

"Do you know who they are?" Falk put his hands out again. "No, of course, you can't tell me. However, if you did know you would have arrested them."

"They may or may not have something to do with a bookshop over in Totnes, Avalon Books. Do you know it?"

"Avalon . . . why, yes, I do. Or rather I'm aware of its existence. Some of my students have purchased books there. I believe they stock my work. Why do you think it's connected?"

"I'm sorry, Professor Falk, I couldn't say."

"I understand."

"Do you think this cross could belong to a member of the group you study?"

Falk paused and cocked his head on one side. "Oh no, I don't think so."

"How can you be so sure?"

"I've studied them for years. I don't remember ever seeing such a thing."

"I need their names, Professor Falk." Riley pressed the point. He pointed at Falk's computer terminal. "I'm afraid if you don't tell me I'm going to have to get a warrant to access your work."

"Do that." Falk stared Riley down. "I can see great interest from the *Guardian*, Liberty, the unions. 'Academic freedom under threat'. It'll make a great story. I fully expect picket lines of students, a sit-in, interest from the broadcast media."

"Your non-cooperation is noted, *Mr* Falk," Riley said, standing to leave. "Please don't attempt to destroy any records or papers you have. To do so would be to commit a serious offence."

"Of course not."

Riley moved to the door. The little glint he'd noticed at the previous interview was back. This time though, despite the man's bluster, it was obvious something was bothering Falk. As Riley slipped from the room he saw

Falk reach up and wipe his forehead, a sheen of moisture glistening in the light.

After returning from Totnes, Calter stayed at the station late, keen to act on the information provided by Wodan. She soon discovered that SPS when in connection with Cambridge, stood for Social and Political Sciences. She'd need to get a list of graduates in SPS for 1989, the year Hedford left. She busied herself with getting contact details for the appropriate department at the university.

A few minutes later, Collier came into the crime suite. He was surprised to see somebody still at work.

"Not got a home to go to?" he said. "Because that's the only explanation I can think of."

"The boss left me to it," Calter said. "She said she needed to get a good night's kip. I wanted to line a few things up for tomorrow."

Calter explained about the visit to Avalon Books, the meeting with the owner and what he'd said about Cambridge.

"Thor, eh?" Collier chuckled. "We could do with a couple of deities on our side. Thunder and lightning beats having to stick to the PACE rules any day of the week."

"I'm going to get the graduation list for 'eighty-nine from the university and hopefully Mr Wodan will give us more details tomorrow, but I wouldn't bank on it. He appeared worried."

"Can we bring him in and charge him with obstruction?"

"I did ask the boss, but she said there didn't seem much point. He was in a pretty distressed state after hearing of Hedford's death. Maybe he'll be more composed when he comes in tomorrow."

Collier nodded and then filled Calter in on other developments. Hedford's flat had been given a thorough going-over. The forensic team hadn't found much, but they had turned up a couple of hairs trapped in the headboard of the bed in the tiny guest room. Long, fair hair, most likely a woman's.

"I'm thinking a casual fling," Collier said. "Somebody he brought back one night. Probably not relevant."

"In the spare room?"

"Maybe the woman was too drunk to do anything and he put her in there to sleep off her hangover." Collier smiled. "Or maybe the bed was firmer. Maybe they just did it in every room. Nowt so strange as folk and sex."

"Anasztáz Róka."

"Sorry?"

"She possessed a key to Hedford's flat."

"What?" Collier reached up and rubbed the short hairs on the back of his neck. "Why didn't I know this?"

"It was filed this morning."

"That's no bloody good. A million and one things have been put into the system, but if nobody says anything how am I to know?"

"Sorry, Gareth."

"So what the heck has Ana got to do with Hedford?"

"We've no idea, but Thor Wodan might know. We'll ask him tomorrow."

"Well, let's hope he lives up to his supernatural billing, hey?"

"We've got a problem, Simon."

The words came in the darkness, Fox still half-asleep on the sofa in the living room as he answered the call on his mobile. He'd dozed off, events whirring in his mind until eventually the cacophony had become white noise. Now a whisper from afar slipped into his consciousness.

"Simon. I said we've got a problem."

The voice sent a shiver down Fox's spine. The man on the phone didn't do problems, or if he did, he simply bull-dozed them out the way. Fox glanced down at his watch, the face glowing in the dark. 11:30 p.m.

"OK." Fox pushed himself up and tried to blink away the tiredness. "Tell me."

"This stuff on the moor. The ponies. I need it to stop."

"The ponies?" Fox blinked again, unsure if he was entirely awake. "I don't think I understand what —"

"It's not just the ponies. There's the girl too."

"The girl?" Fox stared to the far end of the living room, where a rectangle glowed wanly. Through the window he could see the neat lawn bordered by roses, the whole garden painted pale by the light of a half moon. His wife looked after the roses, spending hours pruning the bushes. Nip them in the bud, she'd say, smiling. Fox had no idea what she was talking about.

"The girl on the moor, you idiot."

"The girl . . ." Fox's head spun. He must be still dreaming. Could the man mean the young woman who'd been found at Fernworthy Reservoir? Fox had lost track of where the investigation was now. "What does she have to do with anything?"

"It's complicated, Simon, but remember what you promised me?"

Fox was awake now, the menace in the ghostly voice seeping down the line, Fox's recollection of his promise only too clear.

Whatever the price . . .

"Yes, I do."

"I need you to stop any future investigation, understand? Tell them it's something to do with national security, whatever."

"National . . .?" Fox felt his breathing accelerate. Surely *he* couldn't be involved? "Jesus! I can't do that. Not if it's something you've . . . You can't expect me to put my career —"

"A promise made can't be broken, Simon."

"But Savage, your friends in London, I thought . . ."

"There won't be any friends in London if you don't stop your officers. You deal with this and then I'll deal with Savage, OK?"

"Yes, but . . ." Fox stood and walked across the room to the mantelpiece. He reached out to touch a picture of his wife holding their granddaughter, his hand shaking as he did so. In the darkness the picture was indistinct, his wife ethereal, fading. His hand cast a shadow over the image, the black becoming deeper as he watched the shadow sweep across his wife's face and spread through the room, overwhelming him. He tried to regain his composure. "You have to know I can't do this. What you're asking is impossible."

"You can do this," the voice said, the words hissing through the air. "And you will."

The clock on the wall ticked up to twelve o'clock and then began to chime. The witching hour, Thor Wodan thought. All day he'd been thinking about Martin. Wodan had always dismissed his talk of the occult as the ramblings of a man who'd lost his mind, who'd been pushed to the height of despair by the death of his wife and child. Hedford had blamed those who'd let him down and embellished his stories to show them in a bad light. But now Wodan realised he'd been mistaken. Hedford hadn't been mad. The proof lay in his own death. Irony was the cruellest thing.

He breathed a shaky sigh, all his tears already cried.

Wodan came from behind the till and moved around the room. He reached out and touched the spines of books as he passed by. Each book was a little parcel of magic, literally words of wisdom, but in all the millions of words contained in the room Wodan didn't think there were any that could help him now. He had to choose his own path. Martin Hedford had been a friend and a lover and now came the true test of that friendship.

He stopped in the centre of the room and stared up at the roof lantern and the dark sky above. There was nothing up there, no God to appeal to, no answer in the myriad of stars. The truth lay within himself. Wodan knew he had to go to the police tomorrow and tell them the names of the Satanists. His friend hadn't been deluded, he'd been right. But by keeping things to himself, by not involving the authorities, he'd paid with his life.

Ten minutes later Wodan made a final tour of the shop, re-shelving books and switching off lights as he went. He ended, as he always did, at Avalon. Behind the counter was the control panel for the alarm system. Once he flicked the switch to arm the system he had thirty seconds to leave the shop. It was something he had done so many times before that he could navigate the maze of little rooms in pitch-black. Wodan turned off the final lights in the room and reached for the glowing panel. He stepped out from behind the counter, into the pale rectangle of light washing down through the roof lantern, and then into the dark beyond.

"Thor."

The voice came from his right and at the same time a hand reached out from his left. Someone pushed him in the chest from the front and he felt an arm grasp him from behind. There were four of them, five, more. Shadows in the blackness, pushing him back into the centre of the room. He thrashed out and books tumbled from shelves. Someone kicked his legs out from beneath him and forced him down to the floor.

"You're too late!" Wodan shouted. "Evil never wins!"

"That's where you're wrong," the voice said.

Wodan felt hands grasping at his chest, tearing his clothing apart. His arms and legs were pinned to the ground and all he could do was look up at the people looming above. A gleam of metal flashed and lunged and struck him in the chest. Something cut into him and there was a crunch of bone as a rib shattered beneath the blow. Fingers clawed and pulled at his skin, peeling flesh away from his body. Wodan tried to speak, to scream, but nothing came. The last thing he saw was a silhouette of a man with a towering antler headdress kneeling beside him, the man's hands scrabbling at Wodan's chest and dripping thick with blood.

CHAPTER
TWENTY-THREE

Tuesday 2nd September

She woke to a phone call from the duty sergeant. Thor Wodan was dead.

Savage pulled herself from her bed, grabbed some clothes and went down to the kitchen. The clock on the cooker glowed a cool green. Three a.m. Another call came in as she was getting dressed and she stumbled across to silence the handset.

"Charlotte?" It was DSupt Hardin, not sounding pleased to be awake in the small hours. "Nightmare, this, Charlotte."

"Sir?"

"You visited him yesterday. You and DC Calter. I've seen the action list, so don't try to deny it."

"I'm not trying to deny it, sir. What's the problem?"

"Jesus, woman, he's dead! That's the bloody problem. You should have seen this coming."

"Sir, how —"

"Two police officers visit a man and a few hours later he's murdered. We're going to have to report ourselves to the IPCC. Duty of care and all that bollocks."

As Hardin began to explain his thinking on how they'd handle things, Savage wondered if there was any truth in what Hardin said. She felt a pang of guilt. Thor Wodan had been scared and she'd let him down. She shook her head, wrote a message to Pete, and left the house.

The alleyway leading to the bookshop had been cordoned off and two uniformed officers stood on the pavement. Not that they had much to do; Totnes wasn't exactly buzzing at four in the morning. Savage pulled up and parked in a disabled bay where a set of police cones had been placed. As she got out of the car, one of the officers approached.

"DI Savage?" She nodded. "John Layton's in there waiting for you. They didn't want to move anything until you arrived."

Savage thanked the officer and pushed under the tape that had been strung across the entrance to the alleyway. The passage was dark and Savage had to grope along one wall until she saw a rectangle of light at the far end. Beyond the passage, the lights from the bookshop's front window illuminated the area. Two of Layton's CSIs stood next to a stack of equipment. One of them acknowledged Savage as she went to open the door.

"PPE, ma'am." He reached down into a plastic crate and pulled out a white protective suit, some gloves, bootlets and a mask. "John was most specific."

Savage thanked the technician, clambered into the suit, put on the gloves, bootlets and mask, and entered the shop. As she did so, she looked up at the top of the door. The little bell hadn't rung and Savage noticed there was a catch that could be moved up and down. The catch was in the "up" position, preventing the bell from ringing.

She negotiated the maze of little rooms until she came to the atrium. A white-coated figure stood at the till area, dusting the cash register. The drawer was open. In the centre of the room a huge bookcase had tumbled over. John Layton knelt beside it. From one side a leg and arm poked out. Layton spotted her and stood.

"A PC arrived to investigate the alarm," Layton said. "He assumed Wodan had disturbed a burglar and that some sort of fight had ensued. The officer took a pulse, but it was pretty obvious there was no chance he'd survived."

Books lay strewn across the floor, not just in the vicinity of the bookcase but everywhere. Half of the displays had been cleared, volumes swept from the shelves in a wild frenzy. Savage stepped across the undulating sea of books until she reached Layton. Along with the leg and arm there was a pool of blood.

"There's a lot of blood for a crushing injury." Savage looked down at the crimson stain.

"Yes. We'll need to wait until we can lift the bookcase to know for sure, but I think we'll find that's not the cause of death. The shelves were pushed over to cause confusion, to make it look like some sort of theft."

Layton gestured to the doorway, where the two CSIs from the front of the shop had appeared along with two other officers. They approached the bookcase and began to lift it, Layton taking pictures as they did so. As the bookcase tilted upwards the remaining books on the shelves slid out and tumbled down onto the body. The CSIs manhandled the bookcase and leaned it back against one wall.

Wodan was lying face-down, blood seeping from underneath his chest. Books were scattered everywhere and he was half-buried in a mass of yellowing paperbacks. Layton and one of the CSIs began to remove the books, throwing them to one side. As the books were removed, Wodan's body was revealed. He was almost naked from the waist up, his shirt hanging loose in shreds. Bruises covered his upper arms.

"He was held down," Savage said, pointing at the bruises.

"Where's Nesbit?" Layton said. "He should be here to see this."

It was another thirty minutes before Nesbit turned up, by which time Layton was having kittens.

"Evidence," he muttered to Savage as Nesbit got suited up. "Every minute counts and the sooner we can turn the body over the better."

"Sorry, Charlotte, John," Nesbit said. "I went to the theatre and switched my phone off and forgot to switch the pesky thing on again when I got home. Somebody had to come and knock on my front door. Now then, we want to turn the body, yes?"

Nesbit moved towards the corpse. The CSIs had cleared much of the floor of books, but Nesbit still had to move aside a couple to find space for his bag.

"There's a joke here somewhere," Nesbit said, staring down at a glossy hardback. "But I'm buggered if I can think of one at the moment."

The pathologist knelt and began to examine the body. He touched one arm and moved it slightly. Then he turned his attention to the pool of blood spreading from beneath the chest area.

"This didn't come from the fall or from the bookcase crushing him. There is likely a puncture wound under there somewhere." Nesbit spent another few minutes examining the corpse before asking Layton and one of the CSIs to roll the body onto its back. Nesbit stepped to one side to let them through.

"Shit." Layton and the CSI moved out of the way, leaving the body face-up, one arm held in rigor and pointing skywards. "More than a puncture wound."

What remained of the front of Thor Wodan's white shirt was stained red. His chest was a mass of red pulp, three gleaming white ribs exposed, a gaping hole behind them. Savage swallowed and behind her, one of the CSIs retched.

"Now this is interesting," Nesbit said. "It appears we have a bit of DIY surgery. Look at that flap of skin, it's been cut on three sides of a square and then peeled back and folded over. I'd say something like a scalpel or other razor-sharp instrument must have been used to make the incision."

"While he was alive?" Savage said.

"Oh yes. From the amount of blood, there is no way this was done post-mortem." Nesbit moved his hand to the exposed ribs and then poked his fingers through.

320

"These ribs have been broken. They are no longer attached to the sternum. In fact, looking at the ends, I can see they've been cut much in the same way as would happen in an autopsy."

"Any idea why?" Savage said.

"Well . . ." Nesbit moved his head from side to side and peered into the cavity behind the ribs. "I'd say they did it in order to cut out the man's heart. You see, by the look of things, it's missing."

"My God!" Savage turned away for a moment and tried to resist the urge to vomit. Being sick over one of John Layton's crime scenes wouldn't endear her to the CSI. She swallowed again and looked back at Nesbit. "How the hell . . .?"

"Not difficult, if you know what you're doing. He must have been held down securely because the incision on the flap of skin is very neat. Not something which could be made if he was thrashing around. Which explains the bruises on his arms."

"Two or more people then. Plus the person doing the cutting. And then . . .?"

"Barbarism, Charlotte." Nesbit shook his head and looked at her. "They must have used something like pruning shears to cut the ribs and then a few slices with a long-handle scalpel to cut the heart free. As you can see, the blood has gone everywhere. The man was alive. At least to start with."

Savage turned away again. If there was anything more to know Nesbit and Layton would fill her in later. Right now she wanted to get outside and feel a breeze on her face, to see the sky lightening in the east, know that this sort of darkness wasn't perpetual.

After spending most of the day in Totnes, Savage returned to Crownhill. She stood at one of the whiteboards in the crime suite, pretending to cast her eye over the spider's web of lines John Layton had drawn. Every now and then she glanced away, taking in the people in the room, wondering whether somebody had leaked the information about Wodan. Just a few hours after she and Calter had visited the bookshop, the owner had been killed. Either his murder was an almighty coincidence or one of the team had passed on the lead she'd discovered in Hedford's flat.

DC Enders and DC Calter sat sharing a terminal and arguing about something on the screen. Savage couldn't see either of them being connected to the killings, but maybe she couldn't afford to be so confident. Enders had a young family, three kids, a mortgage. There'd be financial pressures. Was it beyond the realms of possibility he'd taken a bung? Maybe he hadn't even known who he was supplying the information to. DC Calter was single, no family. Savage didn't see her as the type to respond to financial inducement, but perhaps she had a secret lover, somebody she was so besotted with that she would do anything for them.

Gareth Collier sat at a desk on his own sorting through paperwork. The office manager was ex military, rule-bound, methodical. He was also something of a loner. Savage had never seen him joking with other

322

officers and he was always missing from social functions. Was there a more sinister reason than mere social awkwardness?

On the far side of the room DCI Mike Garrett was talking to two indexers. Garrett was working on a case involving people-trafficking. He'd been interested in *Piquet* from the start, ostensibly to share information about missing persons who could possibly be victims. Maybe his interest was for a different reason?

Savage tutted to herself and moved away from the white-board and pushed through the double doors into the corridor. There were twenty-five people working on the case. Junior detectives, indexers, statement readers, ancillary staff. And that was just people at the station. What about Dr Andrew Nesbit and his team, or the CSIs and uniformed officers helping out at crime scenes? Once you thought "conspiracy", you opened a Pandora's Box of paranoia. Anyone could, and maybe should, be a suspect, their intentions questioned, their actions scrutinised.

"Ma'am?" DS Riley came round the corner. "Anything new?"

Riley surely couldn't be a suspect. He'd only been with the force for a couple of years. Before that he'd been up in London. And yet hadn't he been all-too-willing to step over the line to help her?

"Darius," Savage said. "I'm going mad in there. I don't want to believe one of us is involved in all of this. But when I look round the room I can see horns everywhere."

"Horns?"

"The devil." Savage put a finger up either side of her head and waggled them. "Or rather, the devil's accomplices. Fallen angels, demons, ghouls and zombies. I'll be having nightmares about DC Calter turning into a Medusa or something."

"Pete's around at home, yes?"

"Of course. You don't think . . .?"

"That we're targets? I don't want to be melodramatic, but yes, ma'am, it's possible. But I'm not necessarily talking about this case, know what I mean?" Riley whispered the last words.

"Simon Fox?" Savage too lowered her voice.

"Yes. You and Fallon had a little meeting the other morning. Over breakfast. A BLT and an omelette."

"Jesus! How the hell did you know that?"

"One of Davies' little dicky-birds told him, and he in turn informed me." Riley held up his hands. "You don't need to tell me if you've made a move already or if you're planning something, but I'd think about the consequences."

"Shit. Samantha and Jamie." Savage shook her head. "He wouldn't?"

"I don't know." Riley paused and glanced up and down the corridor. "But if I was you I'd give Fallon a call. Get him to provide you with a heavy or two who could watch over your kids, see them to and from their friends' houses, keep an eye on them. Discreetly, of course. I'm sure he'd be happy to oblige."

Savage was sure too. Then she'd be further in his debt. And yet, knowing one of Fallon's muscle men was a few steps away from her children would reassure her.

She nodded and then moved off up the corridor, heading for her office.

"A whole new meaning to the phrase 'Police protection', Charlotte," Fallon said when she explained the situation. "But you're on. Be somebody outside your place from when you leave in the morning until you return at night. Just leave it to Uncle Kenny."

She hung up to the sound of Fallon chuckling down the phone at the irony of the situation. She leaned back in her chair and cursed. She hadn't considered her children in all this. She'd focused on her own feelings, on retribution at all costs. Stupid. Samantha and Jamie and Pete were the most important things in her life. Not Owen Fox, nor his dad. Not police work, not catching criminals, not even bringing Ana Róka's killer to justice.

Savage pushed back from the desk and stood. She'd had enough for the day and, all of a sudden, the place she most wanted to be now was home.

All day, Fox had brooded. It had finally happened, just not in the way he had imagined.

He'd had a call from his son. Savage had visited Owen. She'd gone out of her mind, Owen said. Completely bonkers. She'd pulled a gun on him and then pistol-whipped him.

Savage had to be stopped. And Riley. The DS knew everything Savage did. But knowing was one thing; pulling a stunt like Savage had was quite another.

And now all hell had broken out over in Totnes. A brutal murder in a bookshop. The press were linking the killing with the pony mutilations and the body found on Dartmoor. Chasing information, Fox found out it was far more serious than that. The murdered Hungarian girl was somehow mixed up in it all too. Jesus, Fox thought. What the hell had his friend been up to?

Fox sat in his study staring at the phone. He'd felt certain that Savage would play it by the book. Now it appeared as if she'd gone straight to Owen. The little lamp on his desk flickered and for a moment Fox felt a sudden panic. If the light went out the room would fill with darkness. The nothingness would come sweeping up and around him until black enveloped everything. He took a slow breath and reached out for the lamp's switch. He turned it off and then back on again. Off. On. Off. On. Off. On. Certainty.

Fox tried to steady himself, tried to ignore his trembling hand as it hovered over the switch. Events appeared to be overwhelming him. However fast he ran, the past came after him at twice the speed. A few days ago he'd been concerned about his own future. He'd been selfish. Owen's call had changed all that. Savage was on the rampage and she needed to be stopped.

Fox dialled the number from memory.

"It's me," Fox said when the voice answered. "Simon Fox, the Chief Constable of Devon and Cornwall Police."

"Simon?"

Fox shook his head. He wasn't sure why he'd used his full title. It was as if he needed to reassert his

326

authority over the man on the other end of the line. Gain control. Make the first move.

"I can do it," Fox said. "What you asked."

"Good," the voice said. "Things are hotting up and you'll need to be proactive. Make sure there is no chance I'll be investigated for anything."

"There's a price."

"I know, Simon, and I'm working on it."

"She needs to be warned off. For good."

There was a long pause and Fox wondered whether his words had been misunderstood. On the other hand, perhaps he'd gone too far. But then the voice came back on the line and Fox felt a terrible chill sweep through his body.

"Don't worry. I'm going to send her a message which will leave her in no doubt as to what she needs to do."

Fox hung up and then reached across and turned the light off and then back on again.

Off. On. Off. On. Off. On.

Then he put his head in his hands and began to cry.

"Car, Mummy," Jamie said. "Vroom, vroom."

"Yes. Let me have a go, darling."

"No, Mummy, car! Car!" Jamie's voice went up in pitch. "Car coming!"

Savage sat up, hearing the revving of an engine, seeing a flash of blue Impreza and her daughter on the bicycle in the middle of the road. The car moved in slow motion, getting closer and closer.

"Clarissa!" Savage shouted. "Get off the road!"

"We're playing ponies, Mummy. Clip, clop, clippity-clop."

Savage pushed herself to her feet. The Impreza rolled forward another metre. Clarissa pushed the pedal on the bicycle round half a turn. The tyres on the car squealed on the tarmac. A bell rang out. And then time froze.

Savage found herself floating above the scene, the moorland spread out below as if she was up in Frey's little aeroplane. She looked down. The Impreza was a car length from Clarissa, the driver trying in vain to swerve around the bike. From her vantage point, Savage could see the world in minute detail. She could see the strands of red hair spilling from underneath Clarissa's helmet. She could see pieces of gravel on the road, the individual pieces of grit causing the car to slide. Through the windscreen of the car she could see Owen Fox sitting with a beer can in one hand, a roll-up cigarette in the other.

Then the clock ticked on. The Impreza smashed into the bicycle and Clarissa was catapulted over the bonnet. She hit the windscreen and slid to one side, bouncing off and rolling onto the road. The bicycle smashed down beside her. The Impreza steered out of its skid and roared away down the road, dirt flying from the wheels. Clarissa lay in a heap, broken, dying.

"No!" Savage shouted, sitting up and groping in the blackness. She flayed her arms in front of her, aware of somebody grasping her wrists and holding her. "Noooo!"

"Charlotte!" Pete. Beside her in the bed. "It's just a dream, sweetheart. A nightmare. Shush."

"Yes," Savage muttered, waking fully. "A dream."

She blew out a long breath and then lay down. Pete wrapped his arms around her and soon he was fast asleep again. Savage stared up at the shadows on the ceiling, unable to follow suit. A dream, was that all it was? Or were the images more akin to a flashback? She'd never seen it all that clearly before. She blinked and tried to recall exactly what she'd seen: Clarissa on the bicycle. The Impreza coming down the road. The car hitting Clarissa. Owen Fox with a beer and a spliff in his hands, sitting in the passenger seat of the car.

"Fuck," she said to herself. "Fuck, fuck fuck."

CHAPTER
TWENTY-FOUR

Wednesday 3rd September

"Anything I should know?" Pete said when Savage came down to breakfast on Wednesday morning. "About a man called Owen?"

"Owen?" Savage gulped and then went across to the fridge, opened it, and hid behind the door looking for some orange juice. "Who's Owen?"

"No idea, but you were talking about him in your sleep. Right before you had that nightmare."

Savage shook her head. "Don't think we know an Owen, do we?"

"Well *I* don't. As for you . . ."

"Don't be ridiculous."

"Not ridiculous, just careful. I don't want to lose my wife to some Welshman."

"I prefer Irish men."

"I know." Pete came over to Savage and pushed the fridge door shut. He put his arms around her waist. "Patrick Enders."

"Now you're being daft as well as ridiculous." Savage twisted in Pete's grip. "Now if you don't mind, I've got to get to work."

"Are you sure?" Pete pressed himself against her. "I could pretend to be Welsh. Land of My Fathers and all that. Or Irish, if you prefer."

"When I get home tonight you can pretend to be whoever you want." Savage gave Pete a peck on the cheek and then extracted the orange juice from where he'd squashed the carton between their bodies. "Right now, I need to get going."

Pete let her go and she moved away. He went to wake the children, leaving her alone. Savage took a glass from a cupboard and set it down on the worktop. As she poured the orange juice she realised her hands were shaking.

The crime suite at Crownhill was all but deserted when Savage arrived. DC Enders sat at a terminal and on the other side of the room, two indexers clattered away at their keyboards. Aside from Enders, there were no other detectives present.

"Totnes, ma'am," Enders said. "The DSupt wants to blitz the area around the bookshop. House by house, street by street. He reckons somebody must've heard or seen something."

"So why are *you* still here?" Savage said.

"The overnights, ma'am." Enders picked up a printout and handed it to Savage. "Kingsbridge. There was an RTC on the quayside. An elderly woman was hit by a motorbike. Both escaped with cuts and bruises, but there was some confusion about whose fault the accident was."

Savage frowned. "And is this a good use of your time? Trying to get to the bottom of a minor RTC?"

"I was in early. Kids woke me and I wanted to get out of the house. Bedlam, the holidays, don't you find?"

"Still . . ."

"Read the report, ma'am. It's all there."

Savage looked down at the piece of paper. The report detailed the accident exactly as Enders had described. A PCSO had attended, along with a passing ambulance, although neither casualty required hospital treatment. The PCSO had taken a couple of statements from passers-by.

"I don't see what this has to do with us?"

"Two witnesses, ma'am. The first, a tourist, we're not interested in, but the second . . ."

Savage scanned the report again, looking for the details of the witnesses. Towards the bottom of the sheet she found the statements. She read through until she saw a familiar name.

"Irina?"

"Yes. She's given her full name and her old address. Obviously she's not there now though."

"So it doesn't look as if she's been kidnapped. She simply ran away?"

"She got scared. Probably went to stay with a friend."

"Over in Kingsbridge?"

"Beat me too at first, ma'am," Enders said, smiling. "But as I said, I was in early. I checked the list of friends and acquaintances we have for Ana and Irina. There's a local lad who does the same course as Irina and he lives over that way. His parents run something called the Creekside Guest House in Frogmore. Frogmore's a little village to the —"

"I know where Frogmore is, Patrick. What the hell's Irina doing over there? If she is there, of course."

"She is. I rang the place and spoke to the lad's mother. They're fully booked-up this time of year but Irina's staying in the lodge they have in the garden. Been there all week apparently."

"What are we waiting for then?"

"You, ma'am." Enders grinned, pushed back his chair and stood. "I mean, I was waiting for you. That's why I'm still here!"

Kingsbridge was a small town at the top of the winding estuary that had Salcombe at its entrance. The village of Frogmore lay some three miles to the east, at the head of a small muddy creek. The guest house sat away from the busy A379 and down by the waterside. While Enders knocked at the front door Savage put her head round the side of the building. A lawn stretched to the water, to one side a small log cabin.

"Ma'am?" Enders joined her, gesturing back over his shoulder. "Mrs Hannaford says Irina's gone for the day. The show."

"What show?"

"Kingsbridge Country Fair. The traffic, remember?"

A few miles before they'd reached Kingsbridge they'd been stuck in a jam and Enders had been going on about some agricultural show or other. Savage hadn't taken much notice.

"What on earth is she doing there?"

"Mrs Hannaford says Irina's gone with her son. A day out. They packed sandwiches and everything."

"Sandwiches?" Savage shook her head. "Patrick, do you mind telling me just what the hell is going on?"

Enders shrugged. "No idea, but I guess we'd better get along to the show. I've got the lad's mobile number so we can get in touch if we want."

They drove back to Kingsbridge and found the show field a mile or so north, nestled in the rolling countryside of the South Hams. Traffic sat bumper to bumper, queueing to get into the fair. A couple of large fields had been designated as car parks and it took half an hour before they trundled off the main road and bumped across the freshly mown grass. Enders pulled up alongside a people carrier full of screaming kids.

"And I thought three of the blighters was bad enough," Enders said. "That poor bugger's got five of them."

Savage looked across at the car where World War Three appeared to have broken out on the back seat.

"They'd prefer to be at McDonald's," she said. "Not at a glorified farmers' market."

They got out and strolled across the grass to the entrance gate where a couple of stewards — one young, one old — were checking passes. Savage pulled out her ID and flashed it at one of the stewards. Then Enders showed them a picture of Irina. Had they seen her?

The older steward shook his head and nodded at the river of people streaming through the gate. How the bloody hell was he expected to spot anyone in this crowd? It was more than enough hassle trying to ensure that the young'uns didn't sneak in for free, he explained.

"Wait, I remember her," the other steward chipped in, smiling.

"Aye, lad," the old man said. "You would."

Savage turned to the second steward. Early twenties. Muscles from shifting bales of straw or knocking in fence posts. If he had an ounce of testosterone in him then he'd have had an ogle at Irina, Savage thought. "Go on."

"She were with a guy with glasses. One of them nerd types. Right odd couple, him being all spotty and her an absolute beauty."

"That's her," Enders said. "Did you see where they went?"

"Now you are being daft." The young man turned and gestured to the show ground. A series of marquees lay dotted across the fields and between the tents several areas had been roped off as rings for various events. Thousands of people swarmed in all directions.

Savage took out her business card and handed it to the young steward. "Give us a call if you spot her, OK?"

The man nodded and Savage and Enders walked into the show ground. In a nearby ring a crowd watched children taking part in a Pony Club race. Screams from the sidelines urged on the riders as they hared back and forth across the field, bursting balloons with mini lances. Health and Safety would have had a fit.

"We best take a look around," Savage said. Close by, a large floral display arched over the entrance to the produce tent. "Let's go in here."

Inside the produce tent, there was a calm befitting the serious business of showing fruit and vegetables. A ripple of applause came from the far end, where a group of people crowded round a small stage. Feedback squawked from the PA for a moment before a woman began to announce the prizes for the flower arranging.

Savage and Enders worked their way down the line of displays towards the opening. A rather large cucumber had won a special award. Enders pointed and sniggered.

"W.I.," Enders said. "I can see why they liked that."

Farther on there were onions approaching the size of footballs, while a set of leeks were thicker than a man's arm. There was no sign of Irina.

It was the same story elsewhere. After an hour of traipsing in and out of numerous tents Enders had had enough.

"Parched, ma'am," Enders said, nodding in the direction of an open-sided tent where people milled around with plastic glasses. "And as it happens, there's the bar. We could take a gander over there, couldn't we?"

"Go on then, but shandies, OK?"

Enders shrugged his shoulders in disappointment and headed for the bar. Savage wandered over to the side of the tent, out of the way of the crowds. She sat on an upturned beer crate and, more in hope than in anticipation, looked around for Irina.

Behind the tent was a roped-off parking area for show members. Several men dressed in tweeds sat in picnic chairs next to a big 4X4. A bottle was being passed around, glasses filled, a hamper on the bonnet of the car open and displaying a selection of cheeses. Raucous laughter rang out. Savage caught part of the anecdote. Somebody, it appeared, had been at a pheasant shoot and had accidentally shot one of the beaters below the waist.

"Lends a new meaning to the phrase 'caught short', hey?" said one of the men.

"Waste of a bloody cartridge," the shooter said, before quaffing the contents of his glass. "And you know what? I had to take him to hospital and the bugger bled all over the front seat of my Merc. Not a word of thanks."

"Never mind," the other man said. "At least you can say you bagged a nice brace."

Savage turned, recognising one of the voices. She looked at the man in the middle. Bushy eyebrows, red face.

"Charles Milner, the local MP," Enders muttered at her shoulder, passing her a plastic glass brimming with beer. "Recognise him from when he came for the visit the other day. I knew there was something to be said for socialism."

"Careful," Savage said. "One word from him and you'll be out of a job."

A slab of cheese appeared from the hamper and while Milner set to cutting slices, the others passed the bottle round again. A tin of cheese biscuits was opened and for a couple of minutes the men munched on their food. Milner proposed a toast to something, glasses were filled, and then chinked together. Then Milner hunched over the bonnet, his voice low and inaudible. The other men nodded, smiled. One reached across and patted Milner on the back.

"Those lot live in a different world from the rest of us," Enders said. "Tossers."

"Envy won't —" Savage stopped, mid-sentence. "Shit. Irina!"

"Hey?"

"There!" Savage bent and placed her beer on the floor and then took Enders by the shoulders and turned him. "Three cars over."

A figure stood for a moment by the side of a horse trailer. A girl. Something glinting in her right hand. The girl slipped sideways, heading for the group next to the 4X4, her eyes trained on Milner, the knife now outstretched.

Savage spun and dived down towards her at the side of the tent. Spotting her, Irina hesitated for a second, and then changed direction, running away through the maze of cars.

Savage sprinted towards her, dashing past Milner and his colleagues.

"What the . . .?"

Milner's words were lost as Savage dodged left and then right between the horse trailer and a car. Irina headed down an avenue of vehicles, stumbling through a family picnic, the dad rising and hurling curses after the girl. Savage skirted the group and then ran hard to

338

try to make up the distance. Behind, she could hear Enders puffing along, already out of breath. Irina changed direction, veering ninety degrees along the line of cars and heading back towards the main show ground.

Up ahead a river of people moved along one of the main thoroughfares. Irina glanced back and then one of her arms was jerking out to the side. The knife flashed in the sun as it soared upward and then tumbled down, clattering as the blade hit the top of a car.

"Get that!" Savage shouted back at Enders.

Irina reached the crowd and disappeared into the surging bodies. People were heading for the main ring, where the sharp staccato of a motorbike display rider was attracting attention.

Savage arrived at the path a couple of seconds after Irina. She pushed into the scrum of bodies, aware of shouts ahead as Irina tried to make progress. It seemed to Savage as if everybody was going in the opposite direction to her and nobody seemed in much of a hurry to move out of her way. Then the crowd thinned and Irina was running across a patch of ground, empty because it surrounded an overflowing cattle trough, the ground thick with mud. Savage darted right and then swerved left to avoid a mother pushing a baby buggy. She lost her footing and tumbled over, arms outstretched to break her fall. The ground came up fast and she face-planted, sliding along on her front like a footballer celebrating a goal on a slippery pitch.

"Fuck!" Even without her expletive, people were turning their heads to look. Savage pushed herself up from the mud, aware the stuff had got everywhere; on her clothes, in her hair, splattered across her face.

Up ahead, she could see Irina swinging left onto a bisecting avenue. Savage stood and began to run again. She followed left, the path running down between a row of tents. Irina turned to look back for a moment, and then collided with an elderly gentleman, the two of them falling to the ground. The girl pulled herself up and then, aware that Savage was almost on her, darted towards the nearest tent and disappeared inside.

Fifty metres away a flash of fluorescent yellow caught Savage's attention. Two PCSOs stood at an ice cream stall, ninety-nine ice creams being passed down to them.

"Hey!" Savage shouted. "Over here!"

She waved and then followed Irina into the tent. Inside, a riot of living colour assailed her senses. The air was heady with the perfume of flowers and the earthy smell of greenery. A path wound through floral displays, waterfalls trickled and bubbled, pot plants sat in deserts of gravel. Savage saw the words "Kingsbridge Gardening Club" above one of the displays as she rushed past.

Irina stood down the far end of the tent, cornered next to an impenetrable mass of fern and a trestle table full of dried flowers. Savage walked forward.

"Easy, Irina," Savage said as she got to within arm's reach. "Let's talk about this."

"No way! You're not taking me to them!" Irina shouted at Savage and then struck out with her hand. The blow hit Savage in the face, below her left eye.

Savage stepped forward again and crooked her right foot behind the girl's legs. She pushed her back and Irina fell over, grabbing Savage as she did. The two of them crashed into the display of flowers and the trestles collapsed. Then somebody grabbed her arm, yanking her hard and up and away from the mass of flowers.

"Alright then, madam. Out you come." Savage felt her arm twisted around behind her back and forced upward until she let out a scream.

"Police!" Savage said. She glimpsed a flash of yellow and the next moment one of the PCSOs was standing in front of her. "I'm a bloody police officer."

"Sure you are, love," she said, looking Savage up and down. "Glastonbury branch, is it? Now why don't you keep quiet until we can get someone to take you in." She began to talk on her radio, something about requesting a pick-up car. Savage moved her free hand to reach into her jacket to get her warrant card.

"Look out! She's got a knife!" The PCSO screamed and stepped forward, smashing a fist into Savage's face.

Savage dropped the wallet holding her warrant card to the floor and went limp, allowing the man holding her to grab the free arm and bring that round behind her too.

The female PCSO bent and picked up the wallet.

"Like I said, police," Savage muttered, tasting blood from a cut lip.

"What is it, Mandy?" the man asked.

"Um, not a knife . . ." The woman shook her head and opened the wallet. "Bugger, she *is* one of us. DI Charlotte Savage, Crownhill CID."

Behind her Savage heard a cough and the man muttered a "Sorry, er, ma'am", before he released her.

A crowd of people had gathered and Savage realised they were all gawping. Several were shaking their heads and someone even had their mobile out and was taking a photo.

"The girl," Savage said, groping her way to a nearby chair. "Where is the fucking girl?"

Both PCSOs turned around full circle, all of a sudden keen to help, but their enthusiasm was pointless. Irina had vanished into the oasis of ferns, a few broken stems the only sign of where she had slipped away.

Gareth Collier, the office manager, shook his head. He looked down at his roster sheet. "The DSupt won't like it, Darius. A proper surveillance takes three teams, two-up, to operate twenty-four-seven. That's six people doing sweet FA apart from watching the woman go shopping for new outfits."

"Helen Peacock is our only direct link to what happened up on the moor — the only one left alive, that is," Riley said. "Even if just one officer spends a few hours tailing her we might get something. I'd be happy to do the job."

"Yeah, I'm sure you would." Collier bit his lip, scratched his head and then nodded. "OK. We'll do it, but I'm going to have to disappoint you; DC Calter will be the tail. I think she's more likely to blend in should Peacock decide she needs some new knickers, yes?"

Two hours later and Riley stood next to DI Davies in the queue in the canteen. He told him about the surveillance op.

"Peacock. Tail. Genius, Darius, genius." Davies chuckled and helped himself to several sausages and a couple of scoops of mash. "Anything so far?"

Riley shook his head and reached for a pre-packed salad. He explained to Davies that he'd had a text from Calter. So far Peacock had visited a nail bar, a hairdressers, two shoe shops, and spent an hour having herself measured in a fancy boutique.

"Sounds like she spends a lot of time and money on her appearance," Riley said. "Not that I see the point. The female half of her audience probably couldn't care less. The male half would still fancy her if she wore nothing but a bin liner."

"Nice thought." Davies added a spoonful of peas to his plate and then slid his tray along to the cashier. "Especially those recycling bags. See-through, yes?"

Riley was about to say something when his phone rang. He looked at the display. Calter.

"Helen Peacock is a bad girl, sir," Calter said. "All that dolling herself up was for a reason. She's having an affair."

Calter gave Riley an address in the Peverell area of the city and twenty minutes later he was sitting in the front seat of an unmarked pool car, Calter beside him.

"Which house?" Riley looked across at the terrace of grand Victorian properties.

"Third one along," Calter said. "She went in about forty minutes ago and she'll need to get her hair done again afterwards because I'm guessing a prolonged shagging session is taking place."

Riley felt a frisson of jealousy. "Any idea who he is?"

"No, but I wouldn't mind finding out. He was as dishy as I've seen in a long time. Dark hair, nice smile, a healthy tan, and a great body."

"Is that what you'd like me to write down on your report? Because . . ." Riley paused. The door was opening to reveal Helen Peacock standing there with a man in the shadows. The man stepped forward.

"See what I mean, sir? He's the type of hunk I could play with."

A second tingle of excitement ran down Riley's spine. But this time the feeling wasn't down to Helen Peacock. It was down to the fact he recognised the woman's lover.

"Gotcha!" Riley said. "Professor Falk, our expert in Satanism."

"Falk? He's an *academic?* I don't believe you. I thought they all wore cardigans and little round glasses?"

"Times, evidently, have changed."

"Peacock's married, isn't she?"

"Yes. As to whether Mr Falk is married, I have no idea. What I'm more interested in is the fact Helen Peacock denied having any knowledge or connection to Satanism. That woman's got some explaining to do."

Savage sat on a plastic chair in the St John's ambulance tent, a cup of tea in her hand. The tea was hot, milky and over-sweet.

344

"Get this down you, love," the paramedic had said. "Looks like you need it."

"Understatement of the year, hey, ma'am?" Enders had said.

Now the DC stood beside Savage holding a plastic bag which contained the knife.

"Lucky we were there," he said. "Otherwise the show would've been making headlines for all the wrong reasons."

"Who were the others with Milner?" Savage said.

"A surgeon, a farmer, a land agent and a guy who sells yachts."

"It seemed to be Milner she was interested in." Savage remembered the piercing look in Irina's eyes. "Definitely."

"Yeah, but why, ma'am? What's he got to do with Irina?"

"I haven't a clue." Savage took a sip of tea. "What did you tell Milner?"

"Kept it simple. I apologised for disturbing his picnic and said we were chasing an animal libber. He barely acknowledged me. I don't think he even spotted the girl."

"Good work." Savage took another gulp of tea and then poured the rest into the grass beneath her seat. "Any sign of Irina? I must admit I lost track of her once that idiot PCSO punched me in the face."

"On any other day 'that idiot PCSO' would have been a hero, ma'am. Just unfortunate you turned out not to be some psycho tramp."

"Irina?" Savage ignored Enders' grin. "Where did she go?"

"No idea." Enders held up the plastic bag and opened it so Savage could look inside. "I was too busy looking for this. Once I'd found the weapon I headed for the commotion in the floral tent."

Savage peered into the bag. The knife was a serrated type, long, but with a blunt end. Fine for cutting bread but not much use for stabbing someone with. Unless Irina had managed to slice somebody across the neck, the weapon wouldn't have done much damage.

"What the hell was she up to, ma'am?" Enders took the bag back. "And, more importantly, where the hell has she been all this time?"

"I was wondering if Ana could have been in a relationship with Milner." Savage stood and began to brush some of the mud from her clothes. "If so, then perhaps Irina blames Milner for Ana's death."

"Are you saying *Milner* killed Ana?"

"No. But that doesn't mean Irina didn't think so. We need to find her, ASAP."

"Got a couple of cars touring the lanes around here at the moment."

"OK. What about the boy she was with, have you called him?"

"Phone's switched off. I've sent one of those PCSOs to wait at his parents' place."

"Good. Let's hope we can find Irina soon. For her sake." Savage flicked a final piece of mud from her shirt and pointed to the tent entrance. "And Charles Milner's."

★ ★ ★

In one smooth movement Irina vaulted the gate and rolled behind the hedge. A police car rolled to a stop in the lane. The officer inside clunked the door open and stepped out, then came over to the gate and made a cursory inspection of the field. Irina huddled behind a clump of nettles as the officer shook his head. He then moved to the gate post, undid the zip on his trousers, and urinated, letting out a long sigh.

A minute later, after another glance into the field, he got back into the car. There was a crackle from the radio.

"Nothing here," the officer said.

The crackle came again, Irina unable to hear exactly what the voice said.

"Yeah, of course I checked. Yes in the field, yes in the lane, yes properly. Must have been a duff report, because there's no sign of her. Heading down to Sherford and then Frogmore and then I'm due a break, right?"

The radio operator said something else and then the officer started the car and drove away. Irina extracted herself from the nettles, inspected her forearms for stings, and then went over to the gate. Until the police car had come she hadn't had a clue where she was. Now she knew Frogmore, where the guest house was, lay the way the car had gone. She couldn't return to the little log cabin, but she figured if she carried on down the lane it was unlikely the police officer would retrace his route. She clambered over the gate and began walking in the direction he'd gone.

The lane plunged down a hill and cut deep between high banks. Irina trudged along, beginning to feel hungry and thirsty. The sun was relentless and she began to flag. The stress of the past few days was starting to tell on her. Irina stopped. By the side of the road a stream of water cascaded from a drainage pipe and frothed down into a culvert. The water was unlikely to be clean enough to drink but at least she could splash some on her face. She bent close to the pipe and cupped her hands. The liquid felt cool on her skin. The water gurgled into the drain, the sound comforting. One day, Irina thought, she'd like to live by a stream. Hearing the bubbling of a little brook would be relaxing, the noise would drown out all her cares.

She sighed and stood.

Round the corner and ten metres up the hill a Mercedes 4X4 filled the lane.

CHAPTER
TWENTY-FIVE

According to one of the stewards, Milner had left the show ground.

"Gone home," the man said. "A little bit the worse for wear to be honest."

"Home" turned out to be Caulfield Manor, the ancestral pile Milner had inherited. The manor lay north of the A38, not far from Mortonhampstead. The little town was some ten miles from Exeter and had recently been colonised by London types. You could tell, Enders explained, because they were the drivers who refused to get over on the country lanes.

"Scared of scratching their Chelsea tractors, ma'am," Enders said, as he pulled the car to the side of the road yet again, this time to let a large BMW 4X4 come past. "And the buggers haven't a clue how to reverse either."

Mortonhampstead itself bustled with both cars and people. The better dressed were heading for a late lunch at one of the many eateries, while those clad in waterproofs and walking boots were looking for simpler fare. They took a winding road eastward and then Enders was turning off and up a narrow lane, which twisted up through woodland before entering a wide valley, Caulfield Manor standing at the far end. The house certainly befitted the title of Manor. Built in dressed stone, large windows surrounded a columned porch, and two great chimney stacks towered at each gable end. A gatehouse stood at the entrance to the property and huge iron gates hung open, a driveway sweeping up to the house.

"He's not expecting us, ma'am, right?" Enders said, as he turned off the lane. "Only there's a sign there which says visitors by appointment only."

"No, he's not expecting us." Savage shook her head. "So let's hope he's in."

"Oh, he's in alright." Enders nodded ahead to where a Mercedes 4X4 stood in front of the steps. The number plate read CM1.

Enders pulled up alongside the Merc and they got out. They went up the steps and Savage pressed the bell push. Seconds later the door swung open, Charles Milner standing there in tweeds, face red from drink.

"Yes?" Milner cocked his head on one side, a flicker of recognition in his eyes. "Do I know you?"

"DI Charlotte Savage," Savage said pulling out her warrant card. "And you've already met my colleague, DC Patrick Enders. I wonder if we might have a word about the incident at the country fair?"

"The animal libber?" Milner's eyes narrowed and then he nodded at Enders. "I told your man there I didn't want to press charges, that it was nothing. In my position you expect such things. Now if you'll —"

"I'm afraid this is altogether more serious."

"Then you'd better come in." Milner led them down the hallway and then into the largest living room Savage

350

had ever seen. There were three separate seating areas and a huge fireplace, wood stacked either side of the inglenook. The furniture was a mix of antique and modern and Milner led them over to an old leather three-piece with a buttoned back. He gestured at the sofa and took one of the armchairs for himself. "So, what's this about?"

Savage and Enders sat down and Enders pulled out his notebook. Savage looked around the room once more. There were paintings and tapestries on the walls. All that was missing was a suit of armour in one corner and a little cafe serving cream teas. She was tempted to make some small talk but Milner fiddled impatiently, his eyes glaring at her. There was no reason for him to be nervous and yet his body language suggested he was.

"There was a girl at the fair today. She was armed with a knife and her intention, we believe, was to kill you."

For a moment Milner didn't respond and then he pushed himself up and moved across to the side of the room where there was a small bar area. A couple of clinks later and Milner was walking back and taking his seat again, a glass of sherry in his hand. He sipped the sherry and then nodded to himself as if he'd come to some sort of understanding.

"Anti-fox hunting, I'm assuming? I've been vociferous in my support for the farmers. I opposed the hunting bill, backed the culling of badgers, and I'm also on the board of a well-known pharmaceutical company. I've had threats before, but never anything like this. I guess that's the way the world is going. These nutters will do anything to subvert democracy. We need to be vigilant in our —"

"Mr Milner," Savage said. "Save your rhetoric for the Commons. As far as we know this girl has nothing to do with animal liberation. She's apolitical, in fact she's not even British, so I doubt she has much knowledge of your voting record."

"Not even British . . .? There you go then. She's been radicalised by the Jihadists obviously. Down here, away from London, I'm an easy target."

"She's not a Muslim terrorist, Mr Milner. She's from Eastern Europe. Have you had any dealings with girls from Eastern Europe?"

"No, of course not." Milner licked his bottom lip and then reached for his sherry glass. He studied the amber liquid and then looked straight at Savage. "What are you suggesting, Inspector?"

"I don't know, what am I suggesting?" Savage glanced across at Enders. His pad had a few scrawls of pencil, but it didn't look as if he had gleaned much from the interview so far. "So you're saying you've had no contact with any women from Eastern Europe recently?"

"Inspector, this sounds remarkably like an accusation. If it is, then I'd very much like to know what I'm being accused of. Are you telling me this girl who tried to attack me has been harmed?"

"No, not that we know of."

"Well then, I fail to see what this is all about."

"There's another girl, Mr Milner. She was found dead at Fernworthy Reservoir last week. The girl who attacked you was a friend of hers. I guess she thinks you might have killed her friend."

"Plainly ridiculous. As far as I'm aware no Hungarian girl has crossed my path, recently or otherwise. You say this woman is apolitical, but I think you should look again. This is obviously some ruse, perhaps dreamed up by one of our great newspapers. Quite frankly if it is, then you should be looking at their activities. Post-Leveson, such behaviour is outrageous."

Savage stood up and walked away from the sofa. She gazed through the windows and then turned. Above the fireplace there was a painting, Pre-Raphaelite in style. A girl, hardly more than prepubescent, bathed naked in a lake while from the bankside a man, half goat and half human, watched on.

"The name of the girl found at Fernworthy was Anasztáz Róka. Does that name mean anything to you, Mr Milner?"

"No, of course not. To be honest, Inspector, this is beginning to get a little tiresome. I'm a busy man so unless there's anything else I can help you with . . .?"

"No. Thank you for your time. Come on, Patrick, it's time we left Mr Milner to his work."

Enders rose from his seat, his face puzzled. He nodded at Milner before following Savage from the room. Milner made no attempt to show them out himself. They walked down the corridor, opened the front door, and stepped out onto the porch. They had a good view down the valley now, at the fields either side of the iron fencing. A proper little estate.

353

"You never mentioned Ana's nationality, ma'am," Enders said. "And yet Milner knew she was Hungarian."

"I know."

They went down the steps and Savage stood by the car. To the right of the driveway horses grazed in a small paddock, while to the left a strange strip of grass ran across a field, in one corner of which was a large barn with a curved roof.

"Shit." Savage stared at the green grass. There were no animals in the field and the grass was short. It appeared to have been cut and yet around the edges were large areas of tall scrub. The impression was not unlike a golf course, with the strips of rough either side of the fairway. "Patrick, look at that."

Savage patted Enders on the arm and they walked back to their car.

"Ma'am?" Enders said. He shook his head, not understanding. "Pitch and putt?"

"Look again. That barn, what do you think is inside?"

"No idea. I don't have X-ray vision."

"What about if I said it wasn't a barn, and it's not pitch and putt?"

"Not pitch and putt?" Enders opened the door to the car and got in. "Horses?

"Nope, I don't think so. Let's go and find out, shall we?"

Back at Crownhill, Riley and Calter presented Gareth Collier with the new evidence about Falk and Peacock.

"So, what's the story here?" Collier said, scratching the top of his head. The stubble was extra short and sometimes Riley wondered if the office manager believed in a sort of reverse Samson effect; the shorter his hair, the more effective he was. "Are we saying Professor Falk is involved in all of this?"

"He could be," Riley said. "Peacock definitely lied to us. We need to question her again. There's more to her than meets the eye. She played me like a fish on the end of the line, and it wasn't just feminine wiles."

"Are you certain?" Calter smiled at Riley. "From what I've seen of her, she's got plenty of those."

"Believe me, I'd noticed," Riley said. "It's hard not to."

"People," Collier said. "If we could just get back to the matter in hand."

"Sure," Riley said. "What do you think?"

"I think we've got to play this one carefully." Collier bit his bottom lip, his eyes scanning the board. He picked up a marker pen and scribbled Falk's name next to the picture of Helen Peacock. "I could put a tail on Falk but I don't think the DSupt will wear it, not without some additional evidence. I think the best thing is to come up with some dummy excuse so you can re-interview Helen Peacock. It shouldn't be too hard to think of one. Do you think you can do that, Darius? Pull her string without her pulling yours?"

"I can try," Riley said. "But to continue the fishing analogy, I might need a safety net."

They drove back down the driveway and turned into the lane. Enders cruised slowly along as they skirted the boundary of Milner's property. He took another left and then right and then they could see the pale green of the corrugated iron structure ahead of them.

"Park here," Savage said, pointing at a passing place in the narrow lane. "We can walk along and see if we can find a gateway."

A hundred metres along from where they parked they found a gap in the hedge. The fence behind the hedge had seen better days and Enders pushed the barbed wire down while Savage climbed over.

"He can't see us, can he, ma'am?" Enders said. "Because we don't have a warrant."

"Don't worry, Patrick, I'll take the rap. Anyway if we approach from this direction the building is between us and him."

They walked along the edge of the field until they reached the building. It had a curved roof like a Nissen hut and Savage estimated it was something like twenty by thirty metres. In front of the building, a large area of hardstanding had been laid. The white concrete glared in the sun but here and there darker splodges had spread, black, like oil. To the front of the building two huge doors hung from a cross beam, while to the right there was an ordinary-sized door with a glass panel. Savage approached the small door and peered in, cupping her eyes to reduce the glare. Inside there was a small workshop, boxed off from the rest of the building. Enders pressed his face against the glass alongside hers.

"Not much clue as to what's inside, ma'am. Tractors and farm machinery I expect. Maybe the tosser's collection of classic cars."

Savage tried the door, but it was locked. She gestured along to the pair of larger doors. Enders strode across and put his eye to the crack between the two doors.

"Shit." Enders pulled back from the doors and smiled at Savage. "Now I see what you were on about."

Savage took Enders' place. Shadows filled the interior of the building. Even so, she could easily make out the single object inside. It was a vehicle — in that Enders had been correct — but it wasn't a tractor or an old car. It was an aeroplane.

Back at Crownhill, Savage went to her office. She needed to see Hardin and arrange a search of Milner's place, but first she wanted to get some background information on the MP. She sat at her desk and did a web search. Thousands of Milners came up, but right at the top, with a Wikipedia entry to his name, was one Charles Milner, Member of Parliament for South Devon. She skipped down through the page, quickly absorbing the information. He was one of the landed aristocracy, with remnants of an ancient estate scattered across Devon. Much had been sold off but he still owned several thousand acres of valuable farmland. His great-grandfather had been MP for the same area and Milner had been variously a local councillor and a justice of the peace before he stood in the general election of 1997. While the Tories had been wiped out by the Blair landslide, Milner, a right-wing independent, had snuck under the radar. His anti-EU, pro-farming, pro-fox hunting stance had continued to go down a treat in the rural area he represented.

Savage scrolled back up the page to Milner's early life. He had been educated at a small private school in Devon and then gone up to Cambridge, where he graduated in Social and Political Sciences in 1989.

Shit! Here was the connection to Martin Hedford. Milner had been his contemporary at Cambridge. Milner was one of the Satanists.

In Hardin's office, Savage tried her best to explain what had happened. Hardin listened. Patience was something you learnt when you reached the upper echelons of the police. Still, his head shook back and forth at various points.

"Charlotte," Hardin said when she finished. "Charles Milner is not only a respected member of the community, he's a bloody MP. I can't send a bunch of officers to go snooping around his house without good reason."

"Not a bunch, sir," Savage said. "And not his house. We just need to give the plane a once-over. If Ana was in there then she'd have left traces. Just give John Layton an hour and he'll find something, I know he will."

"And if he doesn't? It could be a coincidence Milner has an aeroplane."

"Come on, sir, you don't believe that? His place is on the flight path Layton worked out. The line runs right over his house."

"Jesus." Hardin shook his head again and then tapped his hand on the table. He reached for his mouse. "This is beyond my pay-grade, Charlotte. I can't make this decision."

"You have to, sir. Milner's an arrogant bastard, used to getting his own way. He'll assume he's above the law. We know different, don't we?"

"Don't start, Charlotte. This job is hard enough without your clever quips." Hardin clicked a couple of times on his screen and then pushed the mouse away. Put both hands on the table in front of him and leaned forward. Whispered. "You really think he kidnapped Ana and killed her? That he's involved with these Satanists?"

"Nigel Frey said the tie-down found in the reservoir could well have come from an aeroplane. Milner has a plane. Irina, the Russian girl seems to want to kill him. Milner also went to Cambridge and studied Social and Political Sciences, graduating in 1989." Savage bit her lip and then held Hardin's gaze. "What more evidence do we need?"

"Right," Hardin huffed. He scratched his chin, puzzled for a moment. "There's something missing here, something important about Milner. For the life of me, I can't remember what it is."

"The Home Office Committee? With respect, sir, his membership shouldn't make any difference."

"No, you're right, it shouldn't. In reality though it does and means I need to get clearance if I'm —" Hardin raised his hands and buried his head in them.

"Sir, what is it?"

Hardin didn't appear to be listening. His hand shot to his keyboard, his fingers a blur as he typed and then thumped the "enter" key. He clicked and then shook his head before swivelling the laptop round so Savage could see.

The screen displayed the website of a local newspaper, the story from eighteen months ago. The lead picture showed Milner as a proud grandparent. In his arms, a newborn swaddled in white fabric. To one side, the mother. To the other side, the father. The story gave further details.

Savage blinked and felt her body jump in an unconscious reflex. She pushed her chair back from the desk and stood.

"Charlotte," Hardin said, as he reached for the phone and waved for her to leave. "Now you can see why I need clearance from the Chief Constable."

Savage nodded blankly, turned away and stumbled to the door. She wrenched the door open and half-fell into the corridor. She rested against a wall for support, closed her eyes and thought about what she'd just seen: Milner with his granddaughter, who was named Milly. The baby's mother; Lauren. The baby's father; Owen Fox.

It's late but Chubber's still up. He's waiting for the light to come. Only then will he feel able to go to bed. The dark brings nightmares and ever since that time on the moor he's had trouble sleeping. Especially now, thinking about the empty shed in the wood.

Don't think about it, Chubber! Don't think about what Antler Man is going to do to you!

360

He can't help it. The thought of being entombed in the ancient grave with worms and maggots eating his skin, rats gnawing at his face, unable to free himself, nothing but darkness and the heavy, heavy stone above. You'd claw, you'd scrape, you'd knock, knock, knock on the stone . . .

Tap, tap, tap.

The window, Chubber!

The window. Chubber rises from the chair at the kitchen table. Midnight's come and gone, but Chubber knows who's there. It'll be Mrs Grately. She's crazy. Wanders the streets in the middle of the night. Whenever she sees Chubber's kitchen light on she comes calling, looking to see if he's got a few choice cuts. He hasn't. And thanks to the police, he doesn't know when he'll get any more. Chubber moves to the window to pull back the blind, expecting to see Mrs Grately's face beaming through the glass, dentures missing, rollers in her hair, nothing but a velour dressing gown to keep her warm against the cold night air.

"I'm sorry Mrs —"

Chubber! It's not Mrs Grately!

No. There's a smile. A leering sneering grimace, behind which a snake's tongue flickers. Above the mouth, the nose and eyes covered with a mask. Above that, a towering head-dress of horns.

Antler Man!

Antler Man taps on the glass again. Points towards the back door. "Open it," he mouths.

Chubber lets out a little bleat. Like a sheep trapped in the corner of a shed. He moves towards the door and, hand shaking, reaches out and shoots the bolt. The door swings wide and Chubber is stepping backwards and the man is stepping forwards and Chubber is falling to his knees.

"Please!" Chubber says, aware as he does so that you don't beg in front of Antler Man. Antler Man gives and Antler Man takes but he does so at his own whim. "I didn't let her out. She escaped."

"We know." Antler Man reaches out a hand and places it on Chubber's shoulder. "Remember what you promised, remember if you don't do what we want you're going to hell."

"She must have fl . . . fl . . . fl . . ."

Spit it out, Chubber.

"She must have flown out." Chubber blurts out the words. He puts his hands out either side of his body and mimes the action of flapping wings. "Tweet, tweet, tweet. Like a little bird."

There's a horrible pause and Chubber wonders if Antler Man is going to get angry. But then there is a strange sound, almost a chuckle, and Antler Man is grinning.

"Forget about her. Get back up to the wood and repair the shed. We're going to need it again."

"How am I . . . ?" Chubber thinks about the bent tin roof, wonders how he can stop a bird getting out.

"Use your initiative, your brain." Antler Man taps his skull head and it's all Chubber can do not to laugh. "Make sure there's no way of escaping and don't let the police catch you this time. Otherwise we'll be in a mess that nobody can clear up, understand?"

Say you understand, Chubber, say it!

Chubber nods. Antler Man smiles and slips backwards through the door into the yard and dissolves into the black night.

Savage awoke with a start. Her side of the duvet was rucked up, her skin clammy and cold. Pete snored lightly for a few seconds before rolling over on his side. He muttered something but in seconds was fast asleep again. She blinked. Tried to remember the dream, but this time there wasn't anything to recall. No Clarissa, no Owen Fox, nothing. She looked over to where a pale glimmer showed behind the curtains, but it was the light from the moon, not the dawn. Savage sighed. She was wide awake. For a few minutes she just lay and stared at the ceiling. Then she decided to go downstairs and get something to drink. Some milk or some juice.

She padded out of the bedroom along the landing, checked the kids, and then went down to the kitchen. The fridge opened with a sucking sound, the light splaying onto the floor. She took out some milk, retrieved a glass from a cupboard and filled it. The liquid felt cool and comforting. She rinsed the glass and stood at the sink for a moment. In the garden everything was monochrome, the moonlight incandescent. All of a sudden she wanted to be out there, to get some fresh air and to look up at the stars.

In the living room the patio door slid open and cool air wafted over her face. The scent was heavy with the smell of seaweed and salt and a hint of damp grass from the cuttings Pete had left on the lawn. She stepped outside and onto the patio. Across the Sound near the breakwater the deck lights of a large tanker glowed orange, and in the still night air Savage could hear the faint rumble of its engines. Then there was another sound, something from round the front of the house. Somebody moving on the gravel drive.

Savage shivered. She was wearing just a slip and nothing on her feet. She turned to go back inside when something glinted to the right of the door. A garden fork. She hefted the fork into her hands and held it out in front like a bayonet. That sound again. She walked across the patio and down a couple of steps to the lawn. The ground beneath her feet was wet with dew and pieces of grass stuck to her soles. She moved across the lawn and skirted a flower bed to reach the corner of the house. A narrow path led down the side past an old oil tank and a little house on stilts Pete had built for Jamie. Savage stopped at the wooden structure and stood in its shadow. The noise came again. Feet on the gravel drive. A voice whispering. One voice or two? She wasn't sure.

She edged forwards, her bare feet on the paving slabs. Now she was at the corner of the garage and could see the driveway. At the entrance to the road a figure moved and then vanished into the lane. Savage walked across the front of the garage, the gravel beneath her feet painful, like stones on a beach. She stood and waited. A minute went by and then another and then a car started some way down the lane. There was a screech of tyres and twin beams of light scythed into the sky and then faded.

Whoever the intruder was, he'd done what he wanted to do. Savage walked across the driveway. She had a hunch that the visitor had been at the front door. Sure enough, in the porch, a small package sat on the step. The cardboard box was a few inches cubed and even in the twilight Savage could read the printed label: FAO Charlotte Savage.

She reached for the package then stopped. This wasn't FedEx or Citylink, this was a personal delivery in the small hours. She left the package on the step and went back round the house, leaving the fork on the patio. Inside she retrieved a pair of latex gloves from a coat and opened the front door. The parcel didn't weigh much and she carried it in and placed it on the kitchen table. She flicked on all the lights, found her phone and took a picture. The box was unremarkable. Brown cardboard, some parcel tape, a white sticky label with her name printed in black ink.

A kitchen knife sliced through the tape and she pulled back the flaps to reveal a small square Tupperware container. On top of the container sat a slip of paper. Savage picked up the paper and read the printed message.

Next time this will be closer to home and somewhat smaller.

Was the message supposed to be a threat? If so, she didn't understand what it meant. She put down the slip and then lifted the container out of the cardboard box. She peered through the translucent sides but couldn't make out the object inside. Something the size of a large orange, but liquid in there too. Her fingers caressed the top of the box and she prised open the lid. She stared down at the dark-red object swimming in blood. For a second she had no idea what she was looking at, but then an image of Andrew Nesbit came into her head. He was standing by the side of a cadaver, holding something in his right hand. Savage closed her eyes and remembered his words.

You wouldn't think it could be so small, would you, Charlotte. Amazing, hey?

Savage opened her eyes and stepped back from the table. The lid slipped from her hand and fell to the floor. She bumped into the sink and reached out and grasped the worktop for support as the room began to spin. She gulped air and tried to pull herself together. Two steps forward and she was looking at the object again. Red and white and not much bigger than her fist.

Thor Wodan's heart.

Plymouth Herald, *January 22nd, 2010*

Body of Hayley Smith Found

The body of Hayley Smith, missing since late November, has been found on Dartmoor. According to police there are no suspicious circumstances. Detective Chief Inspector Conrad Hardin told the Herald that Hayley was found at the bottom of a ravine and it was likely she fell to her death after climbing to the top of a nearby tor. DCI Hardin wouldn't comment on reports that the body was naked. Local MP Charles Milner, whose constituency Hayley lived in, also refused to add to any speculation. "My thoughts are with the family of Hayley Smith. We should all be doing everything we can to alleviate their suffering at this difficult time."

CHAPTER
TWENTY-SIX

Thursday 4th September

The squad meeting on Thursday morning was a sober affair. Savage sat at the head of the table alongside Hardin and Davies and tried to keep awake as the DSupt gave a prolonged briefing. Since her unwelcome present the night before she'd managed barely an hour's sleep. And that had been curled on the back seat of a squad car. Within minutes of calling it in, the area around her house had been swarming with armed officers. Nesbit and Layton had arrived, Nesbit confirming the organ in the Tupperware box was indeed a human heart and very likely to belong to Thor Wodan. Layton had cordoned off the driveway and a portion of the lane and, under an array of floodlights, his team had scoured the ground inch by inch. They had found nothing.

After calling for back-up, Savage had crept upstairs and woken Pete. She had packed a few things for the children and explained the situation to him. It would be wise, she had said, if he took the kids to her parents for a few days. Pete shook his head. He had a better idea. Their yacht. A load of kit from the summer cruise was still on the boat and she was prepped and ready to go. He'd take off for a few days and work his way west to Falmouth. Anchored upriver in some deserted creek, they'd be safe. The kids would think the whole thing was an adventure. Pete, Savage knew, was happier when things were under his control and he was responsible. He'd heard her talk about police cock-ups too many times to allow anyone else to protect their children.

Hardin's speech was building to a crescendo, fist banging the table, voice booming out, face becoming redder and redder.

"We're going to catch these people and we're going to catch them soon, OK?" There was a succession of "yes, sirs" and some vigorous nodding from the younger officers. "Right. Gareth."

"I'm still trying to get the SPS class of 'eighty-nine list from Cambridge but we know Martin Hedford and Charles Milner went there." Collier stood and strode to the whiteboard. "Interestingly, according to the bio on her webpage, so did Helen Peacock. Likely as not, if Thor Wodan is to be believed, there are others who've so far not revealed themselves."

"So if you studied Social and Political Sciences at Cambridge and graduated in 'eighty-nine, you're guilty?" someone shouted out.

"No. Thor mentioned seven people, and Peacock commissioned seven Satanic crosses. We've identified potentially two of them — Peacock and Milner. We need to work on whittling it down, and find out what the connection to Anasztáz Róka is." Collier stopped, then gestured at Layton. "Speaking of which, I believe

John's got some news that might help us. Some *big* news."

"DNA." Layton stood and held up a printout. It showed the familiar barcoding pattern of a DNA sequence in three columns. He pointed to the left-hand column. "Anasztáz Róka's DNA. And in the middle, the DNA from the hair found in Hedford's flat. Identical."

"We know that," somebody said. "She had the key so she was in the flat."

"Yes." Layton scowled. "Of course. But here's the thing. Look at the third sequence. The one on the right is somewhat different. However, I can tell you there is a familial relationship between Ana and this other sequence."

"So who does it belong to, John?" Savage said.

"Well . . ." Layton scowled again, plainly annoyed at having to end his party piece so soon. "It's a father-daughter relationship. The daughter being Ana and the father being Martin Hedford."

"*What?*"

"Yes."

"Figures." Collier was on his feet and pointing at the whiteboard. "Hedford's been in Hungary and we know he lived abroad when he was younger. Ana came to this country recently. My guess is she came to see what had happened to her dad."

"But he had his own family here in the UK," Savage said. "A wife and child. Before they both died."

"So? People split up all the time. Hedford had a child over in Hungary in the Nineties and then came back to the UK and started another family."

Savage nodded. Collier's hypothesis made sense. When Hedford's wife and son in the UK both died in a run of extreme bad luck, he went back to Eastern Europe to reacquaint himself with Ana. She in turn visited the UK when contact with Hedford ceased. Maybe he'd even told her his suspicions about the Satanists.

"So what do we do?" Another voice from the back of the room. "Bring in the ones we know about?"

Collier shifted his stance and rubbed his chin. "The Peacock woman is going to get another visit today. There are, um, issues, with Milner."

"What issues, Gareth?" Savage said. "If one of the obvious actions is to bring him in for questioning then we bring him in, right?"

"It's not as simple as that." Collier appeared increasingly uneasy. "I'm not recommending questioning of Milner at this time."

"Why ever not? He's directly linked to the crimes. Have you gone out of your mind?"

"Not out of his mind," Davies said in a low voice. "Down on his fucking knees with his tongue out."

"I resent that," Collier said. "I'm only obeying orders."

"Exactly," Davies said.

"I'm overruling you, Gareth," Savage said. "We bring Milner in and we question him hard. We try to connect him with Peacock and Hedford. We break him."

"No," Hardin said abruptly. "Absolutely no way."

The room went silent, all eyes suddenly interested in the carpet or the ceiling.

Hardin coughed. "The Chief Constable says we're to steer well clear. He wants a written report from the Operation *Piquet* team ASAP. Without additional evidence, he won't sanction any kind of surveillance on Charles Milner. Understand, Charlotte?"

"No, I don't understand, sir. It's a bloody cover-up. Milner and the Chief Constable are related. Milner's daughter is married to the CC's son. There's a conflict of interest. Simon Fox can't have a say on how this investigation proceeds."

"Don't be ridiculous, woman. Now pipe down and stop being hysterical."

Savage placed both hands flat on the table, intent on pushing herself up and exploding. She began to stand when she noticed Riley sitting impassively, his face inscrutable. He made a small shake of his head. The movement was enough to bring her to her senses. This, Riley was saying, was not the time for confrontation. Savage paused, aware that everybody in the room was staring at her. Then she sat back down.

Carl Denton was pissed off. While Riley and Davies had managed to segue the pony-killing investigation into a full-blown murder inquiry, he was left doing paperwork. Along the corridor a squad meeting was taking place and just about the whole Major Crimes team was in there. Except for him.

"Sorry, son," Davies had said. "DI Maynard is back from his birdfest next week and we need to dot the Is and cross the Ts on the sheep rustling case. Wouldn't want him to think we'd been slacking."

Denton stared at his screen as yet another crime report flashed up. Two sheep missing from a field near Ashburton three months ago. Another theft they could attribute to Creasey, another crime cleared up.

And then there was Calter. Since the debacle with Creasey she'd given him the cold shoulder. All in all, moving to the Agricultural Crime Squad had been a bad idea. The move hadn't prevented Denton from thinking about her, and his heroic deeds in tracking down the pony killings hadn't impressed her. Rumour was she'd recently been on a couple of dates with a helicopter pilot who'd seen action in Afghanistan. The ACS just didn't cut it.

He pulled up the next incident. Sheep missing, Creasey responsible, case closed. Click, check, click. Click, check, click.

Denton sighed and pushed back his chair. He stood, went to the window and looked down into the car park. Creasey was a weirdo and yet it appeared as if sheep rustling was as far as his criminality went. Calter had thought the whole thing was a big joke. Denton had seen the pictures she'd taken of Creasey's little arrangement up in the wood. The snaps had done the circuit of the station in a round robin email and had made the ACS even more of a laughing stock.

A white CSI van pulled into the car park and two CSIs got out. Denton stared at the van. Then he had it. Creasey's place in the woods had been dismissed as merely an illegal sheep slaughterhouse, but what if that wasn't the case? What if DI Savage had been too hasty? Such lowly crimes didn't attract many resources.

Certainly there'd been no crime scene investigation, no CSIs, no John Layton. Aside from Calter's pictures — taken on her phone — there'd been nothing else to properly document what was there, and there'd been no wider search of the area.

Denton went back to his terminal. If Calter's pictures were the only documentary evidence then he needed to look at them again. He'd had a glance when they'd done the rounds but dismissed them. The joke had been on him and the ACS after all. In seconds he had the shots on the screen. Coming from a mobile and having been taken in low light, they were of poor quality. Nobody had enhanced them because there was no need. Creasey's case was a minor one.

Denton stared at the shot of the wooden A-frame. You could barely see anything in the darkness and Calter had focused on the crate of entrails and a pile of sheepskin. He opened a fresh copy in an image-editing program. With a few clicks he'd adjusted the contrast and light levels. The sheepskin and crate were now flared out and almost white with over-exposure, but the A-frame was much clearer. At the top right of the image, wrapped around part of the frame, was some sort of webbing. Denton zoomed in and as he did so, a smile spread across his face. He clicked the program closed, logged off from his terminal and headed downstairs.

The safety net for Riley's visit to Helen Peacock turned out to be DC Jane Calter.

"She might be able to eat you for breakfast, Darius," Calter said. "But I can tell you her charms won't have any effect on me."

Peacock had done back-to-back presenting shifts the previous day, so she had Thursday off. She lived across the river in Cornwall, on the outskirts of the village of Millbrook. Riley and Calter took the chain ferry across the Tamar. Riley never ceased to be fascinated by the journey, even though the crossing took just a few minutes. He left Calter in the car and went up top to admire the view. The chain made a clank, clank, clank, as the ferry gorged itself on the huge links and spat them out again, the chain sinking beneath the swirling waters. Other watercraft using the river risked collision by diving under the bow or else waited to pass astern. The ferry ploughed on regardless.

Back in the car, Riley drove them off the ramp and into Cornwall. They went through Torpoint and then took a succession of lanes which led them around Millbrook Bay and to the village. Peacock's place sat on the edge of the village, behind an imposing brick wall. High double gates and an entryphone system suggested somebody concerned with keeping their home life private. Riley lowered his window and reached out to press the button next to the entryphone grille, but the gates began to open before he'd a chance to speak.

"She's expecting you," Calter said. "And all too eager to let you in. So to speak."

"Very funny," Riley said. "Remember, you're here to protect me, right?"

"I can hold your hand if you like." Calter grinned. "Mind you, that's not the part of your anatomy she's interested in."

Riley wondered about censuring Calter. After all, she was the junior officer and her comments were becoming a little risqué. Instead he gunned the car forward and up the short gravel track and parked in front of the large barn conversion. Huge areas of glass reflected the sunlight and Riley squinted in the glare. They got out of the car as the front door opened, Helen Peacock standing there in a summer dress that left little to the imagination. From behind, Riley heard Calter make a meowing sound.

Riley stepped forward, said "hello" and introduced Calter. Then Helen Peacock was ushering them inside, through a plush hall and into a giant open-plan kitchen-diner.

"We'll sit outside if you don't mind," Peacock said. She indicated a set of patio doors that opened onto a terrace. Beyond, a swimming pool sparkled. "I'll get Jim to fix us some coffee, OK?"

"Jim?" Riley said.

"Yes, he's my husband." Peacock raised a hand and touched between her breasts in the deepest part of her cleavage. "Is that a problem?"

"No. Yes. I mean, we may want to discuss some things in confidence with you. It could be embarrassing — or worse. Do you understand?"

"Don't worry about Jim, I don't keep anything secret from him and he does as he's told. Now, why don't you go and sit outside while I sort out the coffees, OK?"

Riley and Calter went out onto the terrace, where a set of brick benches fitted with cushions surrounded a barbecue pit. From inside they heard Peacock shouting, her strident tones ordering her husband to bring coffee and biscuits onto the patio.

As they sat down Riley glanced at Calter.

"Looks like she knows what she wants and how to get it." Calter smiled and shrugged her shoulders. "Fair play to the woman."

"Coffees won't be long." Peacock strode out, stiletto heels clicking on the slabs. "Now, what's this about? I thought I'd given you what you wanted."

The double entendre again, Riley noted. Not exactly subtle.

"I came to give you this," Riley said, pulling out a little plastic ziploc bag, the Satanic sigil gleaming within. Returning the piece of jewellery was ostensibly the reason for their visit. "We're done with it, thank you."

"Two experienced detectives to bring back a sliver of metal?" Peacock nodded her head. "No wonder the police are strapped for resources. Wouldn't licking the back of a stamp and sticking it inside a jiffy bag have been a little easier?"

Riley glanced across at Calter. The DC was smiling, enjoying the way the woman was using her power. Shit, wasn't Calter supposed to be on the same side as him?

"I also wondered if you remembered anything more about how the item went missing. We're really trying to understand how the cross came to be on the moor."

"As I told you before, I don't remember exactly when it went missing and I've no idea how it reappeared in such a remote location."

"There's a couple of other things, Mrs Peacock." Riley decided to play their trump card. "When I spoke to you before, you denied having any knowledge of anything to do with Satanism. And yet . . ."

Riley paused. A man, somewhat younger than Helen Peacock, was coming out onto the patio bearing a tray. A cafetière, three cups and saucers, and a plate of biscuits sat atop the tray. The man, rather laughably, carried a tea towel over one arm, almost as if he was a butler.

"Ah, Jim." Peacock waved at the table. "Pour the coffees please, darling. Now, what were you saying, Darius?"

Riley stared pointedly at Jim. "Perhaps you would like to wait until we've finished our coffees. The matter is somewhat delicate. You could say confidential."

"If you'd prefer Jim wasn't here you've only to say so, but he knows everything about me. I've no secrets from him, there's no need." Peacock turned to her husband. "Jim, tell them about our relationship."

"Helen's in charge," Jim said as he busied himself passing out the cups and saucers. "I serve her. Whatever makes her happy makes me happy. She is free to do as she pleases while I must do as she says."

"See?" Peacock smiled at Riley, her hand going to her breasts again. "But I can see his presence makes you uneasy. Jim? When you've finished, please go back inside."

378

Riley swallowed. Tried to stay calm and professional. Tried as well to ignore the tingle of sexual excitement he felt. Helen Peacock was quite some woman. He could understand why her husband might be more than happy to do exactly what she wanted.

His duties completed, Jim picked up the tray, nodded at Riley and Calter, and disappeared back inside the house.

"OK. Where were we?" Peacock said.

Riley didn't feel much like skirting around the subject any more.

"You're having an affair with Professor Falk. He's an expert in Satanism and the occult. And yet you told me you knew nothing about the subject. You lied, Mrs Peacock. Lying to the police is a serious matter."

"For the record, I'm not 'Mrs Peacock'. Why on earth would I take my husband's name? As to my relationship with Graham Falk, yes, we're having an affair. I'm not ashamed of it and have made no attempt to deceive anyone or cover up our little get-togethers. Jim knows what I get up to and has no problem with it."

"I don't care what Jim knows or doesn't know," Riley said. "The point is you said you had no knowledge of Satanism."

"I thought you meant practically, you know — animal sacrifice, virgins, dancing sky-clad under the moon. Graham is an *academic*. We may have talked around the subject, but only in relation to his work, to his *theoretical* work."

"So you deny having anything to do with the events taking place on the moor?"

"You mean the death of that poor walker or the mutilation of those ponies?" Peacock shook her head, all the fun and flirtation gone from her mannerisms. "You're mad. Why on earth would I get myself mixed up in something so awful? Now, I'm sorry to cut our meeting short, but unless you've got anything constructive to add I think it's time you went."

"Ms Peacock?" Calter said, pulling out an envelope. "Just one last thing. I wonder if you might take a look at these photographs?"

"What?" Peacock snapped. She seemed taken aback, almost as if she'd forgotten Calter was present. "Sure, show me."

Calter pulled out three pictures; mugshots of Ana and Irina and one of Martin Hedford. She slid them across the tabletop and Peacock bent her head to look.

"Yes." Peacock glanced at Riley and then touched the picture of Ana. "This is the girl who was murdered at Fernworthy Reservoir. I broke the news of the discovery of her body on the lunchtime show. A most unpleasant business. I don't know the other girl."

"And the man?"

"No." Peacock shoved all three photographs back across the table. "I've never met him before in my life."

"That's all our questions," Riley said, trying to contain his excitement. "Thank you, Ms Peacock. We'll see ourselves out."

Riley rose and nodded at Calter. The DC gathered the pictures and together they walked back through the house and out to their car.

"She lied," Calter said as they got into the car. "Helen Peacock went to Cambridge. SPS class of 'eighty-nine. She was a contemporary of Martin Hedford."

"Deeper and deeper," Riley said as Calter's phone rang.

The DC answered it, listened and then hung up. She grinned across at Riley.

"That was Gareth Collier. He's sitting in Starbucks drinking a coffee while watching Graham Falk."

"So?"

"Falk's just taken a call and I think we can guess who it's from."

CHAPTER
TWENTY-SEVEN

Chubber's huffing and puffing all the way up to his little den in the big dark wood. He didn't think he'd be coming here again. Not so soon, anyway. But Antler Man insisted. Chubber's got a job to do and if he doesn't do it he's going down there.

Down where, Chubber?

Hell. That's where Chubber's going if he doesn't do exactly as Antler Man said.

Better concentrate then, Chubber. Better make sure you carry out his instructions to the letter.

Yes. Chubber can do that. Easy peasy feet are cheesy. He walks on, still huffing and puffing but happier now. Before long, he's at the pheasant pen. There's the scaffold all rigged up and there's the little corrugated iron shed. The police said everything would be dismantled, taken away. They haven't done it yet though and that's good. Chubber scans around. There's nobody here. He plunges away from the sheep shed and up towards the feed store.

At the store the roof is still bent back and the girl is still gone and Chubber wonders how he can ever put things right.

Use your initiative. That's what Antler Man said.

Yes, a bit of brain power. He goes to the shed and checks the padlocks. He unlocks them and checks inside. Nothing. That's the problem. Never mind. Chubber's got a box full of tools to do a real fine job and a clean pair of hands to work those tools.

Skilful hands?

Oh yes, very skilful. What was it with the last one? Slaughtered. Skinned. Gutted. Butchered. Twenty minutes, half an hour, max?

Not butchering sheep, Chubber. Not this time.

No, DIY. Shed repair. Making good the roof. Chubber looks up at the hole and wonders how he'll stop a bird from flying free. Then he remembers the pheasant pen. The wire mesh. He could use that. As long as the police stay away he shouldn't have a problem. What was it Antler Man said?

He said if the police turn up we'll be in a mess nobody can clear up.

That's wrong! Chubber's good at clearing up mess. He knows how to dispose of things. For instance, all those guts wibbly wobbly in the plastic crate. Take them into the wood and tip them out. Slippy sloppy down on the ground for the rats and the foxes to eat.

Is that what Antler Man wants if the police should come looking? Their guts all piled up in the plastic crate?

Yes, Chubber's pretty sure it is.

The trek in took a couple of hours. Denton parked his car in the next valley and hiked over two tors until he reached the wood. Approaching this way meant there was no chance of being spotted. In his boots and red waterproof, he was just another walker. Not that there was anybody to see him. The day had started with showers but now a more persistent rain had set in and the weather was keeping all but the hardened outdoor enthusiasts away.

He hit the track a few hundred metres from the turning circle where Creasey parked his van and headed up into the valley. He'd been going for a couple of minutes, daydreaming about Jane Calter, when a crunch of wheels on the gravel scalpings brought him back to reality. Denton turned to see a white van approaching up the track. He dived sideways into a clump of bracken and hid himself as best he could. The van drove up and went past.

Creasey!

Some way up the track the van stopped and Creasey got out. He dragged out a couple of tanalised planks and they clattered to the ground. Next came a holdall and a rusty old toolbox and a gleaming orange bucket. Brand new, Denton thought. B&Q were selling them for a quid a pop. Creasey continued to rummage in the back of the van and then hoisted the planks onto one shoulder, picked up the bucket, holdall and toolbox and kicked the doors of the van shut. He clambered up the bank at the side of the track and disappeared into the forest.

Denton pulled himself up and stood for a moment. He could hear Creasey stomping away up the path, the man's panting getting fainter as he climbed deeper into the wood. Denton pushed through the bracken and walked up the track to the van. He peered in through the rear doors. There was an old tarp and a couple of blue plastic crates.

He moved to the path, his imagination beginning to run wild. They were up there. Girls. Not just one, but several. Creasey had, quite literally, pulled the wool over their eyes. Savage, Davies, Riley — even his beloved Jane — had been completely fooled. They'd completely overlooked the webbing strap on the A-frame. Exactly the same type of webbing which had been found in Fernworthy Reservoir by Frey's divers. For a moment, Denton wondered about calling it in. Somehow the thought of entering the wood alone had taken away his earlier ideas about being a hero. On the other hand, a call would bring dozens of officers and his own contribution would be lost. And what if he was wrong? Then he'd look a bigger fool than ever.

He shook his head and followed Creasey up the path. Twenty minutes later and he came to a little turn-off. He could see Creasey disappearing to the right, trying to manage his load while ducking under low branches. Denton paused to let Creasey get a little farther ahead and then stepped off the path. Within a few minutes Creasey had reached an open area with the remains of an old pheasant pen and a corrugated iron shed. The shed must be where the girls were kept. Last time Savage and Calter had found only an old ewe. That, Denton thought, was a clever double-bluff. He edged forward, Creasey now at the shed. The planks clattered down and Creasey fumbled with the door. Seconds later the door was swinging open, Creasey disappearing inside.

Denton half-expected there to be a scream or something. Silence. He moved to the right and began to skirt the clearing, dropping to the ground when Creasey reappeared at the door. The man looked around and then plunged across the clearing, not heading back the way he'd come, but upwards, deeper into the wood. The door to the shed stood open. It could only mean there was nobody in there. Unless Creasey restrained his victims in some way . . .

What the heck was the man up to?

Denton hesitated for a moment and then ran over to the shed. He looked in, catching a waft of bad air. Sheep shit, urine, rotting straw. Denton stepped inside, his feet squelching in muck. A stack of crates leaning in one corner. Half a bale of hay. A bucket of water. No girls. He began to examine the shed. Although at first sight the building had appeared quite sound he could now see the structure was ramshackle, the wooden framing rotten. No way anyone could be kept here against their will.

Damn. His hunch had been wrong. Creasey was still up to his old tricks, but he wasn't abducting young girls. And no girls meant no impressing DC Calter. The webbing strap was a red herring.

Unless . . .

Denton came out of the shed like a shot. In the distance, Creasey sounded like a herd of elephants as he crashed through the undergrowth. Denton went after him, trailing at a distance, all the time trying to

386

figure out where Creasey was going. After a few minutes Denton saw the outline of a large building, Creasey at one end undoing a set of padlocks on a substantial door.

Denton dropped prone to the ground. This was it! The jackpot. No wonder the others had found nothing. They'd been looking in the wrong place. Creasey had fooled everyone. Everyone but clever old DC Denton.

For a few minutes he lay still. Creasey was in the building, talking to himself. Occasionally a banging floated out, followed by a stream of curses. Was there a girl in there? Was Creasey even now doing something abhorrent to her?

Before he had time to think about the implications Creasey emerged. He pulled the door shut and slid one of the bolts across, neglecting to secure any of the padlocks. Then he lumbered away down through the woodland. Denton rolled to one side and hid behind an old tree stump as Creasey stomped off. He looked at his watch. It had taken Creasey five minutes to get here from the sheep shed. If he'd gone back there for something then Denton had ten minutes to look around. He didn't need that. Just a glance in the building would tell him everything.

As the sounds of Creasey moving away faded, Denton pulled himself up. He moved fast over the ground to the entrance. Three padlocks. That said everything. You didn't use a set of heavy-duty locks for a couple of sheep. He stepped inside. The place was some kind of feed shed. Walls and floor lined with aluminium sheeting, a load of sacks scattered around.

He slipped deeper into the room, having doubts, fumbled in his pocket and pulled out a small torch. He flicked it on and swung the beam around. Plastic sacks, hessian sacks, paper sacks, corn, bird pellets. No sign of any girls. And then he saw them. Over in one corner. He darted across, bent over and picked them up. A pair of tights. Sheer black.

Denton stuffed the tights in his pocket, at the same time bringing out his phone. He moved to the doorway, aware there was no signal. Damn. Never mind, he'd try a text. Sometimes a text could get through when a call couldn't. He composed a short message and was about to send it to DS Riley when he changed his mind. This wasn't something for the Agri Squad. The girl's murder was being investigated by DI Savage and she should hear the news directly from him, not from Riley or Davies. Denton altered the recipient and pressed send.

Outside, a gloom hung under the trees. Thick cloud had rolled across the sky above, and down at ground level every shadow had turned inky black. Denton pulled the door shut and fiddled with one of the bolts, using the torch to help him see. As he slid the bolt across he heard the crack of a stick behind him, hot breath caressing his ear as powerful fingers closed around his neck.

"Chubber's here, boy. Gotta clear things up. All that mess wibbly wobbly in the plastic crate. Tip it on the ground for the foxes, see?"

Denton flailed out with the torch, the beam flashing across the door and into the darkness beyond, the light dimming, the scene fading before his eyes as if the batteries on the torch had all of a sudden failed.

Savage had moped around the station for most of the day. The dressing-down she'd been given by Hardin, not to mention its sexist overtone, had infuriated her, and she hadn't been able to think straight. It was only when Riley and Calter had returned with the new information about Helen Peacock that she'd pulled herself together.

"Peacock, ma'am," Riley said as he stood in the entrance to Savage's office. "She went to Uni with Hedford but when we showed her a snap she denied ever having met him. Then as soon as we leave she calls Falk."

"So what's Falk up to with Peacock?"

"Apart from shagging her, you mean?" Riley grinned. "He had the cheek to call it 'participant observation'."

"Nice work if you can get it."

"Been there." Riley shook his head, the grin gone. "Nearly got myself killed."

"But you're saying Falk is studying the group in some way?"

"He didn't admit anything about this particular bunch, but that's the gist I got from him. He likened it to spending time with a tribe in the Amazon jungle."

"I think you need to have another word with the Professor and point out the seriousness of the situation. If he's got any information he needs to tell us or face a possible conspiracy charge. Meanwhile, we take the Peacock evidence to Hardin and see if he's willing for us to bring her in."

"What about DSupt Hardin, ma'am?" Riley reached over and pushed the door to the office shut. "This business with Fox."

Savage smiled. "The way I see it, if Fox is using his influence to prevent an investigation into Charles Milner he's digging himself into an even deeper hole than he's already in."

"If he's exposed, if the stuff about Owen comes out too, he'll be ruined, likely go to prison also."

"Yes."

"Charlotte?" Riley stepped across the office until he stood next to Savage. He touched her arm. "That would be enough, wouldn't it?"

Savage heard a beep from her phone and, grateful not to have to answer, looked down at the screen.

"It's a message from DC Denton," she said, reading through the text. "He's found some black tights at Creasey's place in the woods. Says they could possibly be connected to our case."

Riley drove while Savage tried to call Denton. By the time they'd reached the forest half a dozen calls had gone through to voicemail.

The barrier at the end of the track stood open and they drove up until they reached the turning circle at the end. Creasey's van sat parked to one side. Savage tried to call Denton once more.

"Still nothing," Savage said. She glanced down at her phone. "But then I've only got one bar. There's probably next to no signal up there."

She gestured up to the woodland where wisps of cloud filtered through the treetops. Above the trees a thicker layer hung blanket-like, sucking the light from the day. A light rain drizzled down.

Savage found the push up from the road easier the second time around. DS Riley wasn't as fit as Calter and he seemed quite happy to take the climb at an easier pace.

"Can you imagine Davies coming up here?" Riley said. "I doubt he'd make it unless he was on a nicotine drip."

They reached the turn off the main path and edged their way along the line of trees. Savage cursed as she slipped and her foot splashed into a leat. Riley put out his hand and caught her under the arm, holding her for a second longer than he needed to.

"Thanks," Savage said. "Falling flat on my face wouldn't have done my appearance any good."

Savage glanced down at her feet. The water in the leat. Something floated on the surface, a red scum.

Riley followed her eyes. "Blood," he said.

Savage crouched to peer under the canopy of leaves. The leat, like all leats, followed the contours, weaving back and forth as it criss-crossed the line of trees. She moved forwards, aware of Riley muttering a "careful" behind her. As they reached the broken-down fence the scene was reminiscent of the last time Savage had been there. Except this time something hung from the A-frame.

"There," Savage said, dropping to her haunches. "Creasey."

"Yes," Riley crouched beside her. "And he's up to his old tricks again."

Creasey stood next to the A-frame, a small knife in his hand. He made repeated slices down the carcass, working at the skin towards the bottom, peeling it away from the meat. Savage noticed the hind legs of the animal, lengths of webbing wrapping several times around them. Much too long for a sheep. At ground level the front legs lay on the plywood board, sweeping back and forth as Creasey worked, the fingers making patterns in the blood.

"Oh fuck!" Savage said, starting to rise. "That's not a sheep he's got strung up there."

"No," Riley whispered as he pushed Savage on the shoulders. "We've got to stay down."

Part of the fence Savage was standing on twanged. Creasey stopped and turned his head, his mouth drooping open at the sight of Savage and Riley. He looked back at the carcass and stuck his knife into the centre of the corpse. Then he bent and picked up a meat cleaver from the floor, his other hand reaching for another knife, this one larger.

"Shit," Savage said.

"Argh!" Creasey yelled.

"Split," Riley said, moving to the right. "And keep your distance from him."

Savage went in the opposite direction, following the broken fence until she came to a section where the posts stood upright, the netting drooping between them. Creasey hesitated for a moment before darting round the A-frame and lurching towards her. For a man who was on the large side he moved fast, covering the ground to the fence in seconds.

"What you doin'?" Creasey said. "Checker check checking up on me was you?"

Savage stood still behind the wire. "Put the weapons down, Mr Creasey."

"Don't like no ghosts sneaky sneak sneaking up on me. This is my domain, understand? My place, my woods, my business."

"And what exactly is that business, Mr Creasey? Bringing young girls up here and dismembering them?"

"You're wrong there, lady. I never membered any girls. But I might make an exception for you. You're older than I like 'em usually but you're still cute."

"That's not a sheep you've got hanging there, Mr Creasey." In the corner of her eye Savage saw Riley pick up a fence post and move away to circle Creasey. She tried not to look. "Who is it?"

"Never you mind, it's you I want now. Chubber's made a big, big mistake, but he'll soon put that right." Creasey moved a couple of steps forwards and poked the wire netting with the cleaver. He seemed to have forgotten all about Riley. "If you'll only stand still a moment."

Riley was behind Creasey now. He braced his feet apart and then swung the fence post. The wood smashed into Creasey's head and the man buckled and fell over. He lay on the ground, comatose.

"Bloody hell, Darius," Savage said. "Did you have to hit him so hard? I think you might have killed him."

393

"Wouldn't be the first time." Riley chucked the fence post away and knelt beside Creasey. He put his fingers to his neck. "No, he's still alive."

Riley moved Creasey into the recovery position. Then he gestured over to the A-frame.

Savage skirted the fence and walked over to the wooden contraption, standing alongside Riley as he looked at the body hanging down.

Close up, it was recognisable as human. Creasey had cut the skin away and rolled the layer down all the way to the chest. Muscle and fat remained. Human the corpse might have been, but Savage was unsure of the sex. She peered down to where the skin lay in folds, looking for the head. She found the back of it. Muzzy brown hair, short. A man's style.

Riley stepped round the frame to approach from the other side. He bent to look at the face.

"Oh fuck," he said, shaking his head and then putting his hand to his mouth. "Don't come round here, ma'am. No need for you to see this."

"Don't be stupid." Savage edged past the corpse and stood next to Riley. She crouched down and peered under the roll of skin. Mud smeared the forehead and one eye bulged out, a mess of bruised skin and blood. The nose was bruised too, bent to one side. The mouth wore a thin grimace, one lip curled back and trapped beneath a front tooth. But it was the scar which caused Savage to gasp. A scar, long-healed, sitting on the left cheek. The scar, she knew, had been caused by a man armed with a cutthroat razor. If it hadn't have been for Savage's quick thinking back then the officer would have bled to death. Her heart began to thump. She knew this man, knew him well. Riley had been right. She hadn't needed to see this.

"Oh no," Savage said. "Denton."

Calter was in a bar in town when the call came through on Thursday evening.

"Have you been drinking?" the desk sergeant asked. "Because if not you need to come in. Now."

"No, not a drop," she said. She'd been planning to go on a long training run the next day so she'd been on orange juice. "What's this about?"

"Thing is," the sergeant said, "if I tell you you'll want a drink so just get in here, OK?"

Half an hour later and Calter was hearing the news about DC Denton along with the rest of the team. A palpable anger and frustration rose in the room, everybody wanting to get on with something, to bash heads, to bring people in. Only there was nobody to bring in. Adam Creasey was in custody and would be questioned in the morning. Not much more to do other than blitz Creasey's place.

Calter volunteered. She'd been there before so it was only right she should be in on the job, wasn't it?

Collier agreed and Calter accompanied Layton and his team over to Glenmore Avenue. It was after eleven before they got started and Layton reckoned the job would take all night.

A couple of hours into the search, Calter helping to fingertip the backyard, there was a knock at the gate. An old woman from three doors up. A Mrs Grately.

The woman was wearing a dressing gown and little else. She'd seen all the activity and wondered what was going on. Creasey was often up late, she said, but he didn't have many visitors. Calter stood at the gate, not allowing Mrs Grately in.

"Lovely man, he is," the woman said. "Always helping people. He never minds if I don't have quite enough money for the meat."

Calter nodded, willing the woman to bugger off so she could get on with the search.

"What's this about? Adam's not in any trouble, is he? If he is I should watch it. Adam's got friends in high places, don't you know? That MP chappie. The one who goes fox hunting."

"What?" Calter opened the gate a little. "Charles Milner?"

"That's him. He was round here just last week with his big car." Mrs Grately lowered her voice. "An assignation with a young girl. Black hair, a pale-looking thing. I don't like to gossip, but he's married, you know? Mind you, she wasn't much of a laugh, she was only half-awake. Or drunk. Shocking what these young lasses get up to. In my day it was half a lager and lime."

"Sorry? Could you repeat that?"

"Lager and lime, love. You must have had it?"

"You said the girl was only half-awake?" Calter shook her head. The general public's capacity for stupidity never failed to amaze her and she feared Mrs Grately was up there with the worst of them. "Was she conscious or not?"

"Not." The woman gave a coy little smile. "She was out for the count. Eyes closed and everything. In fact she was so far gone Adam and Charles had to carry the poor girl to the car."

CHAPTER
TWENTY-EIGHT

Friday 5th September

Fox's morning had been taken up with firefighting. When a police officer died on duty whispers about funding became roars. At a press conference conducted at force HQ the questions from the media came thick and fast.

DC Denton had been single-crewed, was that down to lack of resources?

No it fucking wasn't, Fox wanted to scream, it was because he'd gone AWOL and disobeyed orders.

Four murders in not much more than a week. Was that acceptable?

Did he need to consider his position?

How many more killings before he would resign?

By the end of the conference Fox was in near-despair. His PR adviser wanted to brief him on some new developments, but Fox pushed the man away and headed for some fresh air. Outside, towering clouds built in the sky. Pillars of cotton wool piling on top of each other, turning blacker and blacker.

To one side of the HQ building there was an area of grass, a few trees clustered together. Fox walked round to the trees and hid within them. Beneath their leaves the sky couldn't see him. Nobody could know what he'd done.

His phone vibrated in his pocket. He pulled it out and shrank when he saw who it was. Christ!

The voice on the end of the line was curt and to the point. They needed to meet. The Three Crowns, Chagford. Within the hour.

"Yes," Fox said and hung up.

He moved over and leaned against a tree. He risked a glance upwards. The sky. Poking through. Watching him. Oh God!

"Sir?" A uniformed officer ducked under a tree branch, invading Fox's little haven. The young man cocked his head on one side. "Are you OK, sir?"

"Yes," Fox said. "I'm perfectly fine."

Then he ran for the car park.

Had a bad night, did Chubber. Hard bed and cold room. Bit of a headache. Some doctor came to take a look. Said Chubber would be OK. Don't feel OK though. But the pain in the side of his head is the least of his worries.

Trouble, Chubber, trouble.

Chubber knows it. All down to that night on the moor. Antler Man. Now the police want to know what he's been up to and they're not interested in sheep any longer. He's sitting in another cold room. Bare. Some old dear beside him. An appropriate adult. She's just about the least appropriate adult he can think of. A girl would be nicer. On the other side of the table there's two more adults. Police. One man, one woman. Black and red. Chubber doesn't like the look of the red one. Cold.

Chilly.

Yes, that's it. Not that the black guy is any friendlier.

Black guy?

Yes. This one has black skin. The woman has red hair. They're not too pleased about what he did to the other policeman. The one up in the wood. He's tried to explain to them that the whole thing was a misunderstanding, that he got confused, but without telling them about Antler Man's instructions he hasn't got very far. And he daren't mention Antler Man.

No, Chubber. He wouldn't like that at all.

Chubber stares at the black man. Black men, he thinks, must be like black sheep. He remembers he's skinned black sheep before. Makes no difference. Underneath, they're identical. Black or white, you chop them up the same way, you get the same cuts, and the meat tastes the same. Police officers can't be much different.

The silence hangs in the air. Neither officer has said anything for the past five minutes. Before, there had been questions. Like *Mastermind*, only harder.

"Why did you take the girl, Mr Creasey?" The black man. For some reason he's decided to speak again. Chubber would have preferred if he hadn't. "We know she visited your place and we've found her tights in your feed store up in the wood."

Chubber shakes his head. Girls mean trouble. Best to keep quiet about them.

"Look." The redhead leans forward. Her lips part. The woman doesn't really smile, but Chubber thinks her expression is as close to one as he's going to get. Considering. "You've killed a police officer. It can't get any worse for you, but if you tell us what you know about Ana and Irina we can see you get the kind of help you need. Do you understand?"

Chubber doesn't understand. All he's ever tried to do is to be happy. To make others happy. The little old ladies he gave meat to. The girls he left money for. Didn't those acts of kindness mean he was entitled to some happiness himself?

"The girl." The black man again. He doesn't look like he's ever been happy. The two words come out sounding like an ultimatum. "You need to tell us."

Tell them something, Chubber, anything.

"I didn't kill anybody," Chubber says. He knows that's not strictly correct so he tries again, hoping the truth will win them over. "I didn't kill any girls."

"You killed Detective Constable Denton and then strung him up by the ankles and skinned him. No one else was there, Mr Creasey. This was as cold-blooded a killing as can be imagined. Brutal, premeditated."

"It wasn't me, it was . . . it was . . ."

Chubber! No!

"Antler Man." Chubber blurts out the words without thinking and then realises what he's done. He feels something constricting his throat, almost as if an invisible hand is grasping his neck. "He told me to. He told me to clear up the mess. It was . . . the . . . devil's . . . work . . . I . . ."

Chubber can feel a cold sweat rising. He raises a hand to his forehead and wipes moisture away. Memories of Antler Man begin to return. The horns, the skull with the black eye sockets, most of all, the grating demoniacal voice.

Chubber! Chubber! Chubber!

"No!" Chubber stands. Pushes the chair back. Feels his legs buckle beneath him. Gives in and slumps down again. "I can't. He'll kill me. Antler Man's coming! I tell you, he's coming!"

The woman next to him seems concerned. She reaches across and touches him on the arm.

"Adam, it will —"

"Calm down, Mr Creasey," the redhead says, waving the woman's attention away. "Tell me who this Antler Man is."

Don't, Chubber, don't!

"I can't. I mustn't. He'll know. He'll bury me in the ground. He'll send me to h . . . h . . . hell!"

Chubber's shaking now, gripping the arms on the chair, the whole thing jumping up and down. Tippling, toppling, crashing over. Chubber's on the floor. Face-down on the rough carpet tiles. Antler Man has his heart, hands squeezing. Chubber can hear voices shouting. The redhead, the black guy, the old dear and now others, the room filling with people, hundreds of people, cramming in so tight he can't breathe.

"The devil," he hears himself say, froth bubbling from his mouth. "He's taking me to hhhheeeelllllll!"

And then the blackness.

The Three Crowns in Chagford was an upmarket gastro pub. Not the sort of place where a local could sip a pint of bitter and make it last an hour or two. Fox found Milner in the glazed courtyard, big fat raindrops from the darkening sky just beginning to splatter down on the glass. He was seated at a table over in a corner, his eyes focused on the puddles forming outside. Fox approached the table and gave a polite cough.

"Simon." Milner turned his head but didn't rise, didn't offer his hand. Instead, he nodded at the chair opposite him. "Take a seat. I've ordered for you."

Fox took off his coat, pulled out the chair and sat down. He wasn't used to kowtowing to anyone and didn't like Milner's attitude.

"What the hell were you thinking, Charles?" Fox said. "You can't get away with murder. How are you going to deal with Savage when you're under suspicion? I've tried to stall the investigation but there's only so much I can do."

"Anasztáz Róka's death was unfortunate, I admit. I forced her to take a load of Nembutal and then intended to dump her in the reservoir. She had other ideas. It was all I could do to throw her out and prevent her from crashing the plane. If she'd landed in the water the police would have thought the death was a drug-related drowning. End of story. Case closed."

"And that would have been OK?"

"People die all the time, Simon. Accidents happen. As you well know."

"Don't play games with me. What about the guy on the moor buried alive in the kistvaen? The other girl who's gone missing? The bookshop owner? I've had DSupt Hardin on the phone asking how to proceed. I had to stall him, say I want all the evidence presented to me before any action is taken."

"There isn't any evidence, Simon." Milner shook his head. "None. I suggest you calm down and listen to what I've got to say."

"Listen to . . ." Fox paused. Milner had leaned forward, hands flat on the table as if he was issuing some kind of ultimatum. "Why the hell should I listen to you?"

Milner's voice dropped to a whisper. "Because if you don't, you'll never see Owen alive again."

"*What?*" Fox leaned in too, unsure if he'd heard Milner correctly. "Owen? What's this got to do with Owen?"

"You said that I was to stop at nothing, remember? You said you'd pay whatever it took to get Savage off your back. Too late to chicken out now."

"Chicken out?"

"They've got Owen."

"W — What? Who?" Fox stumbled on his words, not sure of the implication in Milner's voice.

"I thought you knew, Simon? The Satanists have got him. Didn't you get my message?"

Fox was already struggling with his phone, switching it back on again. Within seconds it vibrated and beeped. Fox's hand shook as he looked down at the screen.

"The Satanists? Why?" Fox felt sick. A waft of food odour drifted across from a nearby table. He glanced over. A woman bent to a plate of rare beef, blood oozing from the meat. No, not meat, brains. The white plate wasn't a plate at all, it was a child's skull cracked open in a car crash. The bone gleamed, the woman forked the brains into her mouth and Fox retched. He swallowed back vomit and closed his eyes.

"Simon?" Milner's voice was soft and silky.

Fox blinked his eyes open and stared at Milner. "Are you sure?"

"Yes, Simon. Of course." Milner reached out across the table and patted Fox on the arm. "I'm sorry."

"I must call this in."

"No, not yet. They've made demands. If we're to save the day we need to do exactly as they say, OK?"

"Save the day?"

"Yes. Save Owen."

Fox nodded and then pushed back his chair and stood up. The chair toppled over and other diners looked across at him as he moved away from the table.

"I need air, Charles. I feel sick." Fox turned and staggered from the room, aware Milner was following. The MP stopped to pay the bill, but Fox didn't wait. He headed outside and surged along the street, back towards his car. Rain splashed down around him. He'd left his coat in the pub and within seconds his shirt was sodden. He reached his car, opened the door and slumped in.

"They want Savage." Milner stood by the open door, preventing Fox from closing it. Somehow he'd got there only seconds after Fox. "Bring her to them and they'll release Owen."

"How do you know all this, Charles?" Fox turned sideways. Milner's eyes had widened and his face twitched with excitement. "God, you're —"

"Here's the chance you wanted. Bring us Savage and we'll take care of her. Owen's waiting for you."

"I . . ." Fox faced forward again, staring into the Jaguar's dashboard, for a moment memories of his grandfather flooding his senses. He felt Milner's hand on his shoulder.

"Simon." Fox turned and saw Milner had something in his hand, something wrapped in a small towel. "You'll need this."

Milner pushed the bundle forward and Fox took the towel, feeling the weight of something heavy inside. He nodded blindly and pulled the door shut. He put the package on the passenger seat and started the engine, aware that the towelling had slipped away from the object to reveal the dull grey of gunmetal.

CHAPTER
TWENTY-NINE

PC Ian Narry sat in his car in the driveway to DI Savage's house. Narry yawned. In the last month he'd switched from nights to days and then back again to nights. The change was playing havoc with his circadian rhythms and staying awake tonight was going to be tough.

Narry glanced around. DI Savage had come back a short while earlier. She'd had a brief word with him and then disappeared inside. No offer of a tea or a beer or snack. Luckily Narry had brought along a good supply of nibbles. He'd also brought a magazine. He looked around to check nobody was watching and then reached down under his seat and pulled the mag out. Not exactly allowable reading material at work, but it would keep him awake.

He thumbed through, looking at the photo-sets, lingering over each picture. Lovely. Especially the bird with the double-Ds. In these days of laptops and tablets and mobiles it was good to know you could still buy a good old-fashioned porn mag. Mind you, with his new work partner — a young female probationer — he wasn't going to be able to keep bringing the mags to work. She'd likely go ballistic.

"Sara. No H," she'd said, when they'd been introduced last week.

No H, maybe, Narry had thought at the time, but quite a lot else to be thankful for.

He put the magazine on the passenger seat and leant back. Sara — no H — had a body not unlike the centrefold in the mag. A pair of double-Ds, with a matching set of hips. A real cracker. Pity she wasn't with him tonight.

Narry saw a light go on in the house. The woman. Savage. He shook his head, wondering why he was here. DI Charlotte-fucking-Savage was well known as being able to take care of herself. According to rumour more than one perp had died at her hands. Why the hell did she need to be babysat? The guy who'd killed Denton was in custody after all, locked in some mental ward at the hospital. The bloody nutter was an animal. He'd skinned young Denton alive. It really was about time they brought back hanging.

"Constable?"

Narry jumped. Somebody had banged on the roof of the car. He turned, his mouth dropping open when he saw who was standing by the open window.

"Nice." The man pointed down at the porn mag. "But I have to remind you such material could cause serious offence to female officers. I'd keep it hidden from DI Savage."

"Yes, sir." Narry gulped. He grabbed the magazine and shoved it beneath the seat.

"Anyway, I'm here to tell you you're relieved. The danger has passed and Savage no longer requires protection."

"Really, sir?"

"Yes, but before you return to the station and report back I've got a job for you. I'd like you to go down into Plymstock and grab me a couple of curries from the takeaway. Something medium. Chicken or lamb." The man produced two ten-pound notes. "This should do."

"Yes, sir." Narry took the money.

"In fact, make that three curries." Another ten-pound note appeared at the window. "Get one for yourself, you deserve it."

"Thank you, sir," Narry said, reaching for the key and starting the car. "Of course, sir. Right away."

Savage stood in the garden. To the west a soft pink hue enveloped the low hills of Cornwall. If the old "red sky at night" saying was to be believed, the sky forecast that the thunderstorms and rain of the day wouldn't be repeated tomorrow. The breeze from earlier had died, and now there was but the merest whisper of wind. Still, the air was cooling fast and after a few minutes Savage went inside and closed the patio doors.

In the kitchen her mobile beeped. She picked the phone up and read the text message.

Anchored in the Helford River. Beautiful evening. Kids knackered and already asleep. Beer open. Miss you. Love, Pete.

Pete had texted her the night before from Fowey, but now he'd made it all the way to Falmouth. She wished she was on the boat with her family, being lulled to sleep by the gentle rocking of the ocean. Instead she

409

was here alone. Apart, that was, from her protection officer.

The day had been long and frustrating. Adam Creasey, far from being a distraction for the *Piquet* team, was now occupying a major part of it. The pair of tights found in his shed almost certainly belonged to Ana or Irina and DC Calter had found a witness who said she'd seen Charles Milner outside Creasey's house with Irina. A second interview had led to the woman admitting Irina had probably been forced into Milner's car against her will. To add to the team's problems Creasey was now out of bounds, having been taken ill. When Savage had broken the news to Hardin about Creasey's seizure, the term "duty of care" had come up once again. Savage had given Hardin a detailed description of DC Denton hanging from the scaffold in the wood, told him to stuff his "duty of care", and stormed out.

Savage composed a short reply to Pete and then went to the freezer and pulled out a frozen lasagne. She'd promised DC Calter she'd come out with her on a run some time, but healthy could begin tomorrow. The ready meal went in the oven and a glass of wine came from a bottle in the fridge. She went to the living room and flicked the television on, more in hope than in expectation of finding anything decent to watch.

A few minutes later she jerked awake and blinked. She must've fallen asleep. Somewhere outside she heard a car in the lane followed by a beeping from the kitchen. Not the phone this time, the oven.

She got up from the sofa and went into the kitchen. The oven had turned itself off, a little light flashing in time with the rhythmic beep. Savage pressed the button to silence the noise and then reached for an oven glove. Out came the tray with the chips and lasagne. She placed the tray on a mat and then went to a cupboard for a plate. As she opened the cupboard, from the corner of her eye she noticed the kitchen door swing in the breeze. She'd forgotten to latch it properly when she came in from the garden. She moved across to the door and then stopped. She hadn't come in through the kitchen. She'd been on the patio and had returned to the house by the living room. Her eyes flicked down to the floor, where a lump of fresh grass cuttings had been brought in.

Outside, the orange glow of sunset had gone and the garden stood painted in black and white. Black from dark shadows. White where the glare of a security light shone on the grass. Something had triggered the light. A cat or a badger? Possible, but neither animal could have opened the door.

Savage drew in a breath and held it for a moment. Then she exhaled and moved across the kitchen to the hallway. Was that a creak from upstairs, somebody on the landing, or just the house cooling as night fell?

She slid the soles of her feet across the wood flooring. At the foot of the stairs she peered upward into the darkness. Nothing.

Savage sighed and shook her head, feeling foolish. All this talk of the occult had spooked her. She needed a little of Collier's scepticism. She turned, and as she did so the lights went out in the hallway, and in the living room and kitchen too.

She froze. For a moment it was pitch black, but within seconds she could discern the outline of the door to the kitchen. Somebody — *something* — stood silhouetted against the faint grey light from the garden. Whoever — whatever — it was, filled the doorway. Savage spun and made for the stairs. Behind her there was a grunt and the figure moved after her. She raced up the stairs, turned left and ran along the landing to the second set of stairs which led to the attic rooms where the children slept. These were steeper and she slipped up them, trying to move as silently as possible.

At the top she stood and looked down. The clump of feet sounded heavily on the first set of stairs. Somebody breathing hard. Now the feet dragged across the wooden floor of the landing. Savage stepped back from the stairs. Behind her was a skylight. Anyone looking up would see her against the night sky. She moved away and into Samantha's bedroom. Over on the far side of the room she saw a dim white light flash on and off. The notification alert on Samantha's mobile. Pete had mentioned that in the rush to get away her daughter had left the phone behind. He'd joked she was having with-drawal symptoms. Savage stepped over, pocketed the phone, and then moved to the large Velux window which was set into the sloping roof. She clicked the catch and swung the window open, a wave of cool night air washing over her.

From the floor below she heard an exclamation and the sound of somebody clomping up to the attic. For a moment she hesitated. The pitch of the roof was shallow, but the ground was a long way below. She turned. A man stood in the doorway, clad in black, eyes staring at her through the holes in a ski mask.

Savage dived for the window, sliding out and onto the roof. She rolled over and scrabbled for purchase. But the roof was mossy, damp from the evening dew, and she slipped down towards the edge. Her feet hit the guttering and for a moment she thought it would stop her. Then there was a cracking as the guttering split and fell away from the roof. She tumbled over the edge.

Freefall.

And then she stopped.

Savage came round to blackness and the smell of petrol. For one horrid moment she feared the worst, thinking she might have been hooded and doused in fuel, but then she moved and her head knocked against something plastic, liquid sloshing inside. A moment later and she was aware of engine noise and a rocking sensation. She moved again, finding herself confined in some sort of box-like space.

Not a box, a car boot.

She tried to turn herself over, then realised her hands were bound together in front of her. She pulled hard, feeling the sharp edge of a cable tie digging into her wrists. Whoever had abducted her was taking no chances. The engine noise changed tone and she felt herself being pushed backwards by the car's acceleration, so she let her body relax and slump down.

Savage took a deep breath and tried not to panic. She moved again and felt something pressing into the top of her thigh. Something hard and flat. Samantha's phone! With her hands tied together it was difficult to reach her pocket but she swivelled and managed to get a finger and thumb onto the top of the phone. She pinched and pulled the phone out. As she did so the car braked hard and she was thrown forward, the phone falling from her grasp and tumbling out of reach. She turned over again and scrabbled in the dark but the phone had gone, slipping down beneath a panel to one side of the boot.

Shit!

Savage cursed and then began to move her hands around again. The phone was out of reach but she came across a steel bar. She ran her fingers along the object, realising the cold steel was a wheel brace. She inserted one end between her wrists and using her thumbs applied leverage to the bar, hoping to break the cable tie. The tie cut into her wrists, but the force she could apply with her thumbs wasn't enough. Lying on her side she drew her legs up to her wrists and clamped the bar with her knees. Then she straightened her legs. Pain seared her wrists as the tie sliced into her skin. She twisted again and jerked hard. The tie snapped.

She clenched her fists and resisted the urge to scream as her entire nerve system convulsed. Then she gulped some air and turned around. There was no time for crying or self-pity. She located the bar again and stuffed it into the back of her jeans, pulling her blouse over the top to try to conceal it. Then she picked up the cable tie and looped it round her wrists. Even though it was broken it would, at least for a few seconds, give the illusion of being in one piece.

The car lurched to one side and then braked hard once more. Then they were off-road and bouncing across rough ground, Savage airborne for a moment as the suspension bottomed out and sprang back. The brakes came on again and the car slewed to a stop.

For a moment, there was only silence. Then the sound of a door opening and staying open, somebody moving outside, a click as the boot lid was sprung and a creak as it opened. A torch flashed in, the glare straight in Savage's eyes.

"Charlotte," the voice said, the authoritative tone familiar. "Sorry it has to end this way. I always thought you were an outstanding officer. You will be a great loss to the Force."

Simon Fox stepped away from the car, the glow from the taillights casting a red glow on his features. In one hand he held the torch, in the other, an automatic pistol.

"Simon," Savage said, easing herself into an upright position. "This has to stop now before it goes too far."

"Stop?" Fox put his head on one side. "You're the one who's taken things too far. What happened to your daughter was a bloody accident. Anything else was my fault, nothing to do with Owen. You should have come after me." Fox moved back a couple of paces and waved the gun at her. "Now get out of the boot."

"What's the point of this?" Savage wriggled to the edge of the boot and swung her legs round. She kept her hands tight together, hoping the cable tie wouldn't slip off. "What can you possibly hope to achieve by kidnapping me?"

Fox shook his head. "You don't get it, do you? Milner has Owen. He wants a trade. Owen's life for yours."

Savage finished climbing out of the boot. Night had fallen now and the car sat in a circle of red and white light, the headlights burning a shining path through heather and small boulders, the taillights illuminating a smaller circle with Fox at its edge. He muttered something to himself and laughed again, shaking his head and repeating the same whispered words over and over. Savage realised he was in another place, far away. He'd completely lost it.

"Sir," Savage said, lowering her voice and trying to sound calm. "We can work this out. You need help."

"Oh, very nice." Fox sobered up. "The 'sir' bit. But I'm afraid it's a little late for rules and regulations and doing things by the fucking book. Now start walking."

Fox gestured with the torch, the beam picking out a sheep track edging into the heather. Savage paused but Fox glared at her and raised the gun.

"Where are we going?" Savage said as she started across towards the track.

"Forensics," Fox said from behind her. "There'll be a lot of blood."

"Your car, sir. There'll be hairs, other evidence."

"I'll clean up. I've got a garage. Tools. I like to shut myself away in there. Just me and her. That car is my pride and joy. The thing I love the most. After my family, of course."

Jesus, Savage thought. Fox really had gone crazy.

"Families are important," Savage said, aware her only chance was to keep Fox talking. "I know mine is to me. That's why I've never given up in my hunt for the driver who killed Clarissa. Don't get me wrong, over the years I've dreamed of what I would do to him, but after confronting Owen that's gone now."

"I know you, Savage. You wouldn't set something like this aside, you're not the type of person to forgive or forget. Which means I simply don't believe you."

"Whether you believe me or not, it's the truth. I —"

"Shut up!" Fox shouted from behind and Savage felt a push in her back. "You went to visit Owen, along with a certain well-known Plymouth criminal. Now why would you need Kenny Fallon along on your visit to see Owen? Only one reason. To provide the muscle in case you couldn't hack it on your own. And you couldn't, could you? Owen managed to get away before you could kill him."

"Kenny Fallon helped me track down Owen. He gave information to DS Riley about the panel shop that repaired Owen's Impreza. That's all." Savage kept walking, knowing Fox wouldn't want to go much farther. He'd have to carry her body back to the car. "We visited Owen and he pleaded with me and in the end I couldn't bring myself to hurt him."

"Bollocks. You hit him. You would have done more if you hadn't been interrupted."

"Owen wasn't driving the car." Savage stopped and turned. Now was the time. "He told me it was Lauren, sir. Lauren was the one who killed Clarissa."

"Hey?" Fox stood a couple of paces away, the gun and torch pointing at Savage.

"Your son took the rap for Lauren. He may have been an errant youth at the time but you must have taught him something."

"Owen . . ." Fox stood open-mouthed. "All this time . . ."

"You've been covering up for Milner. I bet he knew. Lauren would have told him."

"So you know he's Owen's father-in-law?" Fox's hand wavered and he began to lower it, the gun now pointing down at Savage's feet. "You're saying Charles knew all along?"

"I can help you, Simon," Savage said carefully. "Help you rescue Owen."

"I . . ." Fox's arm swung down, the gun loose in his hand. He turned his head and stared back in the direction of the car.

Savage slipped the cable tie from her hands and reached behind her for the wheel brace.

"No. I can't risk it." The gun came up, Fox adopting a shooter's stance, arm locked, finger squeezing the trigger.

But Savage had already lunged forward, bringing the wheel brace around from behind her in a wide arc. The brace smashed into Fox's forearm, causing him to spin

418

and fall to the ground. Savage darted away into the darkness, running ten metres and then changing direction. She ran for a few seconds and then dropped to the ground. Fox was climbing to his feet, waving his torch in all directions. The other hand held the gun.

"Savage!" Fox yelled out as he whirled around. "Savage!"

Fox stumbled this way and that for a moment and then set off at a jog, continuing along the sheep track and moving away from her.

Savage wondered about returning to Fox's car. Could he have left his keys there? Could she manage to find her daughter's phone? In the darkness she could see the light from Fox's torch swathing around, hear him still shouting her name. No, it was best she put as much distance between the CC and herself. Savage looked to the sky, where a few stars twinkled through a thin blanket of cloud. She picked the brightest one and began to walk towards it.

A pale tinge began to eat away at the black night, and before long a near full moon appeared from behind dark clouds. East, Savage thought. For the previous hour she'd stumbled around, trying to head in a straight line in the darkness, pretty sure from the occasional glimpse of the stars she was walking south. The moon confirmed it. As her eyes had got used to the night the landscape of the moor had revealed itself. Clumps of heather and boulders, the jagged horizon of nearby tors, an orange glow far off. The glow might have been Plymouth, but she wasn't sure.

After another thirty minutes she recognised the distinctive outline of the city, the lights stopping abruptly as they met the water of the Sound. Nearer and off to her left was a lesser glow. Ivybridge, a small town a few miles from Plymouth, she guessed. She came to a wide track and followed it off the moor, coming to the outskirts of the town a while later. A phone box stood at a junction of two roads. Savage went inside and dialled 101. She told the operator who she was and asked for her call to be transferred.

Half an hour later Riley's car appeared. He parked beside the phone box and got out.

"What's going on, ma'am?" Riley said. "Something about the Chief Constable, is that right?"

"You don't want to know, Darius."

"Where is he?"

"He's up on the moor somewhere."

"You've killed him?"

"No. It was the other way around, actually. He came to my house and attacked me. He took me up on the moor and was going to kill me."

"Bloody hell." Riley shook his head. "He knows we're on to him then?"

"Yes, but that's not the reason he tried to kill me. Milner and the Satanists have taken Owen. They're using him as a hostage. Fox was to bring me to them in exchange for Owen."

"Dead?"

"I'm not sure, but if Fox had killed me then they'd have had something over him. They could've persuaded him to cover everything up."

"It wouldn't have worked."

"Of course not." Savage sighed. "But they're deluded, beyond reason."

"I don't suppose he told you where he was supposed to meet them?"

"No, but I reckon Falk might know."

"Falk." Riley looked downhearted. "I've been thinking, ma'am. Thor Wodan. I might well have inadvertently tipped off the Satanists. You see, I told Falk that we had found a connection between Hedford and Avalon Books. He must've put two and two together. I don't think there was an informer. Falk told the group and they acted on the information."

"Shit." Savage thought of Wodan's heart sitting in the Tupperware box swimming in blood. She didn't know what to say. She tapped Riley on the shoulder and gestured at the car. "Come on, I've spoken to Collier and he's calling in as many bodies as he can. We'll get to the station, run a briefing and see if anybody's managed to find Falk."

"And Fox?" Riley got in and started the car. Looked across at Savage. "He tried to kill you, shouldn't we bring him in?"

"We've got to find him first. And my hunch is he'll be with Milner. Now, I'll work the phone on the way in, you concentrate on driving, OK?"

Riley grinned, floored the accelerator and the car lurched forward.

"Yes, ma'am," he said.

CHAPTER
THIRTY

By the time Savage and Riley got to the station most of the regulars had arrived, summoned from parties, nightclubs or their beds.

"The DSupt told me to pull out all the stops," Collier said as Savage came into the crime suite. "He's headed up to the moor with the mobile incident room vehicle. Hard to credit what he told me is true."

"It is, I'm afraid," Savage said. "The Satanists have got Owen Fox."

"Action points?" Collier had his ubiquitous black marker pen in his hand and he moved to the whiteboard, the pen poised.

"We need to research possible sites where they may have taken Owen. We also need to track down and arrest Professor Falk, Helen Peacock and Charles Milner."

"Falk?"

"He's either one of the group or complicit. Darius reckons he tipped them off about Thor Wodan."

"Right. Any ideas on those sites?" Collier scribbled on the board and then pointed at the map of Dartmoor. A thick red line ran diagonally across the map. St Michael's Ley. Collier's finger traced the line. "Somewhere along there?"

"Fuck knows." Savage looked across to the far side of the room to where Layton stood briefing a group of CSIs. "John?"

Layton nodded and a minute later he came over. "No sign of Falk at his place. I'm preparing to go over there and take the place apart."

"Those ley lines you were on about," Savage said, pointing at the map. "Is it as simple as looking at points of interest on the lines?"

Layton shook his head. There were spurs, he said. Offshoots, branch lines, diverging and converging paths. The Satanists would want somewhere meaningful, but the site didn't have to be on a ley, nor did it have to be on Dartmoor. In fact the ceremony could take place just about anywhere.

Ceremony? Savage wanted to know more.

"You said they've threatened to kill Owen Fox, right? Well, they won't just slot him. There'll be ritual and theatre. We're talking about a sacrifice, after all."

"You think they'll do that to Owen?"

"Yes, I do." Layton shrugged an apology and returned to his team. Collier looked at Savage, expectant.

"Sorry, Gareth, you're on your own. I'm off to the moor." Savage waved at Calter and Enders to accompany her and moved towards the exit. "Try to find Falk, Peacock and the others."

"Sure." Collier's hand went to the top of his head and scratched the stubble. "One other thing, where's the Chief Constable? According to PC Narry the CC came to visit you. Is that right?"

"It's a long story," Savage said, crashing through the double doors into the corridor before Collier could enquire further.

The mobile incident room van stood in a car park on the edge of Princetown. Light spilt from the open door and as Enders pulled the car over Savage could see the bear-like figure of DSupt Hardin hunched over a laptop inside.

Savage left Calter and Enders in the car, got out and went across.

"Sir," she said as she clambered up into the vehicle. "Any luck?"

"I don't want to sound unwelcoming, Charlotte," Hardin said, pointing at the screen where a map of Dartmoor floated in a window. "But I could have done with you being John Layton. I'm here on my own and I can't make head nor tail of these maps and coordinates. I've got teams all over Dartmoor, Frey up in the chopper, and the Assistant Chief Constable is on the phone every five minutes wanting an update." Hardin paused and blew out a long breath. "This is a bloody nightmare. Where the hell is Fox? You'd think he'd be concerned for his son."

"I think he is, sir. He's gone in search of the Satanists."

"What, on his own?"

"Yes, sir. I'll explain later. Have you thought about calling in the rescue group to help?"

"Can't risk it. These Satanists are too dangerous. We've got four armed response vehicles covering the entire moor and I've also got some military bods on standby back in Plymouth. Marines. I hope it doesn't come to that."

"Can you assign us something?" Savage gestured over her shoulder to the car. Calter sat in the rear while Enders stood next to the open driver's door already kitted up in his mountain gear, a GPS unit in his hand. "I've got DC Enders and DC Calter with me."

"Enders?" Hardin looked out through the door. "Thinks he's Edmund Hillary, doesn't he?"

"Who?"

"Never mind." Hardin peered at his laptop. "Merrivale. Where Hedford was found. We've done one pass an hour ago, but it needs rechecking. I expect young Patrick will know how to get there."

"I'm sure he will," Savage said. "Good luck, sir."

Enders nodded when Savage told him where they were off to and ten minutes later they were pulling off the road, the headlights piercing the night, the grey shapes of the stone circle visible in the beams.

"No one here," Savage said. "Too easy."

"Too obvious more like, ma'am," Enders said. "Who's going to frolic stark naked this close to the road? Even in the wee small hours."

"Idiot," Calter said. "They're not frolicking naked. This isn't some New Age lovey-dovey thing. These people are murderers."

"Quiet, you two," Savage said. "Let me think."

The two DCs shut up, the only sound the engine ticking over. Savage peered through the windscreen. Beyond the headlights she could see nothing but blackness. She shivered, remembering how she had run from Fox after escaping from him.

Savage clicked open the door of the car and got out. She was missing something here. Something to do with Fox and his car. She went to the front and placed her hand on the bonnet, feeling the warmth from the engine. No, not here. She walked to the rear of the car and stared at the taillights glowing red. Remembered clambering from the boot, Fox with the gun trained on her. She shook her head. The niggle in her memory was just that, a niggle. She couldn't dig deep enough to recall what was important.

"Let's call in," she said as she returned to the car and got in. "See if the DSupt has any better suggestions."

She reached for her phone but the reassuring slab of screen and electronics wasn't there. Then she had it.

"The Chief Constable's car. I know how to find it."

"You do, ma'am?" Enders leaned over, head cocked, eyes narrowing. "How exactly?"

"Have either of you got a signal on your mobiles?"

"Yes," Calter said, her phone already in her hand. "A weak one."

"Internet?"

"Up here?" Calter stared at the screen. "It's a stretch, but you can try."

"Hand it over then." Savage took the phone, brought up a browser and entered a web address. The site slowly came up, one graphic at a time. She tapped in a

426

username and password and waited. The response seemed to be an age coming but eventually a new page displayed. She tapped once and waited again and then handed the phone back to Calter. "There. That's where Fox's car is. Call in the latitude and longitude to Hardin and get him to send Frey in the helicopter. Patrick? We'll go by car. To the west of Fernworthy. As fast as you can."

Enders rammed the car into gear and they slewed round on the grass before ripping back onto the road. Calter was on the phone to Hardin, reading the figures slowly and then repeating them.

"How did you do that, ma'am?" Calter said as she hung up. "Assuming it wasn't telepathy?"

"It's a long story but my daughter's phone is in the boot of Fox's car. You see she wanted a phone, so the deal was we'd pay the bills as long as she installed a tracker app. She gets the phone and we know where she is. It means I don't have to worry as much as I might."

"Isn't that a bit creepy? I mean keeping tabs on your —" Calter stopped halfway through her sentence. "Sorry, ma'am. I guess I understand."

"Clever," Enders said. "But what I'd like is an app that would allow me to escape from my kids. Maybe some kind of invisibility cloak?"

"You don't mean that, Patrick?" Savage said.

"You haven't met my lot, have you, ma'am?" Enders grinned, but kept his eyes focused on the slither of road winding into the darkness. "Ten minutes to Fernworthy I reckon, but we won't beat Frey in the helicopter."

"Good. Fox is armed and the Satanists may well be too. I'd prefer the lads from D Section dealt with them."

A few minutes later Enders pulled the car off the road once again. The main route into Fernworthy Forest lay up ahead but the phone tracker had indicated Fox was on the western edge somewhere.

"Looks like he's gone cross-country," Enders said, pointing through the windscreen at a stony track leading away from the road. "Shall we follow?"

"Yes." Savage wound her window down and craned her head out, searching the sky for any sign of the Air Operations helicopter. "Turn your headlights off though. Sidelights only."

Enders crawled the car forward, swerving this way and that to avoid potholes and large rocks. After half a mile or so, they came upon Fox's car. The Jaguar was on a grassy rise, long dark streaks in the grass where the wheels had ripped through to the peat.

"Don't think we'll get up there either, ma'am," Enders said as he stopped the car and pulled on the handbrake. "Do we still wait for Frey and the helicopter to turn up or do we go in on foot?"

"We go on foot. If we find the Satanists then we call in one of the armed response units."

Enders killed the engine and they got out of the car. With the lights extinguished the night seemed absolute, just a smudge of grey sky showing them where the horizon was. Savage went to the boot of the Jaguar. It was unlocked and in seconds she'd reached in and found Samantha's phone wedged down behind the rear seat. She pocketed the phone and then the three of them began to walk along the track, feeling their way at first. As their eyes became accustomed to the dark, nearby features sprang up. A large boulder, a patch of bog, a lone tree. The track followed the easiest route across the contours, but led inexorably towards Fernworthy Forest. At first the woodland loomed as a mass of blackness, but soon the individual trees began to reveal themselves, the jagged edges of the pines silhouetted against the dark sky.

Before long they'd reached the woodland. The pines stood thick, an inky blackness seeming to float beneath their foliage. Finding anything beyond the tree line was going to be near impossible.

"Ma'am, there!" Enders grabbed Savage and pushed her down. "Flames!"

Savage stared into the darkness. Enders was right. A flickering light came from deep within the forest, the black shadows momentarily banished by tendrils of golden light.

"Bloody hell," Savage said. "That must be them. Where the hell is Frey? Patrick, give Hardin a call."

"No signal, ma'am." Enders was glaring down at the screen on his phone. "Back near Princetown there wasn't a problem, but out here . . ."

Enders' words trailed off, despondency evident in his tone. Calter said nothing. Savage had to remind herself she was the senior officer, she was in charge. It was up to her to make a decision.

"We get closer. See what's going on, OK?"

Both the DCs murmured an affirmative and then the three of them began to move forward and into the woodland, Savage indicating they should crawl on their hands and knees. Beneath the trees pine needles littered the forest floor, but the surface gave way to soft soil. Before long their clothes were wet and heavy with dirt. They crawled for perhaps fifty metres until the flames were larger, great fingers reaching into a black sky. The wind was increasing, sweeping the fingers back and forth and, high above, air whooshed in the treetops.

Ahead they could see a large clearing, perhaps a hundred metres across. Huge trees circled the perimeter, their boughs painted gold by the glow from the fire, which sat to one side of a large stone in the centre. The fire was piled with branches and the wood crackled and spat as the flames grew higher. Six figures clustered around the stone, faces cowled by the hoods of the dark robes they wore. One of the figures had a headdress topped with a deer's skull, polished antlers gleaming in the firelight. In his right hand he held a wooden staff topped with gold.

"Bloody hell!" Calter said. "On the stone."

Savage stared past the group. There were two people sitting back to back on the stone, ropes binding them together. One was a man and the other, a woman.

Owen Fox and Irina Kryukov.

"To the left," Calter said. "The Chief Constable! What the heck is he doing? Doesn't he know how dangerous they are?"

He'd been partly shielded by the flames, but now Simon Fox walked into view. Some sort of conversation

430

was going on, an argument. Fox raised his fist at the man with the headdress and then shouted at another of the figures. The second figure threw his hood back.

Charles Milner.

"Where's DI Savage?" Milner bellowed at Fox. "She was part of the agreement. No Savage, no deal."

"Let Owen go, Charles," Fox said. "He's done nothing wrong."

"Wrong hasn't got anything to do with it. Quite the opposite in fact." Milner turned his head towards the man with the antlers and then gestured at Owen and Irina. "Tonight we need two souls to send to our Lord. You were to provide one of them in a trade for your son. You failed."

"Take me then. Release Owen and I'll go in his place."

"Oh no, Simon, we need you."

"If you think I'm going to help you then you're wrong."

"I am thinking. I'm thinking of your wife."

Calter prodded Savage. "Ma'am, we've got to stop this." She began to rise from her prone position but Savage reached out and pushed her down.

"No. There's only three of us. We wouldn't stand a chance, look." The man with the antlers had drawn a huge curved dagger. "Patrick, fix our position with that GPS of yours and then get back to where we last had a phone signal and call it in. Go!"

"Yes, ma'am!" Enders rolled on his back for a moment and pressed a button on his GPS. The unit beeped and then the DC was turning and scrabbling away across the ground, disappearing into the black of the woodland.

"Come on," Savage said. "We need to get closer."

"They'll see us," Calter said.

"No. The fire is so bright it will have ruined their night vision. They won't be able to see into the trees."

Within a couple of minutes they were at the edge of the clearing. A clump of bracken provided cover and they hunkered down behind the fronds. Fox was still pleading with Milner but now the man with the antlers had moved nearer to Owen and Irina. The dagger flashed orange in the light from the flames.

"Shit, ma'am. This looks like the finale. How long before Patrick gets help?"

Savage glanced back into the woodland behind them and tried to calculate the distances and time involved.

"Five minutes to run back to where he has a signal, then who knows? It just depends on how far away the nearest team is."

"It's going to be too late." Calter jerked her hand in the direction of the stone circle. "Look."

Antler Man was right next to Owen and Irina, his dagger poised.

"Whatever you do, Jane, stay hidden." Savage began to push herself to her feet.

"Ma'am, don't! I thought you said —"

"No!" Savage stood and shouted. Then she walked out into the clearing.

Milner, Fox and the others turned as one.

"Simon, look who it is," Milner said. "DI Savage. She might just have saved your son."

"Release Owen and Irina." Savage walked across to Milner. Then she turned to Fox. "Sir? If you could help me, I'd be grateful."

"Don't be stupid." Milner laughed and the light from the fire flickered over his ruddy features. "He's not going to help you. He's on our side now, aren't you Simon?"

Fox looked at Savage and then back to where the man with the antlers held a knife at Owen's throat. Then, all of a sudden, he whipped his hand behind his back and brought out his gun.

"Release Owen first," Fox shouted. "And then I'll do it."

"No!" Milner cursed and then stepped to one side so he was between Fox and Owen. "That's not how this works. If you don't kill Savage, then Owen dies. If you shoot me, Owen dies. You've no choice but to do as I say."

There was a flutter of wind in the trees and Fox momentarily glanced up. Then he turned to Savage, the gun outstretched.

"Sir," Savage said. "Even if you kill me this can't end well. Milner will probably still kill Owen and you'll be going to prison for life. Nothing will have been gained."

"Rubbish!" Milner said. "Owen will live and nobody will ever know you killed Savage. We'll get rid of it all. You'll be one of us, Simon. Privileged to walk with Him."

Fox walked a couple of paces towards Savage. "It's the only way, Charlotte. In my position you'd do the same."

Savage shivered as another chill waft of wind swept by. Leaves spiralled upwards and the branches on the trees began to sway. The flames swirled and flattened as a huge gust rushed down.

"He's coming!" The man with the antlers waved his staff and pointed the tip skyward into the night. His other hand pressed the knife harder against Owen's throat. "Lucifer honours us with his presence. He takes our offering and grows stronger and in turn we grow too!"

"But . . ." A woman's voice came from Savage's right. The woman threw back her hood. Helen Peacock.

"Listen!" Antler Man put a hand to his head in dramatic fashion. The wind roared overhead. "He's calling for souls. Kill her, kill her now."

"Go on!" Milner shouted above the wind, his voice barely audible. "Do it!"

Fox stepped nearer to Savage, the gun trained at her head. But his arm was waving madly, fighting against the wind. The flames of the fire weren't rising any more, they were being buffeted to the side, licking across the clearing. Dust spiralled into the air, curling round in a vortex like some sort of djinn.

"You've got three seconds," Milner shouted. "Kill Savage or we kill Owen."

"Please, sir. Don't!" Savage locked eyes with Fox.

"One! Two!" Milner shouted.

"Yes!" Antler Man screamed again. He moved from Owen to Irina, the knife now pointed at her heart. "Take them, my Lord. Take them! I give you both of them!"

434

"Three!"

Savage was about to close her eyes when she became aware of a shaft of light piercing the sky, a beam swathing down and seeking victims to suck into hell. She blinked and for a second she was sure she saw Clarissa's face up there in the brightness. Her daughter spoke, her lips moving in slow motion but the words coming out clear and sweet.

Mummy? You always said everything would be alright, didn't you?

Then a loud crack echoed around the clearing and the man with the antlers yelled something as his right shoulder burst open in a spray of scarlet. A hand went up but the blood came spurting out in a fountain and he dropped the knife and fell away from Irina.

"No!" The man went down on his knees and then tumbled over.

Savage looked at Fox, but he hadn't fired. The gun was dangling at his side, his eyes trained on Antler Man. Then fox raised the gun and two shots rang out in quick succession. Savage dropped to the ground, her hands instinctively going to her head, feeling for the wounds.

Nothing.

She turned on her side and saw Milner standing a few metres away. His mouth had dropped open and he gasped for air, the top half of his forehead a mush of bone and blood and brain.

"I . . ." Milner collapsed to the floor, his body twitching in the dirt. He gurgled twice and then died.

"Ma'am!" Savage rolled over and turned to see Calter running across the clearing. "There!"

Calter pointed into the sky and Savage raised her head, frightened as to what she might see. The wind had a more rhythmical sound now, a *chugga-chugga-chugga-chugga*. From above, a beast seemed to be descending. Dark-blue on the creature's underbelly, yellow on top, a rush of air washing down over her.

Chugga-chugga-chugga-chugga.

She jumped to her feet and stared up. The monster's rotors whirled round and a bright light came shining down.

Chugga-chugga-chugga-chugga.

The Air Operations helicopter!

The aircraft descended to one side of the clearing. The side door stood open, a figure in black riding shotgun, a rifle with a night scope tucked under his arm. When the helicopter was a metre from landing the figure slipped off his perch and hit the ground running, closely followed by two more.

One of the men rushed over to the prone figure with the antlers, a second covered the remaining Satanists, while the other strode across to Savage, his expression hidden by a balaclava.

"He was going for a chest shot," the familiar voice said, looking back to where the first figure crouched over Antler Man. "But it's a result in my book. Hitting anything from fifty metres up in the dark in this wind is a bloody miracle."

"Nigel," Savage said as Frey peeled off his mask. "A little late, but very welcome."

"The Super called it in," Frey said smiling. "Only he needs to go to nav school. In his haste the old fool got part of the coordinates wrong. Luckily your DC Enders came good." Frey turned to the huge stone where Fox and Calter were attempting to free Owen and Irina. "Are they alright?"

"Let's hope so," Savage said. Then she turned and walked across to where the man with the antlers lay.

"He's alive," the armed officer said, pressing down on the man's shoulder with the palm of his hand. "He's losing some blood but the bullet missed his vital organs."

Savage bent and fiddled with the headdress. Calter stepped over to help and they both tugged until the mask came off.

"Graham Falk," Savage said. "He was part of the group all the time."

She stood. Owen and Irina sat on the rock nearby. Both of them seemed barely awake.

"They've been drugged, ma'am," Calter said. "Maybe that's a small mercy. Hopefully they'll make a full recovery."

Savage stared past Owen to where Simon Fox was slipping away into the tree line. Fox stopped and turned. His eyes glistened in the firelight. Then he raised one hand to his head, saluted Savage, and vanished into the darkness.

"A full recovery," Savage said. "Yes, let's hope so."

Epilogue

Monday 8th September

Riley ambled down his hallway and picked up his copy of the *Guardian* from the doormat. Charles Milner had hit the headlines, the MP making a far bigger splash in death than he'd ever done when he was alive. His co-star, Helen Peacock, shared the billing and newspaper editors were rubbing their hands at the prospect of what had already been dubbed "the trial of the century". The image of Milner depicted a red-faced country gent, the sort most readers of the paper would undoubtedly despise. Peacock, on the other hand, looked stunning. Riley shook his head. Why had she got involved? Was it Graham Falk's charisma or something else? The woman had brains, beauty, sexual allure, power. She'd thrown it all away. Riley thought Davies was probably right. Famous people didn't think like normal folk.

The other members of the group weren't so famous. A surgeon, a solicitor and Rasmus Yarnic, the jeweller who'd made the Satanic cross found on Dartmoor. Yarnic, Riley figured, had been playing silly buggers. All that stuff about the Wiccan pentagram on his forearm, the pile of notebooks he'd hoped would obfuscate the details around the Satanic cross. The man, like Charles Milner, had fallen under the spell of his own arrogance.

Then there was Professor Falk. He was in Derriford Hospital recovering from the gunshot wound. Falk's motive was still unclear. According to reports Riley had heard, the man was claiming he'd been on the moor purely as an observer. He was pleading academic detachment. By all accounts that seemed wide of the mark, but there was speculation that, with the right legal team, he'd be able to escape justice. Media interest in the man was huge and there was already talk of a book deal running well into six figures.

All five of the surviving members had been charged with the murders of Martin Hedford and Anasztáz Róka. Other charges were pending.

The University of Cambridge had confirmed that all the Satanists had graduated in 1989. It had refused to comment on speculation that a report from a college investigation into an apparent sacrificial killing of a lamb on Midsummer Common back in 1988 was hushed up so as to avoid negative publicity.

Trying to keep things quiet never worked, Riley thought as he folded the paper. Secrets never stayed secret for ever and lies were always exposed.

A week later, Calter attended the funeral for DC Carl Denton. What seemed like the entire force turned out, dozens of uniformed officers marching in the sunshine, their polished shoes rustling through the first fall of autumn leaves. Inside the church sunbeams streamed through the stained glass but failed to warm the cool air. Calter sat in a pew and shivered as Detective Superintendent Hardin made a speech. He started out in typical Hardin fashion — all bluster and awkwardness — but by the end a fair proportion of officers were in tears, Calter included. The service over, the congregation filed outside. Denton's family were waiting at the entrance to the church, thanking the wellwishers, and as Calter approached his mother stared at her, anger in her gaze. Calter bowed her head, not wanting to meet the woman's eyes. Her son had obviously shared his personal problems with his mother and Calter got the feeling the woman held her personally responsible for Denton's death. Several officers paused to offer condolences to the mother and Calter slipped past behind them and into the graveyard where she wandered alone through the grey stones.

At the police wake afterwards there was talk of Denton receiving some sort of posthumous award, certainly that was what Acting Chief Constable Maria Heldon was recommending. As soon as she was confirmed in post she'd be putting Denton's name forward, she said. Calter remembered Denton's mother at the church, the tears streaming down the old woman's face. A shiny medal on a silk ribbon, she thought, would be no bloody consolation at all.

The day after Denton's funeral, Savage found herself sitting in a briefing room at police headquarters in Exeter with Detective Superintendent Hardin and

440

Maria Heldon. It was looking likely that Heldon would soon be Devon and Cornwall Police's first female Chief Constable. Savage had tangled with Heldon before and felt uncomfortable knowing the woman would be her boss. On the other hand, could she really be worse than Simon Fox?

"Right." Heldon opened a manila file on the table in front of her. "Let's get this over with. As you can imagine, I'm very busy, so if you could be concise."

The meeting had been convened so Heldon could be brought up to speed on the latest developments. The Home Secretary was showing an unhealthy interest in events down in Devon and Heldon wanted to be one step ahead of the game. "Just in case", as she put it.

Hardin summarised the case. In the past week the team had questioned the surviving members of the group and a cohesive story was beginning to emerge. Charles Milner had been the ringleader but he'd been egged on by Graham Falk who, according to other members of the group, had taken on a directorial role, encouraging them to commit ever greater crimes. According to Helen Peacock, it was Falk who'd suggested the first human sacrifice six years ago. Conversely, Falk was claiming that the surviving members of the group were ganging up on him to try to absolve themselves of responsibility for their crimes.

"So there's been six victims plus Ana Róka and Hedford?" Heldon said. Hardin nodded. "Have we identified them?"

"Not as yet."

Hardin explained they hadn't recovered all the remains but, given the willingness of the surviving group members to cooperate, they were hopeful they could establish the victims' identities before long.

He went on. The seven friends had met at Cambridge and Peacock claimed the first incident had taken place just before Christmas in their final year. They'd all gone to a party and been very drunk and, realising their studies weren't going well, they'd decided to try to invoke some black magic. It had been nothing more than a student prank, but when the following summer six of the seven had achieved first-class honours there'd been a tacit agreement to meet each year from then on. Martin Hedford had been the odd one out — he'd only managed a lower second — for that reason, he saw no benefit in taking any further part.

"But what was a joke eventually became murder?" Heldon asked.

"Yes. There'd been goats, sheep, cattle, but one year the ritual went further. It's not clear yet exactly what happened, but Peacock claims the first occasion was an accident. The victim was never supposed to die. When she did and the group covered it up they became beholden to each other. It went on from there."

"And Ana Róka and her father, Martin Hedford?"

"Charlotte?" Hardin turned to Savage. "Over to you."

"Yes, sir," Savage said. She glanced at her notes. "Hedford went abroad after completing his degree. He married a Hungarian woman and they had a child,

Ana. He later split from his wife, returned to the UK and remarried. He had a son with his new wife but when the boy was seven he became ill with a brain tumour. Various treatments were tried but the tumour got progressively worse. At this point his old friends got in touch. Hedford was so desperate he fell back in with them. Perversely it was the need to try and save the boy, along with the fact that several members were down on their heels financially, which prompted the group to use a human victim for the first time in their ritual that year. Even though his son eventually succumbed to the illness Hedford was convinced his participation had extended the child's life."

"But at some point he turned against them?"

"His wife was killed in an RTC. That pulled him to his senses and to assuage his guilt he began to plot the group's downfall. Unfortunately at some point they caught up with him."

"What about the daughter?"

"We're still piecing together her story using her notebook and what we know. It appears Hedford visited Ana in Hungary last year and she knew a little of what was going on. When he went missing Ana came over here to investigate. She had a key to Hedford's flat and found some of the material he'd been working on including a map of sites the Satanists used. She didn't trust the police enough to come to us directly so she enlisted the help of the lads from North Prospect. She paid them to kill the ponies at various sites hoping to draw enough police and media attention to disrupt the Satanists' activities. In the end her plan worked because we found Hedford in the kistvaen at Merrivale, although I don't think Ana had any idea her father was buried up there. Before the pony killings commenced Charles Milner became aware Ana was on to the group and got Falk — in the guise of Antler Man — to set Creasey to watch her. Milner realised she was close to discovering the truth and decided he couldn't allow her to remain free. Creasey and Milner abducted Ana and locked her in the shed in the woods where she was kept for several days. Then Milner and a couple of the others took her to Milner's place and embarked on a night flight over Fernworthy. We believe, from Ana's notebook, that she wanted to try to crash the plane. We don't know exactly what happened up in the air, but my guess is Milner intended to drop her in the reservoir — she was drugged and naked after all — but Ana managed to put up some kind of fight. It was enough to ensure the drop went wrong and she landed in the trees."

"Jesus. To do something like that to a fellow human being." Heldon stared down at her notes, visibly shocked. For a moment, Savage saw the softer side of the woman. Then Heldon looked up, her hard façade back in place. She turned to Hardin. "Right, I think we've finished. But before we wrap up I want to know about Simon Fox. Where on earth is he?"

"We've no idea," Hardin said. "No sign of the man or his car. Rumour is he's in France. He speaks fluent French and his family own a château in the Loire Valley."

Heldon nodded, plainly impressed. "But he's not there?"

"No."

"But it's only a matter of time, right?"

"Yes, of course."

"The question is — what I'm going to be asked by the minister — is what was he doing on the moor seemingly gone AWOL and armed with an unlicensed weapon?"

"We believe he was trying to rescue his son," Hardin said.

"It doesn't make sense." Heldon looked down at her notes again. "According to the reports I have from Inspector Frey, the CC was holding the gun to DI Savage's head. He then shot Charles Milner, who incidentally was unarmed, before disappearing. DI Savage, can you shed any light on the matter?"

Savage swallowed. "The situation was very confused. I don't think Fox knew what he was doing. I think he'd taken leave of his senses."

Heldon snorted. "I find that a little hard to believe, don't you? Phone records show a number of calls between Fox and Milner which were made in the days preceding the incident on the moor. The two had lunch together earlier that day too. There must be something else. After all, the Satanists had taken Owen Fox and intended to kill him. Why would they do that?"

"Fox's son is married to Milner's daughter. We're guessing Milner asked for the CC's help. Perhaps Fox refused and so Milner kidnapped Owen."

"I don't believe it was as simple as that." Heldon paused and the beginnings of a sneer appeared on her lips. "DI Savage, we've tangled before, haven't we? On the previous occasion I found you obstreperous and obstructive. The former I don't have a problem with — it's probably an asset for us women officers — but I will not tolerate the latter, understand?"

"Yes, ma'am." Savage nodded. "I was just —"

"I believe the Chief Constable came to visit you at home before he ended up on the moor. What did you discuss?"

"Not much." Savage swallowed. "He just wanted my opinion on the case as it stood."

"And that was it?"

"Yes."

"And there was no inkling anything else was amiss?"

"No, ma'am."

"I don't buy it, DI Savage. If you're trying to protect Simon Fox because he's your superior officer then I'm afraid your loyalty, while admirable, is misguided."

"Sorry, ma'am. That's how it happened."

"I see." Heldon shrugged. She shuffled her papers and closed her folder. "It's a shame the Chief Constable didn't confide in you. If he had, then perhaps we could have got to the bottom of this mystery. Now we'll have to wait until he turns up. Then hopefully we'll get the truth, won't we?"

"Yes, ma'am," Savage said. "I'm sure we will."

The wait for Simon Fox ended when Savage took a call one evening a few days later. Fox's voice was quiet, almost a whisper. Savage tried to talk to him but he cut across her words. He wanted to turn himself in, he said, but only to her. It would, he said, be apposite if she was the one. He suggested a location to meet and before she had time to protest he hung up.

For a moment Savage stood in her kitchen. It would be an easy matter to phone for back-up, to wash her hands of everything. Fox would simply arrive at the meeting place to find a dozen cars packed with officers while she remained at home.

She put the phone back in its cradle and went to her car.

The rendezvous at Wembury Beach was but a mile or so from her house. She wondered if Fox had been watching her, waiting for the right moment to call. The thought made her uneasy. And yet if he'd wanted to harm her, wouldn't he have done so already?

Savage's MG crawled down the narrow track to the car park. At the far end a lone car gleamed in the sunlight. The car was a Jaguar of deep, deep blue, the tone darker than the sea and with a glossy depth which suggested to Savage that Fox must have washed and waxed the car for hours. Typical of the man, she thought. Appearance counted — and Fox would want everything from the buttons on his uniform to the way the car looked to be perfect. Pity the man hadn't worked on things beneath the surface.

Savage pulled her car over, almost without thinking placing the vehicle across the entrance to the car park. She didn't want any funny stuff like Fox driving off or somebody else turning up unannounced. She clicked the door open and got out. Now she could see Fox sitting in the car, staring forward, out to sea. The sun hung low, light glinting off the surface of the water, several yachts cutting through a light chop, heading for the Sound; a pint or two and home. Something Fox wouldn't be doing for a while. Maybe that was why he'd chosen this spot. A final look at what he'd thrown away.

As she walked across the car park Savage took a moment for reflection too. Taking Fox in now would end the cycle, but she took no pleasure from it. Nothing was going to bring Clarissa back. The feeling of revenge she'd harboured for so long was an angry, bitter thing, which had eaten her up. Now, at the end of it all, there was nothing but emptiness. She'd almost made the same mistake as Fox. Thrown everything away.

Fox wore his uniform. Black. Silver buttons. His cap sat on the dash in front of him, the badge as shiny as the buttons. He'd tilted the seat back a little, relaxing in the last of the day's warmth as he sat cocooned in the car. As Savage crunched the final few metres across the gravel he didn't turn, just waited impassively, eyes forward. Now Savage could hear something. Voices. The car radio. Some sort of sports commentary. Cricket. She reached the car and paused. Fox ignored her, playing a silly game, obviously struggling to hold on to the last vestiges of his superiority.

"Sir?" Savage would humour him. No need for any sort of humiliation. Not now. She tapped on the window. "DI Savage, sir."

Nothing. Just the sound of the radio, a few seagulls wheeling and calling overhead, an engine on a boat humming in the distance.

Savage bent to the window and peered through. Fox sat frozen, his lips parted in a grin or a grimace, a globule of saliva hanging on a thread of liquid which drooled from his chin. She tapped on the glass again, aware as she did so that the low noise wasn't from a distant boat, but rather the sound of the Jaguar's engine purring at low revs. She clicked the door open and a waft of air soured with exhaust poured out. Fox's hands lay in his lap, clutching a tin of boiled sweets. From the radio a spattering of applause rang out, the commentator announcing that bad light had stopped play.

Other titles published by Ulverscroft:

MIDNIGHT IN DEATH
AND INTERLUDE IN DEATH

J. D. Robb

In *Midnight in Death*, Eve Dallas's name has made a Christmas list, but it's not for being naughty or nice — it's for putting a serial killer behind bars. Now he's escaped and has her in his sights . . . While in *Interlude in Death*, when respected Commander Skinner offers her a promotion if she'll give her husband Roarke up to custody, her reaction is furious. Roarke's Irish past is murky, but he's a changed man — so what is the commander after? With Eve and Skinner at one of Roarke's holiday resorts for a police convention, Skinner's thwarted vengeance soon brings death to their luxury surroundings.

ROBIN HOOD YARD

Mark Sanderson

October, 1938: Johnny Steadman, investigative journalist, is called to the scene of a gruesome murder — a man has been tied to his bed, mutilated and left to bleed to death. This is the second time the killer has struck, and it won't be the last. Together with D.C. Matt Turner, Johnny tries desperately to find a link between the victims. When the next Lord Mayor of London is subjected to a vicious anti-Semitic attack, Johnny begins to wonder if the two cases are connected. Against a backdrop of escalating violence in Nazi Germany, he uncovers a shocking conspiracy that could bring the United Kingdom to its knees. But will Johnny live to tell the tale?

THIS LITTLE PIGGY

Bea Davenport

It's the summer of 1984, and there is a sense of unease on the troubled Sweetmeadows estate. The residents are in shock after the suspicious death of a baby, and tension is growing due to the ongoing miners' strike. Journalist Clare Jackson follows the story as the police bungle the inquiry and struggle to contain the escalating violence. Haunted by a personal trauma she can't face up to, Clare is shadowed by nine-year-old Amy, a bright but neglected little girl who seems to know more about the incident than she's letting on. As the days go by and the killer is not found, Clare ignores warnings not to get too close to her stories — and, in doing so, puts her own life in jeopardy.

THE BLACKPOOL HIGHFLYER

Andrew Martin

Assigned to drive holidaymakers to the seaside resort of Blackpool in the hot summer of 1905, Jim Stringer is happy to have left behind the grime and danger of life in London. But his dreams of beer and pretty women are soon shattered — when his high-speed train meets a huge millstone on the line. In the months that follow, as he hunts for the saboteur, Jim is drawn into a beguiling but dangerous world of eccentrics, conmen and cowards. From ventriloquists to funfair salesmen, ticket clerks to dandies, everyone is a suspect . . .

BLACKLIGHT BLUE

Peter May

Enzo Macleod, a Scottish teacher of forensics at Cahors in southwest France, has been using his expertise to crack seven notorious murders described in a book by Parisian journalist Roger Raffin. Having solved the first two, Enzo is diagnosed with a terminal illness, and now he is running out of time to crack the most confounding murder of all. But before he can begin, his daughter is nearly killed, while Enzo himself is mugged — and then arrested, in what appear to be a series of pre-emptive strikes by killers desperate to protect their secrets. Destroying his character, framing him for murder . . . they will stop at nothing to halt Enzo, who must use all his forensic skills to solve the case — before they succeed.

THE ZIG ZAG GIRL

Elly Griffiths

Brighton, 1950: When the body of a girl is found, cut into three, DI Edgar Stephens recalls a magic trick that he saw as a boy. The illusion is called the Zig Zag Girl and its inventor, Max Mephisto, is an old friend of his. They served together in the war as part of a shadowy unit called the Magic Men, formed to use stage trickery to confuse the enemy. Max is reluctant to get involved when Edgar tracks him down, but the revelation that the dead girl is his former stage assistant changes his mind. A similar death follows, based on a trick called the Sword Cabinet. Then Edgar receives a letter warning of another "trick" called the Wolf Trap — the deadliest illusion of all. But who will be the next victim?